Frostborn: The Gray Knight

Jonathan Moeller

ISBN: 1492101397
ISBN-13: 978-1492101390

EPIGRAPH

I am the man that hath seen affliction by the rod of his wrath. He hath led me, and brought me into darkness, but not into light.

-Lamentations 3:1-2

OTHER BOOKS BY THE AUTHOR

A BRIEF PROLOGUE

A letter to the surviving kings, counts, and knights of Britain:

I am Malahan Pendragon, the bastard son of Mordred, himself the bastard son of Arthur Pendragon, the High King of all Britain.

You know the grievous disasters that have befallen our fair isle. My father betrayed my grandfather, and perished upon the bloody field of Camlann, alongside many of the mightiest knights and kings of Britain. Before that came the war of Sir Lancelot's treachery and the High Queen's adultery, a war that slew many noble and valiant knights.

Now there is no High King in Britain, Camelot lies waste, and the pagan Saxons ravage our shores. Every day the Saxons advance further and further, laying waste to our fields and flocks, butchering our fighting men, making slaves of our womenfolk, and desecrating holy churches and monasteries. Soon all of Britain shall lie under their tyranny, just as the barbarians overthrew the Emperor of Rome.

My lords, I write not to claim the High Kingship of Britain – for Britain is lost to the Saxons – but to offer hope. My grandfather the High King is slain, and his true heir Galahad fell seeking the grail, so therefore this burden has fallen to me, for there is no one else to bear it.

Britain is lost, but we may yet escape with our lives.

For I have spoken with the last Keepers of Avalon, and by their secret arts they have fashioned a gate wrought of magic leading to a far distant realm beyond the circles of this world, certainly beyond the reach of the heathen Saxons. Here we may settle anew, and build homes and lives free from the specter of war.

I urge you to gather all your people, and join me at the stronghold of Caerleon. We shall celebrate the feast of Easter one final time, and then march to the plain of Salisbury, to the standing stones raised by the wizard

Merlin.

The gate awaits, and from there we shall march to a new home.

Sealed in the name of Malahan Pendragon, in the Year of Our Lord 538.

CHAPTER 1
THE KNIGHT AND THE FRIAR

The day it all began, the day in the Year of Our Lord 1478 when the blue fire filled the sky from horizon to horizon, Ridmark Arban returned to the town of Dun Licinia.

He gazed at the town huddled behind its walls of gray stone, his left hand gripped tight around a long wooden staff. He had not been here in over five years, not since the great battle against Mhalek and his horde of orcs, and then Dun Licinia had been little more than a square keep ringed by a wooden wall, an outpost named in honor of the Dux of the Northerland.

Now it was a prosperous town of four thousand people, fortified by a wall of stone. Ridmark saw the towers of a small keep within the town, alongside the twin bell towers of a stone church and the round tower of a Magistrius. Cultivated fields and pastures ringed the town on three sides, and the River Marcaine flowed south past its western wall, making its way through the wooded hills of the Northerland to the River Moradel in the south.

Ridmark's father had always said there was good mining and logging to be had on the edges of the Northerland, if men were bold enough to live within reach of the orc tribes and dark creatures that lurked in the Wilderland.

And in the shadow of the black mountain that rose behind Ridmark.

He walked for the town's northern gate, swinging his staff in his left hand, his gray cloak hanging loose around him. When he had last stood in this valley, the slain orcs of Mhalek's horde had carpeted the ground as far as he could see, the stench of blood and death filling his nostrils. It pleased him to see that something had grown here, a place of prosperity and plenty.

Perhaps no one would recognize him.

Freeholders and the freeholders' sons toiled in the fields, breaking up the soil in preparation for the spring planting. The men cast him wary looks, looks that lingered long after he had passed. He could not blame them. A man wrapped in a gray cloak and hood, a wooden staff in his left hand and a bow slung over his shoulder, made for a dangerous-looking figure.

Especially since he kept his hood up.

But if he kept his hood up, they would not see the brand that marred the left side of his face.

He came to Dun Licinia's northern gate. The wall itself stood fifteen feet high, and two octagonal towers of thirty feet stood on either side of the gate itself. A pair of men-at-arms in chain mail stood at the gate, keeping watch on the road and the wooded hills ringing the valley. He recognized the colors upon their tabards. They belonged to Sir Joram Agramore, a knight Ridmark had known. They had been friends, once.

Before Mhalek and his horde.

"Hold," said one of the men-at-arms, a middle-aged man with the hard-bitten look of a veteran. "State your business."

Ridmark met the man's gaze. "I wish to enter the town, purchase supplies, and depart before sundown."

"Aye?" said the man-at-arms, eyes narrowing. "Sleep in the hills, do you?"

"I do," said Ridmark. "It's comfortable, if you know how."

"Who are you, then?" said the man-at-arms. He jerked his head at the other soldier, and the man disappeared into the gatehouse. "Robber? Outlaw?"

"Perhaps I'm an anchorite," said Ridmark.

The man-at-arms snorted. "Holy hermits don't carry weapons. They trust in the Dominus Christus to protect them from harm. You look like the sort to place his trust in steel."

He wasn't wrong about that.

Ridmark spread his arms. "Upon my oath, I simply wish to purchase supplies and leave without causing any harm. I will swear this upon the name of God and whatever saints you wish to invoke."

Three more men-at-arms emerged from the gatehouse.

"What's your name?" said the first man-at-arms.

"Some call me the Gray Knight," said Ridmark.

The first man frowned, but the youngest of the men-at-arms stepped forward.

"I've heard of you!" said the younger man. "When my mother journeyed south on pilgrimage to Tarlion, beastmen attacked her caravan. You drove them off! I…"

"Hold," said the first man, scowling. "Show your face. Honest men have no reason to hide their faces."

"Very well," said Ridmark. He would not lie. Not even about this.

He drew back his cowl, exposing the brand of the broken sword upon his left cheek and jaw.

A ripple of surprise went through the men.

"You're…" said the first man. He lifted his spear. "What is your name?"

"My name," said Ridmark, "is Ridmark Arban."

The men-at-arms looked at each other, and Ridmark rebuked himself. Coming here had been foolish. Better to have purchased supplies from the outlying farms or a smaller village, rather than coming to Dun Licinia.

But he had not expected the town to grow so large.

"Ridmark Arban," said the older man-at-arms. He looked at one of the other men. "You. Go to the castle, and find Sir Joram." One of the men ran off, chain mail flashing in the sunlight.

"Are you arresting me?" said Ridmark. Perhaps it would be better to simply leave.

The first man opened his mouth again, closed it.

"You think he made the friar disappear?" said the younger man, the one who had mentioned his mother. "But he's the Gray Knight! They…"

"The Gray Knight is a legend," said the first man, "and you, Sir…" He scowled and started over. "And you, Ridmark Arban, should speak with Sir Joram. That is that."

"So be it," said Ridmark.

A dark thought flitted across his mind. If he attacked them, he might well overpower them. Their comrades would pursue him. Perhaps they would kill him.

And he could rest at last…

Ridmark shook off the notion and waited.

A short time later two men approached and spoke in low voices to the first man-at-arms.

"You will accompany us," he said.

Ridmark nodded and walked through the gates of Dun Licinia, the men-at-arms escorting him. Most of the houses were built of brick, roofed with sturdy clay tiles, making it harder for an attacker to set the town ablaze. Ridmark saw men at work in their shops, making shoes and hats and aprons to sell to the nearby freeholders.

A memory shivered through him. The last time he had stood here, he had been wearing plate and chain mail, the sword Heartwarden blazing with white fire in his fist, the ground carpeted with slain men and orcs and halflings and manetaurs.

He pushed aside the memory and kept walking, his staff tapping against the cobblestones.

The men-at-arms led him to the main square, fronted on either side by the sturdy stone church and the small castle. They walked through the castle's gates, across the dusty courtyard, and into the keep's great hall. It had changed little since his last visit five years ago.

Though this time dying and wounded men did not lie on rows upon the flagstones of the floor.

The men-at-arms instructed him to wait and left.

Ridmark rolled his shoulders and walked towards the dais, his staff a comfortable, familiar weight in his left hand. A few motes of dust danced in the beams of light leaking through the windows. Tapestries on the wall showed scenes from the court of the first High King on Old Earth, of Lancelot and Galahad questing for the cup that had held the Dominus Christus's blood. Others showed more recent wars, the High King Arthurain fighting against the urdmordar, or the Dragon Knight leading the armies of the High King against the Frostborn.

Idly Ridmark wondered what would happen if he simply tried to walk out of the keep.

Perhaps the men-at-arms would kill him.

The doors opened, and Sir Joram Agramore entered the hall.

He had always been heavyset, but now he verged towards the plump. Peace, it seemed, agreed with him. He had curly red hair and bright green eyes, and wore a long tunic and a mantle, a sword and dagger at his belt.

He stared at Ridmark in silence for a moment.

"Ridmark Arban," he said at last. "God and all his saints. I was sure you had died five years ago."

Ridmark shrugged. "Perhaps God still has work for me."

"He must," said Joram. "But I was sure…the Magistri always say that Swordbearer severed from his Soulblade wastes away. Or kills himself. It just…"

"If grief," said Ridmark, "could kill a man, I would have died long ago."

His left hand tightened against his staff, and he glanced at his hand before he could stop himself. A ring glinted on his finger, the gold still bright despite the five years he had spent wandering the Wilderland. Memories burned through him at the sight of it, good memories, happy memories.

But those memories ended in death.

"Indeed," said Joram. "Forgive me, I did not mean to…I wish…" He sighed and shook his head. "I am not sure what to say to you."

"A knight strives to be courteous to all men," said Ridmark, "and there is no protocol for greeting a disowned exile and former Swordbearer."

"Alas," said Joram, "no."

Ridmark felt a twinge of pity for his old friend. Joram had always been a solid knight, but not man to take the lead in a crisis. "Then tell me of yourself. You are the Comes of Dun Licinia now?"

"No, just a caretaker, I fear," said Joram. "The old Comes died in the winter without any heirs, and the Dux sent me north to oversee the comarchate until he appoints a new man." He shrugged. "It is quiet enough. The occasional band of pagan orcs or beastmen, but nothing like the days of Mhalek."

"You are wed?" said Ridmark. He did not want to talk about Mhalek.

Joram grinned. "How did you…oh, yes, the ring. Yes, four years. You remember Lady Lydia?"

Ridmark laughed. "You talked her around at last?"

"Well, I imagine my new lands helped sway her father, at least," said Joram. "But, aye, we are happy. Two children, so far. God, but they can fill a castle with their wailing!"

Ridmark nodded.

Joram took a deep breath. "If you will allow me to say so…I am glad to see you, Ridmark. What happened to you was unjust, and I think Tarrabus Carhaine forced the Master to expel you from the Order. It was unjust, especially after what happened to Aelia…"

"What is done is done," said Ridmark. He did not wish to discuss Aelia, either.

"Indeed," said Joram. "Ridmark, I must ask. Why have you come here? You were disowned and banished from the Order, not exiled from the High King's realm…but you must know that the Dux Tarrabus still has a price on your head."

"Only the High King," said Ridmark, "can pronounce a sentence of death."

"I think Dux Tarrabus disagrees," said Joram.

"He can think whatever he likes," said Ridmark. "I simply wish to purchase supplies and be on my way."

"Back into the Wilderland?" said Joram.

Ridmark nodded.

A hint of pity went over Joram's face. "Still seeking prophecies of the Frostborn?"

"Aye," said Ridmark.

"Well," said Joram, "at least let me resupply you from my own pantry."

Ridmark lifted an eyebrow. "Dux Licinius might not approve."

"He has forgiven you," said Joram. "He never blamed you for what happened to Aelia."

Ridmark said nothing.

"And if you like," said Joram, "think of it as repayment. For not beating me black and blue when we were squires, the way Tarrabus and his lot used to do."

Ridmark bowed. "If you must."

"I insist," said Joram, clapping his hands. The servants' door by the dais opened, and a pair of halfling women wearing Joram's colors entered the hall, carrying a tray of food and drink. They set the tray on the table and bowed. One of the halfling women glanced at Ridmark for a moment, her eyes like disks of amber in her face, and then left with the other servant. He was always struck by how alien and ethereal the halflings looked.

"Please," said Joram, "sit, sit. You're as lean as a starving wolf." He grinned. "Though I fear I indulge too much at the table, and must confess to gluttony every week."

"There are worse things," said Ridmark, sitting across from Joram, "than gluttony. One never knows if there will be food tomorrow."

"A wise man," said Joram.

Ridmark ate. Joram did set a good table. There was bread with honey, dried fruit, and even a few pieces of leathery ham. He listened to Joram discuss his children and the various problems of governing Dun Licinia.

"Offering me hospitality," said Ridmark, "will get you in trouble with Tarrabus Carhaine."

"Tarrabus Carhaine can..." said Joram, and stopped himself. "I am sworn to the Dux of the Northerland, not the Dux of Caerdracon. If my liege the Dux Gareth Licinius has a problem with my actions, I am sure he will inform me in short order."

"It might get you into trouble with your wife," said Ridmark. "She never did like me."

"That concerns me more," admitted Joram. "But a knight is supposed to be hospitable. And that duty might cause me more...difficultly, I fear."

"Just from me?" said Ridmark. "As soon as we finish, I am returning to the Wilderland. I could very well never return."

He had not expected to return the first time.

"Not from you," said Joram. "From a different, more...troublesome guest."

"How is he a troublesome guest?" said Ridmark.

"I lost him."

"Ah."

"And the Dux," said Joram, "will be upset if I cannot get him back."

"What kind of guest?" said Ridmark.

"A dwarf."

Ridmark frowned. "A noble from the Three Kingdoms?"

Joram shook his head. "No. Well, he was at one time, but no longer. This dwarf insisted upon baptism. He joined the Order of Mendicants and became a friar, taking the name of Caius, after Saint Caius of old."

Ridmark stopped eating to listen. "A peculiar story. I have been to the Three Kingdoms…"

Joram blinked. "You have?"

Ridmark nodded. "They accept the High King, but they are devoted to the gods of the Deeps, the gods of stone and water and silence. I would not expect a dwarf to enter the Church."

"This one has," said Joram. "Brother Caius came here with the idea to preach to the pagan orc tribes of Vhaluusk and the Wilderland."

"A fool notion," said Ridmark.

"He left the town two days ago," said Joram, "and has not been seen since."

"Then he is likely dead," said Ridmark. "This part of the Northerland is relatively safe, but it is still dangerous to travel alone. And the orcs of the Wilderland pray to the blood gods, and their shamans wield black magic and blood spells. A mendicant who tries to preach the faith to them will find his head upon a spear."

"I fear you are correct," said Joram.

"And," said Ridmark, "you want me to find him, don't you?"

Joram sighed. "Am I truly so transparent? Of course, you were always the clever one." He shook his head. "The Dux's letter said I was to treat this Caius with all honor. And if he has gotten himself killed in the Wilderland…"

"The Dux can hardly blame you for that," said Ridmark.

"Nevertheless, I was his host, and he was my guest," said Joram.

"Very well," said Ridmark. "I will find him for you."

Joram blinked. "That's it? I thought you would take more convincing."

"Why not?" said Ridmark. "The dwarf seems valiant, if foolish, and does not deserve to die alone in the Wilderland. I will either find him and bring him back to you, or tell you of his fate."

Or die trying.

"Will that not take time from your…other task?" said Joram. "The search for the Frostborn?"

"Haven't you heard?" said Ridmark. "The Frostborn are extinct." He knew better, but continued speaking. "Joram, you were always a friend to me, and you have shown me kindness now. I know you wished to persuade me…but I have been persuaded. I will find Brother Caius for you."

And, perhaps, he would find his death. But that did not trouble him. He had ranged over the length and breadth of the Wilderland, following the long-dead urdmordar's prophecy of the Frostborn, following the warning the undead dark elven wizard had given him…and he had defeated every foe he had faced in that time.

But perhaps hunting for this strange dwarf would kill him.

And then, at last, he would have peace.

"Thank you," said Joram. "You will have whatever help you require."

"Good," said Ridmark. "This is what I need."

An hour later Ridmark walked to Dun Licinia's northern gate, staff in his left hand, gray cloak hanging from his shoulders, and a pack of fresh supplies on his back. The men-at-arms he had confronted earlier gave him wary glances, but Ridmark ignored them. He stepped through the gate and gazed north, at the flowing River Marcaine, the cultivated fields, the tree-choked slopes, the narrow road…and the great dark mass of the Black Mountain. A mile tall, the Black Mountain stood like a dark fist thrusting from the earth. The high elves of old had considered it cursed, along with the orcs and the beastmen and the halflings and the manetaurs and every other kindred to cross through the lands that became the High King's realm of Andomhaim.

And Brother Caius had gone to that mountain, intending to preach the word of the Dominus Christus to the orcish tribes living in its northern foothills.

Ridmark shook his head, half in admiration, half in annoyance, and started walking. The road lead to the ruins of the Tower of Vigilance, burned during the civil wars of the Pendragon princes fifty years past. It was a logical place for Caius to make camp, though bandits or orcs or other renegades might have taken shelter in the ruins.

He kept walking, and the fields began to thin out, patches of bristly pine forest appearing here and there. Ridmark supposed hardly anyone took the road north. Dun Licinia was the very northern edge of the Northerland, and beyond lay the vast Wilderland, with all its unknown lands and dangerous creatures.

Only a madman or a fool ventured into the Wilderland.

So Ridmark kept walking.

"You!"

He stopped, left hand tightening around his staff.

A stocky middle-aged man in the rough clothes of a freeholder climbed onto the road, his face red with anger. He carried a spear, its head worn but still sharp. The man held his weapon competently, but it would have been the easiest thing in the world for Ridmark to swing his staff and break the freeholder's wrists.

Instead he said, "Have I wronged you in some way?"

"You've been taking my pigs," said the freeholder.

"I have not," said Ridmark.

The freeholder sneered. "Aye, you have. I've seen you lurking in the woods, snatching my pigs when my back is turned. Outlaws, I knew it! Sir

Joram's constable wouldn't listen to me. Well, they should have listened to Peter of Dun Licinia! I have captured an outlaw! You will come with me now..."

Ridmark sighed, stepped forward, and thrust his staff. It caught the spear just behind the head, and sent the weapon tumbling. Peter's eyes went wide, and Ridmark rested the end of his staff on the freeholder's throat.

"Or," said Ridmark, "you could admit that I did not steal your pigs, and let me go on my way."

"Or that," said Peter.

Ridmark frowned. "How many pigs have been stolen?"

"Five. Prime hogs, too."

"When did this start?" said Ridmark.

"Two days ago," said Peter.

Ridmark nodded. Caius had departed Dun Licinia two days ago. Had the dwarven friar gone bandit?

Or, more likely, whatever had killed and eaten Caius was now stealing and eating Peter's hogs.

There were far worse things than pagan orcs in the Wilderland.

"Your pen," said Ridmark. "Show me."

Peter's eyes narrowed. "So you can steal my hogs?"

"God and his saints," said Ridmark. "It's a pigpen. If I wanted to find it, I suspect I could just follow my nose. But I think I know what's been stealing your pigs...and if it's not stopped, it might start eating your family."

That got Peter's attention. "Some horror from the Wilderland? An urvaalg?" He swallowed. "An urdmordar, as the Swordbearers of old faced?"

Ridmark had faced an urdmordar ten years past. It was not an experience he wanted to repeat, but he doubted one of the great spider-devils was stealing Peter's pigs. "Perhaps. Lead on."

Peter nodded and led Ridmark off the road, through a patch of pine trees, and to his farm. A low wall of field stone enclosed perhaps thirty pigs of varying size, their hides marked with a brand. A half-dozen young men, ranging from twelve years to Ridmark's age, busied themselves with various tasks. Peter's sons, no doubt.

Ridmark walked in a circle around the stone pen, ignoring the ripe smell. He examined the muddy ground, noting the mosaic of footprints and hoof marks around the pen.

Some of the tracks led away from the freehold, towards the forested hills.

"What are you doing?" said Peter, following him. "It's mud! Do you think..."

Ridmark lifted his staff, the length bumping against Peter's chest.

"Hold still," said Ridmark, still looking at the ground.

"Why?" said Peter. "You'll…"

"If you move," said Ridmark, "you'll disturb the tracks."

"But…"

"Hold still," said Ridmark.

He followed the tracks leading away from the pen. The land was churned into wet spring mud, with hundreds of footprints, but Ridmark had spent years wandering the wilderness. Given that his meals often came from whatever he had been able to shoot with his bow, he had grown quite good at tracking.

Hunger was a marvelous teacher.

He saw the tracks of three men and two pigs leading into the woods. To judge from the state of the tracks, he suspected the thieves had been here no earlier than midnight. Were they simply common highwaymen, raiding the local freeholds? Perhaps they had taken Caius hostage, and hoped to sell him for a ransom…

Ridmark picked up a slender thread from one of the tracks. It was a long black hair, thick and tough. He lifted it to his nose, sniffed, and tossed it aside.

"What is it?" said Peter, "What have you found?"

"You should arm yourself, master freeholder," said Ridmark, "you and all your sons. Orcs from the Wilderland have taken your pigs."

"Orcs?" said Peter.

"Do exactly as I tell you," said Ridmark, pointing his staff at the freeholder. "Arm yourselves, and keep watch over your fields. And send someone to Dun Licinia to warn Sir Joram. Do you understand?"

Peter nodded and shouted instructions to his sons, and Ridmark drew his cloak about him and walked into the woods, following the trail of the orcs and their stolen pigs.

CHAPTER 2
THE OMEN

Ridmark strode alone through the rocky hills.

The hills of the Northerland were steep and stony, their sides mantled by tough pine trees. Pine needles scraped beneath Ridmark's boots, and the air smelled of sap. The maze of hills created hundreds of small valleys and ravines, and caves dotted many of the slopes. The hills offered hundreds of hiding places for a band of orcs.

And some of the caves even opened into the Deeps, the vast maze of caverns and galleries that stretched beneath the earth of Andomhaim, home to kobolds and deep orcs and dark elves and worse things.

Hopefully none of them had come into the daylight. Some of those creatures had the power to smash the walls of Dun Licinia and kill everyone within the town.

But Ridmark doubted he faced anything so dangerous. He suspected a band of pagan orcs had stolen the freeholder's pigs, and most likely encountered Caius as well. Hopefully they had taken the dwarven friar captive.

If not, Ridmark would avenge his death.

He moved like a silent shadow through the trees, boots making no sound against the uneven ground. The trail continued north, moving towards a tall, steep hill. If the hill had any caves, it would make the ideal base for outlaws. They could see for miles in all directions. Of course, a clever outlaw would realize that the trees could mask a skillful attacker, and would post sentries to keep watch.

Ridmark saw movement in the trees ahead.

He stepped to the side, ducking under the branches of a tall pine, his cloak settling around him. It would help mask his presence. He had received the cloak as a gift, years ago, from the last archmage of the high elven kingdoms, and in times of peril the cloak blended with his surroundings and shielded him from unfriendly eyes.

The branches rustled, and an orcish man stepped into sight.

The orc had a gaunt, lean appearance from long years in the wild, his green skin creased with deep wrinkles, his thick tusks yellowing. His head had been shaved, save for a warrior's black topknot. He wore leather and fur, a short sword at his belt and an axe slung over his shoulder. His eyes, black and hard without any trace of color, roved back and forth. In his hands he carried a short bow of horn and wood.

A brand disfigured the orc's forehead, a burn in the shape of a teardrop.

Or, perhaps, a drop of blood.

Rage burned through Ridmark at the sight of that symbol, and he wanted to step from concealment and bring his staff down upon the orc's skull.

The orc was a Mhalekite.

Mhalek was dead, his claim to be a living god shattered at the Battle of Dun Licinia five years past, but many of his followers had survived. Someday the blood gods of the orcs would return, preached the Mhalekites, and they would sweep the world of the humans and the manetaurs and the halflings and the treacherous orcish kings who had accepted the High King's authority.

The orc walked away, and Ridmark slipped from concealment and followed, moving from tree trunk to tree trunk. The Mhalekite headed to the base of the hill, and a second orcish man came from behind a boulder. Like the first orc, the second wore leather and fur, a bow in his hands and a blood drop brand upon his forehead.

"Did you find anything?" said the second orc, speaking the orcish tongue.

"Nothing," said the first orc. "We are unnoticed. The human vermin and their halfling pets suspect nothing. They will sleep until we cut their throats."

The second orc spat. "Then the Master spoke truly. The hour of blood is come."

"Is Orlacht done yet?" said the first orc.

"Nay," said the second orc. "He still questions the prisoner."

"Orlacht is an idiot," said the first orc. "The Master's wishes are clear. All prisoners are to go to him."

"After the prisoner goes to the Master," said the second orc, "he'll be dead. Or he will wish he was dead. Dwarves have treasure, and we'll never learn where this one hid his gold."

A dwarf? Ridmark moved closer.

The first orc laughed. "This dwarf doesn't have any treasure. He has accepted the god of the humans. He probably gave his treasure away to orphans and widows or some such nonsense."

The second orc snorted. "Then Orlacht will cut off his head out of spite."

The first orc laughed again. "Then better to give him to the Master. He'll suffer more."

Both orcs laughed, and Ridmark took the opportunity to circle around them, hoping to move past and reach the hill. It seemed clear that a group of orcs had taken Caius captive, and if Ridmark acted swiftly, he could rescue the dwarven friar. He moved from tree to tree as the orcs resumed their discussion. Another few feet, and he would be behind them...

A bird called to his right, and both orcs looked in his direction.

They saw him, their black eyes widening in alarm, and Ridmark exploded into motion.

Ever since the Battle of Dun Licinia, he had been forbidden to carry a sword. To the knights of Andomhaim that was a dire sentence, for a sword was symbol of a knight's honor and prowess. But without the symbolism, a sword was simply a tool for killing.

And there were other tools one could use for killing.

Ridmark sprinted at the orcs, his staff in both hands. The first orc raised his bow, but Ridmark was faster. He struck the orc in the forehead, and heard the orc's skull crack beneath the staff's steel-capped end. A quick sidestep, and he smashed the staff's other end against the orc's temple.

The orc toppled motionless to the ground.

The second orc got his bow up and released, and Ridmark dodged, the arrow hissing past his head. The orc threw aside his bow and drew his short sword, but Ridmark charged forward, sweeping his staff in a sideways swing. The staff hit the orc's right knee, and again he heard the snap of shattering bone. The orc fell to his left knee with a strangled groan of pain, and Ridmark whipped the staff around.

The heavy weapon left a crease in the orc's right temple, and the orc fell motionless to the ground, green blood leaking from his ears.

Ridmark looked back and forth, the staff ready in his hands.

There were no more enemies in sight.

The entire fight had taken less than half a minute.

He stopped long enough to examine the dead orcs, but learned little useful. To judge from their clothes, they had come from Vhaluusk, the land of the pagan orcs on the western bank of the River Moradel, but that was no surprise. Many of Mhalek's followers had fled to Vhaluusk after Dun Licinia.

Best to get moving. The longer he lingered here, the more likely it was that another orc would discover the corpses.

Staff in hand, he followed the trail along the hill's slope, moving as fast as he could manage while remaining quiet. The trail ran back and forth, cutting around boulders and patches of pine trees, and Ridmark scanned for any sign of an ambush...

Then voices reached his ears, and he froze.

The sounds came from the top of the hill, and he nodded to himself and climbed up, ducking behind a heavy boulder. A flat hollow filled part of the hill's top, ringed by boulders, and five figures stood in the hollow.

The first was a dwarf in brown robes, his gray skin the color of hard granite, his black beard streaked with white. Most of the hair had receded from the top of his head, and the dwarf himself looked like a statue hewn from stone, his eyes like disks of polished blue marble.

Four orcs stood in a semicircle facing him. Three of the orcs wore leather and fur and carried short swords. The fourth wore chain mail, a massive double-bladed axe in his right hand. His topknot was gray, but the orc still bulged with muscle and stood taller than the others. Ridmark supposed that this was Orlacht, the leader the dead orcs had mentioned.

And that meant the dwarf in the friar's robe was Brother Caius.

"You cannot be serious," said Orlacht, his lips pulling away from his tusks in a sneer.

"I am perfectly serious," said Caius, his voice deep and resonant. He spoke orcish well.

"Then you expect us to renounce the blood gods?" said Orlacht.

"Not immediately, no," said Caius. "But in time."

"In time?" said Orlacht. "The blood gods respect strength and power! They reward the bold and the strong with power and might."

"The blood gods make you spend your lives in a bloody and futile scrabbling for glory," said Caius. "Like throwing red meat into a pack of starving dogs. Or the sacrifices the shamans of the blood gods demand? The woman slain upon altars, or the children burned so their blood may fuel sorcery? How many orcs have perished in this useless pursuit of power?"

"The strong do as they like," said Orlacht, "and the weak perish. This is the way of the world."

"But we are all weak," said Caius.

Orlacht snarled and slammed a fist against his mailed chest. "I am not weak."

"But we are all weaker than something else," said Caius.

"I am not weak!" snarled Orlacht again.

"But you are not the strongest," said Caius. "Do you not know your own history? The dark elves brought the orcs to this world to labor as slaves. Then the dark elves summoned the urdmordar...and the urdmordar enslaved both the dark elves and the orcs alike."

"The sons of Mhalek are a free people," spat Orlacht, "and neither the urdmordar nor the dark elves rule over us now."

"That is only because the High King and his Swordbearers and his Magistri smashed the urdmordar centuries ago," said Caius. "You did not free yourselves. The blood gods love only the strong…but the Dominus Christus accepts all, whether strong or weak."

Ridmark contemplated his next move. The dwarf friar might think to armor himself in his faith, but Ridmark doubted he would sway the Mhalekite orcs. Sooner or later Orlacht would kill Caius, or would haul the dwarf before his mysterious master. Ridmark considered letting the orcs leave and following them, learning more about their master, but decided against it. Orlacht's master, whoever he was, likely commanded many warriors, and if Caius went into their midst, he would never come out again.

Ridmark reached over his shoulder for his bow.

Orlacht spat, but Caius remained glacially calm. "Then you would have us yoke ourselves with the weak, dwarf? Shall we find cripples and cowards and women and treat them as our equals?"

"If you understood me," said Caius, "then you would wish to do it. For you would understand that we are all weak, we are all mortal, and that all strength ends in death. The blood gods offer nothing but misery and shadows beyond death. But the Dominus…"

"Enough!" roared Orlacht. "I will not listen to any more of this preaching. We depart to join the Master at the Tower. Bind the dwarf." He laughed. "Let us see if his preaching will touch the ears of the Master. And gag him! If I hear a word from him, I shall be wroth. Do not fret, dwarf. It will give you time for prayer. If the god of the humans loves you so much, perhaps he will come and save…"

Ridmark raised his bow and released, and an arrow sprouted from the neck of the nearest orc. Green blood flowed over the wound, and the orc gagged and fell to his knees. The remaining orcs whirled, and Orlacht brandished his huge axe and bellowed a curse.

"We are attacked!" he screamed. "Archers in the trees. Take them! Take them!"

The two remaining orcs raced forward, short swords in hand. Ridmark dropped his bow, gripped his staff in one hand and the boulder in the other, and heaved himself around it. The first orc just had time to raise his sword, and then Ridmark caught him across the belly with a blow from the staff. It was not a hard blow, but it was enough to rock the orc, and Ridmark reversed his staff and caught the orc across the knees. The orc stumbled and fell to the rocky ground, and the remaining orc and Orlacht charged at Ridmark.

He dodged to the left, the orc stabbing with his short sword. Ridmark brought his staff around in a two-handed blow, slapping against the flat of the orc's sword. The power of his strike wrenched the weapon from the orc's hands. The orc reached for a dagger at his belt, but Ridmark swung the staff against the orc's throat with all his strength.

The orc fell, windpipe crushed, and Orlacht struck at Ridmark, wielding his double-bladed axe two hands. Ridmark jumped back, the axe blurring before his face, and thrust with the staff, hoping to knock Orlacht off balance. But the big orc kept his swing controlled, moving out of Ridmark's reach. The orc Ridmark had stunned earlier scrambled back to his feet, growling as he waved his short sword.

Ridmark launched a feint at Orlacht's head, and the orc stepped back, axe raised. But Ridmark dashed past Orlacht and struck at the second orc. The butt of his staff plunged into the orc's stomach. The orc staggered, the breath knocked from his lungs, and Ridmark spun the staff in a looping blow, smashing it against the orc's temple.

The orc fell, and Ridmark faced Orlacht alone.

"You think," snarled Orlacht, his black eyes narrowed with rage, "you can defeat me with that little stick?" A crimson light glimmered in his eyes. It was the orcish battle rage, the gift of his blood to make him stronger and faster in battle.

"Yes," said Ridmark, and attacked. Orlacht lifted his axe to block, but Ridmark raised the staff, hooking it behind the blades of the axe, and tugged. Orlacht stumbled forward, and Ridmark slammed his right hand into the orc's face.

The big orc howled in fury, and Ridmark brought the heavy staff down once, twice, three times onto the crown of his head.

Orlacht fell, dying.

Ridmark looked around, seeking any more foes. Caius stood rooted on the spot, gaping at him, but all the orcs were down...

He saw a blur of green in the corner of his eye.

Ridmark whirled and saw the orc he had struck across the temple. He had thought the blow enough to render the orc unconscious, maybe even kill him...but plainly he had been wrong. Ridmark jumped back, just avoiding the tip of a short sword that blurred before his face. He thrust with the staff, driving the orc back, hoping to use his weapon's longer reach to keep his foe at bay.

Caius darted forward, a heavy mace appearing from beneath his robes, and swung. The mace impacted with the back of the orc's right knee. A hideous crunching sound filled Ridmark's ears, and the orc fell with a yelp.

A strike to the top of the orc's head and throat ended the fight.

The orc fell, and Ridmark found himself facing Caius. The dwarf's mace had the peculiar bronze sheen common to dwarven-forged steel.

"Was it really necessary," said Caius in perfect Latin, "to kill them?"

"Perhaps not," said Ridmark, "but they would have done their best to kill me. And once they had killed me, they would have taken you back to their master, whoever he is. I suspect he would not have given you a clean death."

Caius lifted his bearded chin. With his gray skin and gleaming blue eyes, the dwarf looked like a statue, at least until he moved. "It would be an honor to die spreading the word of the Dominus Christus."

"True," said Ridmark, "but would you really want to?"

Caius grimaced. "Not unless I had no other choice. The flesh is weak, I fear, even the flesh of dwarves." He turned. "But do not think me churlish. I am grateful your aid, sir knight."

"I am no knight," said Ridmark.

"I see," said Caius. "Might I know your name, then?"

"Ridmark Arban," said Ridmark.

"Ah," said Caius. If he recognized the name, he gave no sign. "And I am Brother Caius, a priest and a brother of the Order of Mendicants."

"A baptized dwarf," said Ridmark.

"Yes," said Caius, his white teeth flashing in his gray face. "The first of my kindred, I believe."

"If you are a mendicant," said Ridmark, "why do you have a mace?"

Caius shrugged. "It was...harder to give up my old life than I thought. And a son of the Church should not seek out war, but that does not mean we cannot defend ourselves." The dwarf grinned. "And you raised arms in my defense. It would be churlish not to aid you."

"Your aid was well-timed," said Ridmark. "Come. Sir Joram sent me to find you, and you're found."

Caius shook his head. "I desire to continue my journey north."

Ridmark frowned. "Why?"

"I wish to bring the word of the Dominus Christus to the pagan orcs of the north," said Caius, "and that has not changed."

"It has," said Ridmark. "These are Mhalekite orcs, and there are more of them nearby."

"Then they need to hear word of the faith all the more," said Caius.

"They will kill you," said Ridmark. A low wind whipped up around the hilltop, cold and icy.

"I know the risks," said Caius. He sighed. "And I am not a fool, whatever you might think. When I joined the Order of Mendicants, I hoped to meet devout sons and daughters of the Church. But there are few enough among the lords of Andomhaim. I fear your nobles have grown corrupt and complacent, as have the commanders of the Order of Swordbearers and the Magistri."

Perhaps Caius had met Tarrabus Carhaine and his supporters. "That may or may not be, but we need to go to Dun Licinia." The icy wind grew stronger. "Those Mhalekite orcs will move south, and they will attack Dun

Licinia. They people must be warned." He had told Peter to send warning, but Sir Joram might not believe the truculent freeholder.

Caius nodded. "Yes, you are right. I should have thought of it sooner. We must warn Sir Joram Agramore at once." He scowled and looked at the sky. "Though perhaps this snow shall stop the orcs. We never had such weather in the Deeps."

"There is no weather at all in the in the Deeps," said Ridmark, looking at the sky. "But it can't be snowing. There are not enough clouds. It…"

The cold wind became a gale, and thunder rang overhead.

And then the sky filled with blue fire.

Ridmark stared at the sky, stunned, as the sheets of blue fire painted the landscape with an azure glow. He heard Caius repeating a prayer, heard the wind howling around him, but he barely noticed.

"An omen," he heard himself say.

Both dread and a sense of finality settled in him.

"The omen," he said.

He had been warned about that omen ten years ago, fighting the urdmordar that had terrorized the village of Victrix. A year after that, he had undertaken a quest at the behest of the high elves, entering the cursed ruins of Urd Morlemoch. The undead sorcerer that lurked at its heart, the creature that called itself the Warden, had confirmed the urdmordar's mocking prophecy, telling him of the omen, the day blue fire would burst from the slopes of the Black Mountain.

The omen that foretold the return of the Frostborn.

CHAPTER 3
AWAKENING

Calliande opened her eyes.

She saw nothing but utter blackness, felt nothing but the cold stone beneath her back, its chill soaking through her robes. She took a deep breath, her throat and tongue dry and rough. Something soft and clinging covered her face and throat, and she tried to pull it off. But her shaking hands would not obey, and only after five tries did she reach her face, her fingers brushing her cheek and jaw.

She could not see anything in the blackness, but she recognized the feeling of the delicate threads she plucked from her face.

Cobwebs. She was pulling cobwebs from her jaw.

A wave of terrible exhaustion went through her, and a deeper darkness swallowed Calliande.

###

Dreams danced across her mind like foam driven across a raging sea.

She saw herself arguing with men in white robes, their voices raised in anger, their faces blurring into mist whenever she tried to look at them.

A great battle, tens of thousands of armored men striving against a massive horde of blue-skinned orcs, great half-human, half-spider devils on their flanks, packs of beastmen savaging the knights in their armor. Tall, gaunt figures in pale armor led the horde, their eyes burning with blue flame, glittering swords in their hands.

The sight of them filled her with terror, with certainty that they would devour the world.

"It is the only way," she heard herself tell the men in white robes, their faces dissolving into mist as she tried to remember their names. "This is the only way. I have to do this. Otherwise it will be forgotten, and it will all happen again. And we might not be able to stop him next time."

She heard the distant sound of dry, mocking laughter.

A thunderous noise filled her ears, the sound of a slab of stone slamming over the entrance to a tomb.

"It is the only way," Calliande told the men in white robes.

"Is it?"

A shadow stood in their midst, long and dark and cold, utterly cold.

"You," whispered Calliande.

"Little girl," whispered the shadow. "Little child, presuming to wield power you cannot understand. I am older than you. I am older than this world. I made the high elves dance long before your pathetic kindred ever crawled across the hills." The shadow drew closer, devouring the men in the white robes. "You don't know who I truly am. For if you did…you would run. You would run screaming. Or you would fall on your knees and worship me."

"No," said Calliande. "I stopped you once before."

"You did," said the shadow. "But I have been stopped many times. Never defeated. I always return. And in your pride and folly, you have ensured that I shall be victorious."

The shadow filled everything, and Calliande sank into darkness.

Her eyes shot open with a gasp, the cobwebs dancing around her lips, her heart hammering against her ribs. Again a violent spasm went through her limbs, her muscles trembling, her head pulsing with pain.

Bit by bit Calliande realized that she was ravenous, that her throat was parched with thirst.

And she was no longer in the darkness.

A faint blue glow touched her eyes. She saw a vaulted stone ceiling overhead, pale and eerie in the blue light. The air smelled musty and stale, as if it had not been breathed in a very long time.

She pressed her hands flat at her sides, felt cold, smooth stone beneath them.

On the third try she sat up, her head spinning, her hair falling against her shoulders.

She lay upon an altar of stone, or perhaps a sarcophagus. The altar stood in the center of a stone nave, thick pillars supporting the arched roof. The blue light came from the far end of the nave, near an archway containing a set of stairs.

Calliande sat motionless for a moment, listening to the silence.

She had no idea how she had gotten here. Nor, for that matter, did she know where she was.

And, with a growing sense of panic, she realized she could not remember who she was.

Calliande, her name was Calliande. She knew that much. But the details of her past turned to mist even as she tried to recall them. Shattered, broken images danced through her mind. Men in white robes, warriors with eyes of blue flame, armies of blue-skinned orcs...but all of it slithered away from her grasp.

Something, she realized, had gone terribly wrong.

"They were supposed to be here," she whispered, her voice cracked and rasping. "They were supposed to wait here."

But who?

She didn't know.

Her panic grew, her hands scrabbling over the altar's stone surface. After a moment she realized that she was looking for something. A...staff? Yes, that was it. A staff.

Why?

Calliande looked around in desperation, her panic growing.

"They were supposed to be here," she said again.

But through her fear, her mind noted some practical problems. She was alone in a strange place, her stomach was clenching with hunger, and she was so thirsty her head was spinning. Despite whatever had happened to her, she could not remain here and wait for someone to find her.

Calliande took a deep breath, braced herself on the edge of the altar, and stood. Her boots clicked against the stone floor, and her legs felt as if they had been made of wet string. Yet she did not fall, and after a moment she took a step forward.

Something brushed her left arm and fell to the floor.

She looked down at herself and saw that she wore a robe of green trimmed with gold upon the sleeves and hems, and the left sleeve had fallen off, exposing the pale skin of her arm. Once it must have been a magnificent garment, but now it was worn and brittle, the seams disintegrating. The leather of her belt and boots was dry and crumbling, and the few steps she had taken had already split her right boot open.

The clothes looked centuries old.

Her fear redoubled. Was she dead? Had she been buried alive?

Another part of her mind, the cold part that had urged her to find food and water, pointed out that a dead woman would not feel nearly as hungry as she did. Had not the Dominus Christus eaten food in front of his disciples to prove that he was not a spirit?

Whatever had happened to Calliande, she was still alive.

But she needed to take action to stay that way.

She crossed the nave, her boots crumbling further with every step. A thick layer of dust covered the floor, and she glimpsed more cobwebs stretched between the heavy pillars supporting the ceiling. No other footprints marked the dust. It was clear that no one had entered this chamber in a long time. Soot stained the pillars, and here and there Calliande saw piles of burned wood that had once been furniture.

Had this place caught fire?

She saw the first bones after that.

Three skeletons lay in the dust nearby, clad in rusted armor, swords and maces lying near their bony hands. She saw the marks of violence upon their bones. Plainly a battle had been fought here, long ago, and it had been followed by a fire.

How long had she been lying in this place of death?

Calliande reached the archway at the far end of the nave. A skeleton lay slumped against the stairs, clad in the ragged remnants of a robe.

A white robe.

She remembered the image from her dream, and reached to touch the bones.

As she did, the blue light brightened, and a specter appeared on the stairs.

Calliande took a step back in alarm, but the specter made no move to harm her. It looked like an old man in white robes, his head encircled by a tangled mane of gray hair, his eyes deep and heavy and sad.

"Forgive me, mistress," said the specter.

"You can see me?" said Calliande. "Who are you?"

"Forgive me, for we have failed in our sacred charge," said the specter. "The Tower of Vigilance is overrun. The warring sons of the old king brought their foolish quarrel here, and the Tower is taken. I wished us to remain neutral, but the others thought differently…and our Order has paid for it."

"Answer me!" said Calliande. "Who are you? Why am I here?"

But the specter kept talking, and Calliande realized it wasn't really there. Or, rather, it was not a spirit or a ghost. Rather, it was a spell, a final message to her.

Left by the man whose bones now lay moldering at her feet.

"I have no doubt they would kill you simply out of spite," said the old man, "and I have my suspicions of the darker forces behind the strife. But I have activated the defenses of the vault. Sealed it from the inside." He took a deep breath. "Only you can open it."

"But that means…" said Calliande.

That meant the old man had sealed himself inside the vault.

And to judge from the skeleton, he never left.

"Do not mourn for me," said the old man, "for my course is run. I am wounded unto death." She saw the spreading crimson stain across his white robes, and realized that he had been wounded. "You will be safe here, until you awaken."

He closed his eyes and shuddered with pain.

"Mistress, I beg, listen to me," said the old man. "You were right. You were always right, and I should have listened to you as a young man. This war between the Pendragon princes...no, it did not occur on its own. They were manipulated into it. Mistress, beware." His voice grew thicker, his breathing harsher. "The bearer...the bearer of the shadow. You were right about him, too. This was his doing. Everything has been his doing...and he has been laboring in the darkness for centuries before Malahan Pendragon raised the first stone of Tarlion itself. Mistress, please, beware...he will come for you...he..."

The specter vanished into nothingness.

And the blue glow faded.

With a surge of alarm Calliande realized the glow had been part of the spell. And now that the spell's message had been delivered, the light would fade away.

Leaving her alone in the darkness.

"No!" she said, her voice echoing off the walls.

The blue light faded away a moment later, leaving her in utter blackness.

Calliande waved her hands in front of her face, but she saw nothing. For a panicked instant she thought the skeletons would rise around her, rusted weapons gripped in bony hands, but she pushed aside the terror. The cold part of her mind recalled the specter's words, remembered the words about the magical defenses of the vault. If the old man had been correct, her touch ought to open the door.

If he was wrong, she would die of thirst in the darkness.

Calliande started forward, hands held out before her, and put her foot upon the first step. She started to climb, and felt her left boot crumble beneath her. The ruined leather felt like dust between her toes. She kicked it away, lost her balance, and fell, landing hard upon her palms.

The stone stairs were uneven. Perhaps it was safer to crawl.

She worked her way up the stairs step by step. Her robe bunched against her knees, and she tugged it up, only to feel a large chunk of it fall apart in her grasp. The dank, musty air of the vault felt icy against her exposed legs. She kept crawling, her heart pulsing in her ears. Perhaps the stairs would never end. Or perhaps this vault had been sealed so well that she would breathe all the air and asphyxiate in the darkness.

Surely that would be quicker than dying from thirst.

But she kept climbing, the stone rough against her palms. Step by step she went, sweat trickling down her face and back despite the chill, and then…

Her hand brushed smooth stone. She knelt, waving her hands before her, and felt a wall of smooth stone sealing off the end of the stairs. Was this the door the specter had mentioned? Calliande got to her feet, more pieces of her crumbling robe falling away. The stone felt icy cold beneath her touch, and damp with condensation.

She pushed at the door, and nothing happened.

"Open," she said.

Still nothing happened.

"Open!" Calliande shouted, her voice ringing with desperation.

Nothing happened…and then she felt the door shiver beneath her fingers, as if the stone had pushed again her mind.

A low grinding noise filled her ears, and a crack of brilliant white light appeared in the center of the stone slab. Calliande stepped back, one hand raised to shield her eyes, and the slab split in half, its sides retracting into the walls.

Something cold and wet slammed into her feet and shins. She saw water pouring through the crack in the opening door, and realized that the chamber beyond was flooded.

An instant later a waist-high wall of water slammed into her and knocked her over. Calliande tumbled back down the stone stairs, sputtering and thrashing, desperately trying to stop her fall. At last she hit the floor of the vault, the flow of water slackening as it poured down the stairs. She staggered to her feet, the remnants of her robe sodden against her. A desperate chill filled her chest, her body shaking with cold.

If she did not get out of this water, she was going to die.

Calliande hauled herself back up the stairs, grabbing at the wall for support against the cascading water. In the light from the opened doors, she saw that the stairs did not climb more than sixty feet or so.

In the darkness it had seemed so much farther.

Step by step she struggled up the stairs, her limbs quaking from the cold. She saw that the stairs opened into the base of a ruined square tower, its cellar flooded, though the water was draining into the vault. Calliande saw the tower's walls rising nearly six stories over the cellar, its interior long vanished. Pale sunlight leaked through the windows, and she saw heavy clouds streaking the blue sky.

Sunlight.

For a moment a wave of joy washed through her. She had never thought to see sunlight again.

Then the cold struck her. She waded across the cellar to a flight of stone stairs along the wall and heaved herself out of the water. As she did, the sodden remnants of her crumbling robes split apart, leaving only a few rags stuck to her wet skin. Getting out of the cold water helped with the chill, but not very much.

A heavy dread gripped her. The tower around her had obviously been destroyed and abandoned long ago. She was alone and starving, and if she did not find some food soon, she would be in trouble. More urgently, she was nearly naked, and she had to obtain shelter at once. She did not think it was winter, but it was cold, and Calliande feared that she would freeze if she did not find shelter.

But she would find neither clothing nor food in this ruined tower.

Calliande climbed the stairs, her bare feet slipping against the wet stone, one hand braced against the rough wall. The stairs ended in a narrow doorway, and Calliande stepped into a courtyard.

Her confusion increased.

The tower was part of a larger castle, and the castle was abandoned. Once it must have been a magnificent fortress, proud and strong. Now it lay in ruin, the outer curtain wall crumbling, the inner towers empty stone shells. Tough brown weeds covered the courtyard, and here and there a pine tree had thrust its way up through the earth. Calliande saw that the castle's barbican and gate lay in smashed ruin. The fortress had been sacked, burned, and abandoned long ago.

Perhaps even centuries ago.

Her shivering worsened, and not just from the cold.

What had happened to her? How had she awakened in the darkness beneath a long-abandoned castle?

She could worry about it later. Right now she needed to focus on survival. Calliande doubted she would find any clothing in the ruined castle, but perhaps she could find some means of making fire. The brown weeds would burn once she pulled them up. Once she had warmed herself, perhaps she could think more clearly, find a solution to her dilemma.

She turned towards the inner keep, and saw the dark mountain looming overhead.

It rose at least a mile high, a solid mass of black stone rising from the earth like an armored fist. No snow covered its slopes, and Calliande saw the distant shape of ruins atop the mountain.

That mountain was dangerous. She knew it in her bones.

"The Black Mountain," she whispered.

All at once she knew where she was.

The Black Mountain stood on the northernmost edge of the High King's realm of Andomhaim, on the northern border of the lands sworn to the Dux of the Northerland in Castra Marcaine. Castra Marcaine was only a few days' ride from the Black Mountain, and if Calliande could find some garments, she could walk there and subsist on wild plants during the journey.

And if she could remember where she was, then perhaps more of her memories would return.

Like how she had wound up sealed in a vault beneath a ruined castle.

Calliande turned, and saw an orcish man staring at her.

The orc stood in the doorway to one of the ruined towers, clad in fur and leather, a short bow in his hands. Battle scars marked his face and arms, and his black hair had been cut in a warrior's topknot. A strange brand had been burned onto the orc's forehead, like stylized teardrop.

The orc was watching her like a wolf looking at a wounded deer.

And Calliande remembered that she was naked.

She took a step back, trying to cover herself with her hands.

The orc grinned, tusks twitching against his cheeks, and climbed down from the tower's doorway.

"You," said the orc in the orcish tongue, "look cold."

She understood him. Apparently she knew orcish.

"Yes," said Calliande. "If you could bring me some clothing, I would…I would be most grateful."

The orc laughed. "I thought the Master was mad, when he said we would find you in this cursed place. But here you are. And I shall get the reward for laying you at the Master's feet."

Calliande turned to run.

She sprinted across the courtyard, the orc in pursuit. But the ground was uneven and rocky, and Calliande was barefoot. She managed to make it twenty yards before she slipped and landed hard upon her hip. Pain flooded through her, and she managed to roll to one knee.

The orc's hands closed about her shoulders.

Calliande tried to strike him, but she had no strength in her arms, and the orc hauled her to the feet without much effort. He spun her around, jerked her arms behind her back, and tied her wrists together.

"You're fortunate," said the orc. "You're a pretty thing, and I could have some fun with you. But the Master wants you intact and untouched, and I am not fool enough to defy the Master." He laughed. "And by the blood gods, once the Master is done with you, you'll wish I had made you my chattel."

The orc strode across the courtyard, dragging her after, his hand like an iron shackle around her arm.

CHAPTER 4
THE TOWER OF VIGILANCE

Ridmark stared at the blue flames rolling across the sky.

He heard Caius muttering a prayer in Latin, perhaps the fifty-first Psalm, but he did not care.

Fear filled him, and a growing sense of finality. In the last five years, he had hunted for clues, searching for evidence that the prophecies he had received from the urdmordar Gothalinzur and the Warden were false. He knew his former brothers of the Order of the Soulblade thought him a coward and an outcast, wandering the Wilderland in search of phantom foes that might grant redemption. Sometimes he wondered if they were right.

Sometimes he hoped they were right.

But he knew what he had seen.

And now the proof blazed overhead.

The blue flames pulsed once more, and then faded away, seeming to pull towards the Black Mountain to the north. The sky returned to normal, the sun shining through bands of heavy gray clouds.

"God save us," said Caius. "What was that?"

"An omen," said Ridmark. "A sign of their return."

"Return of who?" said Caius.

"The Frostborn," said Ridmark.

It was hard to judge expressions on the dwarf's gray-skinned face, but Ridmark thought he saw a hint of pity there. "The Frostborn are extinct. Your own High King wiped them out two hundred years ago. My kindred marched in that war, and my own father and brother fought alongside High King Ardraine himself. The Frostborn are no more."

"I know what I saw," said Ridmark, looking at the Black Mountain.

"As do I," said Caius, "but I think it was a conjunction of the moons. My kindred have long known that the conjunction of the thirteen moons can produce powerful magical effects. I think this was one of them."

"Perhaps," said Ridmark, "but that is not important. It is a sign, Brother Caius. I was warned against it." He thought for a moment. "The fire seemed to come from the Black Mountain."

"That is an ill place," said Caius. "Many great battles between the dark elves and the high elves were fought here, and then between the urdmordar and the high elves. And between the Frostborn and the High King."

"And the Mhalekite orcs at Dun Licinia," said Ridmark. He looked back at the dwarf. "I promised Sir Joram I would see you safe back to Dun Licinia. The way is clear to the town. Go, now, and you should make it back safely."

"And where are you going, Gray Knight?" said Caius.

Ah. So he had heard of Ridmark after all. "I am going to the Black Mountain. The blue flame seemed to come from there."

"That is folly," said Caius.

"Perhaps," said Ridmark, "but the Frostborn are returning. The lords and knights of Andomhaim must be warned. But they will not believe me without proof."

"So you're off to find proof?" said Caius.

"Aye," said Ridmark. "And a strange coincidence, is it not, that the Mhalekite orcs appear in the woods soon before the omen fills the skies?"

"It is troubling," said Caius.

"I am going to Black Mountain," said Ridmark. "You, Brother Caius, are going to Dun Licinia, to warn Sir Joram about the Mhalekites."

"No," said Caius. "I shall accompany you to the mountain."

Ridmark shook his head. "I fight better alone."

"That is true of neither man nor dwarf," said Caius. "I have taken the vows of a mendicant, but I fought against the dark elves and the deep orcs and the kobolds for decades as a warrior of the Three Kingdoms. I know how to wield a mace." He smiled. "Even the famed Gray Knight himself might benefit from my aid."

"I am not a knight," said Ridmark. He remembered the searing pain of the brand digging into his face. "Not any longer."

Caius shrugged. "As you said, Mhalekite orcs might lurk around the Black Mountain. But Sir Joram seems a phlegmatic sort of fellow, and he might not call to Dux Gareth Licinius for aid without proof. And if both of us go, the odds are better that one of us will survive to warn Dun Licinia."

"You are determined to go with me," said Ridmark, "aren't you?"

"You did save my life," said Caius. "While I look forward to joining the Dominus Christus in glory, I suspect he still has work for me in the mortal world."

"Stubborn," said Ridmark.

Caius grinned. "I understand humans often attribute stubbornness to my kindred."

"If God wants you to live, who am I to argue?" said Ridmark. "Very well. Come if you like. But you will do as I say, understand?"

"You are a captain and knight of renown," said Caius, "or at least you were, and I believe you know what you are doing. Lead on, Gray Knight."

"We'll make for the Tower of Vigilance," said Ridmark. "From there, we'll be able to see all the foothills on the southern side of the mountain."

"If whoever commands the Mhalekites has any brains at all," said Caius, "he'll have seized the ruins of the Tower already. That is a strong fortress, and the High King should never have let it fall into ruin after the war of the princes."

"Aye," said Ridmark. "If Mhalek had thought to seize it, we would not be having this conversation."

But perhaps Aelia would still be alive…

He pushed down that thought at once. Now was not the time to dwell upon it.

"Come," said Ridmark, lifting his staff. "Let us find some answers."

He led the way down the hill, setting a rapid pace.

But Caius had no trouble keeping up.

The ground grew rockier as they drew north, the foothills steeper and the trees smaller. Soon Ridmark found the remnants of a road climbing into the hills, cutting its way back and forth over the slopes. Once it had led to the Tower of Vigilance itself. Taking the road would save time and make for an easier ascent.

On the other hand, if a Mhalekite chieftain had taken control of the Tower's ruins, he would have set patrols along the road. But the orcs would watch for enemy patrols from Dun Licinia, not a ragged wanderer with a staff and a dwarf in a monk's robe.

"That," said Caius, "is a curious weapon you bear."

"It has its uses," said Ridmark, watching the trees. He thought about urging the dwarf to silence, but decided against it. Any sentinels in the trees would see them coming long before they came within earshot.

"I thought," said Caius, "that the sigil upon your face meant you could not bear arms within the realm of Andomhaim."

"Almost," said Ridmark. "It means I cannot carry a sword within the realm of Andomhaim. Other weapons are perfectly acceptable."

"The staff is considered a most unknightly weapon," said Caius.

"It is," said Ridmark, "but I suspect my former brothers of the Order of the Soulblade were wrong. They consider the quarterstaff a weapon for freeholders, for peasants and yeomen. Yet it takes a very skilled swordsman to overcome a capable man with a quarterstaff."

"Indeed," said Caius. "A sword is romantic, but sometimes practical things are better. I am surprised you can hit hard enough with a staff to kill, though."

Ridmark glanced back at him. Caius showed no hint of exertion from the climb, his bronze-colored mace in his right hand. "You are full of questions."

Caius laughed. "Indeed I am. Asking questions is what brought me to the Church, after all. For God is truth, and by seeking truth, we are seeking him."

"Poetic."

"So," said Caius, "how do you hit hard enough to kill?"

Ridmark laughed in exasperation and turned. "Catch."

He threw the staff at the dwarf, perhaps a little harder than he had intended. Caius's free hand snapped up to catch the staff, and the dwarf rocked beneath the weight.

"Heavier than it looks," he mused, and then his peculiar blue eyes widened. "It's made of steel!"

"Aye," said Ridmark. "Wood over a steel core. A blacksmith owed me a favor."

"A potent weapon," said Caius, handing the staff back, "in the hands of a strong man. A weapon much like its owner."

"Oh?" said Ridmark, resuming his climb.

"More than it appears," said Caius. "So you are truly the Gray Knight?"

Again Ridmark laughed in annoyance. "God and his saints. You do not weary of questions. So you have heard the tales about the Gray Knight?"

"I didn't leave the Deeps yesterday," said Caius. "I have spent nearly twenty years in Andomhaim. And ever since the fall of Mhalek, I have heard the stories. A warrior clad in a cloak of elven-gray, a warrior who haunts the wilderness of the Northerland and Durandis and Coldinium. A man who wields a staff, saves travelers from bandits and pagan orcs and worse creatures, and then vanishes as quickly as he appeared."

"A man must do something to keep himself occupied," said Ridmark.

"Indeed," said Caius. "Though I wonder what would drive such a man. But now that I know you are Ridmark Arban, the victor of Dun Licinia and..."

"And what?" said Ridmark, looking back at Caius. "Ridmark the traitor? Ridmark who fled the field? Ridmark who slew..." He looked back at the road.

"I was going to say," said Caius, "a bold and skilled warrior. Orlacht and his lot were capable fighters, and you overcame them single-handedly."

"You helped."

"Minimally," said Caius. "So what drives a man to haunt the Wilderland for five years?"

"Answers," said Ridmark.

The road rounded a hill, working its way along a steep stone slope. Soon, if Ridmark remembered correctly, the Tower of Vigilance itself would come into sight.

"What kind of answers?" said Caius.

"I told you already," said Ridmark. Yet, perhaps prodded by the dwarf's unending questions, he kept speaking. "A long time ago, I slew an urdmordar, a creature who called herself Gothalinzur. She told me that the Frostborn were returning. A year after that, I overcame an undead wizard of the dark elves in the ruins of Urd Morlemoch. He, too, claimed the Frostborn were returning."

"Lies," said Caius, a touch of sympathy in his tone. "Deceits to poison your mind in defeat. The Frostborn were exterminated."

"I thought so, too," said Ridmark. "Then Mhalek said the same thing, before..."

He remembered the scream, remembered the blood pooling on the floor, the pain filling his chest.

Pain that would never leave him.

"Before he died," he finished. "So I decided to find out the truth of it." He turned and look back at Caius. "And both the Warden and Mhalek claimed that blue fire would fill the sky to herald the return of the Frostborn."

"So here we are," said Caius.

"Here we are," said Ridmark. "If you'd prefer not to travel any further in the company of a madman, you are welcome to return to Dun Licinia."

"No," said Caius. "I don't think you are mad. No, I think you are...something else."

"What, then?" said Ridmark, climbing up the road.

But Caius did not answer.

Ridmark took another step, and then stopped.

"What is it?" said Caius.

"Keep your voice down," said Ridmark, lowering his staff so it tapped against the dwarf's burly chest. "Up ahead. See those boulders, just around the curve of the hill?"

Caius nodded. "A perfect place for a sentry."

"Exactly," said Ridmark. "Another few feet, and he'll be able to see us." He looked around, scowling. He supposed they could go around the hill, but that would take hours, and night would fall long before they reached the Tower of Vigilance. Ridmark could scramble up the slope and reach the pile of boulders from behind, but it would be obvious. One mistake, and any sentries would see him.

"A distraction," said Ridmark.

"What did you have in mind?" said Caius.

"You," said Ridmark.

"Me?"

"Keep walking along the road," said Ridmark. "Draw attention to yourself. Sing a hymn or something. While the sentry is watching you, he won't notice me, and I can deal with him."

"I don't like this plan," said Caius.

"You said you like to talk," said Ridmark. "It plays to your strengths."

The dwarf snorted. "I like to ask questions. But very well. I assume you know what you're doing."

Ridmark nodded and climbed the hill, and Caius marched along the world. He began to sing, his deep, rolling voice echoing off the hillside. Ridmark scrambled over the stones, moving from pine tree to pine tree with as much as much silence as he could manage. Caius kept walking, looking for all the world like a friar relieving the tedium of his journey with a hymn.

An orcish man stepped into sight from around the boulders, a short bow in hand, forehead branded with the Mhalekites' blood drop sigil. The orc lifted his bow, taking aim at Caius, and Ridmark charged forward.

At the last minute the orc saw him coming, but it was too late. The first swing of Ridmark's staff ripped the bow from the orc's hand. The second caught the orc behind the knees and sent him sprawling to the stony ground. The orc landed with a grunt of pain and tried to rise, only to find the butt of Ridmark's staff resting on his throat.

"Don't move," said Ridmark in orcish.

The orc growled. "What do you want?"

Caius scrambled up the hillside, mace in hand.

"You were going to shoot my friend," said Ridmark.

"You should not be here," said the orc. "These lands belong to the sons of Mhalek."

"Mhalek is dead," said Ridmark.

The orc growled again. "Betrayed and murdered by the cowardly Ridmark of Andomhaim…though the wretched human paid for his folly."

"Indeed," said Ridmark. "That does not explain why you are here."

"The omen came," said the orc, "just as the Master promised. Mhalek is slain, but the blood gods will come again. We will drive the humans and the halflings from these lands. We will butcher those of our kindred who pray to the weakling god of the humans."

"That is unlikely," said Ridmark.

"Many thousands of us have gathered," said the orc. "And the Master has promised a second sign, a force of warriors that shall make us invincible. Soon the lands of the humans and the faithless shall drip with blood."

"I think not," said Ridmark.

He lifted his staff.

"Are you going to kill him?" said Caius. "He is a prisoner."

"No," said Ridmark. "I'm going to let him go."

He stepped back, staff in hand. The orc climbed to his feet, black eyes narrowed.

"You will let me go? Why?" said the orc.

"Tell your master," said Ridmark, "that we know about his plans. That the men of Dun Licinia are ready for him. Tell your master to turn aside from his folly while he still can. Go."

The orc spat and turned.

Ridmark stretched, tightening his fingers against his staff.

"Ridmark!" shouted Caius.

The orc whirled, short sword in hand, and sprang at Ridmark.

But Ridmark had anticipated the treachery, and met the orc's attack with one of his own. He sidestepped the stab, swinging his staff, and the heavy weapon slammed into the orc's forehead with a crack of bone. The orc toppled, and Ridmark stabbed the end of the staff onto the orc's throat.

The orc died a few heartbeats after that.

"Did you really intend to let him go?" said Caius.

"If he had left without attacking us, then yes," said Ridmark. "I would have let him go. But as you said, a man has a right to defend himself."

"He would have warned the other Mhalekites," said Caius.

"I know," said Ridmark. "But I will not murder a prisoner."

He beckoned, and they worked their way back to the road.

"Your mercy does you credit," said Caius.

"Thank you," said Ridmark.

"But I do not think," said Caius, "that was your real reason."

"Oh?" said Ridmark. "Enlighten me, then."

"The Gray Knight," said Caius. "The man seeking the Frostborn. The man saving travelers and freeholders from bandits and the creatures of the Wilderland. A man who has no trouble risking his life."

"God and his saints!" said Ridmark. "It is just as well that you became a friar, Brother Caius, for you are enamored with the sound of your own voice."

Caius smiled. "Thank you." The smile faded. "But I think, Ridmark Arban...I think you are a man who very badly wants to die, but hasn't yet found anyone capable of killing him."

"All mortals die," said Ridmark.

He remembered the blood pooling on the floor of Castra Marcaine's great hall, remembered that last scream.

"Even those," he said, "who do not deserve it. I suggest we remain quiet now. There may be more scouts in the hills."

Caius gave him a long look, nodded, and Ridmark continued on the road.

CHAPTER 5
SHADOWBEARER

Calliande fought against the orc's grasp.

But the orc was too strong, and whatever had caused Calliande to wake up in a vault below the ruined castle had left her weak and exhausted. The orc pulled her along, her feet slipping and skidding on the rough ground, and she had no choice but to follow.

He pulled her towards the crumbling shell of a tower in the outer curtain wall.

"Kharlacht!" called the orc. "I've found her!"

A second orc emerged from within the tower.

He was huge, nearly seven feet tall, his topknot bound with a gleaming bronze ring. He was young, no more than twenty-five at the most, yet the middle-aged orc seemed frightened of him. The orc wore peculiar armor fashioned from overlapping plates of gleaming blue steel, and after a moment Calliande realized that the armor was of dark elven make, as was the hilt of the greatsword rising over his right shoulder.

Apparently that was something else she knew.

Kharlacht looked her up and down and grunted.

"She is far too young, Ulazur," said Kharlacht, his voice a stern growl. "You've found some lost human wench. The Master will be wroth if you bring her before him."

He turned away. A leather cord encircled his thick neck, and Calliande saw that it held a small wooden cross.

The orc was baptized? Unlike Ulazur, he did not have that peculiar brand upon his forehead.

"I am sure of it," said Ulazur. "That flooded tower in the inner castle. She came out of the water in the cellar."

Kharlacht turned back.

"She appeared right after the great sign," said Ulazur. "After the blue fire. It happened just as the Master said it would. She is the one, Kharlacht."

Kharlacht stooped over her, his huge, hard hand engulfing her chin, and titled her face up to examine it. His black eyes were like disks of stone, and held not a hint of pity or mercy.

"You will tell me your name," he said.

"Calliande," she said, her teeth chattering.

"Calliande," repeated Kharlacht. "How did you come here?"

"I…I don't know!" said Calliande. "I can't remember." She suspected telling the orcs anything would prove unwise.

"She speaks our tongue," said Ulazur. "Unusual for a common peasant. And the Master said she might call herself Calliande."

"Indeed," said Kharlacht. "Very well. We shall speak to Qazarl."

"Do not think to claim the reward, Kharlacht," said Ulazur with a scowl. "You might be Qazarl's kin, but I found her."

"I will not claim the reward," said Kharlacht. Ulazur grinned. "But if she is not the one the Master seeks…then you will answer to the Master for it."

That made Ulazur's smile vanish.

"Come, girl," said Ulazur, yanking on Calliande's arm. "Let us see what the Master thinks of you."

"Where am I?" said Calliande. "Where you taking me?"

"Silence," said Ulazur, raising his hand to strike her.

"The Master wished," said Kharlacht, "for her to remain undamaged."

Ulazur lowered his hand.

"This place is called the Tower of Vigilance in the human tongue," said Kharlacht. The name clicked in Calliande's mind, and she knew he spoke the truth. "Once it was a mighty fortress. It burned when the High King's sons made war upon each other, and now it is a ruin."

"No," said Calliande, "no, that's not right. The Vigilant keep watch here, in case…in case…"

But she could not remember why the Vigilant kept watch.

"As for where we are taking you," said Kharlacht. He looked away. Did she see guilt on his face? "You will see what the Master wants from you soon enough. Bring her."

Kharlacht strode across the courtyard of the ruined castle, Ulazur dragging Calliande after him. They circled the castle's curtain wall, coming at last to the wreckage of the southern gate. Memories flickered within Calliande's mind as she looked at the ruins. She saw the walls standing tall and strong, unmarked by weather and violence. Banners flew from the towers, men in gleaming armor standing atop the ramparts.

But the details dissolved into mist whenever she tried to focus on them.

She was certain she had seen this castle, the Tower of Vigilance, at the height of its splendor. But to judge from the state of the ruins, it had been abandoned for a century, if not longer.

What had happened to her?

Though as she felt Ulazur's fingers dig into her arm, Calliande realized that she ought to be more concerned about what was going to happen to her.

Kharlacht marched up the stairs to the outer wall. A wide turret stretched next to the barbican, offering a splendid view of the foothills below the Black Mountain. A half-dozen orcish men stood there, scowling, and Calliande felt the weight of their gaze fall upon her.

She desperately wanted to cover herself.

At the edge of the turret, gazing down at the foothills, stood a tall figure in a long coat the color of blood. The black-trimmed coat rippled in the icy wind coming down from the mountains. All Calliande saw of the figure in the coat was a shock of dark hair rising over the collar. The wizards of the high elves often wore such coats, indicating their rank and magical prowess.

Evidently that was another fact she had known before…whatever had happened to her.

Though she had no idea what a high elf would be doing among these orcs.

"Qazarl," said Kharlacht.

One of the orcish men stepped forward. He was the oldest orc Calliande had seen so far, his hair and ragged beard white. Unlike the others, he wore neither a warrior's topknot nor armor, but only trousers and a ragged vest. Elaborate tattoos and ritual scars marked his arms and chest.

She recognized the symbols. The orc was a shaman, a priest of the orcish blood gods…and a wielder of dark magic.

"Cousin Kharlacht," said Qazarl, his voice a thin hiss. "You have something?"

"Aye," said Kharlacht. "Ulazur believes he found her."

Qazarl's black eyes shifted to the warrior.

"Yes, great shaman," said Ulazur. "This is her."

He shoved Calliande towards the shaman.

"Her?" A second, younger orc stepped to Qazarl's side. Like Qazarl, his chest and arms were marked with scars and tattoos, though not as many as the older orc. That meant he was still an acolyte, not a full shaman of the blood gods…though he was still powerful and dangerous.

Again she wondered how she knew that.

Ulazur growled at the acolyte, lips pulling back from his teeth. "You doubt me, Vlazar?"

"This...girl is supposed to be the one the Master seeks?" said Vlazar. "He bade us to find a woman of power and strength. Instead you bring us this...huddling peasant girl." He stepped forward, glaring down at Calliande. "What is your name?"

Calliande said nothing, trying not to show any of her fear.

Vlazar backhanded her across the face. The power of the blow knocked her from her feet, and Calliande landed upon the rough stone floor with a cry.

"Enough," said Kharlacht. "This accomplishes nothing."

Vlazar spat. "More crying for mercy, Kharlacht? Why don't you pray to the sheep god of the humans and see if he will save the girl? Or perhaps you can put on lambskin and have Qazarl's wives put you to bed at night?"

The other orcs laughed, even Qazarl.

"Say that again, wizardling," said Kharlacht, his voice deepening and his eyes glowing as rage took hold. Orcs could fly into a murderous fury that made them stronger and faster than all but the most puissant human warriors.

"Do not threaten me," said Vlazar. "I have the favor of the blood gods, and unlike your god, they have power..."

Kharlacht reached for his sword hilt. "We shall see. It..."

"Enough."

The deep voice was calm and resonant, and yet carried a strange echo.

Almost as if it was two voices speaking at once.

Vlazar fell silent at once, and Kharlacht dropped his hand.

The orcs turned to look at the figure in the long red coat.

Calliande felt a shiver of fear. There was something wrong about that figure, something off...

She realized what it was. The gray clouds blocked out much of the sun...but a long black shadow streamed behind the man in the blood-colored coat.

A shadow pointing in the wrong direction.

"Master?" said Qazarl.

"Control your kinsman and your acolyte," said the strange voice. "I need her alive. If you harm her unduly, I fear I shall be...disappointed."

The figure in the blood-colored coat turned, and Calliande found herself looking at a high elf

And there was indeed something wrong with him.

He wore a black tunic, black trousers, and gleaming black boots beneath the red coat. His skin was the grayish-white of a corpse, and black veins throbbed beneath his hands and face, like fingers of corruption digging into rotting flesh. His bloodshot eyes were the color of mercury, of quicksilver, and Calliande realized she could see her reflection in his irises.

"You found her, Ulazur?" said the high elf.

Ulazur made a quick, jerky nod. "Yes, Master."

"Good. Pay him whatever reward was promised, Qazarl," said the high elf. He took several steps forward, and as he did, the orcs backed away. His shadow swept before him like a thrown cloak, and Calliande was desperately afraid that it would touch her bare skin.

But he stopped a few paces away, his strange shadow waving back and forth across the ground like an angry serpent.

"It has been a long time," he said, "hasn't it?"

"Stay away from me," said Calliande.

"Oh, not that long, not really," said the high elf, as if she had not spoken. "Not in the greater scheme of things. Your kindred has walked the face of the world for...what? A thousand years? The blink of an eye." He titled his head to the side. "Though from your perspective, I suppose that is nearly an eternity."

Despite all the strange things that had befallen Calliande, somehow this strange, gaunt creature frightened her more than all of them together.

"Who are you?" she whispered.

The high elf blinked. "You don't remember me? At all?" He laughed. "Ah. But that is delightful. Better than I could have imagined. I have often tried to make mortals forget me. It makes my work so much easier. And you did it to yourself!"

"So you are afraid to tell me who you are?" said Calliande, trying to muster a show of defiance.

The high elf grinned, pale lips exposing yellow teeth. "If I told you my real name, it would make blood pour out of your ears, I am afraid. And we can't have that. I have been called many things, but you used to know me as Shadowbearer."

A shiver of icy recognition went down Calliande's spine, though she could recall no details. Yet she remembered what the specter in the vault had told her. He had warned her to beware the bearer of the shadow.

Had he meant this strange creature?

"What do you want with me?" said Calliande.

"Your blood, your heart, and your power," said Shadowbearer. "In that order, precisely." He grinned again. "I see the frustration in your face. You see, I just told you exactly what I intend to do. In your prime, you would have understood at once. But now it's as if I'm speaking gibberish. How pathetic you have become." He leaned closer, his strange shadow inching closer to her, and Calliande tried not to flinch or look away. "And the most amusing part of all is that you did it to yourself."

"If you know who I am," said Calliande, "then tell me. Otherwise do not weary my ears with your riddling nonsense."

She heard Vlazar's breath hiss through his teeth. Apparently one did not speak in such a manner to Shadowbearer.

But the high elf laughed. "Bravely spoken. If you had your memory, my words would be clear as day. Alas, you maimed yourself in pride, and blinded yourself to wisdom." He clapped his hands together. "But we had best get started, hmm? A year and a month. That is how long I have, starting from the great sign. Thirteen months, and I cannot waste a moment of them. But before our work begins, I have two questions for you. First." He leaned closer, and Calliande shuddered. "Where is the staff?"

"I don't know what you're talking about," said Calliande. She had looked for a staff when she had first awoken, but could remember nothing of it.

Shadowbearer nodded. "I see. Then where is the sword?"

"Sword?" said Calliande. "What sword? I haven't seen any swords."

"I do believe," said Shadowbearer, straightening up, "that you are telling the truth. But let us make certain." He snapped his fingers. "Get her on her feet."

Two of the orcs seized Calliande's arms and jerked her upright. Shadowbearer moved closer, and she saw her distorted reflection in the quicksilver irises of the high elf's bloodshot eyes. Her skin crawled with revulsion as he drew nearer, the red coat hanging around him like a bloody shroud.

"Now," said Shadowbearer, "let us have the truth, shall we? Hold her still. She will likely scream."

His shadow rotated to fall upon her, wrapping around her like icy fingers.

And Calliande screamed.

The shadow had neither weight nor presence. Yet she felt it touching her, felt it sinking into every nook and cranny of her being.

"Now," said Shadowbearer, and she heard his strange voice thundering inside her head. "The staff. Where is the staff?"

"I don't know!" said Calliande. "I don't know anything about a staff."

"Indeed," said Shadowbearer, and made a twisting motion with his right hand.

Pain exploded through her, and Calliande went rigid, screaming. If not for the orcs' grasp, she would have collapsed to the ground. She felt the shadow drilling into her mind and sifting through her thoughts, felt cold, clammy fingers sorting through her memories.

She tried to think of a staff...but she remembered nothing but swirling mist.

"Ah," murmured Shadowbearer. "Clever. Another question. Where is the sword?"

"I...I don't know," said Calliande, shuddering. "The only swords I've seen are with your orcs."

Shadowbearer nodded. "I thought so. Now let us see if you are telling the truth."

Again he made that twisting motion, and agony stabbed through Calliande. She screamed again, her eyes bulging with pain, and felt the talons of his shadow sink into her head. The questing fingers rummaged through her thoughts, seeking for any mention of a sword.

But again, they found only mist.

"So," said Shadowbearer, his shadow sliding away from her. "I am impressed." He turned to the rampart. "You didn't simply erase your memory. That can be undone, after all, with the proper spells. No, you removed it entirely." He laughed. "I cannot view what I cannot find."

"I don't know what you're talking about," said Calliande.

"Of course you don't," said Shadowbearer. "That is the entire point. I admire your forethought, really. You knew this might happen. You knew I would not stop. So you prepared. All this," he waved his hand at the ruined Tower of Vigilance, "and the game with the memories. Very, very clever." He grinned, the expression making his face all the more skull-like. "Very clever...but I have been doing this for a long time, dear Calliande. Longer that you have. I burned the Tower...and I was waiting for you."

"I don't know what any of this is about," said Calliande. "I've never seen you before and I don't know where I am. Please, let me go. Please."

His gaunt face curled in a sneer. "Begging? You are begging for your life?" He laughed, as did the orcs, though Kharlacht remained silent. "How thoroughly you have defeated yourself. Once armies marched at the sound of your voice. Now you are reduced to groveling like a slave girl. You understood the nature of your enemy...but you were too weak to do what was necessary to defeat me. And now even that knowledge has been taken from you."

"I don't understand," said Calliande.

"No matter," said Shadowbearer. "Your understanding is not required. Merely your death. Qazarl!"

"Master," said the shaman with a bow, moving to the red-coated wizard's side.

"We must act at once," said Shadowbearer. "You are prepared?"

"Yes, Master," said Qazarl. "Four thousand of my kin have assembled from Vhaluusk, and they wait outside the walls of this fortress. Food and fodder have been gathered, and we are ready to bring blood and death into the lands of the humans."

"Good," said Shadowbearer. "You are a strong disciple of the blood gods, and you shall succeed where Mhalek failed."

Qazarl nodded, his eyes alight with eagerness, as did the other orcs. Could they not see the faint sneer of contempt of Shadowbearer's face?

This wizard, this creature, whatever he was, was not Qazarl's ally.

Kharlacht looked troubled. Perhaps he saw it.

"I have one task for you first," said Shadowbearer. "A ritual, one that will guarantee victory for your forces."

"What is it, Master?" said Qazarl.

"This," said Shadowbearer, reaching into his coat.

He lifted his hand, and Calliande felt the power of the object in his fingers. Both Qazarl and Vlazar took a step back, and Kharlacht reached for the hilt of his greatsword. Shadowbearer held a lump of white crystal about the size of a grown man's fist, a pale white glow gleaming in its milky depths. The mist in her mind shivered at the sight of the crystal, and suddenly she knew what it was.

"A soulstone," she whispered.

The orcs looked at her, and Shadowbearer grinned.

"Ah," he said. "Your memory returns, does it? Well, not entirely. Otherwise you would know just how much danger you are in."

"Is it true, Master?" said Qazarl. "That is a soulstone?"

"It is," said Shadowbearer, still grinning. "An empty one. Fresh-grown, in fact. Snatched from the caves of Cathair Solas to the north."

"Then," said Kharlacht, "will not the high elves come in wrath to reclaim it? Such a stone is dangerous."

Shadowbearer looked at the hulking orc and said nothing.

"Do not question the Master!" snarled Qazarl, and Vlazar glared at Kharlacht, flexing his fingers as if to cast a spell. "I put up with your peculiar infatuation with the human god because you are blood kin and a skilled warrior. But do not ever presume to question the Master, Kharlacht, for…"

"Actually," said Shadowbearer, "he is entirely correct. The archmage of the high elves is most wroth, and he is coming in fury to destroy me." He smiled. "Not that he could, of course. He has tried ever since the urdmordar ground the high elven kingdoms into bloody dust. Yet I am still here. Nevertheless, he is coming for me."

"Then what shall we do?" said Ulazur. "We cannot fight high elven sorcery."

"No need," said Shadowbearer. "I will deal with the archmage. You, Qazarl, will seize Dun Licinia and kill every man of fighting age within the walls. Keep the women and children as slaves, or kill them as it pleases you." He held out the soulstone, and Calliande felt its power wash over her. "And you, Vlazar, will take this."

"Me?" said the younger shaman, black eyes widening.

"Are you deaf?" said Shadowbearer. "Yes, you."

Vlazar swallowed and took the soulstone from Shadowbearer's hands. "And…and what am I to do with it, Master?"

"Select a suitable escort of warriors," said Shadowbearer. "Twenty or thirty ought to suffice. Take the soulstone and our prisoner," he gestured at Calliande, "and proceed to the circle of standing stones further up the foothills. Do you know it?"

"Yes, Master," said Vlazar. "The dark elves of old once built such places, when they still ruled the orcish kindred as slaves...and they worked mighty sorcery there."

"Splendid. How good to meet a man who knows his own history," said Shadowbearer. "Take the prisoner to the standing stones, unharmed and untouched. When you arrive bind her upon the altar, place the soulstone upon her chest, and kill her. The soulstone will...transform, rather suddenly, after that. Once it does, return here and give me the soulstone."

"I would prefer," said Vlazar, "to join Qazarl and assail Dun Licinia, and spill the blood of the humans!"

"Oh, you will," said Shadowbearer. "Once you return to me with the activated soulstone, you will spill human blood. I promise you that we shall spill more blood than this world has ever seen."

His words echoed in Calliande's head, and another bit of memory floated out of the mist in her head.

"You're...you're going to trap my soul in that crystal," said Calliande. "Why?"

"For power, of course," said Shadowbearer. "Power enough to crack worlds...or, more accurately, to join them." He looked at the sky, his shadow rotating around him, and nodded. "Yes. Begin at once."

"In the name of the blood gods," said Qazarl, "we shall turn Dun Licinia to ashes."

"I shall do as you command, Master," said Vlazar.

"Good," said Shadowbearer. "Oh, and Vlazar? Make certain the girl reaches the altar untouched. She is a pretty young thing, or at least looks like one, and perhaps you wish for some fun before you kill her, hmm?"

Vlazar grinned, and Calliande shuddered at his expression.

"Resist that impulse," said Shadowbearer. "For the magic to work, she needs to reach the standing stones untouched. A little bastard half-orc in her belly would upset the spell. So." His strange shadow rotated to point at Vlazar, and the shaman took an alarmed step back. "Do exactly as I say. Am I understood?"

"Yes, Master," said Vlazar. "All things will be as you command."

"Good," said Shadowbearer. "I shall return. Begin now."

The high elf turned, his shadow rippling and distorting around him, and vanished into nothingness.

For a moment the orcs said nothing.

"This is madness, Qazarl," said Kharlacht. "We might take Dun

Licinia, aye, but the Dux of the Northerland will come for us, along with the Swordbearers and the Magistri. We..."

"Silence," said Qazarl, glaring at the young warrior. "You shall see the power of the blood gods revealed, fool. Perhaps that will at last shame you into forsaking the superstitions of the humans." He made a dismissive gesture. "You will command Vlazar's escort. Select thirty warriors of appropriate strength."

"I do not wish that fool in my company," said Vlazar, glaring at Kharlacht.

"I care nothing for your wishes," said Qazarl. "Kharlacht might pray to the god of sheep, but he is still our strongest warrior, and the Black Mountain is dangerous. The Master will be displeased if the kobolds of the Deeps carry off the woman for their dinner. Stop talking and go."

Vlazar growled, looking back and forth between Kharlacht and Qazarl, and for a moment Calliande thought the rage in his orcish blood would drive him to attack. But at last he shivered, and made a harsh nod. "As you say. Kharlacht, select your warriors. We will leave at once."

"Make haste to fulfill the Master's bidding," said Qazarl. "I will await you at Dun Licinia."

"You two," said Kharlacht, pointing at the orcs holding Calliande. "Bind her. Gently."

Calliande tried to run, but she was still too weak, and Shadowbearer's magical intrusion had left her further weakened. The orcs tied her wrists and ankles together, and then produced a long wooden pole and bound her to it. Two of the orcs hefted the pole and carried it on their shoulders, and she swung from it like a deer trussed up from the hunt.

Or like a goat tied up for the slaughter.

Kharlacht and Vlazar strode from the curtain wall, their warriors carrying Calliande between them.

And from outside the wall, Calliande heard the sound of drums and shouts, the noise of an orcish host preparing itself for battle.

CHAPTER 6
PURSUIT

"I think," said Caius in a quiet voice, "that we are in over our heads."

Ridmark could not disagree.

He crouched behind a mossy boulder, the dwarf friar at his side, and looked at the stone bulk of the Tower of Vigilance.

The ruined castle crowned one of the largest of the foothills. Once its massive curtain wall had encircled the hill's entire crest, the towers of its inner keep rising high against the dark shadow of the Black Mountain. Now the castle was a crumbling ruin, its towers stone shells, its gates broken.

A ruin that provided shelter for thousands of orcs camped outside the wall.

"Three thousand of them, at least," muttered Ridmark, counting the lines of tents. He saw orcish warriors walking everywhere, sharpening weapons and repairing armor. "Maybe even four."

"Aye," said Caius, examining the ruined castle. "They're getting ready to move."

Ridmark nodded, thinking. "They must be preparing to attack Dun Licinia. This isn't merely a warband or a raid. This is an army, as large of one as Mhalek's old followers can muster."

"I head Mhalek raised a great horde," said Caius.

"He did," said Ridmark. "Fifty thousand strong, and they marched out of Vhaluusk and the Wilderland like a storm. They...stop talking."

He ducked behind the boulder, and Caius followed suit. A moment later four orcish scouts marched up the road, each carrying a short bow, their forehead marked with the teardrop sigil of the Mhalekites. Ridmark remained motionless, wrapped in his elven cloak, his hands tightening around his staff.

But the orcs did not see them, and continued climbing the road to the Tower's southern gate.

"Fifty thousand strong," said Ridmark, straightening up, "and they would have burned a trail of cinders and blood from Dun Licinia to Tarlion itself, if Mhalek had worked his will."

"If you hadn't stopped him," said Caius.

Ridmark grimaced. "I was hardly alone." He stared at the castle. "One of Mhalek's remaining disciples must have delusions of grandeur. Or found some old dark elven relic of power. They won't penetrate far into the realm, not with only four thousand warriors. But they will burn Dun Licinia to the ground, and kill God knows how many people."

"Then our course is clear," said Caius. "We must return to Dun Licinia and warn Sir Joram." He shrugged. "Or at the very least one of us must go, if you are so determined to find the truth behind this omen of the Frostborn."

"Even you must think it an odd coincidence," said Ridmark, glancing at Caius. "The blue fire fills the sky...and then an orcish host gathers at the Tower of Vigilance."

"What is this place, anyway?" said Caius.

"The Tower of Vigilance," repeated Ridmark.

Caius snorted. "I know the name, but not its history."

"Fair enough," said Ridmark. He saw hundreds of green-skinned figures moving back and forth below the Tower's outer wall. "Two hundred years ago, after the High King Arthurain the Fifth and the Dragon Knight and the Magistri and the Swordbearers destroyed the Frostborn, some feared the Frostborn they might return. So the Order of the Vigilant was founded, and they built the Tower of Vigilance to watch for the Frostborn. But the decades passed, and the Order became an anachronism. Finally, during the War of the Five Princes, the Master of the Vigilant picked the wrong side. The current High King's father seized the Tower of the Vigilant, burned it, and slew the Order. The castle has been abandoned ever since."

"And now here you are," said Caius, "hunting signs of the return of the Frostborn. Who are extinct."

"And I've found orcs instead," said Ridmark. "God has a sense of humor."

"The Lord works in mysterious ways," said Caius, "his wonders to perform. And while I do not presume to know the mind of God, I hope his plan does not involve you dying in the heart of those ruins. Which you will, if we go any further. I suggest we return to Dun Licinia at once. Sir Joram must be warned...and if the outlying freeholders do not fall back behind the town's walls, they shall be slaughtered."

The dwarven friar was right. The omen Ridmark had sought for five years had filled the sky, and Ridmark knew the answers were somewhere on the Black Mountain. Yet a small army of orcs stood between Ridmark and the Mountain. He did not fear death, and after Mhalek's defeat, he had courted death without hesitation. Yet as weary as he was of life, he was not ready to kill himself...and if he marched into the Tower of Vigilance, that was exactly what he would do.

Besides, he was sure those Mhalekite orcs were somehow connected to the omen.

"Very well," said Ridmark. "We'll make our way back to town. If we start now we should arrive by midnight." He looked at the dwarf. "I assume you have no trouble journeying in the dark?"

Caius smiled, his odd blue eyes glinting in his gray face. "I was a son of Khald Tormen, and I did not see the sun until my twentieth birthday. Your moonlit nights are to me as a cloudless summer day is to you."

Ridmark frowned. "So what is a cloudless summer day to you, then?"

Caius considered it for a moment. "Very bright."

"Indeed," said Ridmark, glancing at the sky. It was not a cloudless summer noon but a late spring afternoon, and the sky was a patchwork of clear blue and harsh gray clouds. "Best we move. Even with your eyes, I wouldn't enjoy finding my way through the hills back to the valley in the..."

A shadow passed overhead, and Ridmark caught a glimpse of sunlight reflecting off something coppery.

"Down!" he hissed.

He pushed Caius against the boulder, and a drake landed a half-dozen yards away.

The serpentine creature was the size of a large dog, through its bat-like wings stretched for a dozen feet in either direction from its slender body. Gleaming copper-colored scales covered the creature from its head to its pointed tail, and talons the color of sooty iron jutted from its paws. Its narrow head rotated back and forth on the end of its long neck, and its gleaming yellow eyes regarded Ridmark with an unblinking stare.

Caius frowned. "Is that a..."

"Drake. A fire drake, yes," said Ridmark. "Spread out your hands. Make yourself look bigger, and start moving to the side." He spread his arms, staff in his right hand, and moved to the left while Caius moved to the right. "And for God's sake don't run at it."

"Small little devil," said Caius, and his deep voice turned the drake's attention toward him. "One good blow from my mace should crush its skull."

"Aye," said Ridmark, "and if you miss, you won't get a second blow, because your head will be on fire."

"Do you think the orcs enspelled it," said Caius, "and sent the beast to scout?"

"Perhaps," said Ridmark. The Magistri of the High Kingdom used their magic for defense, for knowledge, and for far-speaking, but the shamans of the pagan orcs possessed many strange powers. "There are nests of the drakes upon the Black Mountain. Occasionally bold knights will decide to make a name for themselves by slaying a few of the drakes...and usually they wind up cooked within their armor."

The drake had still not moved, its head rotating back and forth between Caius and Ridmark.

"What is it doing?" said Caius. "Why hasn't it attacked?"

"Because," said Ridmark, "drakes aren't afraid of humans, but I doubt this one has ever smelled a dwarf before. It doesn't know what to make of you."

"So he's trying to decide," said Caius, "whether or not to eat us."

"Yes," said Ridmark. "Keep making yourself look larger, and back away around the boulder. If it decides we're too much trouble, it will fly off. Probably try to kill one of the Mhalekites. But if it decides to eat us, we'll have to fight it, and it will breathe fire."

"That would be bad," said Caius.

"Obviously," said Ridmark. He squatted, scooped up a stone with his free hand, and kept backing away. "And if it misses, it will set those pine needles on fire. And if it does, the orcs in the Tower will see the fire..."

"And come investigate and kill us," said Caius. "So what do we do?"

"Keep backing away," said Ridmark. "If we can get behind the boulder, it..."

The drake scuttled forward, its jaws yawning.

"Down!" said Ridmark.

Caius threw himself to the side, and the drake spat a jet of swirling yellow-orange flame. The fire splashed against the side of the boulder, and a patch of pine needles burst into flame, thick black smoke rising into the sky. Caius sprinted at the drake, mace in hand, and the beast opened its jaws for another blast of flame.

Ridmark flung the stone in his left hand. It slammed into the drake's head. The drake snarled and rotated to face him, and Ridmark surged forward. He swung his staff with all his strength, and the shaft struck with enough force to knock two fangs from the drake's jaw. The creature staggered with a scream of pain, and Caius's heavy mace slammed into the joint of its left foreleg. Ridmark heard the bones crunch beneath heavy dwarven steel, and again the drake screamed.

The creature had had enough. It flung itself into the air, wings unfurling, and flew away towards the Black Mountain.

The smoke from the burning pine needles followed it.

Ridmark ducked behind another boulder, as did Caius, and saw the commotion atop the hill. The orcs were moving. They had seen the fire, and they would send at least a single patrol to investigate.

"We had best move," said Ridmark.

"Sound counsel," said Caius.

Ridmark beckoned, pulling up the cowl of his cloak, and led Caius further away from the road, higher up the slope of the hill towards the Tower. He looked at the burning pine needles and muttered a curse. Despite his best efforts, they had left tracks near the boulder. If the Mhalekites had any skilled trackers among their numbers, the orcs would find their trail in short order.

They needed to disappear.

Fortunately, the sun was going down, and the ground grew rockier near the Tower of Vigilance itself.

"This way," said Ridmark. "Step only where I step."

He hurried across the stony hillside as fast as he dared, moving from boulder to boulder and stone to stone. Caius hopped after him, mace in one hand. With any luck, they would not leave tracks for the orcs to follow. Given that the Mhalekites clearly planned to attack Dun Licinia as soon as possible, Ridmark hoped they could lie low until the orcs departed. Then they could slip past their column and head for Dun Licinia.

"There," said Ridmark. They were getting closer to the Tower than he would like, and would need cover soon. "Follow me."

A pair of stubby pine trees jutted from a massive cracked boulder. Ridmark ducked under the trees, the fallen needles gritting beneath his boots, and Caius followed suit. From here, they had a fine view of both the hillside and the road leading to the Tower's southern gate. If any orcs came towards their hiding place, Ridmark would see them long before they saw him.

"A good hiding place," said Caius. He squinted at the curtain wall. "Though if they're clever, I suppose they could mount a siege machine upon the wall and shoot us from a distance."

"If they have any siege machines," said Ridmark, "they're taking them to Dun Licinia. We'd best wait here until we see how they react to the fire." He sat down with a sigh and pulled off his pack. "Do you have any food?"

"Of course," said Caius, lifting his own pack. "Hard biscuits and cheese. I wouldn't venture into the Wilderland without supplies. And you stopped the orcs before they robbed me."

"I don't suppose you have any wine," said Ridmark, reaching for his waterskin.

"I do," said Caius, "but it is reserved for communion."

Ridmark nodded, retrieved some jerky from his pack, and began to eat.

"How long do you intend to remain here?" said Caius.

"Until nightfall," said Ridmark. "Once it's dark, we can make our way back down the hill and back to Dun Licinia."

"That's another four hours, at least," said Caius.

Ridmark nodded. "Then I suggest that you make yourself comfortable."

Caius grimaced. "Small chance of that, I fear."

"Is not hardship good for the soul?"

"True," said Caius, "though, alas, the flesh is never as willing to…"

A war horn rang out, and for an instant Ridmark thought that they had been discovered. But a second horn rang out, and then another, until dozens of blasts thundered over the foothills of the Black Mountain. Drums boomed from the Tower of Vigilance, and Ridmark heard thousands of orcs shouting.

"Quite the racket," said Caius.

Ridmark peered up at the ruined castle. Orcs hurried along the base of the walls, gathering at the southern gate. In their midst he saw wagons pulled by mules, wagons laden with weapons and supplies.

"They're moving out," he said. "And I would wager they are heading right for Dun Licinia."

"We must go at once," said Caius.

"We can't," said Ridmark. "If we leave now, we'll get caught. Not even I can elude that many orcs in one place. We'll wait until dark, or until enough of them leave." He thought for a moment. "Then we can cut through the Tower of Vigilance itself and exit through its northern gate. Another road circles the base of the hill, and we can use it to reach Dun Licinia."

"Just in time to see the town besieged," said Caius.

"Perhaps," said Ridmark. "The Mhalekites might take their time looting the countryside. But if the town falls under siege, we'll head for Castra Marcaine. Dux Licinius needs to be warned, and he can call his Comites and knights to smash the Mhalekites."

He did not look forward to seeing Dux Gareth Licinius again, not at all, and he never wanted to return to Castra Marcaine. But the Dux of the Northerland had to be warned of what was happening in his lands.

"I can think of nothing better to do," said Caius.

"Pity," said Ridmark. "I was hoping you had a better plan."

They sat in silence. Ridmark watched the orcs moving around the base of the castle. A long column wound its way down the road, thousands of orcish warriors marching in a ragged line. The orcs lacked the discipline and the formations Ridmark had seen in the High King's armies, or the baptized orcs allied with the High King. Yet the rage in the orcs' blood let them strike harder and faster than a human man. Discipline always conquered individual valor and boldness, yet the orcs' battle rage was unmatched…

"How do you happen to know this countryside so well?" said Caius, cutting into Ridmark's musings.

He looked away from the marching column. "When Mhalek came, the Master of my...the Master of the Swordbearers sent out scouts. He wanted the countryside mapped thoroughly, didn't want Mhalek to use the terrain against us."

"The Master of the Order at the battle?" said Caius. "That was old Armus Galearus, wasn't it?"

"Aye," said Ridmark, remembering the fierce old man with his bristling white beard. He had been the image of a chivalric Swordbearer, devoted to his code...right up until Mhalek's treachery killed him.

"I suppose you benefited from the maps," said Caius.

"I did," said Ridmark. He shook his head. "They said I won the Battle of Dun Licinia, but as I told you, I was hardly alone. I had a great deal of help."

"Up until the end, at any rate," said Caius.

"Yes," said Ridmark.

He did not want to talk about what had happened after the battle.

They lapsed into silence. Caius lifted his crucifix and began to pray in silence, his bearded lips moving through the words. Ridmark settled against a tree's trunk, held his bow and an arrow ready in his hands, and watched the orcish army march. He wondered why the Mhalekites had occupied the ruined castle. Mhalek himself had avoided it, claiming that dark magic even he could not control lurked within the ruins. Old Galearus had used Mhalek's fear to keep the orcs from flanking the army of Andomhaim, and after Galearus had been killed, the battle had begun far south from the castle.

So why occupy it now? And why abandon it so easily? With a little work, the orcs could have made the place impregnable.

Ridmark sat and waited.

After about two hours he got to his feet. The sun had sunk far to the west, filling the foothills with thick shadows.

"Caius," said Ridmark, and the dwarf looked up from his prayers. "They've moved on." A long column of orcs and wagons moved down the road, and Ridmark had not seen anyone issue from the Tower of Vigilance for a while.

"Foolish of them," said Caius, standing with a grunt. "They could have held the castle. Or at the very least, they could have waited until dawn to march. Now they'll have to camp in the open."

"Perhaps they plan to steal supplies from the freeholders near the town," said Ridmark. "Or perhaps their commander is simply an idiot."

"One can hope," said Caius. "If we must have enemies, let them be fools."

"We are rarely that fortunate," said Ridmark. He watched the column for another moment, and then nodded. "Let's go."

"Now?" said Caius. "There are still orcs on the road."

"Not as many," said Ridmark, "and they're all heading south. If we slip into the Tower and head for the north gate, we can make for Dun Licinia from the northwest."

He stepped out from the trees, staff in hand, Caius following. His heart pounded within his ribs, and he felt unseen eyes gazing at him. Every instinct screamed that the orcs were going to fall upon him, that the Mhalekites would attack.

But the orcs had abandoned the ruins of the Tower, and their warriors marched south.

"This way," said Ridmark.

He picked his way up the slope, keeping a wary eye on the road and the curtain wall, pausing every so often to let Caius catch up. But the orcs continued their march, and he saw no sign of movement within the ruined castle. By the time he reached the top of the hill, the orcish column had vanished around the road.

Heading for Dun Licinia…and for the unprotected freeholders near the town.

Ridmark could do nothing for them now. The sooner he crossed through the Tower of Vigilance, the sooner he could return to Dun Licinia and warn Sir Joram. Or to reach Castra Marcaine to warn Gareth Licinius of the threat to his lands.

Or to rouse Dux Licinius to avenge the people of Dun Licinia.

"Shall we walk to the gate?" said Caius, breathing hard.

"No need," said Ridmark, circling around the exterior of the curtain wall.

The wall was thirty feet high, but it had crumbled into ruin in several locations. Ridmark scrambled up a rubble heap, the broken stones providing easy handholds. He pulled himself to the rampart, helped up Caius, and looked over the ruined Tower of Vigilance. Once a half-dozen tall towers had stood in the center of the courtyard, connected by their own wall. Now only empty stone shells remained, and weeds and even small trees had pushed their way up through the flagstones.

"This was a strong place," said Caius.

"Aye, but no longer," said Ridmark. "Come. Another gate opens in the northern wall. From there we can…"

He fell silent as a flicker of motion caught his eye.

A party of orcs moved around the base of a ruined keep.

"Go," hissed Ridmark, gesturing at one of the towers in the outer wall. "Take cover, now."

Caius hurried into the tower. The door had rotted away long ago, the hinges leaving orange rust stains upon the stone. The tower's interior had collapsed in a pile of moldering timber and broken stone, but the stairs still encircled the wall, and Ridmark braced himself upon the steps, near one of the narrow windows overlooking the courtyard. From here, no one in the yard could see him, but he could see the group of orcs.

Soon the orcs came into sight. An orcish man wearing ragged trousers and a vest led them, his arms and chest tattooed with ritual symbols. At his side walked a tall orcish warrior, almost seven feet high, clad in armor of odd blue steel plates, the hilt of a greatsword rising over his shoulder.

"That's dark elven steel," muttered Caius.

Ridmark nodded. "He must have looted it from some ruin."

"Or slain a dark elven warrior and claimed his armor," said Caius.

That was a worrying thought. A dark elf could live for a millennia, could hone his skills with a sword to unmatched heights. An orc capable of slaying a dark elven warrior would be a dangerous foe.

And if the shaman and the warrior cooperated in battle, they would make for deadly enemies.

"Thirty of them, I think," said Caius.

"Odd they're not leaving with the rest of the host," said Ridmark.

"I know," said Caius. "I think that…" His eyes widened. "Look."

Two of the orcs carried a wooden pole, and a woman dangled from the pole, her wrists and ankles bound with heavy rope. She was naked, her face hidden behind long blond hair, and for a moment Ridmark thought she was dead, that the orcs had turned her into a macabre trophy. But he saw her struggling against the ropes, saw her chest rising and falling as she drew breath.

"A prisoner," said Caius.

Ridmark nodded. The High King's law banned slavery in the realm of Andomhaim, but the pagan orcs often kept slaves, whether orcs from defeated tribes, halflings, or humans captured on raids. If the Mhalekites took Dun Licinia, any survivors would likely find themselves enslaved…or butchered in an orgy of sacrifice to the blood gods. Mhalek had done much the same.

Likely the orcs' prisoner had a similar fate awaiting her.

"There's just one," said Caius. "Strange."

"It is," said Ridmark, watching the woman's pale form as she struggled. Why didn't the orcs have more prisoners? For that matter, why did they have even one? No one lived near the Black Mountain. There had been villages here, but Mhalek had wiped them out. Had some renegades or outlaws made their nest in the foothills, only to fall afoul of the Mhalekites? That made the most sense…but Ridmark had seen no other prisoners. If the orcs had captured slaves, they would have either taken them along to battle or butchered them before abandoning the Tower of Vigilance.

One lone woman did not make sense.

"Something is wrong here," said Ridmark.

"Obviously," said Caius. "No doubt they have a dreadful fate planned for the girl."

"No doubt," said Ridmark, "but why only one prisoner? What was a lone woman doing in the foothills, let along the Tower of Vigilance? There's something deeper happening here."

An odd thought occurred to him. Might the woman know more about the blue fire? The orcs stopped, the blue-armored warrior and the shaman arguing. The shaman glared towards the curtain wall, and for an instant Ridmark feared that they had been discovered. But the shaman stalked away from the warrior, dark eyes glimmering with the crimson light of the orcish battle rage. And as he turned, Ridmark saw the shaman's profile.

"God and his saints," said Ridmark. "I know him."

"You do?" said Caius. "How?"

"His name's Vlazar," said Ridmark. "He was Qazarl's student, and Qazarl was one of Mhalek's disciples. I thought them both slain after the battle, but...we never did find the bodies of all the disciples." Tens of thousands of orcs had fallen like wheat, their bodies rent by blade and lance, their features churned into pulp by the stamping hooves of war horses. "And if Vlazar is here, Qazarl must be commanding the Mhalekites."

"Perhaps Vlazar has a following of his own," said Caius.

Ridmark snorted. "Vlazar is a toad. The Mhalekite orcs respect strength and charisma, and Vlazar is lacking in both. No, Qazarl is commanding the Mhalekites, I'm sure of it."

Though that did not explain what Vlazar was doing here.

After a moment Vlazar and the blue-armored warrior came to an agreement. The group of warriors continued around the courtyard, still carrying the woman tied to the pole. Ridmark watched as they circled around the inner towers, vanishing to the north.

"They're going to the northern gate," said Caius.

"Aye," said Ridmark, rubbing his chin. Black stubble rasped beneath his callused fingers. "Why not join the others? Qazarl marches for Dun Licinia, that is plain. Why not simply..."

The answer came to him.

"They're going to sacrifice the woman," said Ridmark.

"How do you know?" said Caius.

"There are circles of standing stones higher up," said Ridmark. "The dark elves reared them. They believed whatever demon they worshipped was imprisoned within the Black Mountain, and they performed bloody rites upon the high altars. Vlazar is a toad, but he does have magic. He's going to kill the woman upon the standing stones and use her blood to work a spell."

"God and his archangels preserve us," said Caius. "I fear you are right.

We must aid her! But we are only two, and even the Gray Knight cannot prevail against thirty orcs and a shaman."

"Master Galearus once told me," said Ridmark, "that a knight is guided by chivalry, but his mind and his will are his weapons. His sword is merely the instrument of his will. Come, Brother Caius. Let us put our minds and wills to the test."

He led the way from the tower, Caius following, and set in pursuit of the orcs and their prisoner.

He hoped his mind and his will would produce a plan.

After all, Master Galearus's cunning had failed in the end, and Mhalek's treachery had killed him.

CHAPTER 7
THE HIGH ALTAR

Every step filled Calliande with fresh pain.

The orcs departed through the Tower of Vigilance's northern gate and started the steep climb into the highest foothills, just below the Black Mountain proper. The sun dipped to the western horizon, flinging stark shadows across the ravines and the hills. The orcs continued climbing, Vlazar walking in front and barking orders to the warriors every few yards.

The warriors ignored him and looked to Kharlacht for their instructions. The tall orc walked back and forth up the column, speaking in a low voice to his men. Perhaps he planned violence against Vlazar. Or, more likely, he was concerned about the dangers of the mountain. Fire drakes kept nests upon the Black Mountain's slopes, and other creatures, horrors wrought by the black magic of the dark elves, sometimes emerged from secret nests to carry off victims. And tribes of kobolds lurked in the tunnels of the Deeps, and they had no love for orcs.

God only knew what they would do to Calliande.

She swung from the pole, helpless. The ropes bit into the skin of her wrists and ankles. Every step sent a burst of pain up her arms and legs. Despite the chill, sweat dripped down her body as her muscles clenched, trying to support her weight. Calliande gritted her teeth, trying to ignore the pain even as she swung back and forth. She would not cry out. She would not cry out. She…

The orc carrying the front of the pole stumbled, and Calliande bounced.

Pain roared through her shoulders and hips, and a strangled scream came from her lips. The orcish warriors holding the pole glanced at her and kept walking.

Calliande closed her eyes, biting her lip. Bad enough that she had begged Shadowbearer to spare her. She would not show weakness again. She...

Another bounce, and another scream.

"What is this?"

Kharlacht's deep voice filled her ears, and she opened her eyes.

The tall warrior stood nearby, scowling at the orcs carrying her poles.

"We are carrying her as Qazarl commanded," said one of the orcs. "As the Master commanded."

"You are causing her," said Kharlacht, his face impassive, "unnecessary pain."

The orc shrugged. "So?"

"If you wrench her shoulders from their sockets, fool," said Kharlacht, "she could tear a blood vessel. If she hemorrhages to death before we reach the standing stones, it will be hard to sacrifice her upon the altar, will it not?"

"Perhaps," said the orc.

"Cut her down," said Kharlacht.

The orc warrior bristled. "She will escape."

"To where?" said Kharlacht. "Cut her down, or answer to me for it."

The orc shrugged, shifted the pole to one shoulder, and turned. A dagger flashed in his hands, and the blade cut through the rope binding Calliande's ankles. Her legs fell in a tangled heap to the road, her weight sagging against the ropes upon her wrists. Another flash of the dagger, and Calliande fell to the ground. Pain throbbed through her limbs, her muscles clenching, even as the chill of the sweat upon her skin made her shiver.

She tasted blood on her lip from where she had bitten it.

A hand curled around her shoulder, strong and hard, and lifted her to her feet. Calliande found herself looking up at Kharlacht, his face without expression.

"You," he said, pointing at one of the orcs. "Your cloak."

The orc obeyed without hesitation. Kharlacht took the heavy cloak and swirled it around Calliande's shoulders. The thing smelled vile, the leather and wool scratchy against her skin, but it was blessedly warm.

"Keep that closed," said Kharlacht, "until we reach the end."

"And then," said Calliande, "I will never suffer again, is that it?"

Kharlacht opened his mouth to answer, and Vlazar stormed towards them.

"What is this delay?" snarled the shaman. His eyes seemed to burn like coals in their sockets as the battle fury started to come on him. "The Master commanded us to take the human bitch to the altar at once."

"The Master," said Kharlacht, "commanded us to bring her alive and untouched to the standing circle. If she develops a chill or bleeds to death before we even reach the standing stones, you will hardly be able to kill her and work the magic. What do you think the Master will say then?"

"I am a representative of the blood gods!" roared Vlazar. "You will obey me!"

"I care nothing for your wretched blood gods," said Kharlacht, "and I obey Qazarl because he is my blood kin. Your authority means nothing to me."

"Then perish!" roared Vlazar. His eyes blazed with crimson light, and he shoved Kharlacht in the chest. The bigger orc stumbled, and Vlazar lifted his hands and chanted a spell. Fiery light blazed around his fingers, and Calliande sensed malevolent forces coming at the shaman's call.

Kharlacht moved so fast she could barely see it.

She heard the sound a fist striking flesh, and then Kharlacht stood with his foot upon Vlazar's chest, his greatsword of dark elven steel in his hand. The tip rested upon Vlazar's neck, pressing gently into the skin of his throat.

"Strike me again, Vlazar," said Kharlacht.

"Get off me!" snarled Vlazar. He grabbed at Kharlacht's leg and shoved, but even with the aid of his battle rage, Kharlacht was too strong to move.

"Strike me again, Vlazar," repeated Kharlacht, "and you will see what happens."

A hint of fear appeared on Vlazar's face.

"Get off me," said Vlazar. "I am a shaman of the blood gods. Qazarl will be furious with you."

"He will," said Kharlacht, "but he doesn't like you."

Vlazar sneered. "He detests you."

"True," said Kharlacht, "but I am blood kin. He just doesn't like you. And if you get the prisoner killed before we even reach the standing stones, he will like you even less."

He stepped back, the dark elven greatsword in his right hand. Vlazar staggered to his feet, glaring, as if challenging any of the warriors to say anything.

None did.

"Fine," spat Vlazar. "Take the prisoner in hand. See to it that she reaches the standing stones unharmed." He shook a finger at Kharlacht. "But if any harm comes to her, it is upon your head!"

He stalked back to the head of the column, snarling commands at anyone in sight.

"Thank you," said Calliande, huddled within her cloak.

Kharlacht looked at her for a moment, and then nodded.

"I do not care for needless cruelty," he said in Latin.

Calliande answered him in the same language. "You are baptized?"

His free hand started to stray to the simple wooden cross hanging from his neck, but he stopped himself. "I am. My mother introduced me to the god of the humans, the Dominus Christus. I cared little for gods when I was younger, whether the gods of my fathers or the god of the Church."

"What changed your mind?" said Calliande.

"Loss," said Kharlacht.

"Why are you doing this?" said Calliande. "You are not a follower of the blood gods. Why bring me to my death?"

Kharlacht shrugged. "My home was lost to me, when I took this weapon and armor from the dark elven ruin." He raised the greatsword and slid it back into its sheath. "All that is left to me is my blood kin."

"Qazarl," said Calliande. "A brutal and cruel man."

"He is," said Kharlacht with a sigh. "I deny it not. When I was young, I dreamed of becoming a warrior of my clan, of defending my people and village from the beasts and devils of the forest. Instead I carry out the errands of a power-mad shaman who leads his people to destruction at the word of a horror out of legend."

"Shadowbearer," said Calliande.

Speaking the name sent a shiver down her back, even beneath the heavy cloak.

"Shadowbearer," repeated Kharlacht. "He cares nothing for the followers of Mhalek, or for my cousin's people. Yet Qazarl is blinded by his lust and ambition. He will do Shadowbearer's bidding…until the wizard no longer finds us useful and casts us aside."

"You need not do this," said Calliande.

Kharlacht said nothing.

Calliande took a shaky breath, her arms and legs still aching. "You are not a fool. You are baptized, and you know the Dominus Christus commands his followers to offer sacrifices to no other gods, to only kill in defense of life."

"I know this," said Kharlacht. "Vlazar will murder you. But Qazarl is my kin. I must honor my obligation to him. Even…when his will is turned to folly. I am sorry that I must do this."

"Kharlacht!" snarled Vlazar in orcish. "We do not have time to tarry." He turned and grinned, his expression mocking. "If she has so captured your fancy…remember that the Master wishes her untouched. If you have such a fire in your blood for human women, there shall be plenty behind the walls of Dun Licinia."

"I am sorry," said Kharlacht again, ignoring Vlazar's taunts. "We must go."

Calliande felt her heart sink. She had come so close to persuading him. But there was no escape. She was going to climb that mountain, and she was going to die upon an altar with that soulstone upon her breast.

And she would never know why.

"Move!" said Vlazar, turning towards the road. "We have delayed long enough."

Kharlacht opened his mouth to answer…and then closed it, his grim face hardening into a frown.

Calliande followed his gaze. She saw nothing but the dimming sky overhead, the clouds lit by the rays of the setting sun. Kharlacht turned west, shading his eyes. As he did, Calliande saw a metallic gleam overhead, like sunlight reflecting off copper.

Copper? That seemed odd. Why did…

"Down!" snapped Kharlacht, and he shoved her to the ground.

Calliande struck the road just as a lance of snarling flame shot over her head. The blast slammed into two of the orcish warriors, and both men went up in flames with a scream, the horrible stench of burning flesh filling Calliande's nostrils. She rolled to her knees and saw a scaly creature the size of a large dog drop from the sky, copper-colored wings spread behind it, its talons digging into dying, burning orcs.

Recognition welled out of the mists choking her memory.

A fire drake.

The drake turned to face her as Calliande scrambled to her feet. It scuttled over the burning corpses of the orcs as the other warriors shouted. Vlazar fell back, fear on his face, and began to cast a spell. Yet the drake came at Calliande, its unblinking yellow eyes fixed on her.

She did not know if being burned alive would be less painful than dying upon the stone altar, but she was about to find out.

The drake's mouth yawned wide, a harsh yellow-orange light flaring to life behind its black fangs.

A gleaming blue blur struck the drake's neck, and its head jumped off its shoulders. Kharlacht took another step, the drake's blood smoking on the blue steel of his sword, and kicked with a heavy boot. The drake's thrashing body toppled over, smoking blood spraying from its neck to sizzle against the road.

Bit by bit its thrashing stopped.

"Is it dead?" said Vlazar, his voice shrill.

"It is dead, Vlazar," said Kharlacht, wiping the drake's blood from his blade. "You can stop hiding now."

A mutter of nervous laughter went up from the orcish warriors.

"Yes. Yes, of course," said Vlazar, staring at the headless drake. "You fought valiantly." Calliande felt her lip curl in disgust. This craven, cringing coward of a shaman was going to kill her? The indignity of it rankled, even as she recognized the absurdity of the feeling. "You fought…almost as a follower of the blood gods."

"Enough talk," said Kharlacht. "Drakes often hunt in packs. Draw your weapons. You, you, you, and you. Guard the prisoner. You and you and you. Keep your bows out, and have an arrow ready. If anything moves in the sky over us, shoot it, along with any sign of flame. Anything wielding fire in these hills, or above them, is unlikely to be friendly."

The warriors hastened to obey Kharlacht's commands.

"Do as he says," said Vlazar, the sound of clanking armor and rattling weapons drowning out his voice. "I command you to do as he says."

Kharlacht waited until the orcs had arrayed themselves, and then nodded. "Let's get this over with. But proceed slowly. The prisoner is injured, and the Master will be angry if she perishes."

Before she reached the standing stones, anyway.

The orcish warriors resumed their march, Calliande's escorts falling around her.

And to her surprise, she felt somewhat better.

She rubbed her fingers over her mouth and looked at them. She had bitten her lip in her pain, had felt the blood drip down her chin. Yet there was no trace of the cut now. For that matter, the scrapes and cuts on her hands had vanished. The ache in her hips and shoulders from the ropes had faded.

Her body was healing itself faster than it should.

She felt grateful for the lessened pain, but nonetheless alarmed.

Just who was she? Why did Shadowbearer want to kill her upon that altar?

It seemed she would never learn the truth.

Calliande considered running, but knew she would never get away before the orcs caught her.

She kept walking.

An hour later, the dusk faded to night, and they reached the circle of standing stones.

The ring of thirteen menhirs stood atop a high, stony ridge, at the very base of the Black Mountain itself. Strange, grim designs adorned the menhirs' inner faces, carvings that made Calliande's head hurt. The dark elves' sense of aesthetics had not matched human standards of beauty…and the dark elves celebrated the torture and killing of lesser races.

An altar of rough-hewn black stone lay in the center of the circle, its sides likewise carved with alien designs of strange and terrible beauty.

"At last," said Vlazar. "We have arrived." He glared at Kharlacht. "No thanks to your bumbling, I might add. The Master will be wroth that your errors slew two of his followers."

"The Master," said Kharlacht, "cares nothing for us. We are his tools, and nothing more."

His hand strayed to his cross, and Calliande understood his fear. She felt...something lurking within those stones, something that hated all that lived and breathed under the sun. The dark elves of old had built these places to channel and summon black magic, and Calliande felt the lingering echoes within the menhirs.

"This is a mistake, Vlazar," said Kharlacht. "We should not be here."

"Silence," said Vlazar. "This is no place for the spineless followers of the human god. Only the bold sons of the blood gods may tread here."

Yet even he looked nervous.

"You two," said Vlazar, pointing. "Bring her."

The orcish warriors yanked away her cloak, and the cold mountain air felt like a slap against her bare skin. She cringed away from the chill, and the orcs seized her arms. Vlazar strode towards the stone circle, the warriors pulling her after.

They yanked her within the boundaries of the circle...and it flared to life around her.

The earth groaned beneath her feet, and the carvings upon the stones shone with a ghostly green light, painting the circle with an eerie glow. Calliande felt the dark magic stirring within the stones, felt power rising up from within the Black Mountain.

Power rising in response to her presence.

"What is happening?" said Kharlacht, drawing his sword. An icy wind sprang up from the altar at the center of the circle. "Why is it doing that?"

"I...I don't know," said Vlazar. "I am...I am sure it is harmless."

"It's not," said Calliande, and she felt the orcs' grip upon her arms waver. "It's extremely dangerous." She wasn't sure how she knew that, but she was certain of it. "And it might destroy you."

Vlazar looked at her, at the glowing menhirs, and then back at her.

"Bring her," he said.

He strode to the altar, and the orcs wrestled Calliande upon the rough surface and spread her arms and legs. Jagged stone horns jutted from each corner of the altar, and the warriors tied her wrists and ankles to them. She lay helpless and pinned, the hard stone digging into her back and legs.

Vlazar placed the soulstone upon her chest. The crystal felt icy cold against her breasts, and the green light gave it a sinister appearance. She felt the power pulsing within the stone, felt its magic rising in response to the dark power of the menhirs.

If she died upon this altar, with the soulstone touching her flesh...terrible power would be unleashed.

Vlazar strode to the altar, a dagger in hand, and began to cast a spell. Dark magic flared and burned around his fingers. He lifted the dagger, blood-colored fire flickering around the blade.

The dagger that held her death.
She was going to die, and she would never know why.
Vlazar raised the dagger high.

CHAPTER 8
IRON STAFF

Ridmark hurried up the road, Caius following him.

The orcs made it easy to follow their trail. The trees thinned out as the road moved north from the Tower of Vigilance, and soon only a few stunted bushes clung to the hillside. The lack of cover would have concerned Ridmark, but the orcish warriors were in a hurry, and did not bother to look back. Their errand had to be an urgent one.

A dark suspicion formed in Ridmark's mind.

Circles of standing stones dotted the Black Mountain, places of power where the dark elves had worked black magic long ago. Qazarl had to know his small army could not destroy the High King's realm of Andomhaim, could not even defeat the forces of the Dux of the Northerland.

Unless Qazarl had help.

And perhaps by killing the prisoner upon the altar, he hoped to unleash the sort of dark magic that would grant him victory.

Yet if that was what Qazarl intended, why hadn't he come to kill the prisoner himself? Vlazar was hardly the sort of underling one entrusted with vital tasks.

Ridmark stopped.

"What is it?" said Caius.

"They've halted," said Ridmark, looking at the orcish column further up the road. "Take cover. Sooner or later they're going to start looking around."

He ducked behind a boulder. Caius, being shorter, did not need to duck at all. Ridmark peered around the rough stone, watching the orcs. They were having an argument, and the faint sound of their angry voices drifted to his ears.

"Can you see anything?" said Ridmark.

Caius shrugged. "They're fighting over something. I think...yes, I think one of them cut the girl down."

"They're letting her go?" said Ridmark, surprised.

Caius shook his head. "No... they're making her walk. Or they've decided to kill her then and there."

Ridmark's right hand tightened around his staff. If the orcs decided to kill the woman, there was nothing he could do to save her.

"I think," said Caius, "that we...drake!"

Fire blossomed over the orcish column, and Ridmark heard the warriors scream as the flames chewed into their flesh. Coppery scales gleamed as the drake fell out of the sky and landed amidst the orcs. He saw the pale form of the woman, saw her stumble back as the drake advanced on her.

Then the blue-armored orc attacked, his greatsword a blur. The drake's head jumped off its serpentine neck, and its body collapsed motionless to the ground.

"A skilled warrior," murmured Caius.

Ridmark nodded.

Vlazar and the blue-armored warrior shouted at each other for a while, and then some warriors fell in escort around the woman. The column continued its climb, leaving two dead orcs upon the road.

And as they did, an idea came to Ridmark.

"Come," he said, straightening up.

He walked to the dead orcs. The stench of charred flesh and burned hair filled his nostrils. A drake's flame burned hotter than a blacksmith's forge, but over a far larger area. The great dragons of high elven legend had been able to burn entire armies with their breath, and the Dragon Knight's burning sword had laid waste to legions of the Frostborn...

Ridmark examined the corpses. The orc on the left had been badly burned, so Ridmark went to the orc on the right. Some of the warrior's clothes remained intact, so Ridmark pulled off his ragged cloak.

"It is ill to profane the dead," said Caius.

"You'll say a prayer for their souls?" said Ridmark. "They were Mhalekites, followers of the old blood gods. If they were still alive, they would say that the weak deserved to die."

"True," said Caius, "but the Dominus Christus wishes to gather all kindreds to his side. And it is still ill to profane the dead."

"Even if it means we'll save the life of that woman?" said Ridmark.

He went to one knee besides the burned orc and drew his dagger from his belt. It was a heavy weapon, the blade serrated and sharp.

Caius frowned. "I thought you were forbidden to carry a blade."

"A sword," said Ridmark. "This isn't a sword."

Or a Soulblade, more specifically.

He examined the dead orc's right arm for a moment, took a deep breath, and regretted the smell.

Then he lifted the heavy dagger to the orc's elbow and started sawing.

Caius grimaced. "What are you doing?"

"Did you notice the direction?" said Ridmark.

"Direction of what?"

"The drake's attack," said Ridmark, nodding at the headless drake. "It came down from the north. That drake isn't a full-grown adult male. Which means we are close to the nest." The dagger's blade scraped against bone.

"Interesting," said Caius, "but that doesn't explain why you are...mutilating that corpse."

"Because," said Ridmark. He yanked, and the orc's hand and forearm pulled loose. "Drakes feed on burned flesh. It's like dangling raw meat in front of a starving dog." He stood and wrapped the severed forearm inside the torn cloak, and then examined the dead drake. Its blood smelled like charred meat and overheated metal. "And the smell of their own blood drives them into a frenzy."

He picked up the drake's severed head. It was still hot to the touch, and it joined the orc's arm in the cloak.

"So your plan," said Caius, "is to find the drakes' nest, whip them into a frenzy, and then lure the pack into the orcs."

"That is the sum of it," said Ridmark.

"That is stark madness," said Caius.

"Unquestionably."

"We'll likely be killed."

"Most probably."

"So," said Caius. "When do we start?"

Ridmark felt himself smile. "Why, at once." He tucked the grisly package under his arm. "This way."

They continued following the orcs. The pursuit continued as dusk deepened into true night. Ridmark moved quicker as it grew darker, trusting in the night and his elven cloak to shield him from the orcs' eyes. Caius likewise moved with utter silence. For a brother of the order of mendicants, the dwarf moved with the stealth of a master thief.

Ridmark suspected that Caius had known an interesting life before coming to the Church.

A short time later the orcs climbed one more hill and then stopped.

"There," said Caius, reaching for his crucifix. "The standing stones."

Thirteen grim menhirs stood in a ring at the very edge of the foothills, not far from the Black Mountain itself. Strange, alien carvings marked the menhirs, glyphs that made Ridmark's head hurt. A huge black altar stood in the center of the ring. Those stones had stood for long millennia before

Malahan Pendragon had led the survivors of Britain from Old Earth, long before human eyes had ever looked upon the Black Mountain.

Ridmark wondered how many sacrifices had died screaming upon the altar.

"An evil place," said Caius.

"Aye," said Ridmark, his eyes wandering over the hill. A Magistrius had told him once that drakes were creatures of magic, that they preferred to make their nests near places of magic. He hoped the old man had been right...

There.

A narrow cavern entrance opened further down the hill, perhaps a dozen yards below the standing stones. The rocks near the entrance had been charred by flame, and a bush nearby had been burned to charcoal.

The entrance to the drakes' nest.

"Wait here," said Ridmark.

"What are you going to do?" said Caius.

He nodded towards the cavern entrance. "I'm going to annoy the drakes and lure them to the standing stones."

"And in the chaos, you'll snatch the girl and run for it?" said Caius.

"That is the plan," said Ridmark.

"And if the orcs organize themselves into a pursuit?" said Caius.

"Then we'll hide," said Ridmark. "There is an entrance to the Deeps not far from here, perhaps a third of a mile down the hill."

Caius snorted. "The residents of the Deeps are hardly more welcoming than the orcs. We're a long way away from the Three Kingdoms. And you could well get lost in the Deeps."

"Not if I have a dwarf with me," said Ridmark.

"Clever," said Caius, "and reckless beyond measure. You are either a genius of battle or a madman. When will you need my aid?"

"Watch, and strike when the moment is right," said Ridmark. "I suspect you will know the time."

Caius nodded and bowed his head, both hands clasping his crucifix. "God of battles and Lord of hosts, we beseech you to be with your servants. We go into battle to defend the life of an innocent. Let this confrontation end in peace, but if it must not, grant strength to our arms and let our weapons strike justly."

"Amen," said Ridmark.

God, he suspected, had forsaken him the day he had killed Mhalek. But perhaps God would listen to Caius, and perhaps he wanted the woman to live.

Time to find out.

Ridmark pulled up the hood of his cloak and picked his way down the slope. The cave opening grew larger and larger, and he smelled burned flesh. The drakes tended to take kills to the lair, to feed their females and hatchlings.

He wondered how many half-eaten victims he would find within the cave.

Assuming the drakes simply didn't kill him on sight.

Green light flared from atop the hill, and a cold wind blew around Ridmark, tugging at his cloak. Vlazar had started his spell. If Ridmark didn't hurry, the woman was going to die. Fortunately, the green glow drew the orcs' eyes, keeping them from watching for foes. Ridmark abandoned all attempts at stealth and ran for the cave.

He reached the entrance, and the hot, reeking air struck him like a blow to the face. The cave stank of charred flesh and the metallic smell of the drakes' blood. He eased into the darkness and moved around a corner, a fiery glow touching his eyes.

The cave opened into a large chamber beneath the hill, and to judge from the grim carvings upon the walls, the dark elves had once used it for ritual magic. Heaps of blackened bones lay everywhere, and Ridmark saw the charred, half-eaten carcasses of goats. Two dead orcs, no doubt hapless victims plucked from Qazarl's warriors, lay upon the floor.

A dozen adult drakes lounged along the walls, their tails twitching. From time to time one of the drakes breathed a blast of fire, bathing the others in flame. A half-dozen hatchlings occupied a nest in the corner, and as one they glared at him with baleful yellow eyes.

A memory flickered across his mind. Aelia had hated snakes, and one day she had stumbled upon one walking through the courtyard of Castra Marcaine. Ridmark had cut off its head with his soulblade before it could strike her...

The hatchlings shrieked, and the pleasant memory fell away.

Two of the larger adults stirred, moving towards him. If they decided he was a threat, they would challenge him with blasts of flame, hoping to scare him away. If they decided he was prey, they would simply kill him.

Unless he diverted their attention.

Ridmark reached into the bundle, pulled out the burned forearm, and tossed it across the cavern. It sailed past the two drakes and struck the floor, leaving a spatter of green blood in its wake. As one both drakes faced the severed arm, as did every other adult drake.

Ridmark reached into the bundle, his fingers coiling around the hard, leathery skin of the drake's severed head.

One of the larger drakes ripped a chunk from the orc's arm. The nearest drake screeched in challenge and attacked, beating its wings and lashing its forelegs. The other adults moved into the struggle, fighting to establish dominance.

And as they struggled, Ridmark threw the severed head into their midst. It bounced once or twice, leaving smoking blood on the floor.

As one the drakes turned to stare at him, roaring in sudden fury.

Ridmark sprinted for the hillside. He burst onto the hill and veered to the left, and an instant later a raging pillar of flame erupted from the cavern.

He scrambled up the hillside, staff ready in his hands.

A few heartbeats later a dozen angry drakes burst from the cave. Some ran after him, moving with alarming speed. Others beat their wings and took to the air, loosing blasts of flame.

Ridmark ran for the ring of menhirs.

Calliande closed her eyes, the soulstone cold against her chest, and waited for death.

Power stirred around her, currents of dark magic rising in response to Vlazar's spell. She felt the soulstone's power, cold and hungry, waiting to trap her...

She tensed, a prayer to the Dominus Christus upon her lips, and braced herself for the dagger.

Nothing happened.

After a moment, she realized that Vlazar's incantation had trailed off.

"What is that?" he snapped.

Calliande opened her eyes and turned her head.

She saw the menhirs, shining with their eerie glow. Kharlacht stood at the other end of the altar, greatsword in his hands. The other orcs all faced south, short swords and bows in hand.

"What is that?" repeated Vlazar. "Kharlacht?"

"I don't know," said Kharlacht. "It's too dark to see."

Calliande craned her neck. She saw nothing beyond the green glow. Yet the orcish warriors stood at the edge of the stone circle, peering into the darkness.

Then she saw a gout of flame on the hill below, and another.

"Drakes," said Kharlacht. "Lots of them. Your spell must have riled them up." He gestured with his greatsword. "Spread out! Quickly! Otherwise they will burn us all. Archers by the altar, swordsmen by the menhirs! Move!"

The orcish warriors hastened to obey as another burst of flame blazed on the hill. Vlazar stood near the altar, fingering his dagger. Calliande strained against the ropes, wondering if she could get away while the orcs were distracted.

But the ropes held fast.

"Shoot any drake that appears," said Kharlacht. "While they're stunned, swordsmen are to..."

A gray blur shot between the menhirs and came to a stop in the midst of the scattered orcs.

For a wild moment Calliande thought the figure was a warrior of the high elves, a master of sword and spell. But the shape in the gray cloak was not a high elf but a human man. He was tall, in his late twenties or early thirties, with cold blue eyes in a hard face, his black hair close-cropped. Beneath the gray elven cloak he wore leather and wool, and carried a wooden staff capped with steel on either end.

A brand of a broken sword marred his left cheek and jaw.

The orcs gaped at him, and the man raised his staff crosswise before him.

"Who are you?" said Kharlacht, pointing his sword at the newcomer. "Name yourself!"

Vlazar snarled a curse.

"You!" he spat.

"Vlazar," said the man, stepping to the side. "So you remember me?"

"You know him?" said Kharlacht.

"Fool!" said Vlazar. "Do you not recognize the bane of our kindred, the man who betrayed great Mhalek to his doom? That is Ridmark Arban, the fallen Swordbearer!"

The orcs edged away from him.

"You remember me, I see," said Ridmark.

Vlazar sneered. "Do you think I would have forgotten? You wrought great harm upon us...but Mhalek repaid you in kind, did he not? Your soulblade was taken from you. You were cast out from your precious High Kingdom." He grinned. "And you lost that which was most precious to you in the world."

Ridmark said nothing, the staff motionless in his hand.

"Kill him!" said Vlazar. "Kill the man who slew great Mhalek!"

Five orcs charged him, swords drawn back.

And then Ridmark moved.

The staff blurred in his hands, the crack of shattered bone filled Calliande's ears, and two orcs fell limp and motionless to the ground. Another orc stabbed at him, and Ridmark dodged, the staff spinning, and the orc dropped his short sword with a scream of pain. Ridmark's staff slammed into the orc's temple, and the warrior collapsed to the ground.

Calliande watched, stunned, as Ridmark fought his way through the orcs. The battle rage made the orcish warriors stronger and faster, but it didn't matter. Ridmark struck and moved with perfect precision, their stabs and slashes just missing him, his swings and thrusts landing to crack limbs and shatter wrists. The staff must have been heavy, to judge from the force of its impacts, yet Ridmark wielded the weapon as if it were no more than a light branch.

He was the most gifted warrior she had ever seen, with natural talent augmented by years of experience. Not that she remembered any other warriors. But even if the fog lifted from her memory, she doubted she could recall any more skillful warriors.

But he was still going to die.

A half-dozen orcs lay dead around him, but more rushed to face him. Kharlacht stalked forward, greatsword in both hands, and Vlazar lifted his free hand and began to mutter a spell. Ridmark might take half of the orcs with him in death.

But they were still going to kill him.

Then something gleaming and slender flew overhead, and fire erupted across the stone circle.

Ridmark killed another orc, and the drakes attacked.

All of the adults had taken to the air, and they swooped over the stone circle, unleashing their fiery breath. Ridmark threw himself backwards, and a jet of flame slammed into the nearest orc. The warrior shrieked in agony as his clothes and skin went up in flame, and fell thrashing and howling to the ground.

"Arrows!" said the big orc in dark eleven armor. "Arrows! Now!"

The orcs with bows raised them, arrows hissing into the darkness. Two of the drakes fell to the ground, yet more fire poured from the sky. The stone circle dissolved into screaming, burning chaos as some orcs fled, while others tried to fight the maddened drakes.

Which gave Ridmark his chance.

He raced through the mayhem, jumped over a burning orc, and came to the altar. The woman lay upon it, her blue eyes wide with fear and surprise, her blond hair pooled around her head. An odd, fist-sized white stone lay on her chest, nestled between her breasts.

In less dire circumstances, Ridmark suspected he would have found her attractive.

Right now he was more concerned about staying alive.

Especially since Vlazar stood on the other side of the altar, crimson fire burning around his fingers as he cast a spell.

Ridmark raced around the altar, hoping to land a blow, but Vlazar was faster. The orcish shaman thrust out his hand, darkness and flame mixing before him, and a wall of agonizing pain slammed into Ridmark. He stopped with a strangled cry. It felt as if razors had sunk into every inch of his skin, as if his clothes had caught fire.

But it was not real. Vlazar's spell was touching his mind, not his body.

Vlazar shrieked a laugh, his tusks reflecting the harsh glow of his spell.

"Feel the wrath of the blood gods!"

"The same blood gods," rasped Ridmark, taking another step, "that failed to save Mhalek. Those blood gods?" He groaned and forced himself to take another step.

Vlazar gestured, and the pain redoubled. "Mhalek took your heart and your soulblade from you! I shall take your life. Perish! Perish…"

A deep voice rang out, calling to God for strength, and Ridmark saw an orcish warrior collapse. A shape in a brown robe raced across the stone circle, and Ridmark saw Caius throw himself into the fray, his mace rising and falling.

"A dwarf?" said Vlazar, shocked. "Here? Kharlacht!"

And as he flinched, his concentration wavered…and the pain digging into Ridmark lessened.

He surged forward, the staff whistling before him. Vlazar realized his mistake and refocused his spell, but it was too late. Pain surged through Ridmark, but not before his staff slammed into Vlazar's left knee. The shaman fell with a howl, and the pain vanished.

"No!" said Vlazar. "The blood gods will save me! I am strong! I am…"

Ridmark hammered the staff against Vlazar's temple with both hands.

He stepped over the shaman's corpse, yanking the dagger from his belt, and cut the woman's bonds as Caius hurried to his side.

"Good timing, Brother Caius," said Ridmark.

"Thank you," said Caius. "Madam, are you able to walk? We shall have to flee quickly."

The woman grimaced. "I will run until my feet are bloody, if you can get me away from here." She spoke Latin with an odd, formal stateliness. For a brief instant her voice reminded Ridmark of his grandmother's accent.

"We must go," said Ridmark. The drakes would keep the remaining orcs occupied, but not for much longer. Or the drakes would kill the orcs, and then come after Ridmark.

"Thank you," said the woman. "Ridmark Arban. That is your name? Vlazar called you that. My name is Calliande. But I don't know for sure." She gazed at his face, a deep confusion in her blue eyes. "You have the brand of a coward and a traitor…but you have saved me…"

The orc in blue armor, the one Vlazar had called Kharlacht, swept the head from a drake with a single massive blow, his hard black eyes falling upon Ridmark.

"I haven't saved you yet," said Ridmark. "Run!"

CHAPTER 9
THE URSAAR

Every step sent pain shooting up Calliande's legs, the rough ground tearing at her feet, but she ran as fast as she could anyway.

She heard the orcs in pursuit. She didn't know how Ridmark had gotten the drakes to attack the orcs, but his gambit had succeeded brilliantly. Yet it seemed that Kharlacht and the survivors had cut their way free from the drakes.

Belatedly she wondered if Ridmark had a plan beyond the drakes.

"Where are we going?" she shouted.

"Yes, where?" said the odd dwarf Ridmark had called Brother Caius. The dwarf wore a friar's robe, and a crucifix hung from a leather cord around his thick neck. She had never heard of a dwarf joining the Church and turning away from the gods of stone and silence …

But with the fog filling her memories, how would she know? For all she knew, dwarves filled every church in Andomhaim, harmoniously singing all one hundred and fifty Psalms in their native tongue.

"The Deeps!" said Ridmark. "We can slip into the caverns, hide ourselves, and escape once the orcs give up pursuit."

Calliande suspected the orcs would not give up. Shadowbearer did not seem the sort to forgive failure.

And she still had the soulstone clutched in her left fist.

She did not want to touch the thing. The power stirring in its crystalline depths made her uneasy, and she wanted to throw it away. Yet she dared not leave it behind. She knew it was a thing that not should fall into Qazarl's hands.

Or, worse, Shadowbearer's.

So she held the stone and ran as fast as she could.

Ridmark spun around a boulder, caught his balance, and kept running. A narrow path wound its way over the hill, and his boots gripped the stony surface. He shot a glance over his shoulder, saw Caius and Calliande running after him. He was surprised Calliande could keep up – the rough path would tear her feet to shreds.

But if the orcs caught them, they would do far worse.

The path sloped downward, the trees getting thicker further away from the mountain proper. According to the maps Master Galearus had commissioned, the entrance to the Deeps was near. If they gained entrance to the maze of caverns and galleries beneath Andomhaim's surface, they could elude the surviving orcs.

Assuming the orcs did not catch them first.

And assuming they did not encounter greater dangers in the Deeps. The tribes of deep orcs were far more vicious and violent than their surface brethren. Kobolds lurked in the darkness, preying upon both the deep orcs and human settlements upon the surface. And there were other horrors in the deep darkness. The creatures the dark elves had created with their sorcery lurked in the underworld. And the urdmordar themselves, the great spider-devils that had once ruled most of Andomhaim, still spun their webs in the Deeps.

The path dipped into a valley. Ridmark's heart lifted at the sight. The entrance to the Deeps was at the end of the valley, nestled between two wooded hills. Just a little further, and they could reach the cavern.

But the orcs would overtake them first.

Ridmark scanned the path, and saw that it cut between two massive boulders, each larger than the menhirs encircling the black altar atop the hill.

He came to a stop, staff in hand.

"Why have you stopped?" said Caius. Calliande halted next to him, breathing hard.

"Keep going," said Ridmark. "The cavern to the Deeps is at the end of the path, at the bottom of the valley. Wait for me there. I will slow down our pursuers."

"That is madness," said Calliande. "You cannot overcome them alone."

Ridmark shrugged. "I wasn't planning to overcome them, merely to delay them. Stop talking and go."

"You might yearn for your death," said Caius, "but there is no reason to throw away your life so lightly."

"I'm not," said Ridmark, "and if you don't shut up and run, we'll all die anyway. Go!"

Caius sighed, nodded, and urged Calliande along.

They darted between the boulders and vanished into the valley.

Ridmark hurried into the trees off the path. He wrapped his cloak around himself, went to one knee, drew his bow, and waited.

He did not wait long.

A band of orcish warriors raced along the path, weapons in hand. Of the thirty or so orcs that had occupied the stone circle, about half of them had survived the drakes' rampage. That was good. The fewer orcs who survived, the better chance Ridmark had of getting Calliande away and stopping whatever black magic Qazarl intended.

The orcs approached the boulders, and Ridmark had no more time for idle thought.

He raised the bow and released. It was dark, and he had never been more than a mediocre archer, but the arrow slammed into the thigh the lead warrior. The orc roared and fell upon his face, and the other warriors spun and raised their weapons, seeking for their foes.

Ridmark loosed a second arrow. This time his aim was better, and the arrow took an orc in the throat. The big orc in the blue armor, the one Vlazar had called Kharlacht, pointed his greatsword at Ridmark.

"There!" he boomed. "In the trees. Flush out the archer!"

Ridmark moved to the side, walking as silently as he could, the gray cloak hanging around him. Five orcs stormed into the pine trees, making no effort to conceal their footfalls. But Ridmark had spent years living in the wild, surviving by the game he could hunt, and he knew how to move silently. He ducked behind a pine tree, trusting the elven cloak to turn aside the eyes of his enemies, and waited.

The orcs charged past him, likely charging the nest of enemy archers before they could loose more shafts. Ridmark sprang from behind the tree, swinging his staff. The heavy weapon cracked into the back of an orc's head with enough force to shatter bone, and the warrior collapsed without a sound. A second orc turned, only to have Ridmark's staff shatter his jaw and break one of his tusks. The orc fell with a burbling scream, and Ridmark killed him with a single sharp thrust to the neck. He danced past the thrust of another orc's sword and raced for the path, intending to rejoin the others...

"Take him!" Kharlacht's voice boomed, and then the huge orc stood before Ridmark, his dark elven armor gleaming blue in the moonlight. His greatsword came up, and Ridmark knew that massive blade might well tear right through his staff's wood and steel. He struck first, his staff impacting the flat of Kharlacht's blade, forcing Kharlacht's swing away from Ridmark. He reversed his staff and drove the butt for Kharlacht's knee. But the orcish warrior dodged, bringing his greatsword around in a massive sideways swing. Ridmark hammered his staff down with both hands, driving Kharlacht's sword into the ground. He raised his staff, but Kharlacht acted first. The orc raised his right hand from the greatsword's hilt and punched, and Ridmark dodged. Kharlacht's fist missed his face but slammed into his shoulder, and the power of the blow sent him stumbling.

Facing Kharlacht alone would have been a challenge. Facing Kharlacht and a dozen other orcs meant certain death. Ridmark might have welcomed death, to join Aelia at last, but he would not court it without cause.

He had delayed the enemy. It was time to go.

He launched a flurry of swings and thrusts, forcing Kharlacht on the defensive. Battle cries rang out as the other orcs drew near, and Ridmark turned and sprinted into the trees.

The darkened woods swallowed him, and he heard the orcs in pursuit. But Ridmark doubled back, his cloak pulled close to mask his movements. He slowed, though every instinct screamed for him to run, and kept his footfalls silent. The ruse worked, and he saw the orcs running to the path. Ridmark hastened past the boulders and into the valley as fast as he dared.

For a moment he thought he might get away. Kharlacht and his warriors might not know of the entrance to the Deeps …

"There!"

Ridmark glanced over his shoulder and saw Kharlacht standing on the edge of the valley, pointing his greatsword.

He abandoned stealth and ran down the slope.

"I think that is it," said Caius, pointing at the hillside.

Calliande followed his thick finger. The narrow valley ended in a steep cliff face of dark rock, tough trees clinging here and there to the stone. In the center of the cliff face stood a yawning cavern, half-hidden by dangling roots. Beyond Calliande saw a stone tunnel sinking into the earth.

The entrance into the Deeps.

"Come," said Caius. The sound of fighting rang from the edge of the valley. "I do not think Ridmark will buy us much time. We must be out of sight by the time the orcs overpower him."

"You do not think he will prevail?" said Calliande.

"Not against so many foes," said Caius, "and I pray he will escape. But if he does fall, let us ensure his sacrifice was not in vain."

Calliande nodded and followed the dwarven friar to the cavern entrance.

And as she did, she felt a chill. That hardly should have surprised her, given her lack of clothing.

Yet it was not a…physical chill coming from the cavern. She felt it against her thoughts, rather than her flesh. It reminded her of the chill she had felt from the menhirs within the stone circle.

Of the soulstone that still waited in her left hand.

Was the cavern also a place of black magic?

Yet Kharlacht and his orcs would kill her far more quickly than whatever waited inside the cavern, so she followed Caius into the gloom.

"Here," said Caius, stopping just inside the entrance. The floor felt cold and gritty beneath Calliande's feet. "We'll wait here. We can see outside, but we're far enough in that the orcs won't follow us. We'll wait until Ridmark joins us...or until we learn his fate."

They stood in silence. Calliande heard the distant sounds of battle, of orcish voices raised in fury.

"Have you known him long?" said Calliande.

"Ridmark?" said Caius. "No. In fact, I met him just this afternoon."

"I am grateful for the rescue," said Calliande, "though I am curious how you found me."

Did Ridmark and Caius know her? Perhaps they knew who she really was...and they might know how she had been sealed in that cold vault below the Tower of Vigilance.

"Pure chance, I am afraid," said Caius, "or the guidance of the Lord, if you do not believe in chance. I came to the Northerland to bring the word of the Dominus Christus to the pagan orcs of the Wilderland. Ridmark came on some...strange errand of his own. We saw the blue fire filling the sky and followed it to its source, and saw Vlazar leading you away from the Tower of Vigilance. Neither Ridmark nor I would leave you to such a fate...so here we are."

"Blue fire?"

"Aye," said Caius. "The blue fire that filled the sky around noon. It must have been visible for miles. Surely you saw it?"

"No," said Calliande. "I didn't." Had the fire filled the sky at the same moment she had awakened below the Tower? "I think...I think I was underground at the time."

"I see," said Caius. "You were a prisoner of the Mhalekites, then?"

"I don't know," said Calliande. "I...I don't remember anything. I woke up in the darkness below the Tower of Vigilance a few hours ago. Before that...I can't remember anything."

The lines in the dwarf's gray-skinned face deepened. "I see."

"Do you know who I am?" said Calliande.

"I fear not," said Caius. "I have never seen you before, nor have I heard your name. I shall ask Ridmark when he returns."

"If he returns," said Calliande. She had watched him fight against the orcs...but even he could not prevail against so many.

"I think he will, with God's grace," said Caius. "He is...not what I expected. I had heard the name, of course. Ridmark Arban, the coward who fled the field against Mhalek. But I think...I think that was a slander. A calumny raised by his enemies. I have rarely seen a human so bold, and I think the hand of God may be upon him. If he..."

Ridmark sprinted through the cavern entrance.

"You're alive," said Caius. To Calliande's astonishment, he had not even been wounded.

"Not for much longer," said Ridmark, "if we don't keep moving. Go!"

Calliande looked into the cavern. "I'm not sure that is a good idea. There's...some magic here, I think, like the stone circle."

"If we stay here, Kharlacht will kill us," said Ridmark.

He started forward, and Calliande followed him with Caius.

"Won't we need a lantern?" said Calliande.

"No need, madam," said Caius. "The upper levels of the Deeps tend to...provide their own illumination, as it were."

The darkness of the cavern closed around them...but Calliande saw a pale blue glow ahead. The tunnel twisted, turned, and then opened into a high gallery of stone. Stalactites dangled from the ceiling overhead, wet and glistening in the blue glow. The light came from hundreds of enormous mushrooms scattered around the floor, each about the size of a child. The blue glow shone from beneath the mushrooms' veined, translucent caps, transforming them into strange lanterns.

"What are those things?" said Calliande.

"Ghost mushrooms," said Ridmark. "But the dwarves of the Three Kingdoms call them..."

"Lukhaldenmorr," said Caius. He chuckled. "Which translates, in Latin, to 'spirit mushroom', more or less."

Ridmark crossed the gallery, walking around the clusters of glowing mushrooms. A pool of clear water glimmered in the center of the floor, and rough rock ledges rose along the walls. On the far end of the cavern, Calliande saw a narrow tunnel sinking deeper into the earth.

Into the maze of the Deeps themselves.

"Here," said Ridmark, gesturing towards the far opening. "Through here, quickly. If the tunnels beyond branch off, we can hide until Kharlacht gives up. If he doesn't, we can hold off the orcs here easily enough."

"Perhaps we can make this Kharlacht see reason," said Caius.

"He won't stop," said Calliande. "Qazarl is all the kin he has left, and his sense of obligation to his blood drives him."

"Then it can drive him to his grave," said Ridmark.

She followed Ridmark and Caius across the gallery, the floor cold and wet. Her feet ached horribly from the barefoot run across the hills, yet already she felt better, the pain fading with every step, the ache draining from her calves and hips. She lifted one foot, expecting to see a mess of bloody cuts…but the skin of her heel was unmarked.

She was healing, and she did not know how.

But that was a distant concern.

Something about the cavern felt horribly wrong. She sensed the presence of eyes upon her flesh. The orcs staring at her had been bad enough. This was worse. She felt as if something malevolent was watching her, something that wanted to rip her to shreds and watch as she screamed.

Then she heard voices.

"Get behind me," said Ridmark, standing before the tunnel. "We're out of time." Caius raised his mace, and Calliande stepped behind them.

The clatter of armor rang through the cavern, and Kharlacht strode into the gallery, seven orcs following him. He looked back and forth, his greatsword in both hands, and nodded when he saw Ridmark.

"So," he said. "The Gray Knight. I had heard my kin speak of a gray ghost that haunted the wilderness, a gray ghost that did deeds of daring. It seemed their tales hold true."

Ridmark nodded. "I am pleased you think so."

"You fought well," said Kharlacht, "but the chase is over. You cannot prevail against all of us, worthy though you are. Hand over the woman and return the soulstone, and we shall let you live."

Ridmark barked a harsh laugh. "Do you think I will accept that?"

"No," said Kharlacht. "Which is why I shall simply shoot you."

Ridmark gestured at the tunnel. "We can take cover easily enough. And if you come after us, you will have to fight us one by one. You've already lost many of your warriors. Do you want to lose the rest?"

"If I must, then I must," said Kharlacht. "All men die. Better to do so in service of our obligations, rather than of old age in bed."

The chill against Calliande's skin deepened. A violent shiver went through her, and she had to grab at the cavern wall for support. Caius glanced at her, but she shook her head.

And as she did, she saw the rippling before the pool.

The waters were utterly still, yet a patch of air rippled over them. The ripples moved, heading right towards Kharlacht and his warriors. Calliande wondered if exhaustion and pain had caused her to see things…and then a memory rose up from the mist choking her mind.

Before they had been enslaved by the urdmordar, the dark elves had used their black magic to create hideous, mutated beasts, ghastly fusions of animals and the various slave kindreds under their control. Such creatures were stronger and faster than normal animals, and usually impervious to all weapons, save for magic and flame.

And sometimes they had the ability to blend with their surroundings.

"Ridmark! Kharlacht!" shouted Calliande, pointing. "Look!"

She pointed, and both Ridmark and the orcs looked.

And as they did, the blur faded away to reveal a hideous, misshapen creature. The beast looked like a ghastly, deformed hybrid of a bear and an ape, its long limbs and narrow body corded with heavy muscle, its ragged fur standing in greasy spikes, its eyes glowing like sullen coals.

Its claws and fangs were like daggers.

The dark elves called the creatures ursaars, and had once fielded vast armies of them. After the urdmordar had enslaved the dark elves, and the High King and the Magistri and the Swordbearers had smashed the urdmordar, the surviving creatures of the dark elves had scattered to the lonely places of the world.

All that flashed through her mind in an instant.

And then she realized they were going to die. They had neither magic nor enough fire to harm the ursaar, and one of the beasts had the strength of a dozen men.

The ursaar loosed a terrible howl and charged at the orcs, and two of the warriors died in a heartbeat, their heads ripped from their shoulders.

A dozen plans flashed through Ridmark's head.

Part of him wanted to take Caius and Calliande and flee into the Deeps. Perhaps Kharlacht and the orcs would distract the ursaar long enough for them to escape. But he knew the ursaar would not let them go. After it finished with the orcs, it would follow them.

And they had no weapon that could harm it.

Once Ridmark had been a Swordbearer, a Knight of the Soulblade, and he had carried the ancient soulblade Heartwarden. With that sword, he had struck down the creatures of the dark elves, had even slain an urdmordar. With Heartwarden, he could have dispatched the ursaar with a single blow.

But he had failed Aelia, and Heartwarden had been taken from him in disgrace. Now all he had was a staff of wood and steel, useless against an ursaar.

Unless he did something clever.

"Get through the tunnel," he said. "Now!"

The ursaar bellowed and killed another orc.

Caius lifted his mace. "But..."

"Go!" said Ridmark, shoving him towards Calliande. Caius was heavier than he looked, and barely stumbled. But he nodded and urged Calliande to motion, and the two of them vanished down the tunnel.

Ridmark raced into the gallery as Kharlacht dueled the ursaar. The weapons of the other warriors did not slow the ursaar, but Kharlacht's blue greatsword caused the hulking creature some discomfort. Perhaps there was enough of the dark elves' power in the weapon to wound the ursaar. The creature killed another orc, and Kharlacht struck, tearing a gash down the ursaar's flank. Black slime oozed from the cut, and the ursaar whirled, striking with a paw. The blow caught Kharlacht across the chest. His armor turned aside the claws, but the power of the strike drove him to the ground.

The ursaar loomed over him for the kill. The surviving three orcs stabbed at it, but the creature ignored their attacks.

Ridmark slammed his staff across the ursaar's muzzle with all his strength. The creature flinched from the blow, and Ridmark landed two more hits in rapid succession. The ursaar roared and turned to face him, and Ridmark jumped back as Kharlacht scrambled to his feet. He saw the muscles in the ursaar's legs tense, saw it prepare to leap.

He threw himself to the side as the ursaar threw itself forward in a dark blur. It hit the wall with terrific force, so hard that the floor shook beneath Ridmark's boots, a few pieces of stone falling from the ceiling.

Ridmark looked at the narrow entrance to the tunnels, and a wild idea filled his mind.

"Kharlacht!" he yelled. The big orc looked at him, his black eyes glowing with orcish battle rage. "Get in the tunnel!"

The ursaar shook itself and regained its feet.

Kharlacht turned towards the ursaar, raising his sword.

"Go!" said Ridmark. "You can't kill it. Stay here and die, or follow me and live."

The ursaar wheeled, its claws a blur, and tore the head from another orcish warrior. Of the thirty that had gone to the stone circle, only Kharlacht and two others remained.

Kharlacht hesitated, and then nodded. "You heard him! Move!"

The two warriors ran for the tunnel, followed by Kharlacht. Ridmark struck the ursaar across the neck. The beast roared and turned to face him, and Ridmark swung his staff with both hands, slamming the weapon into the creature's knee. His staff could not harm the ursaar, but the impact of the weapon forced the creature's leg to buckle. The ursaar loosed a hideous shriek, and Ridmark sprinted for the far wall.

He stopped next to the entrance of the tunnel.

The ursaar growled, eyes blazing in its hideous, misshapen face.

Ridmark braced himself, sweat dripping down his jaw, his heart hammering against his ribs. For an absurd moment he wanted to laugh defiance at the ursaar. He had danced with death hundreds of times in the five years since Mhalek's defeat.

But he had never thought he would die quite like this.

Then the ursaar threw itself forward in a dark blur, and Ridmark dodged to the left.

He was just fast enough.

He stumbled into the tunnel as the ursaar rammed into the wall with the force of a catapult's missile. The wall creaked and groaned, and he heard the crack of splintering stone overhead.

The tunnel began to collapse around him.

He saw the orcs staring at him in shock, and a piece of stone landed upon one of the orcish warriors, turning his head to mush.

"Run, damn it!" said Ridmark.

Kharlacht and the remaining orc sprinted forward, more stones falling around them. A piece of rock clipped Ridmark's jaw, and another struck his shoulder, dust falling into his face. But he kept running. He saw another gallery ahead, saw Caius and Calliande standing in the mushrooms' pale blue glow. Just a little further...

Ridmark threw himself forward as the ceiling gave way.

He stumbled and fell into the gallery, Kharlacht at his side, and the tunnel collapsed behind them.

They had gotten away from the ursaar.

But they were trapped in the Deeps.

CHAPTER 10
A PACT

Ridmark sat up.

Calliande was at his side a moment later, helping him to his feet. He was surprised that she was still conscious, that she hadn't collapsed from a combination of dehydration, exhaustion, and exposure. Or simple blood loss, if she had cut her foot on a particularly sharp rock.

Yet her grip was steady. Dust caked her face, and droplets of sweat cut paths through the grime.

"You're alive," she said, releasing him.

"Surprisingly," he said.

"Indeed," said Caius. "You are as mad and bold as the tales claim, Gray Knight."

"There are tales about you?" said Calliande.

"Exaggerated stories told by drunken freeholders," said Ridmark, turning towards the collapsed tunnel.

And towards Kharlacht.

Kharlacht was on one knee next to the second orc. A splinter of stone had pierced the orcish warrior's neck, killing him at once. Kharlacht stared for a moment, then shook his head and stood.

"Farewell, Ulazur," he said. "I suppose you will not get that reward after all."

He turned to face Ridmark, greatsword in hand.

"Well," said Ridmark, lifting his staff. "Shall we finish this?"

"It appears we must," said Kharlacht. "You have fought boldly." He shook his head, tusks gleaming in the pale blue glow. "Thirty of us, and I am the only one left. Little wonder you threw down Mhalek. But I cannot relent." He took a deep breath. "I must...you must hand over the woman to me."

"So you can butcher her upon that altar?" said Ridmark.

"So Vlazar can," said Kharlacht.

"Vlazar's dead," said Ridmark.

Kharlacht shrugged. "Then I must return her to Qazarl."

Ridmark looked at the pile of rubble blocking the tunnel. "That will be quite a feat."

Kharlacht shrugged. "The hills below the Black Mountain are riddled with entrances to the Deeps. I shall find another."

"Assuming you don't wander until you starve or die of thirst," said Ridmark.

Kharlacht growled. "The difficulties do not matter. I am bound to blood by Qazarl." He drew himself up. "You will surrender the woman to me, or I will kill you and take her by force."

"Try," said Ridmark, raising his staff.

Kharlacht started forward, and Ridmark moved to meet his attack, but Calliande stepped between them.

"Stop!" she said. "Both of you! Stop!"

Kharlacht froze, as did Ridmark.

"You do realize," said Caius, "that the orc intends to take you back to the standing stones."

"How, exactly?" said Calliande. She pointed at the collapsed tunnel. "He can't dig through those stones with his greatsword. And you're right – if he travels the Deeps alone, with me as a prisoner, we'll wander until we starve. Or we'll wander until something kills us."

"So what do you suggest?" said Ridmark.

"A truce," said Calliande, looking from him to Kharlacht and back again. "We set aside our differences until we return to the surface. Then we go our separate ways."

Ridmark frowned. "And you'll go with Kharlacht?"

"No," said Calliande. She looked at the tall orc. "If you object, I'm sure Ridmark and Caius would disagree."

Kharlacht said nothing, his face expressionless. Ridmark wondered how the orc would react. Would he agree to a truce? Or would he risk everything on a fight?

Or would he agree to a truce...and then betray them later?

"It seems," said Kharlacht at last, "that I have been defeated." His mouth twisted, and he gave a sharp shake of his head. "Vlazar was a fool. I warned Qazarl...but he would not listen."

"Then you will agree to a truce?" said Calliande. "At least until we escape our current danger?"

"I will," said Kharlacht.

"Before I agree," said Ridmark, "I have some questions."

"Very well," said Kharlacht.

"A moment, Gray Knight," said Caius. "I have a question first."

Ridmark nodded, and the dwarf stepped forward, returning his mace to its loop on his belt.

"You wear a cross," said Caius. "Are you baptized, or is that a trophy taken from a slain victim?"

"No," said Kharlacht. "I am baptized. Does that puzzle you? I am told there are entire kingdoms of orcs loyal to the Church and the High King in the south."

"Aye, there are," said Caius, "and I have traveled through them. But baptized orcs are rare this far north."

"Though not as rare are baptized dwarves," said Kharlacht, pointing at Caius's crucifix.

"Indeed," said Caius, "but we are not talking about me. You say you are baptized, but one of our Lord's commands is to have no other gods before him. Yet you were willing to help Vlazar sacrifice an innocent woman to the blood gods of the orcs. Why?"

Ridmark had to admire Caius's cleverness. Perhaps could learn Kharlacht's intentions...and, more importantly, what Qazarl planned to do.

"Because I am bound by ties of blood," said Kharlacht.

"Explain," said Calliande. "If I was to have been slain, I would like to know the reason why."

"That is only fair," said Kharlacht. "Qazarl is my kin, my cousin. My father was a follower of the blood gods, but my mother was baptized. She tried to impress her faith upon me, and I had little interest until...until I suffered some losses. Qazarl is more than a follower of the blood gods. He believed Mhalek was a god incarnate...and even his death at your hands failed to dissuade him."

"Hard to believe a Mhalekite would accept a baptized orc in his service," said Ridmark.

Kharlacht shrugged. "Qazarl and I are the only kin the other has. And I am not unskilled with a sword. If I were weak or cowardly, Qazarl would have had me killed long ago."

"Why take service with him?" said Ridmark.

"Because I have nowhere else to go," said Kharlacht.

"It's a large world," said Ridmark.

"Not for me," said Kharlacht. "For an orc of Vhaluusk, ties of blood and honor are everything."

"What happened to you," said Calliande, "to drive you to Qazarl?"

Kharlacht looked at her, and then sighed.

"Why should you not know?" said Kharlacht. "I was born in a village far to the north, on the edge of Vhaluusk. I was betrothed to Lujena, the daughter of the village's shaman. He did not approve, and when the time came to make my initiation to the fraternity of warriors, he sent me into a ruin of the dark elves to claim a sword." He lifted his greatsword and slid the massive blade back into its sheath. "But it was a trap. The shaman bound a demon of the dark elves to hunt me. I managed to overcome the demon…but not before it killed Lujena." His voice was flat, his eyes like sheets of black stone.

"I am sorry," said Ridmark.

He knew what that felt like.

"The elders of the village blamed the deaths upon me," said Kharlacht, "and I was made outcast. I wandered for a time, seeking a new place in the world…or perhaps I was simply seeking death, and did not find it. I found my way to Qazarl. And now I am here."

"I see," said Ridmark. "Will you tell us of Qazarl's plan?"

Kharlacht shrugged. "Why not? His plan is folly, and you shall learn of it soon enough."

"Indeed it is folly," said Ridmark. "Qazarl cannot have much more than three thousand warriors."

"Almost four thousand, in truth," said Kharlacht, "but you are right."

"He'll take Dun Licinia, if he wants," said Ridmark, "but that will cost him, and he will go no further. Dux Licinius will gather his knights and smash Qazarl's host to pieces. I suspected that the spell at the standing stones would give Qazarl some weapon of black magic, some advantage that might grant him victory."

"Perhaps it would," said Kharlacht. "I do not know what the sacrifice was intended to accomplish. Only that Qazarl said it would somehow…trap Calliande's life and power in that soulstone." He gestured at the pale stone Calliande still carried and shrugged. "But the sacrifice, this entire plan, is Shadowbearer's idea."

Silence answered him.

"Pardon," said Caius, "but sometimes my Latin is not as fluent as I might wish. Did you say Shadowbearer?"

"I did," said Kharlacht.

"You know who he is?" said Calliande.

Ridmark and Caius shared a look.

"According the history of my people," said Caius, "when we first migrated to this world and settled in what would become the Nine Kingdoms, a creature we called the bringer of the deeper darkness appeared to us. He caused the sundering in our kindred, and lured away those who chose to worship the darkness. They became the dvargir, our mortal enemies. But that was fifteen thousand years ago, or so our histories say."

"The high elves have a similar story," said Ridmark. "They lived in peace for uncounted ages, until a creature calling itself the bearer of the shadow appeared among them a hundred thousand years ago." He found it strange to speak of such vast gulfs of time. Malahan Pendragon had escaped from Old Earth and founded the realm of Andomhaim a thousand years ago, and even that seem liked a great reach of centuries. "Those who followed the bearer of the shadow became the dark elves, while those who stayed true to the task that God had given them, to act as the caretakers of this world, remained the high elves. And they have warred against each other to this day, even while the urdmordar consumed the dark elves."

"It seems unlikely that Qazarl's Shadowbearer is the same creature from the legends," said Caius. "Perhaps he is merely a renegade wielder of magic who has taken the name of Shadowbearer to frighten his foes. As a rebel against the High King might call himself Arthur Pendragon, to claim legitimacy."

"Perhaps," said Kharlacht. "But the wizard has power. Qazarl feared him...and Qazarl fears nothing."

"What did he look like?" said Ridmark.

"He is a high elf," said Calliande. Her arms were wrapped tight about herself. Not to conceal her nudity, Ridmark realized, but because the memory of Shadowbearer chilled her. "There's something...wrong with him. I don't know what. His veins have turned black, and his eyes are like quicksilver. His shadow points in the wrong direction. He could reach into my mind and hear my thoughts. I don't know what he wants with me." She shook her head, blond hair sliding against her dusty shoulders. "I don't even know who I am."

Ridmark wondered what she meant by that. But there would be time to figure it out later.

"Whether or not this high elf wizard is actually the Shadowbearer of legend is unimportant," said Ridmark. "Qazarl believes that he is...and Qazarl is going to attack Andomhaim at Shadowbearer's command."

"You speak truly, Gray Knight," said Kharlacht. "Shadowbearer has promised Qazarl power and glory beyond anything Mhalek ever knew." He growled. "Yet it is folly. I think Qazarl and his men are the wizard's tools and nothing more. Once Shadowbearer has achieved his purpose, he will leave Qazarl and his warriors to be smashed by the Swordbearers and the Magistri."

"Then why do you follow him?" said Calliande. "If you are certain destruction awaits?"

Kharlacht shrugged. His expression was...resigned. Like a man who had made his peace with a fatal illness. "He is my blood. I cannot abandon him."

"That is madness," said Ridmark.

"Nevertheless," said Kharlacht. "I do what I must. So." He set himself, tension coming back into his limbs. "Do we have a truce? Or must we kill each other?"

"We have a truce. Until we return to the surface," said Ridmark. "Once we reach the surface, we shall go our separate ways. And you will not try to abduct Calliande. If Qazarl wants to try again, that is his own affair. But you will not turn on us once we reach the surface."

Kharlacht nodded, his topknot bobbing in the mushrooms' eerie blue glow. "I agree. I will swear on the name of the Dominus Christus not raise my hand against you and to defend you and the others in all things until we reach the surface, if you will likewise swear."

"Very well. I, Ridmark Arban, swear in the name of the Dominus Christus not to raise my hand against you and defend you in all things, if you do the same, until we reach the surface. I so swear," said Ridmark.

"And I, Kharlacht of Vhaluusk, swear in the name of the Dominus Christus not to raise my hand against you and defend you in all things, if you do the same, until we reach the surface. I so swear."

"Well, then," said Caius. "I suppose we are all friends now."

"We can have a feast celebrating our amity later," said Ridmark. He looked at Calliande. He wanted to know who she was. Her experiences should have left her exhausted and broken, too shocked and horrified to move, let alone run. Yet she seemed to have recovered, and she had kept him and Kharlacht from killing each other.

But they had to move. Standing around talking in the Deeps was a bad idea. It was nothing short of a miracle that their voices had not already drawn attention.

Perhaps the ursaar had claimed these tunnels as its territory, and none of the other denizens of the Deeps dared to trespass.

"We must turn our attention to survival," said Caius.

"Aye," said Ridmark. "First, food and water. I have some supplies, as does Caius, but I doubt you have any."

Kharlacht shook his head. "I fear not."

"And I know," said Ridmark to Calliande, "that you don't have any food."

She gave him an arch little smirk. "Where would I hide it?"

Again her poise in the face of her trials surprised him.

"Food and water," said Ridmark. "We can stretch what we have between us for a few days, though it will be tight. I hope to reach the surface long before that. If need be, we can subsist on some of the mushrooms, and I can hunt some of the creatures that dwell in the Deeps for meat."

"That assumes," rumbled Kharlacht, "that you know how to get out of the Deeps."

"I don't," said Ridmark. "But we have some advantages."

"For one," said Caius, "I am a native of the Deeps. I know how to survive here."

"And," said Ridmark, "the entrance the ursaar just sealed off was the highest one in the Black Mountain's foothills. We need only to take tunnels sloping downward. Sooner or later we will find one that opens to the surface."

Or so he hoped. Master Galearus's scouts had charted a half-dozen entrances to the Deeps scattered around the Black Mountain. Ridmark thought he could find one of them, assuming the creatures of the Deeps did not kill them first.

And assuming that more ursaars, or worse things, had not set up lairs in the entrances.

"One other thing," said Ridmark. "We need to find you clothing. I don't think you want to walk through the Deeps unclad."

"I already ran through the hills unclad," said Calliande. "But, yes, some clothing would be welcome."

"Ulazur," said Ridmark, "isn't using his."

Calliande blinked, looked at the dead orc, and then back at him.

"I suppose," she said, "that beggars cannot be choosers."

Ulazur smelled unpleasant, and was twice Calliande's size, but she was grateful to claim his clothing. She was desperately tired of being naked in front of so many men. Ulazur's leather armor was too large and too heavy for her, but she pulled on his trousers and his worn tunic and his boots, pulling the straps tight to compensate for their size.

"Will it suffice?" said Ridmark.

She took a few cautious steps in the heavy boots and nodded. "I would gratefully accept rags. They will suffice."

"Good," said Ridmark. "It is well past sundown by now, but I want to find a different place before we rest. The sound of the cave-in will have made noise." He shook his head. "Between the collapse and our argument, it's a miracle we have not drawn attention already."

"Perhaps this section of the Deeps is deserted," said Kharlacht.

"Perhaps," said Ridmark, but Calliande heard the doubt in his tone.

"What manner of creatures are we likely to encounter?" she said.

"Kobolds," said Ridmark. "There are tribes of them, preying on each other and any humans and orcs and halflings they capture. More creatures of dark elven magic like the ursaar, perhaps. And spitfangs - lizards with a poisonous bite. They can grow as large as wolves, and twice as mean. Come." He lifted his staff and stepped forward. "Follow me. Do not speak unless absolutely necessary. Sound travels a long way in these caverns."

Caius fell in at his side, and Calliande followed them both. Kharlacht brought up the rear, and he moved with surprising silence. They walked through the gallery of stone, past the fields of glowing mushrooms, and into maze of narrow tunnels. Patches of glowing lichen, perhaps related to the mushrooms, provided light here and there, though Calliande often had to take careful steps and feel with her hands to keep from falling. From time to time Ridmark and Caius stopped and conferred in whispers, discussing the way ahead.

At last Calliande heard a faint rustling sound. As they moved deeper into the tunnels, the sound grew louder, and she realized it was the noise of splashing water. The tunnel widened into a large cavern with a rocky floor. A narrow stream of water fell from a gash in the ceiling and poured across the sloping floor to vanish in another tunnel. Dense banks of glowing mushrooms lined the stream's banks, and Calliande saw misshapen, eyeless fish darting back and forth in the clear waters.

"Here," said Ridmark. "We'll stop here for the night."

"Is it safe?" said Calliande.

"Not particularly," he said, "but safer than the rest of the Deeps. The stream will help mask our sounds." He pointed to a broad ledge against one wall. "That is as defensible as a location as we are likely to find, and we can camp there."

They climbed to the ledge. Ridmark paced in a circle, and nodded to himself, satisfied.

"We'll camp here," he said. "I'll take the first watch."

Ridmark and Caius shared out some dried meat and slices of bread. Calliande found that she was ravenous, and ate the food with a will. She settled against the rock wall, trying to sit as comfortably as she could manage.

A bed would have been nice, but it was still more comfortable than that black altar.

But had she ever slept in a bed? She didn't know. Perhaps she would die in these tunnels, as she had almost died in that black vault below the Tower of Vigilance.

The grim thoughts chased each other around her mind until she fell asleep.

CHAPTER 11
LOST MEMORIES

Ridmark stood motionless upon the ledge, both hands upon his staff.

He wore his elven cloak wrapped around him, the cowl pulled up. He did not know if it would fool the sensitive eyes of the Deeps' denizens, but he would not cast aside any potential advantage. Still, the cavern remained quiet, save for the constant murmur of the water. He saw no sign of any creatures, and none of the blurring ripples that marked the presence of an ursaar or an urvaalg, or worse, an urvuul.

Odd that it had been so quiet.

He remembered the first time he had entered the Deeps, over nine years ago. The high elven archmage Ardrhythain himself, the archmage who had taught the knights of Andomhaim to wield Soulblades as Swordbearers and magic as Magistri, had come to Dux Licinius's court at Castra Marcaine. Ardrhythain had asked for a Swordbearer to perform a dangerous task, and Ridmark had volunteered. In pursuit of that task, he had traversed the Deeps and entered the ruins of Urd Morlemoch.

And there he had met the dark elven wizard who had warned him of the Frostborn, the undead creature called the Warden, confirming the prophecy from the urdmordar Ridmark had slain…

He shook aside the recollections. This was hardly the time to dwell upon the past.

Still, he remembered the Deeps holding far more dangerous creatures than this.

Perhaps Calliande was right, and they had entered a deserted region.

He looked at the woman where she lay sleeping against the stone wall, wrapped in the orc's clothes. There was indeed something strange about her. He had hoped to question her, once they stopped, but she had drifted off to sleep at once. No doubt her ordeals had exhausted her, and he could only image the tortures the Mhalekites had inflicted upon her.

As if she felt the weight of his attention, her blue eyes opened. She climbed to her feet, making little noise despite her heavy boots, and joined him.

"You cannot sleep?" said Ridmark.

"Actually," said Calliande, "I feel quite refreshed. Should we not be silent?"

"The water will mask the sound of our voices," said Ridmark. "You could not have been asleep more than three hours."

She shrugged. "I cannot explain it. I heal quickly. Too quickly. I should have bled to death or torn my feet to shreds. But I'm still alive, and I can stand."

"Who are you?" said Ridmark.

She sighed. "I hoped you knew."

"You don't know who you are?" said Ridmark.

"I fear not," said Calliande.

He waited.

"I don't remember anything that happened before this morning," said Calliande.

"You took a blow to the head?" said Ridmark.

"Maybe. I don't know," said Calliande. "I woke up in a vault below the Tower of Vigilance. I was alone, and it was dark. There was a...a spell, an image, that warned me against Shadowbearer. I managed to find my way out of the vault. I was wearing a robe, but it was...ancient, and it fell apart. I climbed my way out of the cellar, naked and freezing...and Kharlacht and his friends found me."

"I see," said Ridmark.

She gave him a hard look. "You don't believe me?"

"No," said Ridmark. "I believe you. You have no reason to lie about it."

Yet it was a most peculiar tale.

"The Tower of Vigilance burned," said Ridmark.

"I noticed," said Calliande. "What happened? It must have been a strong castle once."

"It was," said Ridmark. "The Order of the Vigilant founded it to keep watch for the Frostborn. Yet it became clear the Frostborn were extinct, and the Order dwindled. A century ago the sons of the High King fought each other for the throne of Andomhaim in the War of the Five Princes. The Master of the Vigilant backed the wrong Pendragon, and the current High King's father burned the Tower. It has been abandoned ever since."

A flicker of fear went over her face. "His father? Then...how long ago did the castle burn?"

"Ninety years ago," said Ridmark.

The fear sharpened. "Ninety years?" she whispered. "You mean I might have been lying down there for…ninety years?" She looked at him. "When…when was the Tower of Vigilance built?"

"The year of our Lord 1256," said Ridmark. "The year the Dragon Knight and the High King destroyed the Frostborn."

"What year is it now?"

"1478," said Ridmark.

"God have mercy," said Calliande. "I might…I might have been lying in that vault for two hundred years?"

"Perhaps," said Ridmark. "But for a two hundred year old woman, you're looking remarkably hale."

She tried to smile. "Thank you. But a spell of some kind could have sustained me…left me in sort of a hibernation."

Ridmark shrugged. "It is possible. Though I do not know enough about magic to say for certain. I am no Magistrius."

"But if it is possible," said Calliande, "if I slept in that vault for two hundred years…then everyone I ever knew is dead. My father and mother. My brothers and sisters. My husband and children, if I even had them." She rubbed her face for a moment. "An entire life, lost to me…and with my memory gone, I would never know it."

"It is," said Ridmark, "a peculiar sort of memory loss."

"What do you mean?"

"When I was a boy, I knew a man who lost his memory," said Ridmark. "A horse kicked him in the head, and he forgot his own name. But he also forgot how to talk, to feed himself, how to do anything else, and eventually died of his injuries. But you remember your name."

"Calliande," she said. "At least, I think that is my name."

"And you can remember how to walk and dress yourself," said Ridmark. "You remember how to speak…in fact, you speak in both Latin and orcish."

"That is odd," said Calliande, her brow furrowing. "I wonder if I know any other languages."

"And you are enduring this situation with remarkable calm," said Ridmark. "You have more steel in you than I would have expected. I know men and women who would hide weeping in a corner, had they endured what you have endured."

"I cannot say that prospect has no appeal," said Calliande, "but…if I surrender I die, and I have no wish to die. Not yet."

Ridmark could not say the same.

"I suspect the damage to your memory was caused by a spell," said Ridmark. "If we seek out a Magistrius, he may be able to reverse the spell."

"Assuming we get out of the Deeps alive," said Calliande.

"There is that," said Ridmark.

They stood in silence for a moment. Ridmark watched her profile as she gazed at the waterfall. She claimed to have awakened in a vault below the Tower of Vigilance. The Order of the Vigilant had been founded to guard against the potential return of the Frostborn, until the Magistri and the nobles of Andomhaim had decided that the Frostborn were extinct. Ridmark had once thought that, too.

Then he had heard both Gothalinzur and the Warden speak of the future...

"Do you know anything about the Frostborn?" said Ridmark.

Calliande frowned. "The Frostborn?" She thought for a moment. "No. I cannot recall anything. They...tried to destroy Andomhaim, did they not? And the High King and the Dragon Knight destroyed them, wiped them out. Beyond that, all I know is what I've heard since I've awakened."

"You were sleeping below the Tower of Vigilance," said Ridmark. "I would make sense that you would know about them."

"Perhaps," said Calliande, "but if I do, I can remember nothing of it. Why do you want to know?"

"Ten years ago," said Ridmark, "I fought and slew an urdmordar named Gothalinzur. She claimed that the Frostborn would soon return, and she was kidnapping freeholders to use as a larder once they arrived. The year after that, I undertook a quest into the ruins of Urd Morlemoch. The dark elven sorcerer imprisoned within that evil place claimed he saw the return of the Frostborn in the heavens, in the position of the thirteen moons. Five years ago, I fought Mhalek, and he claimed that the shape of the world was changing, that the Frostborn would arise again."

"But if the Frostborn are extinct," said Calliande, "how can they return?"

"I have spent the last five years," said Ridmark, "trying to find the answer to that question."

They lapsed into silence.

"Mhalek," said Calliande. "Who is he?"

"You don't know?" said Ridmark.

Calliande shook her head. "Qazarl mentioned him...but I cannot recall the name."

Ridmark considered that. It seemed that certain facts jogged Calliande's memory, dug the recollections out of her mind. That meant she had most likely never heard Mhalek's name before.

And that meant she had been sealed in that vault for five years, if not longer.

"Mhalek was an orcish shaman, a powerful one," said Ridmark. "He was once a subject of the king of Khaluusk, a baptized son of the Church. But he left the Church and turned to black magic, and started worshipping the old orcish blood gods. In time he came to believe that he was a blood god, incarnated in mortal flesh, and went north to raise an army from the pagan orcs of Vhaluusk. He invaded the Northerland, but was defeated at Dun Licinia."

"What happened to him?" said Calliande.

"I killed him," said Ridmark.

He remembered the final confrontation with Mhalek, remembered the screams, the blood upon the floor of Castra Marcaine…

Calliande took a deep breath. "You said…you said you slew an urdmordar."

"I did," said Ridmark. "Gothalinzur. At the village of Victrix, ten years ago."

"Urdmordar are mighty foes," said Calliande, "and can only be slain with magic."

"I was once a Swordbearer, a Knight of the Soulblade," said Ridmark, "and I carried the soulblade Heartwarden. I killed the urdmordar with that sword."

"But you were expelled from the Order," said Calliande. "The brand on your left cheek."

Ridmark nodded.

"Can…can I ask why?" said Calliande.

What could he tell her? That his arrogance and misjudgment had cost him everything? That he deserved his punishment and worse? That the forgiveness Dux Gareth Licinius and Sir Constantine Licinius had offered had only made his guilt worse?

"I made an error," said Ridmark, staring at the waterfall.

"Thank you for my life," said Calliande.

He blinked in surprise and looked back at her.

"Whoever you are or whatever you might have done, you saved my life," said Calliande. "And at great risk. You didn't even know who I was. You still don't. But you rescued me nonetheless."

"I know what the Mhalekites are like," said Ridmark. "I would not leave anyone to their cruelties."

"Thank you," said Calliande. She hesitated, and touched his arm. "And…once this is all over, once we've escaped…I will try to help you find the Frostborn. If I can be of any use."

Ridmark inclined his head. "And I will help you find your memory. If I can."

She smiled at him once more and went back to lie down. A moment later Ridmark saw that she had fallen back asleep. Apparently her strange vigor had at least some limits.

An hour later Caius awoke with a grunt. The dwarf looked at the sleeping Kharlacht, nodded, and walked into a patch of tall mushrooms, no doubt to relieve himself. A moment later he returned to the ledge and knelt in silent prayer for a time.

Then he joined Ridmark.

"Anything?" he said in a low voice.

"Nothing," said Ridmark. "If anyone is watching us, they are skilled at stealth."

Caius nodded. "Calliande is…rather comely, is she not?"

"God, the archangels, and all his saints!" said Ridmark. "The tales claim that all friars are meddling matchmakers, but I had not thought that impulse would extend to a member of the dwarven kindred."

Caius grinned. With his gray skin and marble-like blue eyes, he seemed at home in the gloom of the Deeps in a way that Ridmark and the others did not. "Well. I have grown sentimental in my old age." His smile faded. "What did she say?"

"She doesn't remember anything before waking up in a vault below the Tower of Vigilance yesterday afternoon," said Ridmark.

"So she woke at the same time," said Caius, "the blue fire filled the sky."

"I thought as much," said Ridmark.

"Do you think she is telling the truth?" said Caius.

"If she is a liar," said Ridmark, "then she should choose a less implausible story. I believe she is telling the truth." He scratched his chin, the stubble rasping beneath his thumb. "My guess is that someone in the Order of the Vigilant left her beneath the castle, bound with a spell. When the Order was destroyed, their records burned with the castle…and all knowledge of Calliande was lost."

"That seems reasonable," said Caius. "Though why bind her like that?"

"I have no idea," said Ridmark.

"You believe the Frostborn will return," said Caius. "Perhaps…she knows something of it?"

"I thought that, as well," said Ridmark.

"Or perhaps…she will be the means of their return?" said Caius.

Ridmark shook his head. "I don't see how. She is a strange woman, true, but not malicious."

"She might not remember to be malicious," said Caius.

"Maybe," said Ridmark. "But I doubt the lack of memory would change her basic virtue."

Caius shrugged. "Are we not all shaped by our experiences? Are we not the sum of our memories? The sages of the dwarves say that just as the thousand blows of a hammer shape a blade, so to do the thousand experiences of a man shape him."

Ridmark grunted. "If you want to debate philosophy, Brother Caius, wait until we return to the sunlight."

Caius grinned. "I shall remember that! That stone she carries, the one Vlazar had. Do you think it is truly a soulstone?"

"I do," said Ridmark. "It looks like the ones bound to the blades of the Order's Soulblades. But larger. Much larger. I wonder if that means it is more powerful."

"It may," said Caius. "I know little of soulstones."

"I know that the high elves alone know the secret of their making," said Ridmark, "and so far have only shared finished stones with the Order of the Soulblade."

"I fear that is all I know, as well," said Caius.

"That soulstone has power," said Ridmark. "We'll keep it away from Qazarl. And this Shadowbearer, whether he is truly the figure of legend or some renegade with delusions of grandeur."

Caius tugged at his gray-streaked beard. "Do you think Vlazar altered Calliande's memory?"

Ridmark snorted. "Vlazar? No. If he had tried, he would have either failed utterly or reduced her to a drooling imbecile. He couldn't have managed such a precise spell."

"A Magistrius would have the skill," said Caius. "But from what I understand, your Magistri are forbidden the use of such a spell."

"Aye," said Ridmark. "The Order of the Magistri may only use magic for defense, for knowledge, and for communication. Any other use is forbidden." He shook his head. "Well, we have many mysteries. What is one more?"

"I can take the next watch," said Caius, "if you wish some rest."

"I do," said Ridmark. "Keep an eye on Kharlacht."

"I shall," said Caius.

Ridmark crossed to the wall, placed himself between Kharlacht and Calliande, and sat down. He propped his staff against the wall, loosened his dagger in its sheath, and rested against the rock. Both Kharlacht and Calliande remained motionless. Ridmark watched Kharlacht for any sign of treachery, but his eyes kept straying to Calliande.

The questions gnawed at him. Who was she, and why had she awakened without her memory?

And what did she have to do with the Frostborn?

He drifted to sleep.

###

Morning came, or at least whatever passed for morning in the sunless world of the Deeps.

Calliande awoke to see Ridmark distributing food. Neither sleep nor exhaustion seemed to have left their mark on him. Black stubble shaded the hard line of his jaw, and his eyes were like blue shadows. The brand was a harsh scar upon his cheek.

What had he done to earn it? He was fearless and clever in battle, the exemplar of a Knight of the Soulblade. What could he have done to earn expulsion from the Order?

Perhaps his crime had made him that way, had left him uncaring of his life and eager to risk it.

Still, Calliande owed him her life. If he did not wish to speak of it, she would not press him.

But the curiosity would not leave her.

"I think," said Caius, "that our best option is to follow the stream for as long as possible. We are high in the foothills, and water flows downhill."

Kharlacht grunted. "When Qazarl led his folk down from Vhaluusk, we passed a stream flowing from a cave mouth, not far from here. Perhaps this is the same stream."

"We may hope so," said Caius. "Unfortunately, it is just as likely that it flows into one of the great underground seas. Not even my kindred have mapped them all."

"It is in the hands of God," said Kharlacht.

"We could always take the other cavern," said Calliande, "near the waterfall." Another tunnel yawned there, one that sloped higher into the hills. "Perhaps it will circle down."

"It might just as easily keep going up," said Ridmark. "And I do not think we should enter the Deeps below the Black Mountain itself. A place the dark elves regard as sacred is no place to linger. If the stream proves impassable, we will double back."

No one argued. His plan was sound, Calliande thought. And Ridmark Arban had a...mantle of command about him, a cloak of authority. This wanderer was a man accustomed to giving orders. She expected Kharlacht to argue, but the orcish warrior only nodded.

"Caius, walk with me," said Ridmark. "Kharlacht, take the rear, watch for anyone following us. Calliande, keep your eyes open."

She nodded, getting to her feet, and stifled a laugh of admiration. Of the four of them, she was the least useful, and she knew it. She had no weapons, and would not know how to use them if she did. Yet Ridmark still gave her a task, still made her feel like a part of a larger whole.

Why had the Order of the Soulblade expelled such a man?

They gathered their possessions, left the stone ledge, and entered the stream's tunnel. At first Calliande feared they would have to wade through the icy water, but the stream only occupied perhaps a third of the floor. They walked in silence, the only sound the splashing of the water, the only light coming from the patches of glowing lichen and the occasional ghost mushroom. From time to time Calliande saw light within the stream, and she wondered if spirits frolicked beneath the water.

Or perhaps the souls of those who had died here, wandering forever in search of an exit.

But she realized the light only came from strange, luminescent fish.

The cavern widened, patches of mushrooms providing additional light. Finally it opened into another gallery. The stream rushed ahead into another tunnel, and six more passages opened off from the gallery. Heaps of rounded objects lay scattered across the floor, and an odd, musky smell filled the air.

Bones. The rounded objects were bones.

Kharlacht drew his sword with a steely hiss, and Ridmark walked to one of the piles and picked up a bone with his free hand.

"Murrag," said Caius, squinting at the bone.

The word sparked no recollection in Calliande. "What is a murrag?"

"They're somewhat like sheep," said Ridmark, "but with thick scales in lieu of fur, and large eyes to see in the gloom down here."

"Think of a fat, lazy lizard with a surly disposition," said Caius.

Calliande looked at the scattered bones. "Quite a lot of fat, lazy lizards."

"Aye," said Kharlacht. "I know little of the Deeps, but we have entered the lair of a predator, I am sure of it."

"What manner of predator?" said Ridmark.

"I don't know," said Caius. "That smell...I think it's dung."

"Dung?" said Ridmark. "Yes, I know it. It's spitfang dung. I've smelled it before. We..."

Calliande saw the wall ripple.

For an alarmed moment she thought it was another ursaar. But these ripples looked as if the colors of the stone wall were flowing together. With a shock she realized that a shape on the wall was changing colors, altering itself to match the hue of the wall.

And then she could see the creature.

It was the lizard the size of a dog, with webbed feet and an ornate crest around its neck. Huge fangs jutted from both its upper and lower jaws, and its eyes gleamed like faceted jewels.

The lizard scuttled forward, its jaw yawning wide.

"Ridmark!" shouted Calliande.

Ridmark spun.

"Spitfang!" he said. "Down!"

Calliande ducked, and just in time. The lizard spat a gobbet of yellow slime. It arced over her head to spatter against the floor, and she heard it hissing and sizzling. The spitfang surged at her with an angry hiss, and Calliande backed away.

Then Ridmark was before her, his staff whirling, and the heavy wood cracked against the side of the lizard's head. The spitfang hissed again, and its long tail cracked like a whip. Ridmark caught the tail on his staff, and it coiled around the length of wood. He wrenched the weapon back with enough force to knock the spitfire off balance, its claws raking against the floor.

The spitfang hissed, the glands on the side of its neck bulging as it prepared to spit again.

Blue steel streaked before Calliande's eyes, and the blade of Kharlacht's greatsword sheared through the spitfang's neck. Its head rolled across the floor, dribbling yellow slime, while its body went into a thrashing dance. A few heartbeats later its tail uncoiled from Ridmark's staff, and the body went limp.

Ridmark yanked his staff free, and Calliande let out a long breath.

"Good timing," said Ridmark.

"Ugly thing," said Kharlacht, shaking the lizard's blood from his dark elven blade. With its death, the spitfang's strange camouflage faded, revealing mottled scales of gray and brown. "So ugly I can see why they disguise themselves."

"The disguise helps capture prey, too," said Caius. "The dark elves use them as war beasts."

Calliande stiffened. "Then we're near a stronghold of the dark elves?"

"Possibly," said Ridmark. "Kobolds also use them as war beasts. They're unreliable, though. The scent of a certain kind of ghost mushroom can drive them berserk. And wild packs sometimes wander the tunnels."

"Packs?" said Calliande. One of these things was bad enough. She did not want to see a dozen of them.

"If there was a pack," said Caius, "we would be fighting them already. There was just the one, and we stumbled into its lair."

"And a lone spitfang," said Ridmark, turning the corpse over with his boot, "means an escaped war beast."

An elaborate rune had been branded upon the lizard's neck.

"Kobolds," said Caius. "That is kobold script."

Kharlacht grunted. "Tunnel rats."

"Yes, but dangerous ones," said Ridmark. "We'll need to avoid them."

"And if we can't?" said Calliande.

"Then we fight," said Ridmark.

He led the way further into the Deeps, and Calliande and the others followed.

CHAPTER 12
RAIDERS

The next day Ridmark saw the carved arch.

The stream flowed through a winding, wide tunnel, its floor dotted with pale clusters of ghost mushrooms. Most of the mushrooms shone with a blue glow, but from time to time he saw one that emitted a bloody red light. He made sure to avoid those. The red ghost mushrooms were highly poisonous, and their smell drove spitfangs into a berserk frenzy.

But he saw no more spitfangs. From time to time he saw a murrag. The fat lizards were the size of sheep, their leathery scales hanging in loose folds around their bodies as they grazed among the mushrooms. The beasts were harmless unless provoked, but they could kick with enough force to shatter bone.

"Some murrag steaks," said Caius, "would be most welcome."

Calliande frowned. "You eat those things?"

"Of course!" said Caius. "Murrag meat is a delicacy among the nobles of the Three Kingdoms."

"Indeed," said Ridmark, "but we have no way to cook it, and I doubt it would be pleasant raw."

"Alas, no," said Caius with a sigh, and they kept walking.

Ridmark's stomach rumbled. He was used to traveling on light rations, but sooner or later he would need to eat enough to recover his strength. If they did not reach the surface soon, they would have to start hunting.

He was considering how to cook the murrag when he looked up and saw the archway.

It had been carved out of the rock of the tunnel. Writing covered its surface, and Ridmark squinted at the characters.

"Dwarven glyphs," he said.

"Aye," said Caius.

"Can you read them?"

Caius snorted. "Of course I can. The language is archaic, but…ah. It says that this arch marks the outer boundary of the stronghold of Thainkul Agon."

"I didn't know the Three Kingdoms extended this far east," said Ridmark.

"They don't," said Caius. "The Three Kingdoms were once the Nine Kingdoms, but my people took bitter losses in the long wars with the dvargir and the dark elves and the urdmordar. Three kingdoms remain of the original nine…and I think this was an outpost of one of the lost six kingdoms."

"A ruin, then," said Ridmark.

"Aye," said Caius. "And a good place for a stronghold. The stream would provide water. Harder to starve out in a siege."

"And a ruin," said Ridmark, "where anyone or anything could have settled in the last thousand years."

"I fear so," said Caius.

"Perhaps it is abandoned," said Kharlacht. "We have seen no one else."

"Someone branded that spitfang," said Calliande.

"It might be dangerous to enter," said Caius.

Ridmark thought it over.

"No," he said at last. "No, we'll keep going. If we have to double back, we'll lose another day. More, if the tunnels near the waterfall and the spitfang's lair are dead ends. Perhaps this ruin will be as abandoned. If not, we'll try to sneak past or negotiate with any residents."

"Assuming the creatures within," said Kharlacht, "are even capable of negotiation."

Ridmark offered the orc a tight smile. "If not, you'll get to put that greatsword to use. Let's go."

He walked under the arch, the others following.

The cavern beyond showed signs of long-ago habitation. The floor had been smoothed, and the stream's channel straightened. The light grew brighter, not from the clusters of ghost mushrooms, but from glowing stones set in niches upon the walls.

"Glowstones," said Caius, pointing.

"Are they things of magic?" said Kharlacht.

"Nay," said Caius. "We make them with chemicals, by bathing a prepared stone in a solution of salts mined from the lower tunnels of the Deeps."

"Your kindred are skilled with stonework," said Ridmark. "Changing the channel of the stream must have been a tremendous effort."

"We are," said Caius. "Among my kindred, it is said that the gods of the deep places created stone to house us, iron to serve us, and gold to feed us."

"Yet you left your gods for the Church," said Calliande.

"I did," said Caius. "Our gods offer neither joy nor hope. They have made my kindred stern and humorless and cruel, and we spend our lives futilely striving for power, looking forward only to an eternity of oblivion as we sleep in the darkness. I find the word of the Dominus Christus much more joyful. But come! We can have such a discussion later." The melancholy faded from his voice. "And if you think this stonework is impressive, wait until you see the ruin proper."

The tunnel sloped downward. From time to time they passed steles carved with dwarven glyphs. Caius said they were milestones, showing the distance to the Stone Heart in the Three Kingdoms, the place where the dwarven kindred first entered the world.

Then the tunnel ended in a gate.

Or, at least, it had been a gate. Once the massive gates of dwarven steel would have presented an impregnable barrier to any intruders. Now they lay broken and twisted upon the floor, their bronze edges glimmering in the light of the glowstones. Beyond Ridmark saw a tall hall of worked stone, its ceiling supported by thick pillars carved in the likeness of armored dwarven warriors.

"Thainkul Agon," said Caius. "Or what is left of it."

"I wonder what happened here," said Calliande.

Caius shrugged. "The dvargir attacked. Or the urdmordar. Or perhaps the dark elves. Dwarven steel is strong...but an urdmordar's strength could rip it, or dark elven magic could twist it."

"I hope the attackers did not linger," said Calliande.

"No," said Caius. "No, this happened long ago. My fear is that whoever has taken up residence in the ruins since will prove unfriendly."

"Let's find out," said Ridmark.

He led the way into Thainkul Agon, his staff ready. The stream flowed through the center of the pillared chamber, disappearing into another opening in the far wall. The carvings of the dwarven warriors armor stared down from the columns, grim and silent. The only noise came from the splash of the stream in its channel. Clusters of ghost mushrooms grew at the edges of the water, and glowstones shone in the ceiling overhead.

In places Ridmark saw signs of violence. Cracks on the pillars from where axe and mace blows had struck. Gouges on the floor from the fall of armored warriors. Bones lying scattered in the corners. Yet the signs were old. Time had weathered the gouges on the floor, and the bones were crumbling.

"I suspect," said Ridmark, "that this place has been deserted for a long time."

"It feels that way," said Caius. "I wonder why? It is a defensible place, with ample water."

Kharlacht kept his sword in hand. "Perhaps a dangerous creature has taken up residence here, one strong enough to frighten away any rivals."

"Perhaps," said Ridmark.

The stream entered an archway, the tunnel beyond sloping down at a steep angle. Stone stairs ran along either side of the stream, and Ridmark descended, the wet stone gritting beneath his boots. He saw a hazy glow at the end of the stairs. Ridmark kept walking, and stepped onto a stone balcony overlooking an empty space. The others came to a stop around him, and he heard Calliande's startled inhalation of breath.

"My God," she said.

The tunnel opened into a vast natural cavern. The stream fell from the balcony in a waterfall, glittering in the light of glowstones overhead. A thick forest of ghost mushrooms, some as tall as trees, filled the cavern's floor, their red and blue spores glowing in the air. Stone houses stood on terraces lining the cavern's walls, their facades carved with elaborate glyphs and reliefs.

A dozen smaller tunnels broke off from the larger cavern, the stream vanishing into an elaborate carved arch.

"It's beautiful," said Calliande.

"Aye," said Ridmark, "and I can see why no one else has settled here."

"Why?" she said.

Kharlacht answered. "The tunnels there and there, my lady. Do you see? The gates of dwarven steel have been smashed, as in the outer hall. This cavern might have water and food, but it is not defensible."

Ridmark nodded. He saw that Caius had moved further down the balcony, gazing at the wall. Hundreds of dwarven glyphs marked the stone, along with an odd, stylized diagram that looked like...

A map?

"You've found something?" said Ridmark.

"I believe so," said Caius. "This inscription records the founding of Thainkul Agon." He snorted and ran his hand over the glyphs. "I have never understood why humans leave records in paper. Stone is so much more durable."

"Indeed," said Ridmark, "but what does the inscription say?"

"This was a border stronghold of the kingdom of Khald Rigis, founded ten thousand years ago to ward away the dark elven kingdoms under what is now the northern Wilderland." He gave a sad shake of his head. "But it was overrun, and Khald Rigis fell to the urdmordar long ago. Now it is just another empty ruin." His gloomy expression brightened. "But there is a map. See?" He pointed at the diagram. "Our guess was right, Gray

Knight. That stream flows to the surface. Assuming the tunnel hasn't been blocked, we need only follow it."

"How far?" said Ridmark.

"Less than half a day," said Caius. "If we start now, we may depart the Deeps before nightfall."

"Good," said Ridmark. "Then if we hasten, we might reach Dun Licinia before Qazarl."

Or, if the town had already fallen under siege, they could go to Castra Marcaine and summon aid from Dux Licinius.

"This way," said Caius. "There are some stairs here."

The dwarf led the way to a narrow switchback stair that cut its way along the wall to the cavern floor. The steps were narrow and damp, and Ridmark kept one hand on the stone wall for balance. They reached the cavern floor, and the wet, musky smell of the ghost mushrooms filled Ridmark's nostrils.

Along with the faint smell of rotting meat.

He looked around and spotted the skeleton slumped against the wall.

He first thought it was the corpse of a human, perhaps of a child. But human children did not have fingers that ended in claws or long snouts filled with fangs. Nor did they have gray-scaled skin.

"What is that?" said Calliande.

Ridmark prodded the bones with his staff, the scraps of scaly skin rattling. "Kobold." He noted the cracked ribs, the craters in the elongated skull. "Someone cudgeled him to death. About a year ago, I'd guess."

"Qazarl said tribes of kobolds live in the Deeps near the Black Mountain," said Kharlacht, scanning the mushrooms.

The mushrooms were large enough to provide cover for an ambush.

"Let's not wait around to meet them," said Ridmark.

He took a step towards the stream, and a gray shape appeared from behind the stalk of a mushroom.

The creature was the size of a large child, albeit a child with scaly gray skin, long black claws, a slender waving tail, and the elongated head and unblinking yellow eyes of a lizard. An elaborate crest of red scales rose from its neck and the top of its head, twitching as the creature drew breath. It wore amulets and bracelets of polished bone and stone, and carried a short bow in its clawed hands.

A kobold.

"Greetings," rasped the kobold in orcish.

Kharlacht and Caius lifted their weapons, Calliande stepping behind them. Ridmark raised a hand to stop them.

"Greetings to you," said Ridmark in orcish.

"I am Crotaph," said the kobold, "speaker for the clan of the Blue Hand." Ridmark saw that a four-fingered kobold hand, completed with claws, had been inked in blue paint across the scales of the kobold's thin chest. "You are trespassing upon the tunnels of the Blue Hand."

"That was not our intent," said Ridmark. He glimpsed movement in the shadows of the mushrooms, and knew that other kobolds lurked just out of sight. "We fled our foes upon the surface, and the entrance collapsed behind us. We wish to return to the surface, and then will never trouble you again."

"Our shaman had a vision," said Crotaph. "The spirits spoke to him, and told him of four strange travelers from the sunlight lands. A human, an orc, and a dwarf, and a woman who burns like the fire at the heart of the earth."

"Perhaps the shaman ingested the wrong kind of mushrooms," said Caius in Latin.

Fortunately, Crotaph did not understand. "The shaman said you would enter into the ruins, and here you are. Great is his power, and the spirits heed his will."

"Good for him," said Ridmark. "But what do you want with us?"

"You trespass upon our territory," said Crotaph, "but the shaman and the Warchief will allow you to pass. But you must pay a tribute."

"What manner of tribute?" said Ridmark. "Gold? Food? I imagine food is more valuable than gold down here."

The kobold trilled, his crest expanding as he showed his fangs, and Ridmark realized that was the kobold equivalent of a grin. "Many things have value, gray warrior. Many things. But you have one thing of great value." A clawed hand pointed at Calliande. "The woman, and the white stone she carries. You will surrender them to us, and we shall allow you and the dwarf and the orc to leave our lands in peace."

Calliande stiffened, her hand falling to the pouch where she kept the soulstone.

"What does your shaman want with me?" she said.

"The shaman has great power," said Crotaph, "but your power is greater. He will take your power, and lead the Blue Hand to glory and strength."

"Absolutely not," said Ridmark.

Crotaph's head turned towards Ridmark, his forked tongue flickering over his fangs. "You spurn the Blue Hand's generous offer? Think carefully before you make such a rash choice."

"An offer, is it?" said Ridmark. "Then I will make you an offer of my own, Crotaph of the Blue Hand. We will pass through your tunnels and never return, and you will not hinder us."

"And in exchange?" said Crotaph.

"I will leave you in peace," said Ridmark. "And if you try to oppose me, I will bring ruin upon you."

Crotaph hissed, bearing his fangs, his claws flexing against his bow. "You are one man with a stick."

"Last chance," said Ridmark, glancing at the nearby mushrooms. There were five concealed kobold archers, he thought. Maybe six.

"Impudence," said Crotaph. "We will teach you humility."

"Get ready to duck on my word," said Ridmark in Latin to the others.

Kharlacht raised his greatsword, Caius hefted his gleaming mace, and Calliande tensed.

"Kill them!" shouted Crotaph. "Leave the woman alive!"

A half-dozen kobolds appeared in the surrounding ghost mushrooms, bows drawn and aimed.

"Now!" shouted Ridmark.

He threw himself to the stone floor as the others fell, arrows hissing past them. He saw one arrow slam into Kharlacht, only to shatter against the blue steel of the orc's armor. Ridmark rolled, came to his feet, and charged the nearest kobold archer. The kobold shrieked a war cry and started to draw another arrow, but Ridmark was too fast. The first swing of his staff knocked the bow from the kobold's hands, and he reversed the weapon.

The length of the staff slammed against the side of the kobold's head with bone-shattering force, and the archer fell limp to the ground.

Ridmark sprinted along the edge of the mushroom cluster, catching the second archer. The kobold tried to turn, aiming at Ridmark at the last moment, but Ridmark's staff smashed into his face. The kobold stumbled back with a snarl, its fangs broken, and the staff came down and cracked his skull.

The kobold fell in a limp heap to the ground.

"Kill them!" screeched Crotaph. "Take the woman! The shaman commands it!"

But Ridmark darted around the stalk of a towering mushroom and killed a third archer. To his left he saw Kharlacht cutting down another kobold, while Caius stood guard over Calliande, mace in hand. Kobolds were dangerous opponents, but preferred to attack from ambush, using arrows fired from a distance. They hated to fight hand-to-hand, and often fled if faced with strong opposition. If Ridmark and Kharlacht and Caius put up a stiff enough resistance, perhaps the kobolds would flee.

Though that depended on whether or not they found their shaman more frightening than Ridmark and Kharlacht.

"Take them!" shouted Crotaph. Ridmark turned towards him. If Ridmark struck down their leader...

"Ridmark!"

Ridmark saw a score of kobolds emerge from the mushrooms. The kobolds wielded clubs and axes with stone heads, their crests flaring as they hissed and shrieked battle cries. Kharlacht hurried to stand alongside Caius, his blade running red with kobold blood.

Ridmark joined them, and they met the kobold charge.

Calliande backed against the stone wall, her eyes fixed on the fighting. The screams filled her ears, the grunts and shrieks and the sounds of cracking bone and splitting flesh. The chaos swirled before her eyes, the bodies falling to the ground, the blood splashing over the stone.

And all the blood came from the kobolds.

She watched with a detached, horrified fascination as Ridmark and Kharlacht cut their way through the kobold mass. Kharlacht fought with brutal power, his massive arms driving his greatsword with such force that he often cut a kobold in half. Those few kobolds who got close enough to strike found that his dark elven armor turned their blows, giving Kharlacht all the time he needed to slay his attackers.

But Ridmark was faster.

He moved through the kobolds like a wolf among sheep, his staff a blur in his hands. She had seen firsthand how heavy the thing was, yet he swung and thrust the weapon as if it were no more than a light branch. Every blow either disabled or slew a kobold, and their strikes came close to touching him, so close, but they never seemed to connect.

He and Kharlacht were warriors without peer.

Caius stood before her, striking any kobold that drew too close, but few ever did. Ridmark and Kharlacht were simply too skilled for the kobolds. Calliande suspected that they would prove more than a match for their opponents.

Even so, she wished she could help them. She hated feeling so useless, so helpless.

So weak.

For some reason it felt like a foreign sensation, something she had not often experienced. Though she had felt nothing but weak and helpless since awakening in that vault.

Something arched over the melee. For a moment Calliande thought it was another arrow, but it was moving too slowly.

It landed at her feet with a crack. It was a clay sphere, wisps of smoke rising from its broken edges.

"Calliande!" said Caius. "Get…"

The sphere exploded with a brilliant light, and then everything went black.

###

The blast from the smoke bomb erupted in a flash of white light and a thick ring of gray haze. It was disorienting, but it surprised the kobolds as much as Ridmark, and Ridmark did not hesitate. He tore through the stunned kobolds, striking right and left with his staff. He heard Kharlacht bellow a war cry, smelled the hot tang of kobold blood filling the air. Ridmark struck down another kobold, and looked for more opponents to fight.

But there were no opponents left.

He spun, seeking through the haze, but saw the kobolds fleeing in all directions. The battle was over...

"Ridmark!" Caius began to cough. "Ridmark!"

He hurried through the haze and found Caius on his hands and knees at the base of the cliff, coughing.

"You're wounded," said Ridmark.

"No," said Caius with another cough. He snatched his mace and staggered to his feet. "No. Smoke bomb. Kobold trick. Thought they'd kill me. But they..."

"Where's Calliande?" said Ridmark.

"They took her," said Caius, "along with the soulstone. I'm sorry."

Ridmark cursed and turned as the smoke thinned, but the cavern was deserted.

The kobolds were gone, as was Calliande.

CHAPTER 13
THE SHAMAN

Calliande swayed back and forth.

Dreams floated through her mind as she swayed.

She saw a field of cold gray ice beneath a sky the color of hard iron, haunted by creatures with eyes of blue fire.

A great army gathered, the banners of the Pendragons flying overhead, Swordbearers in the van, swords of white light burning in their fists.

A bitter argument with an old man, her oldest friend and closest advisor.

A staff of twisted oak and a sword of red gold.

Fog swallowing her mind.

Cold stone closing around her, darkness swallowing her.

And then a gaunt high elf in a long red coat, his eyes like quicksilver, laughing at her as his shadow fell upon her like an avalanche.

Calliande screamed, realizing that she had made a mistake, a terrible mistake, but it was too late, and the shadow laughed at her...

###

Her eyes shot open.

"No! I will not allow it!" she shouted in the high elven language. "You will not open another gate, Incariel! I know you brought them here! I know who you really are! I know what you are! And I will not allow you to summon them again."

For a moment, the fog in her memory wavered, and she could see the shape of her life, like mountains visible through looming mist...

She reached for them...and the fog swallowed them once more.

Calliande screamed in raw frustration. She had been close, so close. But bit by bit, facts started to penetrate her rage.

She was in an uncomfortable position. Her legs were mashed against her chest, her face pressed against her knees, the rough wool of her trousers scratching against her chin. Her arms were pinned against her chest, and she kept swaying back and forth.

She was in a net.

Calliande managed to turn her head, and then almost wished she hadn't.

A kobold warrior walked alongside her, tail waving, an obsidian-tipped spear in his clawed hands. His head rotated to face her, his tongue flickering over his fangs.

"So," hissed the kobold in orcish. "You are awake."

"Where are you taking me?" said Calliande. "I demand you let me go at once!"

"We have not raided the surface for too long," said the kobold warrior. "Mushrooms and murrag meat are not fit food for a warrior. Flesh, human flesh, is succulent." He clicked his fangs. "And then the flesh of young human females is the most succulent of all." His clawed hands reached into the net, closing around her right wrist. "The shaman wants you alive…but you do not need your hand. Yes…"

His claws tightened against her skin, and Calliande screamed and tried to pull away. Her efforts only made the net sway more rapidly. The kobold loosed a rasping laugh, and Calliande felt the razor-sharp claws bite into her skin…

The butt of a spear slammed into the kobold's head, and the warrior sprawled to the floor of the cavern.

"Fool!" snarled Crotaph, his crimson crest flaring with his anger. "The shaman commanded that the human woman come alive. Alive, and untouched! Do you wish to explain to the shaman that we failed because you could not control your damned belly?"

"But…" started the warrior, and Crotaph hit him again.

The warrior did not get up again.

"I am understood?" said Crotaph, his head turning back and forth. "The human female is to be unharmed! Or you shall answer to the Warchief…and pray that he does not hand you over to the shaman for punishment."

A rasping grumble of assent went up from a dozen kobold throats. Calliande saw that her net hung from a pair of poles carried by four kobolds. Other kobolds screened their flanks, guarding the narrow tunnel.

She saw no sign of Ridmark or the others. Had they been killed?

"Where are you taking me?" said Calliande.

She did not expect an answer, but Crotaph turned towards her nonetheless.

"To the village of the Blue Hand," said the kobold, his strange yellow eyes regarding her. Calliande wondered if this was how a mouse felt as a snake slithered closer.

"Where are the others?" said Calliande.

Crotaph's crest flattened, his tail coiling, and something in Calliande's mind informed her that it was the kobold equivalent of a shrug. "Still in the ruins of the dwarves, most likely. The shaman commanded that we bring you before him. He said nothing of your companions, and they are puissant warriors."

Calliande felt a surge of hope. Ridmark and the others were still alive.

"They will come for me," said Calliande. "Your warriors cannot stop them. If they catch up to us, you will all die. Let me go, and I will make sure we never trouble you again."

"If they catch us," said Crotaph, "we will likely perish. But we are almost to our village. And once you enter the village of the Blue Hand, you shall never leave." He hissed, forked tongue darting back and forth. "Our village is strong, and your companions will never force their way past our defenses. If they enter by stealth, the shaman's magic is strong. They cannot stand against his spells."

"Many others have said the same," said Calliande, "and they are now slain. Have you heard the stories of the Gray Knight?"

"I have," rasped one of the kobolds carrying the poles. "Years ago, we raided a village on the surface. We would have taken the women and children back as food, but the Gray Knight intervened, and many of us were slain. Perhaps you ought to warn the shaman, Crotaph, if the female's companion is truly the Gray Knight."

"Silence," said Crotaph. "You speak of fables. The Gray Knight? Perhaps you think the Dragon Knight will descend into the Deeps to slay us, or that Saint Michael will use his god's magic against us. Now stop talking and move! The longer we tarry, the quicker our foes will come upon us."

Crotaph moved at a loping run along the tunnel. The kobolds dropped to all fours while running, their tails stiffening for balance. The kobolds carrying Calliande remained upon two feet, but still moved at an impressive speed. The jouncing ride reminded Calliande unpleasantly of hanging from Vlazar's pole.

Still, at least she had clothes this time.

And she had to find a way to delay. Ridmark and the others would come for her. If she could just find a way to slow down the kobolds long enough for Ridmark to catch up to them…

Of course, it was hard to do anything at all, trapped as she was. All she could do was swing back and forth, the constant rocking making her grateful that she hadn't eaten very much today.

Perhaps she could use that to her advantage.

The kobolds turned a corner, the tunnel growing wider, stalagmites jutting from the floor like the teeth of some half-buried beast. Calliande saw a large stalagmite approaching, its sides glistening with moisture. She threw herself to the right as hard as she could. The net held her fast, but as kobolds passed the stalagmite, she slammed into the cold stone.

That rather hurt.

The force of the impact wrenched the poles from the hands of the kobolds, and they fell in a heap. Calliande clawed at the net, trying to untangle herself. Her hands found the top, and she yanked it open. She staggered to her feet, a wild hope flaring in her chest. She could break free, run down the tunnel and escape before the kobolds...

A half-dozen obsidian spear points came to rest against her chest. The top of the kobolds' heads only reached her stomach, but she had no doubt the creatures could drive their weapons through her flesh.

"Do not move," said Crotaph.

"You won't strike me," said Calliande. "Your precious shaman wants me alive and unharmed."

"True," said Crotaph, "but alive and untouched can also mean alive and unconscious. Fight us again, and I will have you drugged. You won't enjoy that."

"Fine," said Calliande.

"We should bind her, Crotaph," said one of the warriors.

"Why bother? We have almost reached the village," said Crotaph. "If she runs, drug her. Come."

The kobolds prodded her with their spears, and Calliande had no choice but to follow them. The air was thick with the smell of smoke and the dusty odor of the kobolds' scales, and Calliande realized they were almost to the village of the Blue Hand.

"Your shaman must be very powerful," said Calliande, "if you fear him so. The gods of the kobolds must be with him."

She did not expect an answer, but Crotaph said, "The shaman is a god."

"A god?" said Calliande. "He claims to be a god?"

"He is a god," said Crotaph.

She made herself laugh. "Mhalek of the orcs claimed to be a god as well, and the Gray Knight slew him."

Crotaph hissed. "The orcs are fools, and their blood gods are shadows. The shaman of the Blue Hand has power. A century ago he came among us, and he has protected us ever since. Not even the dark elves dare to cross his magic. The world will fall at his feet, and the kobolds of the Blue Hand shall make slaves of all other kindreds."

"Mhalek," said Calliande, "said the same."

At least, she assumed so.

Crotaph growled, and said no more. A flickering light danced on the walls of the cavern, and Calliande realized it was firelight. The tunnel widened, and opened into a large gallery, larger than the great cavern of Thainkul Agon.

The kobold village filled most of the space.

A stockade of piled stones surrounded it, with a gate made from lacquered mushroom planks. Herds of murrags grazed in the mushroom fields outside the walls, guarded by kobolds with short bows. A dozen kobolds prowled the ramparts, bows in hand. The gate opened, and Crotaph led her inside. Beyond she saw dozens of ramshackle houses built of loose stone and mushroom caps. Tunnels cored the cavern walls, no doubt leading to additional houses and storerooms.

And in the village she saw kobolds, hundreds of kobolds. The kobold females were almost identical to the males, thought smaller and with intricate patterns of striped scales on their sides instead of crests upon their heads. Everywhere she saw kobolds going about their business, making weapons or tools, tanning hides, cooking, or simply talking.

But as one, they fell silent as she entered and stared at her with unblinking yellow eyes.

The biggest kobold Calliande had yet seen forced his way through the press. He was tall enough to reach her shoulder, and wore an elaborate mantle fashioned of bones and polished stones. He was fat, his belly and limbs swollen so badly that the scales had cracked in places. Unlike the others, he carried a short sword of actual steel in his belt.

"Warchief," said Crotaph, bowing and lowering his crest.

"Crotaph," growled the Warchief, glaring at Calliande. "You have lost many warriors."

"A dozen, at least," said Crotaph. "Some may yet return. But we have been successful." He gestured at Calliande. "The shaman's visions were true, and we have found the woman."

"So I see," said the Warchief. "A useless skinny little thing. If we butchered her here and now, she wouldn't give more than a mouthful to a score of warriors. Human females provide the best meat when they are plump."

Calliande shuddered.

"The shaman wants her," said Crotaph.

The Warchief's crest deflated.

"Yes," said the Warchief. "What the shaman of the Blue Hand desires, the shaman of the Blue Hand gets. You have done well, Crotaph, and you have my gratitude." He pointed at the other warriors. "You. Follow me. Bring the human."

Again the warriors jabbed her with their spears, and Calliande followed.

The Warchief lumbered across the village to the cavern wall, and climbed a rough set of steps hewn into the rock. As they climbed, Calliande saw the village spread out beneath her. A large enclosed pen occupied the space below the stockade wall. Scores of spitfangs filled the pen, some sleeping, some pacing, a few fighting. Bones carpeted the ground beneath them, and Calliande wondered how many victims had met their end beneath the spitfangs' claws and venom.

She saw quite a few kobold skulls among the bones. Perhaps those who angered the Warchief and the shaman went to the spitfangs.

The stairs ended before a yawning cavern mouth. A dozen human skulls hung over the entrance, yellowed and ancient. From within Calliande saw the flickering glow of a fire, and smelled the stench of rotting meat.

"Inside," said the Warchief. "The shaman of the Blue Hand awaits you."

Calliande did not want to go into that reeking cave, and the very thought of taking another step filled her with terror. But the Warchief and a dozen kobold warriors blocked the way back.

She took a deep breath, wincing at the smell. She had to delay. She had to find a way to buy time until Ridmark found her.

Assuming Ridmark could find a way past so many kobolds...

Calliande turned away from the Warchief and took a cautious step into the cavern.

The smell of rotting meat grew stronger. She walked deeper into the cave, the fiery glow growing brighter. She saw designs chalked into the wall, elaborate sigils and interlocking circles, and felt something stir in her mind. She recognized at least some of those designs.

The cave opened into a small, round chamber. A firepit had been dug into the center of the floor, and the glowing coals within it filled the chamber with a bloody glow. Several tables lined the walls, holding books and scrolls written in Latin, high elven, and dark elven. A couch of dried mushroom planks sat on the other side of the firepit, piled high with cushions.

Upon the cushions slouched an ancient kobold wrapped in a worn robe of murrag leather. Deep wrinkles scored his face and neck, his scales cracked and dull. The yellow eyes that turned towards Calliande were filmy, and the kobold had lost half his fangs. She heard the steady whistling rasp of breath through his nostrils.

And she felt magical power radiating off him like the heat from the firepit.

His clawed hands were blue. At first Calliande thought they had been painted or tattooed, but then she realized that they were glowing with a pale blue light. Some part of her fog-choked memory realized that meant the shaman had tremendous power over the magical element of water. He could freeze or boil any liquid with a thought, including the blood in an enemy's veins, and could conjure water elementals of tremendous power.

Little wonder the kobolds worshiped him as a god.

For a moment Calliande and the shaman stared at each other.

"Calliande," rasped the ancient kobold.

Something about his tone, his accent, sounded familiar.

"You know me?" she said in orcish.

The shaman sighed. "Do not weary my ears with that barbarous and uncouth tongue," he said in perfect Latin. "Use the speech of the High Kingdom. It has been far too long since I have heard it."

"Very well," said Calliande in Latin, surprised. "Then I will repeat my question. You know me?"

"Indeed," said the shaman. "I know you very well, Calliande." The kobold tilted his head to the side. "A more urgent question is whether or not you recognize me."

"No," said Calliande. "I've never seen you before."

"Ah." The shaman sounded disappointed. "I would have assumed you would see past appearances, beyond the mere flesh. But I was wrong. To think I used to admire you. But now I see that you are as weak as all the others."

Two realizations came to her.

The first was that this kobold knew who she was.

The second was that he didn't realize that she had lost her memory.

Which meant if she handled him carefully, she might be able to obtain some useful information. She needed to play for time...and perhaps she could get the shaman to tell her who she was.

"Indeed?" said Calliande. "Do not presume to lecture me on weakness. I will not tolerate such nonsense from a petty wielder of simple magic crouching in his hole."

"Your threats are meaningless," said the shaman. "I know your powers have not returned, at least not in full strength. Otherwise the Warchief's pet thugs would not have been able to capture you so easily."

Calliande raised an eyebrow. "Perhaps I permitted myself to be captured. Perhaps I simply wanted to see you for myself."

The shaman shrank back into the cushions. Who had Calliande been that she could cause fear like that?

"No," said the shaman at last. "No, if you wanted me dead, you would have done it already."

"I don't recognize you," said Calliande. "Why would I wish you dead?"

"If you knew who I truly was," said the shaman, "then you would attack me at once."

"Then who are you?" said Calliande.

The kobold shaman hissed and drew himself up. "You knew me as Talvinius."

Calliande could not remember if she had heard that name before. Yet Talvinius was certain that he knew her.

And Talvinius was not a kobold name.

"You've changed," she said, trying to think of something to say.

Talvinius wheezed with laughter. "Changed? Yes, I would think so." His tongue flickered over the broken fangs. "The centuries have not been kind to me, no?"

Centuries? He had known Calliande centuries ago?

"They have not," said Calliande, hoping to lure him into telling her more.

Talvinius croaked his laugh. "I once lusted for you, you know. I thought to lure you into my bed. But you were always too focused upon your duty, so concerned with your great and holy cause."

"You are mad," said Calliande, "if you think I would willingly take a kobold into my bed."

Talvinius sneered. "But I was not always a kobold."

"No?" said Calliande. "You claim you were once human? That you are not merely a mad kobold claiming to be a man I once knew?"

Again Talvinius laughed. "Is that what you think, dear Calliande? That I am merely a mad kobold? Oh, but this is delightful. I was once human, a Magistrius of the Order."

"Human?" said Calliande. "And then you accidentally transformed yourself into a kobold? A likely tale."

"Do not mock me," growled Talvinius. "Not after what I have endured. But...ah, I understand now. You slept for too long. You know nothing of the Eternalists. That is modern history, too new for an ancient hag like you."

"First you lust for me, and now you call me a hag," said Calliande. "Amazing that your honeyed tongue never lured me into your bed. But your fables intrigue me. Just what is an Eternalist?"

"There were those among the Magistri," said Talvinius, "who came to question the restrictions placed upon our Order. Defense, knowledge, and communication. The three uses of magic permitted by the law of the High King and the Church, the three uses ordained by our treaty with Ardrhythain. Practically speaking, this narrowed us to spells of warding, healing, divination, and telepathy. But magic...magic could be used for so much more. For far greater purposes."

"Humans are not to be trusted with power," said Calliande. "We are a fallen race, and our hearts turn towards cruelty and tyranny. We must shepherd the power of magic well, and guard is closely. The Magistri are to be the servants of humanity, not its rulers."

Those words had felt so familiar, as if she had spoken them a thousand times before.

"The same trite sermons as always," said Talvinius. "Two hundred years and you have not changed. You slept...but some of us dreamed of more. Some of us had the vision and courage to realize that the Church's scriptures and histories are merely fables, that such places as Rome and Jerusalem and Athens never existed. Perhaps even Malahan Pendragon himself was but a legend, a lie concocted by the clerics who feared the power of the Magistri. Magic possesses the power to change humanity, Calliande, to make us as strong as the urdmordar, as powerful as the dark elves...and as long-lived as the high elves."

"Eat of this tree," said Calliande, "and you surely shall not die."

"That is a misquotation and you know it," said Talvinius. "Humanity is at a disadvantage, Calliande. The dwarves can live for five hundred years, the dark elves for a thousand, and the high elves even longer. The urdmordar are effectively immortal. If humanity is to survive, it must be guided...and who better to guide it than Magistri gifted with immortality?"

"And so these Eternalists of yours," said Calliande, "were Magistri who tried to find a way to live forever using magic."

"Yes," said Talvinius. "Great strides were made. But in time word of our experiments leaked out, and the High King, the Church, and the Masters of the Magistri turned against us. Most of the Eternalists were killed, the rest scattered. I fled here to the Deeps...and in time, my body grew old. I had no choice left..."

"So you turned yourself into a kobold?" said Calliande. Then the answer came to her. "No...you expelled your spirit from your flesh and possessed a living kobold." She frowned. "Why a kobold?"

"Because," said Talvinius, his voice sour, "a kobold was all I could manage. Expelling one's spirit and seizing control of another body is a rather...arduous process, to say the least. Had I more time to prepare...but my final illness came quickly, and so I seized a kobold's body for my own."

Calliande felt her lip curl in disgust.

"And that is why the Magistri and the High King turned against you," she said. "You were trying to possess other people in your experiments."

"They were only peasants," said Talvinius. "Dumb brutes, ignorant and savage and unlettered. They exist only to serve their betters. And if their betters chose to spend their blood in pursuit of immortality..."

"That's monstrous," said Calliande. "They are living men with hearts and souls, and you had no right to steal their lives to extend your own."

"I had every right!" said Talvinius, pounding one arm of his couch with a clawed fist. "And I did it." He cackled. "Two hundred years, Calliande, two hundred years after you hid yourself in that vault in pursuit of your phantoms, and I am still alive. All my contemporaries died long ago. Yet I am still here."

"And in such a glorious form, too," said Calliande. "How long have you lived in that kobold's body? When was the last time you were able to rise from that couch?"

"The kobolds worship me as a god," said Talvinius. "They provide whatever I require."

"You're pathetic," said Calliande, "and you've made yourself into a monster. I don't know whether you are more pitiable or contemptible."

"Then destroy me," said Talvinius. "Strike me down, and send my rotted soul screaming down to hell...assuming such a place is not just another fable of the Church. Do it, Calliande. Do it now."

Calliande hesitated.

"I thought not," said Talvinius. "I suspected your powers had not returned. And I now know your memories have not come back to you. Very well played, I might add. I was not sure...and you learned quite a bit from me, I suppose. But if you have come into my lair without your powers, then I know you have not regained your memories."

Calliande felt her mouth go dry. "How?"

"Because," said Talvinius, "if you had your memory, you would not have come here...because you would know how much danger you are in now."

"You're going to kill me?" said Calliande.

"Kill you?" laughed Talvinius. "I suppose this body wants to kill you. Two hundred years, Calliande ...and you are just as lovely as the day you buried yourself alive. I suppose I should desire you. But I wear the flesh of a kobold...and I want to feast on you, not ravish you. I wonder how your flesh and blood would taste against my tongue. But I'm not going to kill you. I'm going to take you."

"Take me?" said Calliande. "How..."

But then she understood, and she turned to run.

It was too late. Talvinius crooked a finger, and white mist swirled around Calliande's feet. A heartbeat later a block of thick ice encased her feet and shins. The thick boots kept the chill at bay, but Calliande could not move. She pulled at her legs, but the ice held them fast.

"It will be demeaning, I suppose," said Talvinius, "to wear the flesh of a woman."

"I thought you could only claim the flesh of a kobold," said Calliande, trying to wrench free of the ice.

"That was a century ago. I have practiced since then," said Talvinius. "And I shall have the aid of the empty soulstone you carry. Did you think I would not sense an item of such power? Ah, but you lost your memory. With the aid of that soulstone, I shall leave this decrepit carcass behind and claim your body for my own…and then all your power shall be mine. What wonders and terrors I shall wreak upon the High Kingdom!"

Calliande struggled to free herself, and Talvinius began casting a spell.

CHAPTER 14
FANGS

Ridmark turned, the remaining smoke thinning.

"What are you doing?" said Caius.

Ridmark ignored him for the moment. There was a great deal of sand and dry silt on the floor of the cavern, no doubt left from the occasional flood of the stream.

That meant anyone passing through the cavern would leave footprints.

He paused at the base of the cliff and examined the marks upon the ground.

The answers came to him easily enough. Calliande had been standing there when the smoke bomb had gone off. The fumes had stunned her, and the kobolds had dragged her across the cavern as Ridmark and Kharlacht struggled against the remaining warriors.

Caius walked to his side, Kharlacht following. "What are you…"

"Quiet," said Ridmark, holding out his staff to block their path. "And hold still. You'll foul the trail."

He worked his way across the cavern. There was less sand further away from the stream, but there were enough mushroom spores and silt upon the floor that he could follow the kobolds' trail. If he read the signs right, he suspect they had carried away Calliande in a net.

The trail ended at a narrow cavern entrance, the tunnel beyond sloping upward.

Ridmark stopped, grimaced, and beckoned the others forward.

"What happened to Calliande?" said Caius. "The smoke bomb overpowered me, and when I awoke…"

"The kobolds took her," said Ridmark, "this way. Clever of them. They distracted us, and then snatched her while we were fighting."

"But why?" said Caius.

Kharlacht shrugged. "Perhaps the same reason Shadowbearer commanded Qazarl to slay her upon the altar."

"You are going after her?" said Caius.

"I am," said Ridmark. "And no lectures about how I wish to throw my life away, Brother Caius. I told Calliande I would help her." He hesitated. "There is no need for you to accompany me. Follow the stream to the surface, and go warn Sir Joram of Qazarl's attack."

"By now Sir Joram likely knows more about Qazarl's attack than we do," said Caius. "I shall not abandon a comrade in arms and a woman in need."

Ridmark nodded. "I would be glad of your aid." He looked at Kharlacht. "You have no need to accompany us. Return to the surface and rejoin your kin."

Kharlacht shook his head. "I will follow you."

"Why?" said Ridmark. "You have no obligation to do so. Once you leave the Deeps, you are released of your oath to aid us."

"I have no wish to see Calliande fall into the hands of the kobolds," said Kharlacht.

"You would prefer to hand her over to Qazarl yourself?" said Ridmark.

He expected anger, but Kharlacht only shook his head. "I do not wish her ill. And I am bound by my word. I swore I would see you returned to the surface, that I would not harm Calliande…and if I let her remain in the hands of the kobolds, I would bring her harm."

"That would be the kobolds' doing, not yours," said Ridmark.

"But the responsibility would be mine," said Kharlacht. He looked at Caius. "As in the Dominus Christus's parable of the traveler beset by brigands."

"Very well," said Ridmark. "Then let us waste no more time in talk."

He led the way into the tunnel, Caius and Kharlacht following. The cavern floor sloped up, lit by patches of ghost mushrooms clinging to the floors and walls, and Ridmark saw signs of the kobolds' passage, the scratches of claws upon stone, the occasional fallen scale.

After a third of a mile he saw signs of a scuffle, droplets of blood upon the ground. Ridmark dropped to one knee and sniffed.

"Kobold," he said. "Not human."

"Perhaps Crotaph suffers from dissension in the ranks," said Caius.

"Indeed," said Kharlacht. "Among the clans of Vhaluusk, a chieftain is often hard-pressed to keep his authority, especially when there are desirable captives available."

"Given that kobolds eat humans," said Ridmark, "I think we had best hurry."

He saw no sign of any human blood. If the kobolds had come to blows over Calliande, they had not harmed her.

But nor had she been able to escape in the chaos.

The tunnel widened around them, the ceiling getting higher. A faint breeze brushed Ridmark's face, and he smelled the dusty odor of kobold scales in the air.

A lot of kobold scales.

Ahead he saw the glow of firelight in the distance.

"Wait here," he said. "I think the village of the Blue Hand is just ahead."

"Risky to go alone," said Caius.

"Of course it is," said Ridmark. "We have done nothing but take risks for the last three days. But it is less of a risk for me than it is for either of you. I can move with greater stealth than you or Kharlacht." He tugged at his gray elven cloak. "And I have this. If I'm careful, I can get close enough to scout the village and return."

Caius sighed. "Your plan is madness...but it is sound, as always. We shall wait here for your return."

"If I don't return by the end of the day," said Ridmark, "assume that I am dead, and return to Dun Licinia to warn Sir Joram. And to warn the Magistri and the Swordbearers about that soulstone. Such a thing is far too dangerous to remain in the hands of a kobold shaman. And Shadowbearer may try to claim it."

"Go with God," said Caius.

Ridmark nodded, drew his cloak around him, and hurried forward.

The tunnel opened into a vast cavern, larger than the chamber of the waterfall in Thainkul Agon.

The village of the Blue Hand occupied most of the cavern.

A stockade wall of rough stone encircled the village, kobold sentries standing guard upon the rampart. Beyond the wall Ridmark saw houses and workshops of loose stone, roofed by dried mushroom caps. Hundreds of tunnels marked the cavern walls beyond the stockade, and Ridmark realized the kobolds had tunneled into the stone like ants.

Finding Calliande would prove a challenge.

For some reason, his mind flashed back to the desperate days before the Battle of Dun Licinia. Master Galearus and the other chief nobles and Magistri were dead, slain at parley by Mhalek's treachery. Ridmark had taken command of the host because there was no one else left to do so. His men had been badly outnumbered and demoralized...but he had turned the tables and defeated the Mhalekite horde.

He had snatched victory from the jaws of defeat by turning his foe's weaknesses against him.

Perhaps the kobolds had a similar weakness.

Of course, his victory against Mhalek had cost him everything.

What might a victory here cost?

Ridmark ignored the thought and moved closer to the village, creeping from stalagmite to stalagmite. Murrags grazed among the mushrooms, tended by kobolds armed with bows. Ridmark avoided them and came to the intersection of the cavern wall and the stockade. It was the obvious place for anyone to scale the wall, but the kobolds had posted no guards there.

A weakness.

Ridmark climbed the rough wall and pulled himself up to the ramparts.

At once he saw why the kobolds needed no guards on this corner of the wall.

A fenced pen sat below the stockade, holding at least one hundred and fifty spitfangs. Most of the creatures were sleeping, their scales blended to match the gray stone around them. Others were awake and prowling, and a few snapped at each other.

None of them had seen Ridmark yet.

He climbed back down the wall. Had he delayed any longer, the spitfangs would have detected his scent. The resultant noise would alert the kobolds.

He leaned against the wall, wrapped in his cloak and watched the village.

Where would they have taken Calliande? The largest building within the stockade looked like a long hall, no doubt the seat of whatever chieftain ruled the village. Yet the shaman had sent Crotaph to kidnap Calliande, not the chieftain, and Ridmark suspected the shaman ruled the kobolds of the Blue Hand. The kobolds worshipped an odd smattering of gods – the orcish blood gods, the great darkness of the dark elves, and some offered sacrifices to the urdmordar.

Was the shaman of the Blue Hand in fact a priest of an urdmordar? That was a worrying. Few creatures were as dangerous as an urdmordar matriarch in her full might…and only magic could harm an urdmordar.

Ridmark had no such magic at hand.

His eyes fell on a large cavern entrance, higher than the others. Human skulls hung from the entrance, and he saw strange symbols carved into the wall nearby. A dim glow of firelight came from within that cave, visible through the pale radiance of the ghost mushrooms.

The shaman's chambers. Ridmark was sure of it.

A plan formed in his mind. It was bold, and could well work. It was also reckless, and might get him killed.

But that would be no great loss. If he had died the day he had faced Mhalek, then Aelia would still live.

Ridmark slipped from the cavern and returned to the tunnel leading back to Thainkul Agon. Kharlacht and Caius awaited him, weapons in hand. To his satisfaction, neither the orc nor the dwarf noticed him until he was only a few feet away.

Kharlacht growled. "Do not startle me like that. I almost cut off your head."

"Then pay better attention," said Ridmark.

"Did you find her?" said Caius.

"I believe so," said Ridmark. He examined the wall, and then walked towards a cluster of red-glowing mushrooms. "She's likely in the shaman's cave, which overlooks the village proper."

"How many kobolds are in the village?" said Caius.

"Hundreds, certainly," said Ridmark.

He yanked one of the red-glowing ghost mushrooms from the wall.

"Those are poisonous," said Caius.

"They are," said Ridmark, "but I wasn't planning to eat one."

He dropped the mushroom, picked up a pair of rocks, knelt, and started to grind the mushroom to glowing red powder.

Kharlacht and Caius stared at him in befuddlement.

"The red ghost mushrooms are poisonous," said Ridmark. He examined the powder for a moment, nodded, and plucked another mushroom from the cluster. "What other properties do they have?"

"The scent of them," said Caius slowly, "drives a spitfang to madness."

Ridmark nodded. "And the Blue Hand kobolds have a pen full of spitfangs in their village. Perhaps a hundred and fifty of the beasts, if not more."

"So your plan," said Caius, "is to drive the spitfangs to madness, loose them upon the kobolds, and snatch Calliande away from this shaman in the chaos?"

"Essentially," said Ridmark, squinting at the pile of glowing powder. "No plan of battle survives contact with the foe, and I will adapt as circumstances dictate. But that is what I intend."

"Madness," said Caius.

Kharlacht threw back his head and roared with laughter.

Both Ridmark and Caius stared at him.

"Madness, yes," said Kharlacht, once he had mastered himself. "But madness with a purpose. It is the same thing you did to my warriors, when you loosed the drakes upon us. A bold and reckless plan, a plan that should not have succeeded...yet here were stand." He shook his head, a few loose hairs from his topknot brushing against his jaw. "My kin would say the blood gods have given their favor to you. But I do not follow the blood gods, and I think the Lord has placed his hand upon you, as the scriptures say he did with the Assyrians of Old Earth."

"I hope not," said Ridmark, "considering what happened to the Assyrians of Old Earth. Now stop talking, and start grinding mushrooms."

Both the orcish warrior and the dwarven friar obeyed, and soon they had an ample pile of powdered mushrooms. Ridmark examined the pile for a moment, and then nodded.

"Is that enough?" Kharlacht said.

Caius snorted. "That's enough to drive every spitfang from here to the Three Kingdoms mad."

"Good," said Ridmark. He scooped the powder into a leather pouch and dusted off his hands. "Wait here until I return with Calliande. If it becomes obvious that I am not going to return, head for the surface. Kharlacht, you are released to return to your people…and Caius, you must go to Dun Licinia and warn Sir Joram, or go to Castra Marcaine if the town is already under siege."

"I will accompany you," said Kharlacht.

"Why?" said Ridmark.

"Four hands are better than two," said Kharlacht, "and if something goes awry, you will need aid."

That, or Kharlacht wanted to seize Calliande and make his escape while Ridmark was occupied. But Ridmark would not show hesitation or doubt before the orcish warrior, and Kharlacht was right. If something went awry, Ridmark would need help.

"Very well," said Ridmark. "But you, Brother Caius, will remain here." Caius opened his mouth to object. "Someone needs to warn the town if we fail…and I do not think you can climb that wall fast enough."

"You have a point," said Caius. "I will remain behind."

"Good," said Ridmark. "Kharlacht, come. Do not make any noise."

He led the way up the tunnel, the orcish warrior following.

Calliande struggled against the ice binding her legs.

"Strange, is it not?" said Talvinius. "The magic of the Frostborn proved useful. They are, of course, utterly extinct, and you and the Order of the Vigilant wasted your lives pursuing a phantasm. But even their petty spells have proven potent." He cackled. "Of course, you don't remember any of that."

He gestured again, and the block of ice ripped free from the floor and slammed into the wall. The impact knocked Calliande's breath from her lungs, and white mist swirled around her wrists. It hardened into shackles of ice, pinning her arms to the cave wall.

"Are you going to beg, dear Calliande?" said Talvinius. "That would be enjoyable."

"Why waste my breath?" said Calliande. "You've already made your intentions quite clear."

"Indeed," said Talvinius. "Shall we begin?"

The ancient kobold picked up a cane, heaved himself to his feet, and limped towards her.

Ridmark beckoned, and Kharlacht followed.

They wove their way through the fields of mushrooms, dodging from tree-sized mushroom to tree-sized mushroom to avoid notice. The kobold guards did not see them, and if the murrags saw them, the fat lizards remained apathetic. For all his muscled bulk, Kharlacht moved with a manageable degree of stealth.

They reached the base of the wall. Ridmark went first, scaling the wall. He pulled himself up to the rampart, looked around, and nodded.

Kharlacht followed a heartbeat later, massive greatsword gripped in his right fist.

Ridmark looked over the wall. The spitfangs remained calm, most of them asleep. He reached for the pouch hanging at his belt. He would start with the prowling spitfangs, and then move to the sleeping beasts as they awoke.

And then he would enter the village and get Calliande back.

Or he would die. But for Calliande's sake, he hoped to live.

He took a step forward, and a kobold appeared over the edge of rampart. The creature had a pointed stick in one hand, no doubt a prod used to keep surly spitfangs at bay.

The kobold froze in surprise. Ridmark drew back his staff to strike, but he would not be able to land a blow in time.

The kobold opened his mouth to scream a warning.

Talvinius limped closer, his dusty scent filling Calliande's nostrils. She also smelled the sickly, rotting smell of illness pouring off the ancient kobold.

"You don't have much time left, do you?" said Calliande.

Talvinius's broken fangs clicked together.

"No," said Talvinius. "This body...this body has lived long beyond its natural span. I convinced the wretched kobolds that I was a god, and they offered me blood sacrifices on a regular basis. Their stolen lives have sustained me for decades...but the decay can only be postponed for so long."

"That's monstrous," said Calliande. "You murdered kobolds to sustain yourself."

Talvinius spat upon the floor. The smell of sickness grew sharper. "They are only kobolds. Lizards with overlarge brains, and nothing more. Vermin to be exterminated...or harvested, as need be."

"It's still murder," said Calliande.

"How simplistic," said Talvinius. "I have moved beyond such childish moralizing."

"Which has served you so well," said Calliande, "since you're trapped in the body of a dying kobold." She scowled. "You are loathsome, Talvinius. You had the power of magic, you had the responsibility to use your power for good...and you abused it utterly. How will you account for yourself when you stand before the throne of God on the day of judgment?"

"Another childish story," said Talvinius, gazing up at her. "See if your myths will save you now."

He reached into her pouch and drew out the soulstone, his claws clicking against the crystal.

"At last," he murmured. "I didn't think you would have one of these with you. A delightful bonus. Once I claim your flesh, this will make me all the more powerful."

He began to cast a spell, ghostly blue fire dancing around his clawed fingers.

The kobold drew breath, but Kharlacht moved faster.

He seized the kobold's throat and drove his blade forward in a blue blur. The steel sank into the kobold's chest and burst from his back, red with blood. The kobold thrashed for a moment, and then went limp.

Ridmark let out a long breath and nodded his thanks to Kharlacht.

Kharlacht pulled his blade from the dead kobold and let the corpse drop to the rampart.

Ridmark tugged on a leather glove, reached into the pouch, and started to throw handfuls of the powder into the spitfang pen.

The reaction was immediate.

A dozen of the spitfangs lifted their heads. They turned in a circle, growling and hissing, and attacked each other. Several threw themselves at the sleeping spitfangs. Dozens of the creatures awakened and fought back, and Ridmark kept throwing handfuls of the powder into the pen. Soon the spitfangs were embroiled in a massive melee, shrieking and howling, bursts of poisoned spit flying back and forth.

The pen's door flew open, and a dozen kobolds hurried inside, jabbing at the enraged spitfangs with sticks. The lizards barely noticed.

Ridmark needed to turn the spitfangs' attention to the kobolds. But how? What could lure...

He looked at the dead kobold.

Ridmark kicked the dead kobold into the pen. The body flopped across the stony ground. Three spitfangs jumped upon the corpse and began ripping at the dead flesh. The air filled with the scent of kobold blood.

And the spitfangs went mad.

The creatures surged forward, tore apart their kobold herders, broke through the gate, and swarmed into the village of the Blue Hand. Cries of alarm and shouts of rage erupted from the village, and Ridmark saw the kobold warriors rush to meet the threat of their maddened war beasts.

And in the chaos, no one noticed the gray-cloaked human and the orcish warrior standing upon the walls.

"You made a mess," said Kharlacht.

"That was the point," said Ridmark. "Follow me and stay away from the spitfangs. With luck, we can get to the shaman's cave before anyone sees us."

He dropped from the wall and into the pen, and Kharlacht followed.

Ridmark hurried into the melee.

Talvinius finished his spell, his thin, shaking limbs reaching for Calliande's head. For a terrible moment she thought he would rip out her throat, despite his intention to claim her body for his own.

But instead his clawed fingers brushed her temples, as gentle as a lover's touch.

And she felt the touch inside her mind.

Calliande flinched.

"Yes," whispered Talvinius, "you understand."

He spoke, his gray tongue rasping against broken fangs, but she heard his voice inside her mind.

"You are mine."

She felt the icy fingers of his power sinking into her thoughts, felt the cavern filling with darkness around her.

No, the cavern wasn't filling with darkness. She was falling into the nothingness, Talvinius's dark magic driving her spirit from her flesh.

Calliande screamed, her body trembling, fighting to drive the alien presence from her mind.

"No," whispered Talvinius. "You cannot stop me. You don't have your power. You made yourself weak, Calliande...you made yourself weak to save the world."

Calliande screamed, fighting against Talvinius's presence...but his cold fingers sank deeper into her mind.

Ridmark raced across the village, making for the narrow stone steps threading up the side of the cavern wall.

"Intruders!"

Ridmark whirled and saw a kobold warrior lunged at him with an obsidian spear. He parried the blow and reversed his staff, the heavy wood smashing against the kobold's temple. The kobold fell limp to the ground.

But three more rushed to take the warrior's place.

Ridmark met their attack, his staff spinning as he blocked their thrusts and swings. Their assault drove him back, but Kharlacht threw himself into the fray. The swing of his blade took the head from a kobold, and his next strike opened a kobold from throat to navel. Ridmark broke the wrists of another, and the warrior stumbled back with a shriek...only for a maddened spitfang to leap upon him.

For a moment the mayhem cleared around them.

"Go!" said Ridmark, and they ran for the stairs.

Calliande shuddered, Talvinius's laughter ringing in her mind.

And as his cold hands reached into her thoughts, some of the mist clouding her memory swirled.

Rage rose up to devour her fear.

"You," she spat. "You betrayed the Order of the Vigilant. You promised to stand guard against the Frostborn! Instead you are crouching in this hole, feeding on the blood of kobolds like a damned leech! You were once a Magistrius, a wielder of magic...and instead you have chosen to become this contemptible shell!"

"Silence!" snarled Talvinius. "You are mine! I shall wear your flesh, and I will never die!"

"No!" said Calliande. "I will see you brought to account for what you have done."

"Unlikely," sneered Talvinius, "since you cannot even lift your hands."

The alien presence in her mind redoubled, and Calliande shuddered. Her rage increased, burning hotter until it seemed as if she had been wreathed in fire. She felt her herself snarling, her body straining against the shackles of ice.

Talvinius's ragged crest collapsed in sudden fear.

And all at once the icy shackles binding Calliande's wrists vanished.

She grabbed Talvinius's wrists, yanking his clawed hands away from her face. The soulstone fell from his grasp and rolled away across the floor.

"What is this?" shouted Talvinius. "It is not possible!" The blue light around his hands began to dim, fading beneath a sudden white radiance. "It is not possible! No! No! Stop! Please, please stop!"

White light filled the world, and Calliande felt herself fall.

A sptifang lunged at Ridmark, jaws snapping, and he dodged a blob of venomous spit. He drove his staff in a high swing, catching the spitfang in the teeth, and the creature fell yowling to the ground. Another blow from his staff snapped its neck, and the sleek lizard went limp.

Two more kobolds rushed them, and Kharlacht's sword took the head from the first. Ridmark stepped around the second, his staff slamming into its knee. The kobold stumbled, and Ridmark brought his staff down onto the warrior's crest.

The chaos raged through the village, the kobolds fighting their enraged spitfangs, but more and more warriors had spotted Ridmark and Kharlacht. If they did not fight their way to the shaman's lair soon, then they never would...

A massive thunderclap rang through the cavern, so loud that the floor shook. Every last kobold and spitfang turned to look at shaman's cave, and a blazing beam of white light erupted from the entrance.

An instant later a white fireball shot from the cavern and landed in the midst of the melee. In the flames Ridmark saw an ancient kobold, thrashing in his death throes as the white fire chewed into his flesh.

"The shaman!" screamed a kobold. "The shaman has fallen!"

The spitfangs shrieked and resumed their attack, and Ridmark ran for the stairs, Kharlacht a half-step behind.

Calliande's eyes opened.

Her cheek rested against warm, rough stone, and the sullen glow of a fire filled her eyes. She sat up, and found herself on the floor of Talvinius's cave. The rock around her was blackened, as if it had been exposed to tremendous heat, and a scorched trail led out of the cavern.

There was no sign of Talvinius.

The air was heavy with the smell of burned flesh.

Calliande suspected that Talvinius would not trouble her again.

She got to her feet, head spinning. What had she done to him? Her rage had risen up in her like an inferno, burning through the fog of her memory, and then…

She looked at the smoking char on the floor.

Had her rage manifested as fire and struck down Talvinius?

It seemed impossible.

The sound of screaming reached her ears, along with the shrieks of enraged spitfangs. Something was happening in the village. Had Talvinius's death thrown the kobolds of the Blue Hand into chaos?

If so, this might be Calliande's only chance to escape.

A gleam of light caught her eye, and she saw the empty soulstone lying near the firepit. Calliande scooped up the crystal, stuffed it into her belt pouch, and headed for the exit.

She reached the top of the narrow stone stairs and saw that the spitfangs had somehow broken out of their pen and had gone berserk, hunting their kobold masters. Calliande considered hiding until the fighting died down, but this might be her only chance to get away.

She sprinted down the stairs, one hand gripping the wall for balance. A kobold female emerged from one of the caves, hissing at her, but Calliande kept running.

Her eyes widened.

Ridmark and Kharlacht fought back to back at the base of the stairs, driving back the kobolds with every step.

Ridmark whipped his staff in a circle, striking down another kobold, and saw Calliande.

She dashed down the steps from the shaman's cave, her blue eyes wide with fright and strain. Yet she was alive. Kharlacht cut down the last kobold, and Calliande ran down the last steps and joined them.

"Are you hurt?" said Ridmark.

She shook her head, eyes haunted. "No. I don't know how…but no."

"What did you do to that shaman?" said Kharlacht.

"We can trade stories later," said Ridmark. "Run!"

He ran for the gate, the others following. The kobolds had started to gain the upper hand against the spitfangs. A kobold lunged at Ridmark, and he knocked the warrior out of his way with a sharp swing of his staff.

Ridmark ran through the gate and sprinted through the field of mushrooms. Still he saw no signs of pursuit. The spitfangs would keep the kobolds occupied, but once they pacified their war beasts, they would realize what had happened.

They would want revenge.

Best to be gone from the Deeps by then.

He headed into the tunnel leading from the kobolds' cavern, weaving his way around the clusters of glowing mushrooms. Soon he saw Caius waiting, his mace ready.

"You're alive!" Caius said. "Truly, the age of miracles has not passed from the world."

"Evidently not," said Ridmark. "And if we don't keep moving, we're not going to stay alive. Go."

They resumed their run, heading for Thainkul Agon.

CHAPTER 15
PARTING

Calliande's chest burned, her legs aching with every step.

But she kept running.

The thought of several hundred angry kobolds proved an excellent motivator.

They had left Thainkul Agon, following the stream into its downward-sloping tunnel. The tunnel curved back and forth, the stream splashing in its channel. The air smelled of wet and mold, and thick clumps of glowing mushrooms lined the tunnel. Calliande ran on, her heart pounding, her legs throbbing. She was tired…but not as tired as she thought she would be.

Whatever strange power that had let her heal quickly, that had allowed her to drive back Talvinius, was still working.

At last Ridmark raised his hand and stopped.

"We can rest here," he said, squinting up the tunnel. "We'll have ample warning if the kobolds are after us. And I think we could benefit from some rest."

"Aye," said Caius, his gray face dark from exertion. He let out a long breath. "I once ran all day and fought deep orcs all night. Ah, but that was a hundred years ago. I am too old to keep up with you children."

Calliande looked at the dwarf. She suspected Caius was at least two centuries old…but if Talvinius had told her the truth, she might be older than him.

Ridmark passed out some food, dried meat and hard bread, and they sat against the cavern wall. Even Kharlacht sat down with a sigh, the blue steel of his armor clanking. Yet Ridmark remained standing, watching the tunnel for any pursuit.

"How did you do that?" said Calliande.

"Do what?" said Ridmark.

"Get into the village," said Calliande. "It must house five hundred kobolds. How did you fight past them?"

Caius chuckled. "He did not, my lady. Do you recall how red ghost mushrooms drive a spitfang to madness?"

Calliande nodded.

"Ridmark ground up a large number of red mushrooms and threw the powder into the spitfangs' pen," said Caius. "In the resultant chaos, he and Kharlacht slipped into the village and escorted you to safety."

"Much as he did," said Kharlacht around a mouthful of bread, "at the standing stones." He shook his head. "Only a madman would think to use a nest of fire drakes as a weapon."

Ridmark looked at her. "What happened in the village? We had come to rescue you...but you were already rescuing yourself. What happened to the shaman?"

Caius frowned. "I thought you slew him."

Ridmark shook his head. "No. We fought our way to the heart of the village....and then a blast of white fire erupted from the shaman's lair. It threw him to the ground, and if he wasn't dead from the fire, the landing certainly killed him."

Calliande hesitated. She did not want to speak of what had happened. But Ridmark and Caius had risked their lives to save her, and Kharlacht had proven himself honorable.

"I don't know," said Calliande at last. "The kobold shaman...I don't think he was a kobold, not truly. He claimed his name was Talvinius, and that he was once a member of the Order of the Magistri."

Caius frowned. "A kobold Magistrius?"

"No. Well...after a fashion," said Calliande. "He said he had once been a member of the Order of the Vigilant, but became something called an Eternalist. When his body died, he sent his spirit into a kobold's body to survive. That was why he sent Crotaph after us. He wanted to claim my body, to send his spirit into my flesh." She touched the pouch at her belt. "And he wanted the soulstone."

Ridmark and Caius shared a look.

"What is an Eternalist?" said Kharlacht.

"An order of heretics within the Order of Magistri," said Ridmark. "Or they were. They arose soon after the Frostborn were destroyed. They chafed at the restrictions the laws of the High King and the Church placed upon magic, and wished to expand their powers. Eventually they came to believe that the Magistri were the natural rulers of all men, and found willing allies in nobles who wanted to turn their peasants and freeholders into slaves, just as the lords of Rome on Old Earth ruled over an empire of slaves. There was civil war, but the Eternalists were defeated. The Order of the Magistri was reformed, and the Eternalists were all slain or went into hiding."

"Except for this Talvinius," said Kharlacht, "who has lurked here ever since."

Caius sighed. "I am not surprised the Eternalists found an audience for their lies among the lords of Andomhaim. I came to the High King's realm hoping to find zealous sons of the Church. Instead I found that the nobles are more interested in wealth, the Swordbearers in their prestige, the Magistri in their power, and the priests in their concubines."

"True," said Ridmark. "But some of the nobles are good men. Dux Gareth Licinius is a valiant and true lord." He was silent for a moment. "And my father."

Calliande blinked. Ridmark had never spoken of his family. A memory rose from the fog of her mind. He had said that his name was Ridmark Arban...and the head of the house of Arban was also the Dux of Taliand, the oldest and most prestigious duxarchate in the realm of Andomhaim.

Which meant that Ridmark's father was one of the most powerful men in the High Kingdom.

"Aye, Dux Gareth and Dux Leogrance are good men," said Caius, "but I fear they are a minority."

"Are good men not always a minority?" said Ridmark. "Did not God tell Abraham that he would spare the cities of the plain if only ten righteous men could be found within their walls?" He waved his hand. "But we have more immediate concerns than history and theology."

"History and theology are the immediate concerns of every man," said Caius.

Ridmark made an exasperated sound and turned back to Calliande. "How did you escape him?"

"I'm not sure," said Calliande. "He was...powerful. He cast a spell on me, and I felt his spirit try to take control of my body. I got so...so angry. Not just from what he was doing to me, but from how he had abused his magic, how he had taken something that was to be a sacred trust and twisted it into something profane. It felt like a fire was erupting inside me. Talvinius started to scream...and when I woke up he was gone. Probably burning on the floor of the cavern."

The men considered this in silence for a moment.

"Are you a Magistria?" said Ridmark at last.

"I don't know!" said Calliande, striking her fist against her leg. "I don't know. I didn't cast a spell, yet magic must have killed Talvinius. I think Talvinius knew me before...before whatever happened to seal me below the Tower of Vigilance. The way he spoke to me, I must have been a Magistria. But I cannot recall anything of magic, any knowledge of my past." She shuddered. "And if he knew me, if he was an Eternalist...that means I was in that vault for at least a hundred and fifty years. He spoke of the Frostborn as if he had seen them…and that means I could have been asleep for two centuries. Everyone I ever knew is dead. My mother and father, any brothers and sisters. If I had a husband and children. They are all dead…and I cannot remember them."

She wanted to weep for the family she had lost…assuming she had even had a family.

For she could not remember.

"I am sorry," said Caius. "If you like, when we stop I can say prayers for the repose of their souls."

Calliande nodded. "Thank you."

"But there is another concern," said Kharlacht. He stood. "How do we know that you are not Talvinius?"

Calliande blinked. "What?"

"Talvinius burned on the floor of the cavern," said Ridmark.

"Aye, but if this sorcerer was an Eternalist, a changer of flesh," said Kharlacht, "he might have taken Calliande's body before his old flesh perished."

Calliande opened her mouth, closed it, a panic growing inside her. She had no way to disprove the orc's suspicions, no way to prove who she really was.

She didn't even know who she really was.

"Doubtful," said Ridmark. "If that was Talvinius, we would be dead. Once he occupied Calliande's body, he would have commanded his followers to slay us, or brought his magic to bear."

"Perhaps he wished to gain our trust," said Kharlacht.

"To what end?" said Ridmark. "Calliande already had the soulstone. And we are a disgraced knight, a baptized orc, and a dwarven friar. If Talvinius wanted to find useful tools, he could certainly have done better than us."

Caius laughed. "I fear your argument is correct."

"Thank you," said Calliande.

Kharlacht nodded after a moment. "As you say."

Ridmark looked up the tunnel. "We have rested enough, I think."

"You hear the kobolds?" said Caius, scrambling to his feet.

"Not yet," said Ridmark, "but they are following, I have no doubt. Come."

They stood, and followed him along the bank of the stream.

Ridmark squinted into the gloom.

"I see light ahead," said Caius. "Moonlight, I think."

Kharlacht sniffed the air. "And I can smell trees."

"The surface," said Calliande. "I have never been so glad to see it. I have spent far too much time underground."

"Be on your guard," said Ridmark, staff ready. "Another ursaar might lair in the entrance."

But the others hurried forward, even Caius, eager to see the surface again. Ridmark kept watch, his eyes and ears straining for any sign of attackers, but the cavern seemed deserted.

Then the entrance yawned before them, and they stepped onto a ledge overlooking a steep valley. The stream rushed past and fell in a white waterfall, flowing away to the River Marcaine to the south. The stars blazed in the night sky overhead, and three of the thirteen moons shone.

All of them, Ridmark noted, glowing with the color of the flames that had filled the sky the day he found Calliande.

"The surface," said Calliande, her face relieved as she gazed at the sky.

"And this, I think," said Ridmark, turning to face Kharlacht, "is where we part ways."

His fingers tightened around his staff. If Kharlacht would attempt treachery, he would do it now.

But the orc remained impassive, his expression solemn. Perhaps even sad.

"Aye," he said. "I gave oath to see you safely to the surface, and so I have done. I am now obliged to go to my kin."

"Qazarl, you mean," said Calliande.

Kharlacht nodded. "You are a valiant warrior, Gray Knight, and could I work my will I would fight under your banner rather than Qazarl's. But I am bound by blood, and I must follow him."

"You needn't follow him," said Ridmark. "You could leave him and come with me."

"And do what?" said Kharlacht. "Wander the wilds seeking wrongs to right? I have no place within the realm of Andomhaim, just as I have no place in Vhaluusk. And I could not forsake my blood."

"You will do what you must," said Ridmark.

"You understand what that means," said Kharlacht.

"And you will not try to abduct Calliande again?" said Ridmark.

"I will not," said Kharlacht. "I gave my sworn word." He sighed. "When we next meet, it shall be on the field of battle. May God go with you, Gray Knight."

"And with you, Kharlacht of Vhaluusk," said Ridmark.

Kharlacht nodded and walked away. Ridmark saw him picking his way over the side of the steep hill, moving from rock to rock. Soon he vanished into the pine trees coating the hill.

"Come," said Ridmark, looking at the sky. "It's about midnight. We'll find a place to rest, and then head for Dun Licinia tomorrow at daybreak."

Assuming Qazarl had not already destroyed the town.

Ridmark, Calliande and Caius ascended to the hill's crest, and Ridmark looked around. The combined light of the three moons and the stars was enough to identify some landmarks, and the dark mass of the Black Mountain blotted out a portion of the sky.

"Southwest," said Ridmark. "We're southwest of the mountain, and directly west of Dun Licinia. About a half-day, maybe three-quarters of a day. We'll reach it tomorrow."

"What will become of me?" said Calliande.

"I doubt Qazarl or Shadowbearer will forget about you," said Ridmark. "Once I've warned Sir Joram and Dux Licinius about Qazarl, I can take you to Tarlion, to the Tower of the Magistri there. If you were once a Magistria, they should have records of you. And if some sort of spell blocks your memories, they can remove it. I believe Sir Joram has a Magistrius in his service at Dun Licinia, though I cannot remember the name."

"His name is Alamur," said Caius. "A man much in love with the sound of his own voice, if you will forgive my bluntness."

"I see why you would not get along," said Ridmark. "Nevertheless, he is a Magistrius, and perhaps he can help you."

Calliande wrapped her arms around herself. "I am not sure I wish to speak to any Magistri, if Talvinius is representative of their Order."

"The Eternalists are extinct," said Ridmark, "and Talvinius spent the last century hiding in the darkness of the Deeps. I would not trust anything he said."

"I suppose not," said Calliande.

"We'll camp here tonight," said Ridmark, "and make our way to Dun Licinia in the morning."

They made themselves as comfortable as they could within a ring of pine trees. Ridmark took the first watch, and soon both Calliande and Caius had fallen asleep. The fighting in the Deeps, Ridmark suspected, had taken more out of Caius than the friar had let on.

He watched Calliande for a moment, considering what to do about her.

He had sought for evidence of the Frostborn for five years...and on the very day he had seen the omen that heralded their return, Calliande had awakened in the vault below the Tower of Vigilance. And if Talvinius had been telling the truth, she had been in that vault since the defeat of the Frostborn.

Her memories might hold the answers Ridmark had long sought, the truth about the return of the Frostborn.

Perhaps he should to travel with her until she regained her memory.

He had planned to travel to Urd Morlemoch, to force the Warden to reveal the truth of his prophecy, but Calliande might hold all the answers he needed.

Assuming she was willing to share them with him.

For once she regained her memory, she might refuse to have anything to do with him. He had been expelled from the Order of the Swordbearers, branded with the mark of a traitor and a coward. The Magistri shunned Ridmark, as did the Swordbearers, and if Calliande truly had been a Magistria, she might well shun him once she recovered her memory.

She would be right to do it. He deserved death, for what had happened. Someday it would come to him, and then he could rest.

But only after he had warned the realm against the return of the Frostborn.

Ridmark stood motionless until Caius awoke to take the watch, and then fell into a dreamless sleep.

The next day they broke camp and headed across the foothills for Dun Licinia.

CHAPTER 16
BURNING FIELDS

An hour later, Ridmark saw the first plume of black smoke against the blue sky.

"A large fire," said Caius.

Ridmark nodded, scanning the pine trees for any foes.

"Are there any freeholds this far from the town?" said Caius.

"Several," said Ridmark. He smelled the burning wood now. He could not smell burning flesh, which was good. He glanced at Calliande, saw her tight, worried expression. "It's dangerous this far north, but bold freeholders claim lands here, try to make a living. Worth it, if he can pull it off...but he's always at risk from pagan orcs or kobolds or worse things."

He found a path heading through the trees and took it, trying to move quietly. Though it hardly matter – Caius could move quietly enough, but Calliande simply had no ability at stealth. Ridmark suspected the countryside was crawling with Qazarl's scouts by now, and he would prefer to avoid them. He thought he could take four or five of the Mhalekites in a straight fight, but any more than that could simply overwhelm him.

Or they could just shoot him from behind a tree.

The path ended in a large clearing at the base of a hill. Once the clearing had held a freehold, terraces climbing the sides of the nearby slopes, a pair of large barns overlooking a set of sheep pens. But now the barns burned, flames devouring their walls and rafters. A house built of fieldstone stood behind the barns, its interior and roof ablaze.

There was no sign of any living thing.

"Those fires couldn't have been started more than an hour past," said Caius.

"Aye," said Ridmark. "But I don't think the orcs killed anyone." He strode into the clearing. "You see these tracks?" He pointed. "Sheep and pigs. Recent tracks, too. I think the freeholder and his family got out before the orcs came." He looked at the burning barns. "Hopefully they reached Dun Licinia before Qazarl's scouts caught them."

"They lost everything," said Calliande, voice quiet. "This place must be the work of decades"

"Men can rebuild farms," said Ridmark. "Only the Dominus Christus can rebuild dead men." He beckoned the others back to the trees. "Best to get away from here. The orcs might return, and..."

Even as he spoke, he saw a movement from behind a tree.

"Down!" shouted Ridmark. Calliande and Caius ducked, and an orc came into sight, a short bow in hand. The arrow buzzed past Ridmark, and he sprinted forward, staff raised. The orc took aim, and Ridmark swung just as the orc released. The end of the staff caught the orc in the face, knocking the Mhalekite back. Ridmark sidestepped, reversing the staff, his strength and momentum driving the length of wood and steel against the Mhalekite's temple.

The orc fell motionless to the ground.

"Ridmark!"

Ridmark saw three orcs charging towards Caius and Calliande. Caius had his mace, but the dwarf was only one man, and Calliande had no weapons.

They would overwhelm Caius in short order.

Ridmark charged as the orcs closed around Caius, and flung his staff like a spear. It tangled in the legs of the nearest Mhalekite, and the orcish warrior went down in a heap. The orc stood as Ridmark approached, and he threw a punch, rocking the Mhalekite, but the orc roared and swung his short sword. Ridmark ducked, grabbed his staff, and slammed the weapon into the orc's knees. He did not have enough momentum behind the blow to do much damage, but the Mhalekite staggered back. Ridmark drove the butt of the staff into the orc's belly. The Mhalekite doubled over with a groan, and Ridmark brought his weapon down onto the orc's head.

The warrior fell dead to the ground.

The final orc faced off against Caius, short sword ringing against the dwarf's mace. Caius launched an attack, pushing the orc back with vigorous strokes. The Mhalekite dodged right into the path of Ridmark's next blow.

The orc joined his companions upon the ground.

Ridmark turned in a circle, staff raised, but saw no other attackers.

"Scouts, likely," he said. "They doubled back to see if anyone returned to the freehold."

"A cruel tactic," said Caius.

"Mhalek was fond of it," said Ridmark. "I should have realized what was happening. Are either of you hurt?"

"I am unharmed," said Caius, and Calliande shook her head.

"You," said Ridmark, pointing at her, "need a weapon."

"I don't know how to use a sword," said Calliande. "And I'm not strong enough to get much use out of a weapon like a mace or a club."

"No," said Ridmark, stooping over one of the dead orcs, "but it doesn't take much strength to stab."

A sheathed dagger rested on the dead orc's belt. It wasn't orcish work, but the sort of dagger carried by men-at-arms of the Dux of the Northerland. Undoubtedly the orc had stolen it. Ridmark examined the weapon, and then handed the blade to Calliande.

"Take this," he said.

"And do what with it?" said Calliande. "I can't fight alongside you like Caius or Kharlacht. I am useless."

"Stop speaking folly," said Ridmark. "I don't expect you to fight alongside me...but if the orcs try to take you again, you will need to defend yourself."

Calliande hesitated, and then took the dagger and clipped the sheath to her belt.

"We had best move on," said Caius, "before more of Qazarl's men find us."

Ridmark led the way into the trees.

Calliande walked onward, following Ridmark's lead.

They had seen a dozen more burning freeholds. From time to time they passed bodies lying untended on the ground, both Mhalekite orcs and men wearing the clothes of freeholders and laborers.

"Qazarl has likely divided his host," said Ridmark, "sent them to burn out the countryside around Dun Licinia. He must be anticipating a long siege."

"A poor strategy," said Caius. "That gives Sir Joram more time to prepare, to pull in the freeholders and supplies from the countryside."

"His goal isn't just Dun Licinia," said Ridmark. "He wants to find Calliande."

Calliande closed her eyes for a moment. She had caused this. All the death and destruction they had already seen, and all the death and destruction to come. It had been unleashed because of her.

And she didn't even know why.

"Kharlacht must not have returned to him yet," said Caius. "Otherwise he would know what happened to Calliande."

"Or," said Calliande, "he might have killed Kharlacht for his failure, before giving him the chance to speak in his defense."

Another death upon her shoulders. Kharlacht had taken her to the standing stones to perish upon the altar, to fuel whatever black magic Shadowbearer intended. Yet Kharlacht had been kind to her, had helped her escape from Talvinius's grasp. She did not wish him ill.

She certainly did not want him to die.

"Perhaps not," said Ridmark. "Even if Kharlacht returned to Qazarl and told him everything, it would still take time for Qazarl to recall all his raiding parties. At least an entire day, if not longer."

"So we have that long," said Caius, "until Dun Licinia falls under siege."

"Aye," said Ridmark. "Let us put that time to good use."

He set a brisk pace through the trees. Calliande winced with every snap of a twig beneath her feet, every crackle of dry pine needles. But she did not know how to move with stealth as Ridmark and Caius did, and the heavy orcish boots certainly did not help. She dreaded the noise she made, feared that every step would bring enemies down upon their heads.

But whether through luck or Ridmark's skill, they encountered no other orcs. The day wore on, and as noon gave way to afternoon, they emerged from the trees and onto a dirt road. A river ran alongside one side of the road, flowing away to the southwest.

"The River Marcaine," said Ridmark. "We've made good progress."

"How much farther, do you think?" said Caius.

Ridmark gestured. "See for yourself."

They followed the road around a stand of pine trees, and Calliande saw the town of Dun Licinia for the first time.

A stout stone wall fortified the town of about four thousand people, and beyond the rampart Calliande saw the tower of a keep, the twin bell towers of a stone church, and the rounded turret of a Magistrius's tower. The town's gates were shut, and men patrolled the walls, crossbows in hand. Green banners emblazoned with white harts flew from the twin octagonal towers guarding the northern gate, and after a moment Calliande realized that the white hart upon green was the sigil of the Dux of the Northerland.

Apparently she had known the Dux.

Or one of his ancestors, more likely.

"God has been with us," said Caius. "The town has not yet fallen."

Ridmark nodded. "Sir Joram was never the most formidable man on the practice field, but he is smart and diligent. We should speak with him at once. He'll need more information…and the fact that you're still alive will likely be the first piece of good news in days."

Caius snorted. "I never thought I would hear anyone say that."

Calliande hesitated. "What will you tell him about me?"

"The truth," said Ridmark. "Why should I not?" He thought for a moment. "Joram is not a fool. But do not tell the full truth to anyone but him. If anyone asks, you were taken captive by the orcs, and Caius and I rescued you and brought you back to Dun Licinia."

Calliande smiled. "That's true enough."

"Aye," said Ridmark. "But don't tell anyone about the soulstone, save for Sir Joram. I think that might prove too much of a temptation for many men, especially for the Magistri. Like a woman carrying a bag of gold alone on a deserted road. Best not to expose anyone to the temptation."

Calliande nodded. "Do not put a stumbling block in another's path, is that it?"

Caius grinned, his teeth flashing in his graying beard. "Well spoken."

Ridmark led the way to the northern gate of Dun Licinia.

Men-at-arms patrolled the walls, along with peasant militia equipped with leather armor and short bows.

And all of them pointed their weapons as Ridmark.

"Hold!" shouted their leader, a grizzled man-at-arms in his middle years. Ridmark remembered him from his previous confrontation at the gate.

It had only been a few days ago, but it seemed much longer.

"I need to speak with Sir Joram at once," said Ridmark. "I have news about the Mhalekites."

"You'll stay where you are," said the man-at-arms. "Sir Joram has ordered the town sealed, and…"

"Thomas!" bellowed Caius, stepping to Ridmark's side.

The grizzled man-at-arms blinked. "Brother Caius?"

"Stop being obtuse and let us into the town," said Caius. "Sir Joram Agramore sent Ridmark to find me. And just in the nick of time, too, else those Mhalekites would have given me a red smile below my chin." He stroked his beard. "Assuming they could have gotten through my beard, of course."

Some of the militiamen laughed.

"And he also rescued this woman," said Caius, gesturing at Calliande, "who had been taken captive by the orcs. Truly, without the valiant intervention of the Gray Knight, both I and this fair lady would lie dead. Now stop blustering and let us inside. We have news about the orcs that Sir Joram must hear."

Thomas scowled, but shouted an order, and the gates of Dun Licinia swung open with a groan.

"Nicely said," said Ridmark.

"Thank you," said Caius. "I may talk all the time, but it all that practice has occasionally proven useful."

Calliande laughed.

Ridmark walked through the gates with the others, a pair of militiamen falling in around them. The entire town had been mobilized for a siege. Bundles of arrows and crossbow bolts had been stacked against the wall, along with rows of spears and shields. Women worked in the streets, some preparing bandages for the wounded, others carrying baskets of food. The militiamen led them to the square, and Ridmark saw Sir Joram Agramore speaking with a pair of men-at-arms. He had traded his tunic and mantle for plate armor and chain mail, his sword and dagger ready at his belt.

His eyes widened in astonishment as Ridmark approached.

"This man demands to speak with you, sir," said one of the militiamen, "and..."

"God and all his saints," said Joram. "You're still alive!" He grinned. "And you found Brother Caius, too."

"Good to see you again, Sir Joram," said Caius. "I fear the orcs of the Wilderland were not particularly receptive to the message of the Church."

"It seems not," said Joram. "When we first received word of the raids on the outer freeholds, I was sure that you both were slain." He clapped Ridmark on the shoulder. "It is good to see you again. I have sore need of your aid, if you are willing to provide it."

"But sir knight," said one of the men-at-arms, "he is branded..."

"The Mhalekites will make no such distinction," said Joram. He glanced at Caius. "Did you stir them up with your preaching? I thought we had taught Mhalek's followers a lesson five years ago. I didn't think there would be enough left of them to mount an attack, but it seems that I was wrong."

"Brother Caius didn't stir them up," said Ridmark. "Something else did."

Joram frowned. "What happened?"

Ridmark nodded. "We had best speak privately."

Calliande listened as Ridmark told the entire story to Sir Joram.

They had gone to the keep's great hall, the chamber decorated with the tapestries of Lancelot and Galahad seeking the grail and of the Dragon Knight fighting the Frostborn, and Joram had sent away his guards. It was clear that he trusted Ridmark, and she wondered about that. Ridmark had been expelled from the Order of the Swordbearers, carried the brand of a coward and a traitor upon his face. Yet Joram was willing to believe anything he said.

Given the bold deeds she had seen Ridmark do, she wasn't entirely surprised.

"And then we parted ways with Kharlacht and made our way here," said Ridmark.

"An incredible story," said Joram. "Had any other man told it to me, I would call him a charlatan or a madman. You are many things, Ridmark, but you were never a liar."

"I fear I am not imaginative enough to come up with such a fable," said Ridmark.

Joram snorted. "Perhaps not." His green eyes turned to Calliande. "I am sorry for the ordeals you have endured, my lady. As long as you choose to remain in Dun Licinia, my hospitality is yours, and you shall be my honored guest. Though Dun Licinia is hardly a safe haven at the moment."

"Thank you, my lord knight," said Calliande, touched by his kindness.

"And…you can remember nothing of your past?" said Joram. "Nothing at all? No reason why Qazarl and this…Shadowbearer creature might have wished you ill?"

"None, my lord," said Calliande. "I wish I could tell you more. I dearly wish I knew more myself. Other than what Talvinius told me, I know nothing. And Talvinius might have been lying."

"I have come to suspect," said Ridmark, "that Calliande was once a Magistria of great power in the Order of the Vigilant, one who sealed herself away to awaken once the Frostborn returned."

Calliande blinked. Had she truly been someone like that? A woman of power and strength, one with the foresight to wait until the Frostborn had returned?

Of course, if true, her foresight had been flawed. The Order of the Vigilant had dwindled, the Tower of Vigilance had burned, and she had awakened alone in the darkness with her memories lost.

"I suspect Qazarl and Shadowbearer wanted to slay her with the soulstone upon the altar in order to unlock her power, and claim it for themselves," said Ridmark, "to help achieve some dire purpose."

Joram frowned. "Like breaking the walls of Dun Licinia?"

"Or something greater," said Ridmark.

"Such as the return of the Frostborn, perhaps?" said Joram. He sighed. "Ah, Ridmark. I thought the Frostborn extinct, and your quest some mad attempt at redemption. But after the strange things we have seen…who can say? Still, we only face Mhalekite orcs. If the Frostborn had returned, the rivers would freeze in the heart of summer, and men would be found dead with their blood turned to ice. Or so the tales say." He looked at Calliande. "This soulstone. May I see it?"

Calliande hesitated and drew out the stone, its rough sides cold against her fingers. She felt the power stirring within the stone, the raw arcane force.

"It looks like an overlarge piece of quartz," said Joram, voice quiet. "But...ah, I am no Magistrius, but even I can feel the power in the crystal. Put it away, please, my lady." Calliande complied. "It seems certain that Qazarl will assail Dun Licinia, once he learns that you and the stone are within our walls."

"I could ride south," said Calliande, "lure him away from the town." She did not want to leave the Dun Licinia, but she did not want any more people to die because of her.

Ridmark shook his head. "Qazarl will assail Dun Licinia with or without you. If you leave now, you will only fall into his hands."

"Then we must prepare to meet the attack," said Joram. He hesitated. "Ridmark...your aid would be welcome."

"I shall fight," said Ridmark.

"I would also welcome your counsel," said Joram. "I have never commanded so many men at once. I served as the army's quartermaster in the war against Mhalek, not as its commander."

"Are you asking me to take command of the defense?" said Ridmark. "The men will never accept orders from a man expelled from the Swordbearers."

"No," said Joram, "but if you want to give any advice to the town's commander...I think you will find him most receptive. And grateful."

Calliande realized that Joram was terrified.

"So be it, then," said Ridmark. "You've done well, so far, by gathering the freeholders and as much food as you can manage."

"Aye," said Joram. "We've enough food to feed the town and all our fighting men for three months. Four, maybe, if we tighten our belts. But the battle shall be over long before that."

"How many fighting men do you have?" said Ridmark.

"Three hundred men-at-arms," said Joram. "The town's garrison, sent from Dun Licinia to guard against orcish and beastmen raiders from the Wilderland. Another four hundred militia gathered from the townsmen and the freeholders."

"Qazarl as between three and four thousand orcish warriors," said Ridmark. "He might have gathered additional allies from the beastmen packs, or from the kobolds."

"We irritated the kobolds on our way here," said Caius.

"But with seven hundred men," said Ridmark, "you should be able to hold long enough for Dux Gareth to send aid from Castra Marcaine."

"If any aid comes," said Joram.

Ridmark frowned. "Did you send riders to Castra Marcaine?"

"I did, as soon as we realized the scale of the Mhalekite threat," said Joram. "But they may not have gotten through. Qazarl has dispersed his host into many raiding parties, and they might have killed my messengers."

"We'll need to trust to more than your messengers' skill," said Ridmark. "You have a Magistrius here, do we not?"

"Aye, Magistrius Alamur," said Joram with a grimace. Apparently the man was just as unpleasant as Caius had said.

"The Magistri can converse with each other over long distances," said Ridmark. "And I know Dux Licinius has Magistri at Castra Marcaine. Tell Alamur to send a message to the Dux's Magistri. They can warn the Dux of the danger, and he will send troops."

"Alamur refuses to heed me," said Caius.

Ridmark blinked several times. "Why?"

"I don't know," said Joram, scowling in frustration. "The man has been nothing but trouble ever since Dux Gareth sent him to Castra Marcaine. He is arrogant, and refuses to cooperate on even the simplest of tasks. He spends days locked up in his tower with his books, and refuses to emerge to aid in the governance of the comarchate." He smacked his right fist against his left palm. "I have no Swordbearers here, and you know the beasts of the dark elves can only be slain through magic or flame. Last month an urvaalg attacked one of the outlying freeholds. Had Alamur roused himself sooner, we might have saved the freeholder and his family. Instead, our learned Magistrius only struck down the urvaalg once it drew near to the town."

Something in the knight's story woke the anger in Calliande, the same rage she had felt while facing Talvinius. A Magistrius ought to use his power for good, not selfishly, and the prospect of a Magistrius neglecting those in his care infuriated her.

"But you are acting as the Comes of Dun Licinia," said Ridmark. "Command him to aid in the defense of the town."

"I tried," said Joram. "He refused to recognize my authority, and said he would only obey a command from either the Dux or one of the Masters of the Magistri. Not from me."

"The idiot," said Ridmark. For the first time since Calliande had met him, he looked angry. He had fought Kharlacht's warriors and Talvinius's kobolds with icy calm, but now he looked angry. "We will need the help of a Magistrius, and not just to send messages. Qazarl has the black magic of a pagan orcish shaman, and I doubt he's a weakling. We must have Alamur's help."

Joram shook his head. "He refuses to give it."

"Then," said Ridmark, "let's go persuade him."

CHAPTER 17
A BARGAIN

Ridmark left the keep and walked to the Magistrius's tower. Caius, Calliande, and Sir Joram followed him, trailed by a pair of Joram's men-at-arms.

The tower stood behind Dun Licinia's stone church. The Magistri often resided in high towers to study the position of the thirteen moons, since the conjunctions and positions of the moons altered the effects of certain spells. Alamur's tower looked little different than the others Ridmark had seen, tall and round with the bronze tube of a telescope jutting from the roof.

He knocked several times, but no answer came.

"Caius," said Ridmark, "would you lend me your mace?"

"Why?" said Caius.

"Because," said Ridmark, "I'm going to break down the door."

"But he is a Magistrius," said Joram. "You…"

"You can't break down his door and compel him," said Ridmark, "because you are a knight in service of Dux Gareth Licinius of the Northerland, and that would reflect poorly on the Dux. You, Brother Caius, cannot do it, because you are a mendicant friar and friars can only fight in defense of their lives. I, however, am a disinherited exile expelled from the Order of Swordbearers for cowardice and desertion. No one is responsible for me, and my actions reflect upon no one. If the Masters of the Magistri dislike what I am about to do, Sir Joram, you can tell them to take it up with me."

Calliande blinked. He could not tell if she was impressed or disgusted.

"As ever," said Caius, "you make a persuasive argument."

He handed over the mace.

The mace was quite a bit heavier than it looked, as most dwarven weapons were. Ridmark stepped back, raised his arm, and hammered the mace against the door.

After the fifth strike, the door splintered away from the lock.

"Thank you," said Ridmark, handing the mace back to Caius.

He pushed aside the ruined door and climbed into the tower, the others following. The first floor held a richly furnished living room, overstuffed chairs surrounding a gleaming table. The second held a dining hall, and the third held the Magistrius's luxurious sleeping chamber.

The top floor contained the Magistrius's workshop, library, and observatory. Wooden shelves groaned beneath the weight of books and scrolls, and worktables held jars and bottles and a variety of peculiar instruments. Another table held an elaborate bronze astrolabe, next to the bronze telescope.

In the center of the room stood the furious Magistrius Alamur himself.

The Magistrius was a tall man of regal bearing, clad in a gleaming white robe with a black sash. He had a close-cropped gray beard and gray hair, and his dark eyes flashed with fury. Joram and the men-at-arms looked nervous. They had broken into the home of a Magistrius, one of the wielders of the potent magic taught by the elven archmage Ardrhythain himself, masters of mysteries beyond the reach of most men.

Ridmark was less impressed.

In his dealings with the Magistri as a Swordbearer, he had found them conceited and pompous...and often less knowledgeable and less powerful than they liked to claim.

"Joram Agramore!" thundered Alamur. "What is the meaning of this egregious intrusion? You have invaded my home! This will draw the wrath of the Order of the..."

"I broke into your home," said Ridmark, his staff tapping against the polished wooden floor. "Sir Joram is just here to make sure I don't hurt you unduly."

Alamur's bearded face twisted into a sneer. "Yes, I know you. The branded man, the renegade the peasants like to call the Gray Knight. The man who fled the field of Dun Licinia to save a woman, and utterly failed."

Calliande gave him a sharp look.

"I am that man," said Ridmark.

Alamur smirked. "Then what does the Gray Knight wish of a Magistrius?"

"Nothing complex," said Ridmark. "Only your duty."

Alamur raised his eyebrows. "Duty? It is the duty of a Magistrius to defend the realm from black magic. It is a duty of a Magistrius to shepherd the people of the realm, to guide the nobles in their tasks, to urge them to wise decisions." He cast a disdainful look at Joram. "It is not the duty of a

Magistrius to assist the nobles in every petty brawl with a ragged orcish warband."

"This is hardly a petty warband," said Ridmark. "These orcs are Mhalekites."

"Any fool can brand a sigil upon his forehead," said Alamur. "Mhalek is dead...as you ought to know...and his followers were destroyed. These orcs that have Sir Joram so concerned are nothing but brigands. If Sir Joram were competent, he could have defeated these attackers without bothering his betters."

Joram looked away from the older man's glare. Ridmark saw the source of the problem. Like all knights of the realm, Joram had spent his life in awe of the Magistri. It would have been difficult for him to defy one.

"The attacking orcs are at least three or four thousand strong," said Ridmark. "And they are led by Qazarl, one of Mhalek's disciples."

Alamur sniffed. "A thug with a sword, no doubt."

"A shaman, strong in blood sorcery and dark magic," said Ridmark. "If you do not oppose him, his spells will wreak havoc on Sir Joram's men."

Alamur laughed. "A wretched little hill shaman is not worth the time of a Magistrius."

Ridmark tilted his head to the side, considering the Magistrius.

Something was...off. Ridmark had dealt with the Magistri before, and they had usually been as pompous and arrogant as Alamur. Yet they had been eager to flaunt their powers, to prove their prowess by smashing creatures of dark magic. This utter refusal to fight was unusual.

But Ridmark did not need Alamur to fight.

"Fine, then," said Ridmark. "If you will not fight, then at least send a message. There are Magistri at Castra Marcaine."

The Magistrius offered a patronizing smile. "Yes, I know. I have been there. Recently. Unlike you, I imagine. Castra Marcaine is the closest thing to civilization in the wretched Northerland."

"Send a message to the Magistri there," said Ridmark. "Bid them to warn Dux Licinius about the Mhalekites."

"I most certainly will not," said Alamur.

"Why?" said Ridmark. "Because it is beneath the dignity of a Magistrius?"

"Yes, but that is not the reason," said Alamur.

"Will you deign to share it?" said Ridmark.

"If I must," said Alamur. "I will not trouble the Dux of the Northerland with so petty a concern." He stepped forward, his smirk changing into a glare. "And I will not trouble the illustrious Dux with the ranting of Ridmark Arban, the man who slew his daughter."

A spasm of rage and grief and endless sorrow went through Ridmark. But none of the emotion touched his face.

"My failure," said Ridmark, "does not excuse your failure to do your duty."

"You are pathetic," said Calliande.

All eyes turned to face her. Ridmark was certain that she was speaking to him. He had stopped Mhalek, but he had failed in the most profound way possible, and...

But she stepped towards Alamur.

"A Magistrius is supposed to wield magic in the defense of the people of the realm," Calliande said. "All you do is lurk in this tower and nurse your injured pride."

Alamur laughed. "Who is the girl, Gray Knight? Some country bumpkin dressed up in orcish rags? Or a whore in costume? You have a taste for...orcish tarts, as it were?"

"Such comments," said Caius, face stern, "are unworthy of a child, let alone a Magistrius."

"Do not lecture me, dwarf," said Alamur. "You..."

"Be silent," said Calliande, her voice hard with icy contempt. "You were sent to Dun Licinia because you were the weakest, were you not? The least skilled...the least popular among your brothers and sisters?"

Alamur's face went hard. "Do not speak so to your betters, woman."

She turned away from him, and a strange expression went over her face as she looked at the Magistrius's shelves.

Calliande heard Ridmark and Alamur continue their argument, but something else drew her attention.

She sensed something...wrong.

Something rotten.

Ever since they had set foot in the tower, she had sensed the currents of magical power rippling around her. Alamur worked magic here, powerful magic. The currents of power felt both familiar and...benign, somehow. Vlazar's magic had been dark, like shadows mixed with burning blood, and Talvinius's magic had felt like rotten fruit, like a dead animal eaten away by corruption. The magic within the tower, by contrast, felt warm and strong, like the wall of a castle defended by bold men.

Yet she felt something dark within the warm aura.

A shadow.

"The Masters of my Order shall hear of these grievous insults to the Magistri," said Alamur. "As shall Dux Licinius, Sir Joram. It seems clear to be that you are not fit to act as the Comes of Dun Licinia. Perhaps you are not even fit to clean your own stables."

"If Dun Licinia falls and Qazarl kills everyone within the walls," said

Ridmark, "then neither the Masters nor the Dux shall hear your complaints."

Calliande walked closer to the shelf. The Magistrius's shelves held books and scrolls, written in both Latin and high elven, and a variety of odd curios – a tasseled manetaur spearhead, a stone with a fish's skeleton imprinted upon it, an old orcish war helm.

A scroll, tucked between the helm and the spearhead, caught her eye. The corruption radiated from it.

"Be reasonable, Magistrius," said Caius. "We must all stand together, or we shall perish together. That has been the history of Andomhaim. The High King and his nobles fought together against the orcs. Ardrhythain taught your people magic, and the Magistri and the Swordbearers stood as one against the urdmordar and then the Frostborn."

"Threats worthy of a Magistrius's efforts," said Alamur. "Not this rabble of hill orcs. If Joram is even marginally competent, he can handle them without my aid."

Calliande gazed at the scroll, fascinated. It had been fashioned of old leather, and she glimpsed strange symbols upon its surface.

"Then think of the words of the Dominus Christus," said Caius. "You are mighty, Magistrius, and we are to look after the weakest among us…"

Alamur laughed, his voice full of scorn. "Do not throw the words of the Church at me, dwarf. The Church is an instrument to keep the peasantry in their place and nothing more. The idea that its laws should bind a Magistrius is ludicrous. And I will not take part in your little backcountry brawl. The blood of a Magistrius is worth that of a thousand lesser men."

"You are eaten up with pride and arrogance," said Caius. "You should turn your back on them, lest they devour you."

Calliande picked up the scroll. The leather felt icy cold beneath her grasp, and seemed to radiate dark magic. She unrolled it, the scroll creaking, and looked at the black symbols marching across its surface. The characters were dark elven, but the language was orcish, and…

"Pride is merely the word the weak give to the confidence of their betters," said Alamur. "You ought to…wait. What are you doing? Put that down at once!"

Calliande looked up from the leather scroll, and saw the Magistrius hurrying towards her, a hint of fear on his haughty face.

And suddenly she understood what he had done.

She wondered if Talvinius had looked like Alamur, before he had taken the body of that kobold.

"Put that down, you foolish girl," thundered Alamur. He reached for the scroll, and Calliande took a quick step out of his reach. "You will injure yourself. That scroll…"

"That scroll," said Calliande, holding it up so the others could see it, "was written by Qazarl, wasn't it?"

A stunned silence fell over the others.

"Preposterous," said Alamur. "Sir Joram, the girl is obviously addled. Remove her from my presence at once."

"This is written in orcish," said Calliande. "The characters are dark elven, but the language is orcish. It is a magical incantation for a spell that draws its power from the blood of a sacrificial victim."

"As if you would have the learning of the Magistri," said Alamur.

"She's right," said Caius. "I can read dark elven characters, and she speaks the truth."

"And how would you know, dwarf?" said Alamur. "Have you dabbled in dark arts?"

Caius smiled. "It is simply the education given to all dwarven nobles before we come of age. The dark elves were our foes long before the humans ever came to this world, and a warrior must understand his foes if he is to defeat them."

"And that is what I am doing," said Alamur, "understanding my foes in order to defeat them."

He was starting to sweat, Calliande noticed.

"Indeed?" said Ridmark. "Your foes, you say? The foes you said were beneath your notice? The foes you would not trouble yourself to fight? If they are beneath your notice...then why do you have a scroll of orcish blood magic in your library?"

"And one," said Calliande, "that looks as if it was written recently?"

"I do not have to answer any questions," said Alamur. "If you have complaints, direct them to the Masters of my Order in Tarlion. Otherwise cease wasting my time and wearying my ears with..."

"Ah," said Ridmark, tapping his staff against the floor. "I think I understand."

They looked at him.

"You didn't want to come here," said Ridmark. "Dun Licinia was beneath your dignity. But the Masters of your Order sent you anyway, and that rankled. And then you found Qazarl...or Qazarl found you? He is a strong shaman, and he offered you power. Some spells of blood magic, spells that would let you take revenge on those who wronged you and claim your rightful place in the Order."

"This is a calumny," spat Alamur. "You have no proof for any of this!" He smirked. "And I have never spoken to Qazarl in my life. I would not demean myself by speaking with such a creature."

"No, I suppose you wouldn't," said Ridmark. He had the same calm expression Calliande had seen on his face right before he killed someone. "But would it demean you to speak with Shadowbearer?"

Alamur flinched. "How do you know that name?"

"Because," said Calliande, "I heard him give commands to Qazarl."

"And it is very strange, is it not," said Ridmark, "that Qazarl is fighting for Shadowbearer...and you refuse to fight against Qazarl, while having a spell of orcish dark magic within your study?"

"Magistrius," said Joram, "this is a very serious charge. At the very least, I will have to contact the Dux and his Magistri, and let him know about these allegations. He will..."

Panic flashed over Alamur's face. "No!"

He flung out his hands, and Calliande felt the surge of magical power.

"Ridmark!" she shouted. "He's casting a spell..."

White light pulsed around the Magistrius, and invisible force erupted from his fingers. The force of the spell slammed into the others, driving them to the floor, the tower creaking around them. The impact knocked Calliande from her feet, the scroll tumbling from her grasp. Alamur loomed over her, and for a moment she feared that the Magistrius would kill her. But he only snatched up the scroll and headed for the stairs.

And as he did, Ridmark thrust his staff.

He caught Alamur across the ankles, and the Magistrius lost his balance and fell with a surprised bellow. Ridmark came to one knee as the scroll tumbled from Alamur's hand. The Magistrius sat up with an enraged hiss, lifting his hand to cast another spell.

"Ridmark!" shouted Calliande as she felt the magic gather. "He's going to..."

Ridmark seized Alamur's hand and bent the fingers back.

The sound of cracking bones was quite loud, and Alamur's astonished scream even louder.

The Magistrius might have been powerful...but clearly he was not used to pain.

Ridmark knelt next to Alamur and rested his staff across the Magistrius's throat as Calliande and the others stood. She felt the surge of power as Alamur began another spell, but Ridmark pressed his staff against the older man's throat. Alamur gagged, and the magic faded that away.

"None of that," said Ridmark. "I don't want to accidentally kill you."

"Is everyone all right?" said Joram, looking around. "Lady Calliande?"

Alamur's eyes went wide at the name. He hadn't recognized her...but he knew her name. Did he know who she was?

"Who am I?" she said, standing over him. His dark eyes rotated to face her. "Tell me. If you know who I am, tell me. Tell me now!" She kicked the staff in frustrated rage, and Alamur gagged again. At once she felt guilt...but then she remembered that this man had been plotting with Shadowbearer.

And apparently he had been willing to betray every man, woman, and child within the walls to their deaths.

"I don't know," he rasped. "He mentioned…he mentioned you when he came to me. He said that the shape of the world would soon change, now and forever, and that the Frostborn would return." Ridmark's face went motionless, his blue eyes cold and hard. "He said that your death would inaugurate the great change, and that a man of my skills and power would rise high in the new order…"

"If you served him," said Ridmark.

"Yes," whispered Alamur, his eyes full of terror. "Don't hurt me. Please don't hurt me. I'll…I'll tell you anything you want."

He tried to cringe away like a terrified dog, but Ridmark held him fast.

"God and the archangels!" spat Joram. "You betrayed us, Alamur. Like one of the Eternalists of old. An enemy of the realm threatens to destroy the town, and you betray us for…for what? A scroll of gibberish?" He gestured at the scroll. "I will be well within my rights to have you hanged for treason."

"No," said Ridmark. "He's going to do something for us." He leaned closer to the Magistrius. "You're going to send a message to the Magistri of Castra Marcaine, right now. You will tell them of Qazarl's attack, and you will tell them to ask the Dux to send aid immediately."

"Or?" said Alamur, a hint of his defiance returning.

"Or I'll kill you," said Ridmark.

"That would be murder," said Caius.

"Yes," said Ridmark. "It would. But a lot more people will die if we don't receive help from the Dux. So, Magistrius. Either send the message to the Dux's Magistri, or prepare to account for your treachery before the throne of God. Decide now."

Calliande watched as the last hint of defiance drained from the Magistrius.

"Yes," said Alamur, closing his eyes, "yes, yes, I'll do it."

"Calliande," said Ridmark. "Watch him. Warn me if he tries anything."

Calliande nodded, and felt the power gathering around Alamur as he cast a spell. His eyes opened, shining with white light, and he spoke.

"Brothers!" he said. "It is I, Alamur of Dun Licinia! A strong force of orcs marches against the town, led by a powerful orcish shaman. If we do not receive aid at once, the town shall fall. Warn the Dux. We must receive aid."

The light faded from his eyes, and Alamur slumped back against the floor, sweat dripping down his face.

Ridmark looked up at her.

"It is done," said Calliande. "He sent the message." She was not entirely certain how she knew that, but she was sure of it.

In her previous life, it was plain she had known a great deal about magic. Did that mean she had been someone like Alamur, cold and arrogant and filled with spite? She hoped not. But if she had once wielded magic...could she do so again? She would no longer feel so helpless.

And she could aid Ridmark against Qazarl.

"Sir Joram," said Ridmark. "I suggest that you restrain the Magistrius and put him under arrest. Bind his hands and blindfold him – it will make it harder for him to work his spells. You can also have one of the priests treat his broken fingers." He thought for a moment. "If you like."

"You heard the Gray Knight," said Joram to his men-at-arms.

Ridmark got to his feet and removed his staff from Alamur's neck. The Magistrius began coughing and wheezing, and the men-at-arms hauled dragged him away.

"That was unpleasant," said Sir Joram as they stepped out of the tower.

Ridmark looked around. The sun was disappearing over the hills to the west. He would have to tell Joram to keep close watch on the ramparts. Qazarl might try to sneak warriors over the wall in the darkness, warriors who would then attempt to open the gates.

"It was," said Ridmark. "I hadn't intended it to become so violent. I had simply hoped to bully Alamur into sending a message to the Dux."

"But you didn't know," said Calliande, "that he was a traitor. That he had sold out the town to Shadowbearer and Qazarl." She gave a vicious shake of her head. "That he was no better than Talvinius."

"Would you have killed him?" said Caius.

"If he had tried to attack us again?" said Ridmark. "Without hesitation."

"If he had refused to cooperate?" said Caius.

Joram frowned. "The Magistrius betrayed the realm during a time of war. As the Comes of Dun Licinia, I would have been well within my rights to have him hanged. Indeed, I would almost have been obliged to do so. A traitorous Magistrius could provide powerful aid to the enemy. I would prefer to keep him for trial before his Order, but if he tries to escape during the fighting...I will have him executed."

"Forgive me, my lord knight," said Caius, "but the question wasn't for you. If he had refused to cooperate, Ridmark, and if he had offered no further resistance, would you have killed him?"

Ridmark was silent for a moment. He felt the dwarf's strange blue eyes on him, felt the steady weight of Calliande's gaze.

"No," said Ridmark at last. "No, I would have let Joram imprison him. I am not a Swordbearer any longer, I am not a knight...but I am not a murderer. At least, I am not a murderer again. There is already too much innocent blood upon my hands."

Calliande opened her mouth, and he saw the question in her eyes.

And the blast of trumpets rang out from the ramparts, echoing over the town.

"The enemy is within sight of the walls," said Joram. "May God be with us."

CHAPTER 18
SIEGECRAFT

Ridmark followed Sir Joram to the walls, Caius at his side. He had sent Calliande to the keep, and to his relief, she had agreed without argument. She was neither a knight nor a man-at-arms, and the ramparts would be no place for her. Some of Kharlacht's orcs might have survived the battle at the standing stones, and they would recognize her. They might try to snatch her off the walls and take her back to Qazarl, or at least steal the soulstone. She would be safe in the keep.

Assuming the town did not fall.

Sir Joram climbed to the ramparts between the twin watchtowers of the northern gate. "What news?"

Thomas, the middle-aged man-at-arms who had challenged Ridmark earlier, bowed. "My lord knight. The enemy gathers north of the town. They are keeping out of bow range so far, and I suspect they are digging in for a siege."

Ridmark looked over the battlements and saw Qazarl's host.

Thousands of orcish warriors waited at the edge of the cleared fields to the north. Most of them wore leather armor, as had the Mhalekite orcs Ridmark had faced so far. Yet many wore chain mail and carried heavy axes. Dozens of banners flew over the orcish host, a black field with a single massive red drop in the center.

He remembered seeing a much larger army in this valley five years ago.

"Four thousand," said Joram, squinting at the host in the dimming sunlight. "It looks like you guessed right, Ridmark."

Ridmark nodded, watching the orcs assemble their camp.

"No siege engines, it seems," said Caius.

"Aye," said Ridmark. "The orc tribes of the Wilderland rarely have the

161

skill to build catapults or ballistae. But ladders are easy enough to assemble. I expect they will build a few dozen ladders and then try to overwhelm us in a single rush." He scratched his chin. "Or Qazarl will try something clever, send raiders to open one of the gates."

"My lord knight," said Thomas, glaring at Ridmark. "Will you listen to this outcast?"

Joram shrugged. "He defeated the Mhalekites once before, Thomas. I am inclined to heed his counsel."

Thomas scowled, but had no answer for that.

"My lord!" said another man-at-arms, pointing over the battlements. "Look!"

"What manner of creatures are those?" said peasant militiaman. "It looks like a lizard that walks as a man."

In the midst of the orcs Ridmark glimpsed gray-skinned figures the size of large children, tails coiling behind them. The shapes wore black veils to shield their large eyes, and carried spears and axes with obsidian blades.

"Kobolds," said Ridmark. "This is my doing. We annoyed them when we passed through the Deeps, and I suspect Qazarl welcomed them with open arms."

Thomas blinked. "You passed through the Deeps? And you're still alive?"

"Oh, aye," said Caius with a grin. "It was a pleasant afternoon stroll, that's all. Hardly worth the mention."

Ridmark rested his left hand on the rough stone on the battlements. "This is a problem."

"Obviously," said Joram. "The enemy has greater numbers."

"It's more than that," said Ridmark. "Orcs see in the dark as well as we do, but they have keener noses. But kobolds have superior night vision. I think Qazarl will try to send them over the wall to open the gate in the night."

"We will have to remain vigilant," said Joram.

"Aye," said Ridmark. "I suggest patrols all night along the ramparts. Split the men into two groups, and keep them sleeping near the northern and the southern gates."

"The Mhalekites are massed to the north," said Joram.

"Which would make it all the easier for some kobolds to slip south and scale the wall there," said Ridmark. "Or Qazarl could launch an assault upon the northern wall, and try to send men to take the southern gate while we are distracted."

Joram let out a long breath. "Your counsel is sound. I will see it done, and prepare the men to fight."

"We must delay," said Ridmark. "That is the best strategy. Delay until the Dux arrives from Castra Marcaine with help."

"So be it," said Joram.

Ridmark looked at the men on the walls, at the bundles of supplies in the small square below the gate. Joram had done everything right, but there was one thing they could not prepare to face.

Qazarl's magic. Or, worse, Shadowbearer's magic, if the renegade high elf wizard chose to join the fight on his minion's side.

The defenders would simply have to wait and see.

Calliande climbed to the rooftop of the keep and looked over the town of Dun Licinia.

It looked...new.

From what she had heard, Mhalek had been defeated here in a great battle five years past, his horde of orcish warriors smashed. Most of the houses had been constructed of brick, their roofs covered in clay tiles. The keep, the church, the Magistrius's tower, and the town's wall had been built of stone. Most of the men were at the walls, preparing to fight, and most of the women were preparing food and bandages and arrows. Everyone else was in the church, praying for God and the Dominus Christus to watch over their husbands and sons and brothers, to see them safely through the battle to come.

Calliande hoped that God was listening.

She hoped that they all did not die within the next day.

And she hoped, above all, not to fall into Shadowbearer's clutches again.

She shivered and leaned against the battlements, the stone rough and cool beneath her bare hands.

Sir Joram's majordomus had found new clothing for her, thank God. Ulazur's foul-smelling clothes had been preferable to going naked, but it felt good to wear proper clothing. The majordomus had found her a green gown that almost fit, with a black leather belt and boots that did not hurt her feet. She had kept the dagger Ridmark had given her, it sheath clipped to her belt. She did not know how to fight, but his counsel of keeping a weapon near at hand was sound.

Calliande's eyes turned towards the northern wall, to the men standing guard there.

And to the orcish host, just visible in the trees beyond the cleared fields.

The defense was in Ridmark's hands now. Sir Joram was in command, but she could tell the man was not comfortable in the role. He would defer to Ridmark. Indeed, he could have done much worse. Calliande had seen Ridmark fight, and if he wielded the defenders as skillfully as he wielded his staff, he could hold off the Mhalekites for a long time, perhaps long enough for aid to arrive from Castra Marcaine.

But even the Gray Knight might not be able to hold off the Mhalekites long enough.

Because Qazarl had magic and Ridmark did not.

Had Ridmark still been a Swordbearer, it would have been different. The power of a Swordbearer's Soulblade could deflect hostile magic, could shield Ridmark long enough to cut down the orcish shaman. But Ridmark had been expelled from the Order of the Swordbearers, though Calliande did not know why. If Alamur had not been a traitor, he could have blunted the power of Qazarl's magic. Perhaps it was just as well – she had sensed the strength of Qazarl's magic and of Alamur's, and Qazarl was the stronger.

But Shadowbearer was mightier than both men put together. Shadowbearer had claimed that the high elves were hunting him. If he escaped and joined Qazarl, Dun Licinia would fall in short order.

Not even Ridmark could stand against Shadowbearer's power. He might not be able to stand against Qazarl's power.

Ridmark needed magic of his own.

And Calliande had to find a way to give it to him. Because if she did not, the town would fall...and Shadowbearer would claim her once more.

The stone altar awaited her within its ring of standing stones.

She sighed in frustration and gripped the battlements.

It made sense that she would have magic of her own. She knew more about magic than she ought, and she had the ability to sense magic.

If she could sense magic, could she not use it?

Perhaps she had been a Magistria of the Order of the Vigilant, sleeping away the centuries beneath the Tower of Vigilance until the Frostborn returned.

A darker thought occurred to her. Perhaps she had been an Eternalist like Talvinius. The Eternalists had been obsessed with immortality, and perhaps she had sealed herself away beneath the Tower to extend her life.

Calliande hoped not.

But no matter who she had been in her previous life, she would find a way to aid Ridmark.

If she could.

For the hundredth time, Calliande closed her eyes and tried to summon magic, tried to remember something, anything that would help her cast a spell.

Nothing happened.

She sighed in frustration and headed for the stairs. Useless, she was utterly useless. Both Shadowbearer and Talvinius had thought to claim her power, whatever it was. But what good was her power if she could not find a   way   to   use   it   to   help   the   others?

Sir Joram had given her a small, but comfortable, guest room on the keep's highest level, furnished with a narrow bed and a chair. Calliande sat upon the chair and closed her eyes, staining against the mist filling her mind, trying to remember something that might prove useful against the enemy.

Nothing came.

Night fell, and Ridmark strode the circuit of Dun Licinia's ramparts, Caius trailing after him. He felt weary, but he did not want to sleep. Likely Qazarl would use his kobold allies in an attempt to seize the gates tonight, and Ridmark wanted to be ready.

"Gray Knight."

A stocky, middle-aged man stood near the battlements, wearing leather armor with steel studs and holding a worn wooden spear with a sharp steel head. It was Peter, the belligerent freeholder who had accused Ridmark of stealing pigs from his herd.

"I fear I was unable to find your hogs," said Ridmark, ignoring Caius's puzzled look. "Most likely the Mhalekites ate them long before I crossed your path."

"Aye, I thought so," said Peter. He scowled and spat over the wall. "Damned pagan orcs. Well, the warbands came down from the hills, and one of them set fire to my barn. My sons and I fought them off. Don't think the green bastards expected to find fighting men. We rounded up all our folk and all our livestock and got within the town." He shook his head. "I suppose God was with us. Hardly anyone in the outer freeholds made it to the town alive."

Ridmark nodded. "It is good you escaped. Stay vigilant. The Mhalekites will likely make an attempt on the town tonight."

Peter grimaced. "Do you think we can win? There are so damned many of the orcs. Not as many as the first time the Mhalekites came, but still too many."

"You were here for the first battle?" said Ridmark.

"Aye," said Peter, a grin flashing behind his graying beard. "I was a man-at-arms for the Dux Gareth Licinius. When Mhalek slew Galearus and the other commanders, I was sure we were done. But then you took command and whipped the Mhalekites." The freeholder looked almost embarrassed. "If I had known who you were, I wouldn't have accused you of taking my pigs."

"I am grateful for that," said Ridmark.

"Brother," said Peter to Caius. "Would you give us your blessing? It cannot hurt to have God on our side before the battle."

"God watches over us all," said Caius, "but of course." Peter and the nearby militiamen went to their knees, and Caius started to speak in formal Latin. "In the name of God the Father, and God the Son, and God the Holy Spirit, I ask God, the archangels, and all the saints to…"

A flicker of motion caught Ridmark's eye.

Four of the moons were out tonight, throwing pale silvery-blue light over everything. He saw no sign of motion outside the walls, nor any unusual activity from the Mhalekite camp. Yet the uneven ground offered plenty of cover for someone skilled at stealth.

"Go, with this blessing," said Caius, "and put your trust in God."

The men started to rise, and again Ridmark saw a flicker of motion at the edge of the battlements. A small black shape appeared there, and Ridmark realized what it was.

A kobold's claw.

"Stay down!" he shouted as Peter and the nearby militiamen started to rise.

Three kobold warriors appeared atop the battlements, short bows in hand, and released. The arrows buzzed over the heads of the kneeling men, missing them by inches. Ridmark surged forward, his staff coming up, and swung with all his strength. He caught the nearest kobold in the stomach, and the power of his blow knocked the warrior off the battlements. The remaining kobolds hissed and lunged at him with clubs, their crests flaring. Ridmark parried the blows, reversed his staff, and drove the butt into a kobold's chest. He heard ribs crack, and his next blow knocked the kobold from the wall.

The last kobold flew at Ridmark, shrieking, only to land upon the spearheads of Peter and his men. The kobold fell to the rampart, twitching, and Peter finished off the warrior with a quick stab and twist.

"Kobolds!" said Peter. "Creeping up on us in the dark. Why…"

"To the northern gate," said Ridmark, "quickly." He pointed at one of the militiamen. "Run to the southern gate as fast as you can and put them on alert. Then find Sir Joram and tell him what is happening. He's likely at the keep."

"What is happening, sir?" said the militiaman, blinking in surprise.

"The kobolds are trying to creep into the town and open the gates," said Ridmark. "Go!"

The militiaman ran for the stairs, and Ridmark raced along the ramparts, Caius, Peter, and several militiamen following. He doubted those three kobolds had been the only infiltration party. Qazarl would have sent several, all heading for either the northern or southern gates.

The northern gate came into sight, the twin octagonal towers dark against the star-strewn sky. Ridmark saw the guards standing atop the towers, watching the Mhalekite host to the north.

Then he saw one of the watchmen fall limp from the tower to crash against the ramparts.

"Foes!" roared Ridmark at the top of his lungs. "Foes are in the towers! To arms! To arms!"

He raced for the door to the tower and found it standing half-open. A dim light came from the guttering fire in the hearth, throwing light over two dead militiamen upon the floor, kobold spears jutting from their backs.

Three kobold warriors stood over the dead men, moving to the steel windlass that operated the gate.

Ridmark fell upon them like a storm. His first blow landed with terrific force against the side of a kobold warrior's head. Bone cracked, and the warrior fell motionless to the ground. The other two turned to attack him, only to meet the charge of Peter and his men. Steel spearheads stabbed, and the kobolds fell back, retreating up the stairs.

"Peter," said Ridmark. "Stay here and guard the windlass. If the kobolds get the gate open, the orcs will charge the town."

Peter nodded, and Ridmark raced up the stairs, Caius following.

He heard the creak of a bow and shouted a warning, throwing himself against the wall. An obsidian-tipped arrow skipped off the stairs, and Ridmark hurried forward. The next turn around the stairs revealed the kobold archer, crest flared in challenge. Ridmark's staff crushed both the crest and the kobold's skull, and the archer tumbled limp down the stairs.

He reached the turret and found a pair of kobolds standing over the signal fire. One of the kobolds held a pouch of blue powder. Ridmark suspected the powder would turn the fire blue, giving the Mhalekites the signal they needed to charge the gate.

He rammed into the first kobold, knocking the warrior to the ground and sending the pouch flying away. The second kobold sprang at Ridmark with a shriek, claws and fangs reaching, only to meet Caius's mace. Bone cracked and broken fangs flew, and the kobold fell dead to the turret.

Caius let out a long breath. "Clever of them."

"Aye," said Ridmark, "and this isn't over yet. Follow me."

He hurried back down the stairs to the guard room, where Peter and his sons still defended the windlass.

"Stay here," said Ridmark, "and keep anyone from opening the gates."

Peter nodded. "Gray Knight...if you had not come when you did, those kobolds would have shot us before we even saw them."

Ridmark clapped Peter on the shoulder. "It seems Brother Caius's blessing was indeed effective."

He hurried into the night, the dwarven friar following.

An hour later, Ridmark stood with Brother Caius and Sir Joram in the street below the northern gate. A steady stream of men-at-arms and militiamen came to Sir Joram to offer reports.

Qazarl had been thorough.

A dozen small groups of kobold warriors had crept up to the town's walls, using the darkness to mask their movements. Four men had died at the northern gate, three at the southern, and six more at various points along the walls.

"A grim night," said Sir Joram, shaking his head.

"And it could have been much worse," said Ridmark. "If the kobolds had gotten even one of the gates open, the Mhalekites would be butchering us in the streets now."

"Aye," said Joram. "I've given strict commands for the men not to burn torches upon the walls, to preserve their night vision, and for a dozen men to guard the windlasses. The doors are to be locked and barred, and only opened with the proper passwords."

"Those are good precautions," said Ridmark. "I would also suggest putting some of the women and children to work patrolling the streets. If the kobolds can't get into the gatehouses, they might think to slip into the town and start fires."

"The women and children will be able to fight," said Joram.

"Perhaps not," said Ridmark, "but they could warn the reserves."

"Very well," said Joram. "It will be done." He took a deep breath. "Three days."

"To what?" said Ridmark.

"Until aid arrives," said Joram. "It takes a week for a man on foot to reach Castra Marcaine from here, but men on horseback can make the journey in three days. We have three days to hold until aid arrives."

"Perhaps four," said Ridmark, "if the Dux's men face any difficulty getting here."

"I know," said Joram. "So. Three days at the earliest and five days at the latest. Do you think we can hold that long, Ridmark?"

Ridmark looked at the walls.

"I suppose," he said, "that we are going to find out."

Again Calliande tried to summon power.

And again nothing happened.

The sounds of fighting from the wall faded. She suspected that Qazarl had launched a raid to seize the gates, just as Ridmark had predicted.

Fortunately, it sounded as if the attack had been repulsed.

Her mouth twisted in a scowl. Men were fighting and dying on the walls...and here she sat, battering her mind against her faded memory.

Useless, so useless.

She tried again, but exhaustion took her, and she sank into a black and dreamless sleep.

CHAPTER 19
ASSAULT

The next morning, Ridmark awoke to the sound of drums.

He stood, working through the stiffness in his cold arms and legs. The town was full to overflowing with refugees from the nearby freeholds, and there were no beds left. So he had simply wrapped himself in his elven cloak and gone to sleep in a doorway near the northern gate. He had spent years camping in the wilds, and the doorway was more comfortable than many nights he had spent in the forests and hills of the Wilderland.

The drums boomed over the walls.

Had Qazarl launched an all-out assault?

Ridmark took his staff and hurried to the ramparts. The men-at-arms and militiamen on the walls stirred, pointing over the battlements. Ridmark saw Qazarl's army drawn up at the edge of the trees, sorted into columns around their siege ladders. Yet so far the orcs remained motionless.

He crossed to the rampart between the gate towers and found Sir Joram and Brother Caius. Joram did not look as if he had slept at all, his heavy-set face shaded with red stubble. Caius remained calm as ever, his lips working in a silent prayer as his right hand rested on the handle of his heavy mace.

"Ridmark," said Joram. "I take it the drumming woke you?"

"Aye," said Ridmark. "It just began?"

"Only a few minutes ago," said Joram. "They are trying to intimidate us, plainly." He struck his fist against the pommel of his sword with a scowl. "Would that I had more horsemen. Then we could sally forth and teach these Mhalekites some respect!"

"Let them drum until their arms fall off," said Ridmark. "Delay is our ally, and their foe."

The drumming stopped.

"It seems they figured that out," said Caius.

"Sir Joram!" shouted a militiamen. "Look!"

Joram moved to the battlements, Ridmark and Caius following.

A group of thirty orcs moved towards the northern gate. The lead orc carried a spear with a white banner.

"A parley?" said Joram.

"Likely they want to demand our surrender," said Caius.

Ridmark pointed. "Qazarl is with them."

The orcish shaman strode in the midst of his guards. Ridmark had last seen him five years ago, just before Mhalek's defeat, and Qazarl had changed little in that time. The shaman still had white hair and a long white beard, his tusks rising from his jaw like twin jagged daggers. He wore trousers and a loose vest, and tattoos and scars in the shape of arcane sigils marked his arms. Even from a distance, Ridmark sensed the aura of confidence around the shaman. Qazarl had always been one of Mhalek's most powerful disciples, and the past five years had only increased his strength.

"One good bow shot," said one of the men-at-arms, "and we could rid our foes of their leader."

"No," said Joram. "I am a knight of the realm of Andomhaim, and I will not murder a man under a white banner of truce."

Caius nodded. "Honorable."

"It is," said Ridmark. Galearus had been honorable as well, and Mhalek had used that to murder him and all his lieutenants. "And even if we were not honorable, it would not matter. Mhalek was powerful enough to shield himself from weapons of steel and wood. It would not surprise me if Qazarl had learned the spell as well."

The orcs stopped just out of bowshot of the walls.

"Hear me, human dogs!" roared the hulking orc in chain mail carrying the banner, speaking in accented Latin. "I am Mzalacht, warrior of Vhaluusk, and I speak for this host! Qazarl, the most faithful disciple of the living god Mhalek, demands your surrender. Lay down your arms, open your gates, and your lives shall be spared! Resist, and you shall all perish!" The orc herald glared up the walls, while Qazarl himself remained impassive. "Who speaks for Dun Licinia?"

"I speak for the town!" said Joram, putting one foot upon the battlements. "I am Sir Joram Agramore, the Comes of Dun Licinia. By the authority of Gareth Licinius, Dux of Northerland, and by the High King Arthurain Pendragon, the seventh of his name, I command you to leave our lands and return to your homes at once! For you have trespassed upon the lands of the High King and brought fire and sword unlawfully and unjustly against his people."

Mzalacht laughed. "Cringe behind your walls and invoke the name of your precious High King, Joram of Andomhaim, but your High King will not save you. Your Dux cannot save you. You are at our mercy, and cannot escape."

"Bold words," said Joram, "considering that you are outside our walls, and your one attempt to break in failed miserably."

"You might have repulsed one attack," said Mzalacht, "but can you repulse another? And those that will follow? We have greater numbers, and even the weakest orc warrior has the fierceness and strength of seven crawling humans."

"We shall put that to the test, will we not?" said Joram.

Mzalacht launched into a string of roaring, rambling threats. Ridmark's eyes scanned the embassy, and settled upon Qazarl. Why bother with a herald? Qazarl was not a fool. He knew that aid was almost certainly on the way from Castra Marcaine. Why take the risk of attacking the town now? Shadowbearer might have promised the orcs victory, but there was no sign of the renegade wizard...

Then Ridmark understood.

Qazarl was launching the attack because Vlazar had failed to kill Calliande...and Calliande and the soulstone were within the town's walls.

The orcish shaman lifted his head, as if he felt Ridmark's gaze...and Ridmark saw the shock of recognition as Qazarl's black eyes widened.

The shaman stepped forward, raising his hand, and Mzalacht fell silent.

"Ridmark Arban!" said Qazarl, his rasping voice rolling over the field.

Joram looked at Ridmark and nodded.

Ridmark climbed onto the battlements, his gray cloak snapping behind him in the breeze.

"Qazarl of the Mhalekites," said Ridmark. "Making a pilgrimage to the site of your master's greatest and final defeat?"

Qazarl laughed. "Mhalek fell at Castra Marcaine, Ridmark Arban. As you know full well."

Ridmark said nothing.

"So you became the famed Gray Knight?" said Qazarl. "Surprising. I heard that Swordbearers severed from their precious Soulblades lay down to die. And after what happened at Castra Marcaine, I thought you would have curled up in a corner to weep until death took you."

"As you can plainly see, I did not," said Ridmark. "Or has your mind grown so addled with age that you can no longer discern truth from delusion?" The men near him laughed. "Or given that you followed Mhalek to his defeat, perhaps your judgment was never sound."

"What is happening now is none of your concern," said Qazarl. "Run off, and I shall let you live with your misery and dishonor."

"And then you would have one less man to kill," said Ridmark. "Since you have so far failed to take Dun Licinia, your threats do not worry me."

Qazarl sneered. "Do you truly think this is about Dun Licinia? This wretched little town is nothing. Are you so blind that you cannot see what is happening? The shape of the world is about to change. A new order is arising, and a new power will rule the earth. The wise, the strong, will align themselves with the new power. The weak will be crushed and swept aside like chaff."

Ridmark felt a chill. The urdmordar he had slain ten years ago, the urdmordar who had first predicted the return of the Frostborn, had said much the same thing.

"This new power. Shadowbearer, I assume?" said Ridmark. "A poor choice. Given that he has abandoned you here to die."

Qazarl laughed. "Blind, pitiful fool. Vast powers are in motion, powers that you cannot possibly comprehend. Your realm of Andomhaim is riddled with corruption, and your High King's throne sits upon a dais of rotten wood. Very soon now it shall all come crashing down."

Ridmark decided to take a gamble. "Perhaps all that is true...but it's not going to happen. Not yet, anyway."

"And just why not?" said Qazarl.

"Because," said Ridmark, "I have Shadowbearer's empty soulstone and you do not."

Qazarl said nothing.

"And I would wager every gold coin in Andomhaim," said Ridmark, "that your precious new order is not going to arise without that soulstone."

"Perhaps," said Qazarl, "you are more perceptive than I thought. Ridmark Arban, the Swordbearer without a sword. Instead of a Swordbearer, you have become the Gray Knight. And the Gray Knight loves to save people, does he not? Defend them from the monsters of the wild, the creatures of dark magic? Like a broken, pale shadow of a true Knight of the Soulblade."

"Does this have a point?" said Ridmark. "Surely you did not come all this way to weary my ears with your feeble attempts at poetry."

"I will make you a simple bargain," said Qazarl. "The soulstone and the woman both. Hand them over to me, and I will leave Dun Licinia in peace."

"And if I do not?" said Ridmark.

Qazarl grinned. "Then I will take Dun Licinia by storm and put its people to the sword. I will butcher every last defender upon its walls. I will take the children, and kill them in front of their mothers. Then I will hand the women over to my warriors, and once they have taken their pleasure, I will have the women killed. Dun Licinia will be ashes, and its people will be butchered meat."

A murmur went up from the defenders of the wall. Ridmark saw

Qazarl's game well enough. None of the men upon the wall desired to fight, and most simply wanted to tend their farms and workshops in peace. By giving them a way to buy peace, Qazarl had a chance to get everything he wanted without a fight.

And then he would likely kill everyone in Dun Licinia anyway, once he claimed whatever strange power resulted from Calliande's death upon the stone altar.

Ridmark opened his mouth to answer, but Joram spoke first.

"You insult us with this offer!" said Joram, sweeping his arm over the battlements. "These are the men of Andomhaim, valiant and true! Do you think they will buy their safety with the blood of an innocent woman? Perhaps such things are common among the followers of the blood gods, but we will not debase ourselves so. If you wish to claim this woman, brigand, then throw your men against our walls. Justice and honor are with our cause, and God shall lend our arms strength!"

The men cheered in response. Qazarl remained silent until the echoes died away.

"So be it!" he said. "We shall settle this through force of arms. Pray to your God, and see if he will deliver you."

Qazarl snarled an order to his escort, and the warriors turned and marched back towards the waiting army.

"Nicely spoken," said Caius.

"Thank you," said Joram, wiping sweat from his brow. "I feared our men might lose heart at his offer. Perhaps I should have guards put around Calliande, just in case one of our men…loses faith."

"Not yet," said Ridmark. "I think you will need every man here."

Drums boomed from the Mhalekite army, and the roar of thousands of orcish voices filled the air. Six columns of orcish warriors marched forward, three on either side of the northern gate. The warriors at the center of the columns carried heavy siege ladders, tall enough to reach the top of the ramparts, and broad enough for two men to climb abreast. Other warriors with heavy shields screened the orcs with the ladders.

"I think," said Joram, "that you are correct." He turned and raised his voice. "To battle! To battle! All men to their stations! Spears and swords in front, archers behind! To battle!"

The clatter of armor and shields rose from the ramparts as the men arranged themselves to face the oncoming orcs. Shouts and the tramp of running boots came from the streets of Dun Licinia as the reserve companies rushed to the northern gate.

"Ridmark, Brother Caius," said Joram. "You are both doughty warriors, and I have no lawful authority over you."

"We certainly will not run from the fight," said Caius.

"I would expect not," said Joram. "I ask only you go where the fighting is the fiercest. Your skills could help us hold off the Mhalekites."

Ridmark gave him a tight smile. "It shall be as you say. Come, Brother."

Joram shouted additional commands as the columns approached the wall. The militiamen and the men-at-arms responded with more efficiency than Ridmark would have expected. The men-at-arms were professional soldiers, but the militiamen were townsmen and freeholders. Still, Ridmark suspected that most of them were veterans of the war against Mhalek.

He supposed he had led these men in battle five years ago.

Ridmark walked west along the wall, keeping behind the archers, Brother Caius following after. Men-at-arms raised crossbows, while the militiamen lifted short bows.

"Here," said Ridmark. "We'll make our stand here."

"Why here?" said Caius.

"Because," said Ridmark, pointing, "we're closer to the gate tower here. Any orcs who gain the wall will try to take the gate. We'll stop them."

"I should have seen it," said Caius. "I shall never get used to warfare upon the surface. It is simpler in the Deeps. But it would be better not to have war at all."

"Tell that to Qazarl," said Ridmark.

Caius sighed. "I tried."

"Archers!" boomed Joram's voice. "Release!"

The archers released, and the crossbowmen squeezed their triggers. Scores of arrows and bolts hissed from the walls and slammed into the advancing orcs. The warriors with the shields caught many of the missiles, the steel heads thudding into the thick wood. But some of the quarrels and arrows struck the orcs carrying the ladders. One of the ladders wavered and came to a stop as the arrows pierced the orcs carrying it.

But the other five ladders kept advancing.

"Release at will!" shouted Joram.

The archers kept a steady stream of arrows, while the crossbowmen reloaded and cranked their heavy weapons. The crossbows were more powerful, but took too long to reload. Ridmark guessed that the men-at-arms might have a time to fire one more volley before the orcs scaled the ladders.

"Spears and swords!" came Joram's voice. "Ready!"

The men-at-arms and militiamen moved closer to the ramparts. The crossbowmen reloaded and loosed another volley, and Ridmark heard more roars of pain and fury rise from the orcish warriors. More had died...but far more were coming.

The orcs reached the walls, and the ladders thumped against the battlements.

"Stand fast!" roared a nearby sergeant, and the orcs scrambled onto the ramparts.

The first warriors met a wall of steel and arrows. One orc caught four arrows in the chest and tumbled backwards, while the warrior next to him took a pair of spears in the gut. But more orcish warriors scrambled up the ladder, roaring in fury, their black eyes gleaming red as the orcish battle rage took hold. One orc threw himself forward and crashed into the militiamen, striking right and left with his short sword. Green blood splattered as a man-at-arms struck with a sword, but the orc whirled and impaled the man-at-arms.

The man-at-arms fell, the orc charged into the line, and Ridmark moved to attack.

The length of his staff slammed into the orc's face with enough force to break bone, but the orc was in the grip of battle rage. The warrior shook off the blow and charged, and Ridmark sidestepped, swinging his staff with enough force to shatter the bones in the orc's left shin. Rage or not, the leg could no longer support the orc's weight, and the warrior collapsed with a howl.

A militiaman brought down his spear with a yell, and the warrior went still.

More orcs scrambled up the ladder, fighting the beleaguered militiamen, and Ridmark saw Qazarl's host charging across the field. If they did not find a way to disable or destroy those ladders, the orcs would swarm up to the ramparts and drive the defenders from the wall.

And in the resultant chaos, Qazarl could carry out his threats upon the town's women and children.

"To the ladder!" shouted Ridmark, and threw himself into the fray. In the tight quarters, he did not have enough room to swing his staff properly, but he had enough space to jab and thrust. His blows stunned the orcish warriors, permitting the men-at-arms and armsmen to land killing blows with their swords and spears. Caius fought at his side, shouting exhortations to the men, his heavy mace landing bone-crushing blows. Step by step they drove the orcish attackers back, the ramparts growing slippery with green and red blood.

They reached the ladder.

"Push it over!" shouted one of the men-at-arms, seizing the end of the ladder.

"No!" said Ridmark. If they pushed over the ladder, the orcs could simply raise it up again. "Grab it and pull it over the ramparts. Quickly!"

He seized the top rung and started to pull. It was too heavy to lift himself, but a dozen other men saw the wisdom of his plan and hurried forward. Together they began to jerk the ladder upwards inch by inch. The orcs below howled in outrage and seized the bottom rung, and the ladder slid back towards the ground. Caius dropped his mace and grabbed the ladder. The dwarf's sturdy strength, coupled with the efforts of the militiamen, proved too much for the orcs on the ground. The ladder ripped free of their grasp and toppled backwards over the rampart. It landed in the street below with an echoing clatter.

The men loosed a ragged cheer.

"Thank you for your efforts, Brother," said one of the men-at-arms. "We would not have gotten the ladder over the wall without your strength. Truly, they breed strong backs in the Three Kingdoms."

Caius grinned. "And they breed valiant fighters in Andomhaim."

"Come!" said Ridmark, picking up his staff. "We can help drive the remaining ladders from the wall. Archers!" He pointed his staff at the militia archers and the men-at-arms with crossbows. "Stay back and loose at any orcs attempting to pull back the ladders. The rest of you, follow me."

Ridmark strode forward, Caius and the others following him in grim silence.

The fighting was over by mid-morning.

Ridmark had led the men-at-arms and militiamen along the western half of the northern wall, pushing back the orcs and pulling their ladders into the town one by one. Once the last of the ladders had been pulled up, the archers had been free to turn their full attention to the orcs below, and the Mhalekites had retreated in disarray to the trees.

The defenders had not fared as well along the eastern half of the northern wall. Joram's counterattacks had pulled two of the three ladders over the wall, but at the third, Qazarl unleashed some sort of black magic. A dozen men fell dead in a heartbeat, and the orcs fortified themselves upon the rampart. Only when Ridmark led the defenders from the western half to join Joram's men did they finally force the orcs from the wall.

The Mhalekites fell back to the trees to prepare another attack.

Ridmark stood on the rampart with Caius and Joram. Below came the groans and cries of the wounded, and dead orcs lay strewn about the ground below the wall.

"How many?" said Joram, his voice hoarse.

"Perhaps two hundred of the foe dead," said Ridmark. "Thirty or forty more, if some of their wounded perish."

Joram sighed. "We lost forty men, and suffered another forty wounded. Of those, thirty should still be fit to fight…and the rest may not live out the day."

"The Mhalekites had a rougher time of it than we did," said Caius. Specks of drying blood stained his gray, stone-colored skin. He looked at the dead orcs and sighed. "May God have mercy on them, and save them from an eternity as slaves of the cruel blood gods."

"The Mhalekites indeed suffered greater losses," said Joram, "but they can afford to spend blood. A dozen more such assaults will wear away half of Qazarl's host…but they will destroy us utterly."

"Then we must delay them at all costs," said Ridmark, "and hold until aid can come from Castra Marcaine."

Joram nodded, and they went to prepare for the next assault.

CHAPTER 20
A CHALLENGE

Three days after the fighting began, Calliande hurried through the nave of Dun Licinia's stone church, her hair tied back, the sleeves and hem of her dress spotted with blood. Tapestries hung on the church's thick stone walls, showing scenes from the scriptures. One showed the Dominus Christus healing the ten lepers, and another displayed him creating loaves and fishes to feed the multitude. Still another showed him healing the eyes of the man born blind, or commanding the paralytic to rise and walk.

Calliande prayed for such miracles now.

Close to a hundred wounded men lay upon the church's stone floor. The most severely wounded, those unlikely to live out the day, lay upon cots. Those likely to survive lay upon blankets on the floor. Men who needed only some patching and stitching but could still fight sat on benches near the thick pillars that supported the roof. Groans echoed off the walls, and the air smelled of blood and sweat and urine, even with all the doors and windows open. Women from the town moved about their tasks, tending and feeding the wounded men. The keep's staff of halfling servants had been moved to the church, and now worked to clear away bloodstains, change bedding, prepare bandages, and when the end came, to carry away the bodies.

And Calliande was in charge of it all.

She did not know how she knew as much about medicine as she did, but she knew things. How to clean a cut with mold and boiling wine, and how to suture it closed. How best to set a broken bone, and how to give a man the right kind of drugs to sleep as she closed his wounds. Yet she knew all those things, and as the first of the wounded had come to the church, the knowledge had risen unbidden into her mind. Soon she found that none of the townswomen or the priests knew as much about medicine as she did, that without her aid, men would die who might otherwise have lived.

So she had taken charge of the wounded, and found that the priests and women were grateful for someone to tell them what to do. Calliande labored among them, stitching wounds, winding bandages, applying poultices, and helping to carry unconscious men. It was grim, tiring work, but better than sitting alone in her room, trying to summon magic that she might not actually possess.

And she no longer felt so useless.

A wounded militiaman sat upon one of the benches, stripped to the waist. His right shoulder was a hideous bloody wound, and a deep gash went down his ribs to his belly. An orc had stabbed him in the shoulder, and as the militiaman had struck down his foe, the orc's short sword had sliced along his ribs.

"What is your name?" said Calliande as she examined the wound. Best to keep them talking. It helped distract them from the pain.

"Bann," said the militiaman with a grunt.

"An interesting name," said Elaine, the matronly woman assisting Calliande.

Bann grinned. "My father was mad for the tales of the Old Earth, Lancelot and the High King Arthur and his knights. Named me for one of them." He snorted. "Suppose if I had cut down that Qazarl, I might have been made a knight myself."

"You fought valiantly," said Calliande. "All your wounds are in the front."

"I did!" said Bann. "Not to boast, but I did. And even the Gray Knight himself said I fought well."

Calliande nodded. Sir Joram Agramore commanded the city's defense, and the men respected their Comes…but they followed Ridmark. Even Sir Joram followed Ridmark. She would not have thought an exiled Swordbearer could win their loyalty, but she was not surprised. Had Ridmark not snatched her from terrible danger, brought her to safety through fierce perils, relying only upon his wits and courage and his skill at weapons? Little wonder the defenders of Dun Licinia followed him.

Little wonder he had taken command of the host of Andomhaim five years ago to defeat Mhalek.

Again she wondered why such a man had been expelled from the Order of the Swordbearers.

"Wine," she told Elaine.

"You're going to tell me this won't hurt very much?" said Bann.

"Actually," said Calliande, "this is going to hurt a lot. But alternative is to wait until your wounds putrefy, and then you die raving and screaming of a fever. Which will hurt a great deal more."

Bann grimaced. "Best we get on with it, then."

Calliande washed out his wounds with a mixture of boiling wine and mold. Bann gritted his teeth, sweat pouring down his face, but did not scream. After the wounds were cleaned, Calliande closed them with a needle and thread. Still Bann remained silent, though the muscles in his jaw jerked with every jab of the needle.

After he leaned against the cool stone pillar, gasping. "I don't suppose you have any of that wine left?" His voice was a croak. "Because I would dearly like to get drunk just now."

"We do," said Calliande, and Elaine handed over a clay flagon. Bann took it with his good hand. "Drink up. That should take some of the edge off. I would give you more, but we have to save the stronger medicines for those with grievous wounds."

"As you should," said Bann, draining half the flagon in one gulp.

"The wound should heal cleanly," said Calliande, "if you don't rip out your stitches. What is your profession?"

"Stonemason," said Bann. He finished off the wine.

Calliande nodded. "You'll be able to swing a hammer again. It will take some time to regain your strength after the stitches come out, but you should recover completely."

She had not often been able to say that today.

Bann nodded, eyelids heavy as the effects of the strong drink took hold. Calliande forced him to drink a large amount of boiled water, lest blood loss and the drink conspire to dehydrate him. Then Bann lay upon a blanket on the floor, closed his eyes, and went to sleep.

"He will recover, I think," said Elaine.

Calliande nodded. "With God's favor, and if he doesn't rip out his stitches, he will recover." She sighed. "We can say that of too few men."

"But more than we could without your aid, Lady Calliande," said Elaine.

"Don't call me that," said Calliande. "I don't know if I am noblewoman or not. For all I know I was a freeholder's daughter before the orcs took me captive."

But she doubted it. No one would trouble to put a freeholder's daughter into a centuries-long magical sleep.

"If not nobility of blood, then nobility of spirit," said Elaine. "Without your aid many of these men would have died." She blinked. "Including my husband."

"Your husband?" said Calliande, alarmed. She could not remember Elaine's husband. Was her short-term memory starting to fail as well?

Of course, the last three days were a blur of blood and screams and tears.

"He lost two fingers," said Elaine, "when his left hand was caught between his shield and an orc's sword." Calliande remembered him, a blustery, jovial merchant with a paunch who had made jokes even as the putrefaction set into his wounds. "He shouldn't have been fighting at all, the fat old fool, but he would not stand by while the younger men fought for our lives. Not after that shaman threatened to kill us all. And after he took his wound, he hid it and fought on." Elaine blinked again, her eyes bloodshot. "When I saw him, I was sure he would die. The putrefaction had set in. But you thought to use that mushroom to treat the wound. He will live."

Calliande shrugged. "It was...something I remembered, that is all. It is well for us the mushrooms were growing in the alley behind the warehouses. We could hardly leave the town to forage in the woods."

"It was the mercy of God," said Elaine, "that brought you to Dun Licinia. You and the Gray Knight. I would not think a man with a coward's brand could fight so fiercely. If we are to be delivered from this peril, he will find the path. Sir Joram is a good man, of course, but he is not a warrior. Not the way your Gray Knight is."

Calliande blinked. "My Gray Knight?"

Elaine only smiled in answer, and then Calliande heard a commotion on the other end of the nave. She turned her head, fearing that more wounded had arrived. Some of the men on cots stood, and Calliande wondered if the orcs had broken into the church...

Then she saw that Ridmark had come to visit the wounded.

She watched as he moved through them, face grave as he spoke. He listened to their stories and praised their valor. He remembered how each man had taken his wound. The men stood straighter around him, and even the badly hurt tried to stand until he urged them down.

He was good at this. He was the son of the Dux of Taliand and had been born to command, but some nobles were cowards and ineffective. But Ridmark, Calliande thought, had been born to lead men into battle the way an eagle had been born to rule the skies. He could have conquered Andomhaim, had he wished. The histories of Old Earth told of a man called Alexander of Macedon, a ruthless tyrant who had carved an empire of blood founded entirely upon his fearlessness and iron courage, a man whose name still echoed two thousand years later on a world far from Old Earth. Ridmark Arban could have become such a man.

Instead he walked through the church with the brand of a coward upon his face, speaking to the wounded.

He crossed to join her, his staff tapping against the stone floor.

"Calliande," he said.

"Ridmark," she said back. "It is good you are unharmed." She saw spots of dried blood, green and red both, upon his leather jerkin. Dark circles ringed his deep blue eyes, which seemed colder and harder than she remembered. He looked unchanged, but she could see that the fighting had worn on him.

"Thank you," said Ridmark. He looked at Elaine. "Mistress Elaine. Your husband is well, I hope? Sir Joram had to order him from the wall before he fainted."

"He is, Gray Knight," said Elaine. She did a curtsy. "Forgive me, but I must see to the wounded."

Ridmark nodded, and Elaine hurried away, leaving Calliande alone with Ridmark, or at least as alone as they could be in the crowded church. She saw what the older woman was doing, and was mostly amused. Perhaps a little annoyed.

And part of her, more than she would have thought, was grateful.

"How are things here?" said Ridmark. "Sir Joram wanted to visit the wounded, but he feared to leave his post, lest Qazarl launch another assault. So I offered to go in his stead."

"As well as can be expected," said Calliande. "Those we can save, we save. Those we cannot save…we make them as comfortable as we can and wait for the end."

Ridmark nodded. "I have seen field hospitals before, more than I care to recall. You are doing good work, Calliande." He almost smiled. "If we live through this, Sir Joram might well ask you to start a hospital in Dun Licinia."

"Perhaps I will," said Calliande. "Assuming my memory never returns, I will need to learn a trade in order to support myself."

But that was an idle fantasy and she knew it. She still had the empty soulstone. No doubt dark secrets lurked in the swirling mists of her memory.

And Shadowbearer would still be looking for her.

"You could simply wed," said Ridmark, "and have your husband support you."

Calliande laughed. "Indeed? Yes, I would be a prize indeed. A woman with no memory and no wealth, pursued by a renegade high elven sorcerer for reasons she has forgotten." Her laughter faded. "And I might have a husband and children, long dead. I…may have just forgotten them."

"Some of your memory has returned," said Ridmark, "if you recall so much of medicine."

"It is like the other parts of my memory that have returned," said Calliande. "It came only because I needed it. I remembered I could speak orcish because Ulazur and Qazarl and the others only spoke orcish. I remembered I could sense magic because I had that soulstone sitting upon my chest. And I remember I knew something of medicine because I saw so many wounded men. But who taught me to speak orcish or to stitch wounds? I fear I cannot recall."

"If we live through this," said Ridmark, "I will help you to find your memory, if I can."

Calliande shrugged. "Will you not be busy pursuing the Frostborn?"

"They are connected, somehow," said Ridmark. "Your memory and the Frostborn. I do not know how, not yet. I am sure you were put into that sleep because of the Frostborn. Caius thinks I am mad, and Joram thinks I am addled with grief…but the Frostborn are returning. How, I do not know. Perhaps they will be resurrected, or they are simply in hiding…but they shall return." His blue eyes regarded her without blinking. "And you are at the center of it somehow, though I cannot see how."

"I wish I knew," said Calliande. "I wish I could tell you."

"I know," said Ridmark. "But you have comported yourself well. Most women – most men, for that matter – would have been broken by the trials you have experienced since awakening. But not you."

"No," said Calliande. She frowned. "I suspect…I suspect I have lived through worse. But cannot remember it. I do not know if that is a comforting thought or not."

He almost smiled. "I hope you have the opportunity to find out." He glanced at the church doors. "I should go. Qazarl could launch another assault at any moment."

He turned to go.

"Ridmark," said Calliande.

He looked back at her.

"Thank you," she said. "For my life."

This time he did smile, and his blue eyes turned a touch less cold. "You already thanked me for your life, the night we escaped from the ursaar. No need to do it twice."

"You rescued me from the kobolds since then," said Calliande.

"By the time I arrived," said Ridmark, taking a step closer, "it seemed you were well underway to rescuing yourself."

"I would have gotten away," said Calliande, "only to die on the spears of the kobold warriors." She stared at him for a moment, and then shook her head. "I don't understand you."

"What is there to understand?" said Ridmark.

"That brand on your cheek," she said. "You ought to be a craven, a traitor…and you are none of those things. None of them at all. What did you do to get that brand?"

"No one has told you yet?" said Ridmark. His eyes did not turn cold, but…distant. Lost, even. "I should have died here, Calliande. Five years ago, when we faced Mhalek. It would have been better if I had died during the battle. Mhalek would have been defeated, and…much evil would have been averted."

"No," said Calliande. "Never say that, Ridmark Arban. Never. If you had died, I would be dead, Caius would be dead...and God alone knows how many men and women and children within these walls would be dead."

"You almost make me believe it," said Ridmark.

"I believe it," said Calliande, "and I believe in you."

He stared at her, and Calliande felt her heart hammering against her ribs. With a sudden surge of fear, she realized that he wanted to kiss her. And she wanted him to kiss her. She wanted him to do it, right here, and damn the witnesses.

"Calliande," he said, voice rough. "I..."

He leaned forward...and the blast of trumpets echoed outside the church.

Both their heads snapped to look at the church's doors. They knew what the trumpet blasts meant.

Qazarl and the Mhalekites had launched another assault.

"Go," said Calliande. Her throat was dry as dust, and she licked her lips. "Go. They need the Gray Knight. Be careful."

"I am always careful," said Ridmark.

But she knew that was not true.

Ridmark ran through the streets of Dun Licinia, his cloak snapping behind him.

Bit by bit the unfamiliar feelings Calliande had inspired in him drained away.

Not unfamiliar, not really. But...forgotten. He had not felt like that in a long time.

For a brief moment, she had almost made him feel like he was a better man than he really was.

But Ridmark knew better.

For it would have been so much better if he had died here after the orcs were defeated. Mhalek would not then have fled to Castra Marcaine, but would have fought to the bitter end.

And then Aelia would still live.

The trumpets rang over the town, accompanied by the distant boom of the Mhalekite war drums. Ridmark forced all thoughts of the past and of Calliande from his mind. Battle was coming, and he needed all his attention focused on the present.

And perhaps he would die in the fighting, and finally meet his just punishment.

Ridmark ran up the steps to the rampart overlooking the northern gate. Sir Joram stood there, stern in his plate armor, Caius waiting at his side. A cluster of sergeants of the men-at-arms and militiamen waited around their Comes, staring to the north.

At the motionless Mhalekite host.

"Ridmark," said Caius.

"They're not attacking?" said Ridmark, gazing at the orcs. He saw that they had formed themselves into columns around a new set of siege ladders, but despite the constant booming of the drums, they had not yet advanced.

"No," said Joram with a scowl. "I suspect they are trying to intimidate us, to play for time."

"But why?" said Caius. "Time is not on their side. The longer they delay, the more likely it is that aid shall arrive from Castra Marcaine."

"They want to distract us, not intimidate us," said Ridmark, his mind racing through the possibilities. "Qazarl has something planned, and he doesn't want us to notice it. More kobolds over the wall?" He glanced at the sky. "No, it's too bright, and kobolds don't see as well in daylight."

"Perhaps a tunnel?" said Joram.

"I would have noticed the vibrations from the digging," said Caius. "And they have been here only three and a half days. Some of my kindred could have constructed a mine beneath the walls in that time, aye. But these orcs from the Wilderland? Never."

"Reinforcements," said Ridmark. "Qazarl must have reinforcements coming down from the foothills of the Black Mountain, and he wants to mask their approach."

"And," said Joram, "if he has reinforcements, he might have sent them to assail the southern wall while he holds our attention from the north."

"It could be even simpler," said Ridmark. "Qazarl might have split his remaining warriors and sent some of them under cover of darkness to assail the southern wall. If we wait for an attack, and he launches a second attack from the south...he might be able to force his way into the town."

"A desperate move, surely," said Joram.

"It's been three days, and we've taken losses, but the town has held," said Ridmark. "If Qazarl doesn't do something dramatic before the Dux's men arrive, he's going to lose. Assuming he survives the defeat, he'll have to report back to Shadowbearer. And I suspect that would be fatal."

Joram pointed at a militiaman. "Take a message to the southern gate. The sergeant in command is to exercise extra vigilance, and call for reinforcements at once if anything at all seems amiss. Am I understood?"

"Yes, lord knight," said the militiaman with a bow, running for the southern wall.

"That is all we can do for now," said Joram. "We wait until aid arrives, or until Qazarl throws more warriors at..."

The drums stopped.

Ridmark watched the enemy lines, expecting the Mhalekites to begin another assault.

Instead a procession of a dozen orcs marched from the lines. Mzalacht marched at their head, again carrying the lance with the white banner.

"An embassy?" said Caius. "Now?"

"The same reason as before," said Ridmark. "Delay."

The orc herald stopped at the same place as before. Dead orcs dotted the ground here and there. The retreating Mhalekites had sometimes taken their dead and wounded back with them, but sometimes they had not, and dozens of slain orcs lay upon the fields.

The stench was becoming a problem.

"Men of Dun Licinia!" boomed Mzalacht in Latin. "For three days we have struggled, and for three days you have fought valiantly. Again and again you have repelled our assaults."

Joram climbed upon the battlements, armor clanking. "If you have come to state the obvious, do not weary our ears." Laughter rang up around him. "For three days we have repelled you, and we shall repel you for three and thirty more!"

Cheers answered his defiant shout, the defenders shaking their spears and swords at the embassy.

"You can defy us for as long as you wish," said Mzalacht once the shouts had subsided, "but we shall grind you down in the end. Yet why should you die, men of Andomhaim? You will make excellent slaves. We wish to preserve your lives."

"Then turn around and march back into the Wilderland," said Joram, "and we shall all die of old age in our beds."

"Ridmark," murmured Caius, voice low. "Look. There, in the trees, behind the second ladder on the left."

Ridmark followed the dwarf's pointing finger. In the trees, just behind the orcish army, he saw signs of motion. The orcs were working on something. More ladders, perhaps? Maybe siege engines? Yet he doubted the Mhalekites had the engineering skill to build catapults or ballistae.

"They're digging," said Ridmark at last.

"But why?" said Caius. "If they want to dig a tunnel to undermine the wall, that's far too great a distance."

A dark suspicion stirred in Ridmark's mind. "A spell. There are some burial mounds in those woods. Leftover from an old orc kingdom the urdmordar destroyed and enslaved centuries ago."

Caius snorted. "If Qazarl wanted to rob tombs, there are better ways to go about it."

"He might need some old bones for a spell," said Ridmark. "Or there might be something of old magic buried in the mounds. God and his saints, but I should have thought of this earlier. The orc shamans were stronger in the old days, before the High King's realm reached this far north. They learned their dark magic directly from the wizards of the dark elves."

"Or the urdmordar, when it amused the spider-devils to teach their pets sorcery," said Caius. "So it is written in the histories of my kindred. If only Alamur were not a traitor. He might be able disrupt Qazarl's efforts, or at least sense the spell and tell us its nature."

"Aye," said Ridmark. He turned towards Joram, intending to warn him of the threat, but Mzalacht's next words stole his concentration.

"To end this siege," thundered the orc, "Qazarl, the loyal disciple of great Mhalek, proposes a trial by combat. We have chosen a champion, and we suggest that you choose a doughty warrior from among your number. Let him come forth, escorted only by a herald, and meet our champion halfway between your walls and our warriors."

"And the outcome of this duel?" said Joram.

"If our champion is defeated," said Mzalacht, "we shall withdraw from the field and return to Vhaluusk."

"And if our champion is defeated?" said Joram.

Mzalacht laughed. "Then you lay down your arms, open your gates, and become our slaves."

Joram scoffed. "Do you really expect me to accept this ridiculous offer? Our position is strong, and we can hold for months. How much longer will your food last?"

"Joram," said Ridmark, voice quiet.

The knight looked down at him.

"Let me accept this challenge," said Ridmark.

"That is folly!" said Caius. "The orcs almost certainly intend treachery."

"I agree with the good Brother," said Joram.

"No, they don't," said Ridmark. "Well, they do, but not at the duel. Qazarl's up to something in the trees. Some trick...probably a spell, I think. The trial by single combat is only a gambit to buy more time. Qazarl knows help is coming from Castra Marcaine, and he know he has to get inside the walls before it arrives."

"Then why would we aid his distraction?" said Caius.

"Because," said Joram, "distraction plays to our advantage."

"The longer I draw out this duel," said Ridmark, "the longer we have for Dux Licinius's men to arrive."

"Are you sure about this?" said Joram.

"Yes," said Ridmark. "I will delay for as long as I can. And when I am victorious...well, we will see what Qazarl has in mind."

"You are so certain you can prevail?" said Caius.

"I am," said Ridmark.

But he wasn't, not really. He knew the extent of his skill and abilities, and doubted any single orcish warrior could defeat him.

But he had been wrong before.

He remembered Aelia screaming, remembered the blood…

"Very well," said Joram. "Do as you think best."

Ridmark nodded and headed for the stairs.

CHAPTER 21
THE DUEL

The town's gate boomed shut behind Ridmark and Caius with an air of finality.

It sounded rather like a coffin's lid closing.

"You don't have to do this," said Ridmark.

"Nonsense," said Caius. "You are permitted a witness and a herald, to ensure that the trial is fair."

"True," said Ridmark. "And a priest to administer the last rites, if I am mortally wounded?"

"Well," said Caius. "Yes."

"Then let's get on with it," said Ridmark.

He walked away from the gate and towards the Mhalekite host encamped at the edge of the trees. In the distance he saw the foothills and the dark mass of the Black Mountain itself. He knew the orcs were too far away for a bow shot, yet nonetheless his skin itched, and he felt the urge to take cover.

Ridmark stopped a dozen paces from the orcish embassy. Mzalacht looked him up and down and sneered.

"You are the champion?" said the herald. "The ragged Gray Knight and his pet dwarf? You are the best that Dun Licinia could muster in its defense?"

Ridmark shrugged. "If I die, no great loss."

"And it is my wish," said Caius, "that you repent on your sins, and join us in brotherhood and amity in the Church."

Mzalacht spat. "Pathetic. We ought to kill you here and now, and insist that the humans send out a worthier champion."

Ridmark met his eye. "Try."

Mzalacht looked away first.

"So be it," said the orc. "Remain here until our champion and his attendants arrive."

"Attendants?" said Ridmark. "The agreement was that we would come alone to the field."

Mzalacht laughed. "Fear not, Gray Knight. You have your dwarven priest, do you not? The champion requires his attendants. But they will not harm you."

The herald turned and walked towards the Mhalekite host, his guards following.

"Can you see what they're doing in the trees?" said Caius, once Mzalacht and his party were out of earshot.

"Not from here," said Ridmark. "There are too many orcs blocking the view."

Another roll of drums came from the Mhalekite host, and the orcs started to cheer, thrusting their weapons into the air. Four orcs emerged from the army and walked towards him. The orc in the center was tall, almost seven feet, and wore only trousers and boots. Bruises marked his chest, and...

"Ah," said Ridmark, understanding.

Caius looked at him.

"Kharlacht," said Ridmark. "The orcs' champion is Kharlacht. It seems Qazarl decided to rid himself of two problems at once."

As they drew closer, Ridmark saw that Kharlacht wore an iron collar, two chains hanging from it. The orcs accompanying him held the chains on either side, while Mzalacht followed them, still carrying the spear with its white banner.

They stopped a dozen paces away.

Kharlacht's eyes met Ridmark's. The big orc looked utterly tired, both in body and spirit.

"Behold!" roared Mzalacht. "Our champion. He betrayed the sons of Mhalek, aiding our foes and helping our enemies to escape our wrath! Now he shall redeem himself by striking down the champion of the humans...or he shall perish upon this field!"

The orcish army roared, their cheers struggling against the jeers and shouts of the defenders upon the wall.

"You've looked better," said Ridmark, once the shouting faded away.

"Aye," said Kharlacht.

"Perhaps you should not have returned to Qazarl," said Ridmark.

Kharlacht grimaced, deep lines etching his green-skinned face. "Perhaps. But I could not betray my kin, and I returned to Qazarl. He was...wroth."

"I can imagine," said Caius.

"He would have killed me on the spot," said Kharlacht, "but his advisors convinced him that I might be useful later."

"Silence!" said one of the orcish warriors with the chains. "You will not..."

Kharlacht growled, seized the chain, and yanked the warrior close. His hand closed hard around the orc's throat, and the warrior's face began to turn a darker shade of green.

"Do not presume," he snarled, "to threaten me."

Both Mzalacht and the other orc drew their swords and pointed the blades at Kharlacht.

"Release him!" said Mzalacht.

"You're going to kill your champion for me?" said Ridmark. "That does seem to defeat the purpose."

Kharlacht let the warrior go. "Bring me my armor and weapons and be gone. Now!"

The orcs unlocked the collar around his neck and produced a gambeson. Kharlacht pulled it on, and Mzalacht handed him a canvas sack. Kharlacht removed the blue steel plates of his armor from the sack and donned them one by one, covering his torso and arms in a carapace of steel. At last Mzalacht handed Kharlacht his massive dark elven greatsword, and then took a judicious step back.

The two orcs who had held Kharlacht's chains walked away, while Mzalacht drew a circle in the earth around Ridmark and Kharlacht.

"This circle defines the boundaries of the trial," said Mzalacht. "Forty paces wide. If you are forced outside the circle, you lose the duel. If you flee outside the circle, you lose the duel. Otherwise the trial by single combat shall continue until one of you are unable to continue and submits by raising your left arm." The herald grinned. "Or until one of you are slain. Are these terms acceptable?"

"They are," said Caius, "though I shall be watching for treachery."

"As shall we, dwarf," spat Mzalacht. "The blood gods shall grant us victory."

Caius smiled. "But your champion does not even pray to the blood gods. They may be...disinclined, shall we say, to favor your side?"

Mzalacht sneered. "Then both our champions can perish. The blood gods do not favor the weak." He stepped out of the circle, as did the other two orcs.

"Caius," said Ridmark, both hands on his staff.

"May God be with you," said the dwarven friar, stepping out of the circle.

Leaving Ridmark alone with Kharlacht.

"Begin!" roared Mzalacht. "Fight! Fight, and know that the honor and the glory of your kindred go with you!"

Kharlacht lifted his greatsword in both hands and strode forward with a slow, steady pace. Ridmark shifted his staff to one hand and walked to meet him. He was not certain he could defeat Kharlacht in single combat. Ridmark was fast and strong…but so was Kharlacht, and his greatsword was a more potent weapon than Ridmark's heavy staff.

They stared at each other for a moment, Kharlacht's sword held in both hands, Ridmark's staff resting low at his side.

A deathly silence fell over both the town and the fields as the defenders and the Mhalekites waited for the combat to begin.

"You don't have to do this," said Ridmark.

Kharlacht shook his head. "I must. It is my duty to my blood."

"This trial by combat is a sham," said Ridmark, "and you know it as well as I do. If I kill you, Qazarl will not retreat to the Wilderland, and if you kill me, Joram will not surrender the town."

"I know," said Kharlacht.

"Qazarl is only doing this to buy time," said Ridmark, "to finish whatever spell he is working in the woods."

"I also know this," said Kharlacht.

"What is he doing?" said Ridmark. "If you are willing to tell me." If he survived the trial, he could bring the information back to Sir Joram.

"That I know not," said Kharlacht. "Some spell of black sorcery, I am sure. He had his warriors digging up the old burial mounds for days. He found…something, some relic, and then called me forth to fight as champion."

"He cares nothing for you," said Ridmark.

Kharlacht scowled. "And you do?"

"I respect you as a worthy foe and an honorable man," said Ridmark, "which is more than Qazarl can say."

Kharlacht said nothing.

"He will cast you aside," said Ridmark, "when this is done. If he prevails, he will have you killed. If he is defeated, he will blame his defeat upon you and kill you for it."

"But he is my blood kin," said Kharlacht, "all that is left of it in this world. I cannot forsake him. Not until he has forsaken me."

"You are loyal beyond reason," said Ridmark. "No man would blame you for turning your back upon Qazarl."

"Perhaps not," said Kharlacht, "but I would know."

Ridmark thought of Aelia and Mhalek, the great hall of Castra Marcaine ablaze with the crimson glow of Mhalek's black magic. "I understand that."

"You, too, are an honorable and a worthy foe," said Kharlacht. He sighed. "I regret greatly that the bonds of blood require that I kill you."

"And I regret," said Ridmark, lifting his staff, "that I must kill you."

For the first time Kharlacht smiled, the hard, merciless smile of a man who had nothing left to lose. "If you can."

He surged forward, his greatsword a blur of blue steel as he struck.

But Ridmark saw the blow coming and stepped to the side, the dark elven greatsword falling past him to hit the ground. Had the sword struck him, the power of Kharlacht's blow would have cut him open from neck to navel. Ridmark swung his staff, hoping to land a hit on Kharlacht's head. But Kharlacht ducked, the edge of Ridmark's staff brushing his topknot, and lashed his sword at Ridmark's legs. The swing did not have much power behind it, and Ridmark lowered his staff and deflected the blade. He launched a thrust at Kharlacht, hoping to catch the orc in the throat, but Kharlacht snapped his sword up and sent the thrust bouncing away.

They stepped apart, weapons raised.

Ridmark heard a distant roaring. For a moment he thought it was the sound of his blood rushing through his veins, but then he realized it was the cheering. The Mhalekites were shouting "victory" in orcish, over and over again, while the defenders upon the wall of Dun Licinia were bellowing Ridmark's name in defiance.

Kharlacht advanced, and Ridmark took a step back, his mind racing through potential attacks. The orcish warrior was stronger than Ridmark, and almost as fast. His huge greatsword gave him reach to match the length of Ridmark's staff, and his dark elven steel protected him from blows to the chest and stomach.

No armor on his throat or head, though. Or upon his legs. And while his sword matched the reach of Ridmark's staff, it was a slower weapon. Ridmark could grip his staff anywhere, and Kharlacht could not do the same with his sword. In the time that it would take Kharlacht to retract his sword and prepare the massive weapon for another blow, Ridmark could adjust his grip on the staff and land two or three quick hits.

At least, he thought he could.

If he was wrong, at least he would die quickly.

Ridmark thrust his staff towards Kharlacht's face. Kharlacht retreated, sword deflecting the staff. The orc beat aside Ridmark's next attack and charged, his greatsword sweeping in a vicious sideways cut. Again Ridmark dodged, the blade just missing him to strike the ground. Kharlacht's stroke was neither sloppy nor hasty, and at once Kharlacht regained his balance, his weapon coming up to block.

But in that brief moment, Ridmark had a chance to strike.

He shifted his grip and thrust, and the end of his staff slammed into Kharlacht's left wrist. The big orc grunted and staggered, and Ridmark thrust again, his staff striking Kharlacht's left leg. Kharlacht jumped back, his sword coming up in guard, and Ridmark circled away.

"You fight well," said Kharlacht. He opened and closed his left hand several times and then put it back on the hilt of his sword.

"Thank you," said Ridmark.

"But you are alone," said Kharlacht. "You have no nest of drakes to unleash against me. No pack of spitfangs to drive into a frenzy. Only your own strength and wit to wield. Will that be enough?"

"We shall find out, will we not?" said Ridmark. "But if it was so easy to defeat me, you would have done so already."

"Indeed," said Kharlacht, and the orcish warrior flew at him. Ridmark backed away as fast as he could manage, trying to keep Mzalacht's circle in sight. He glimpsed Caius saying a prayer, saw Mzalacht and his guards laughing in anticipation. Trying to block Kharlacht's sword with his staff was an invitation to disaster, but Ridmark could not keep dodging. Kharlacht's furious attack would not last forever, but he needed to only land one hit to cripple Ridmark.

But Ridmark saw the way Kharlacht's huge sword could become a weakness. At the nadir of his swings, before he could draw back the weapon, Kharlacht's balance was slightly off. And if Ridmark struck the flat of Kharlacht's blade then, he could land a quick hit on the orcish warrior.

Kharlacht swung, and Ridmark dodged and lashed his staff against the flat of the greatsword's blade. The orc staggered, tightening his grip to keep from having the sword knocked away, and for a moment he was open. Ridmark jabbed his staff, and the end slamming the steel plates covering Kharlacht's stomach. Kharlacht stumbled with a grunt, the breath exploding from his lungs. Before he could catch his balance, Ridmark struck again, aiming his staff for Kharlacht's right knee. Kharlacht swept his sword in a wide arc, deflecting the staff and forcing Ridmark to step back.

He circled around the orcish warrior, forcing Kharlacht to turn to keep him in sight.

"This is a useless strategy," said Kharlacht. "Your weapon cannot penetrate my armor. It will not even dent dark elven steel."

"No," said Ridmark. An idea came to him. "But you have no armor about your throat or head, do you? Which seems unwise. A man can live without a few fingers, but he cannot survive with a crushed windpipe."

"Indeed," said Kharlacht, and attacked.

His sword came at Ridmark in a sideways swing, but not quite as fast as before. The weight of his armor and sword was slowing him down and draining his stamina. Ridmark dodged the first swing, the second, and then the third, Kharlacht driving him towards the edge of the circle. By the sixth swing, Kharlacht's movements had slowed just enough for Ridmark to slap his staff against the flat of the orc's blade. Kharlacht stumbled, and Ridmark reversed his staff and drove the end at the warrior's throat.

Kharlacht saw the blow coming and stepped back, sword coming up to guard his face.

But Ridmark's attack had been only a feint, and he reversed the staff, driving the end towards Kharlacht's right knee. At the last instant Kharlacht realized his peril and jumped back, which kept the staff from shattering his kneecap. Still the blow landed with a loud crack, and Kharlacht stumbled with a grunt of surprised pain. Ridmark whipped his staff around and swung the weapon into Kharlacht's midsection. Again Kharlacht's armor absorbed the hit, but the power of the strike knocked the orc on his heels. He stumbled back several steps, breathing hard, his sword held out before him to ward off any attacks.

Ridmark circled to his left, and Kharlacht turned to keep him in sight.

The shouts of the defenders grew louder, the bellows of the orcs angrier and more ragged.

"I admit," rasped Kharlacht, his tusked face tight with strain, "that I underestimated you at first."

"Oh?" said Ridmark.

"I thought you a madman with a stick," said Kharlacht. "A true warrior, I believed, carried a sword. Not an axe, not a spear, and certainly not a quarterstaff. A sword."

"When I was a squire, first learning the sword," said Ridmark, "I grew arrogant in my skill. This displeased my father, who sent me to spar with his bailiff, a low-born man who had never carried a sword in his life, who fought with a quarterstaff. I boasted I would teach this impudent peasant his place, and show him that a knight of Andomhaim could defeat any low-born churl."

"What happened?" said Kharlacht.

Ridmark felt himself smile. "The bailiff gave me such a thrashing that I could not sit down for a week."

Kharlacht threw back his head and roared with laughter. Ridmark could have ended the fight then, could have thrust his staff and crushed the orc's throat, but he did not.

He already had a heavy burden upon his conscience. No reason to add to it.

"It seems," said Kharlacht, recovering himself, "that you have learned that lesson well."

"I did," said Ridmark. He kept circling, Kharlacht turning to keep him in sight. "There was one other lesson that man taught me, one both applicable to single combat and to leading a host of fifty thousand men."

"What lesson is that?" said Kharlacht. He kept turning, wincing as his weight shifted upon his bruised leg.

"The key to victory," said Ridmark, "is to apply your strength to your enemy's weakness, and to do so without mercy."

"And how will you apply that lesson here?" said Kharlacht, resignation settling over his features.

"You cannot hit me," said Ridmark, "but I can hit you."

He charged at Kharlacht, his staff spinning. Kharlacht got his sword up, but again and again Ridmark landed minor blows, his staff darting through the brief instants Kharlacht took to recover his balance. None of the blows were particularly serious. But every one of them caused Kharlacht pain, drained away a bit of his strength and endurance.

And every blow that struck his right leg made him wince.

At last Ridmark's thrust caught Kharlacht's right knee, and the orc stumbled. Ridmark sidestepped, reversing his staff, and swung the weapon against the back of Kharlacht's knee. The orcish warrior bellowed in sudden pain as his leg folded beneath him, and Ridmark swung his staff with all his strength.

The staff caught Kharlacht across the forearms, knocking the dark elven greatsword from his hands. Kharlacht reached for the weapon, and Ridmark's next thrust slammed into his forehead.

It was not enough to kill him, not even enough to render him unconscious, but it was enough to send him sprawling to the ground.

Ridmark rested the butt of his staff on Kharlacht's throat.

One brief flex of his arm, and he could crush Kharlacht's windpipe.

Kharlacht blinked, his black eyes swimming back into focus.

"Do it," he rasped. "You vanquished me fairly and without trickery." He closed his eyes and relaxed. "Do it, and send me to join Lujena." Ridmark wondered who that was. One of Kharlacht's dead kin, perhaps? The one who had inspired such loyalty to family in him? "Do it and end my misery."

Ridmark said nothing.

Utter silence had fallen over the field. He saw Mzalacht and his guards staring at him, aghast. No doubt they had expected Kharlacht to prevail. The defenders watched in silence from the ramparts. He saw Caius watching him, expression solemn.

The orcish army remained motionless. Yet beyond the trees Ridmark caught glimpses of activity. Qazarl was up to something, and the trial by combat had gained him time to prepare it.

Perhaps it would be best to simply kill Kharlacht and force Qazarl to show his hand.

"I accept," said Ridmark, lifting his staff from Kharlacht's throat, "your surrender."

Kharlacht opened his eyes, frowning.

Ridmark shifted his staff to his left hand and extended his right. After a moment, Kharlacht took it, and Ridmark pulled him to his feet.

"You have fought well and with honor," said Ridmark, "and therefore, I accept your surrender."

Kharlacht blinked. "But...I did not..."

Ridmark turned to Mzalacht. "I have prevailed in this trial by single combat, and by the terms of the agreement, Qazarl and his warriors shall withdraw from this siege and return to the Wilderland."

Mzalacht's mouth opened and then closed again, and then he looked to his warriors, as if for assistance.

"I was defeated," said Kharlacht. "By Qazarl's own word, he must withdraw from the field."

The herald spat. "You deliberately lost the fight, you are a weakling coward enslaved to the god of the humans, and…"

Kharlacht growled, his eyes glazing red with the orcish battle fury, and the ground jolted beneath Ridmark's boots.

He looked around, as did the orcs and Caius. Again the ground shook, and a cold wind sprang up from nowhere, tugging at Ridmark's cloak. The wind stank of sulfur and carrion, of dead things left in the dark.

Mzalacht began to laugh. "Behold! The wrath of the blood gods come! In Mhalek's name, Qazarl has awakened their wrath. You shall perish! You…"

A pillar of blood-colored fire erupted from the trees behind the Mhalekite host.

Ridmark saw movement between the town and the orcs.

All across the field, the dead orcs were beginning to move.

Ridmark turned in astonishment, while Caius muttered a prayer. The dead orcs were standing, getting to their feet, picking up whatever weapons lay at hand. Most had hideous wounds marring their torsos and faces, and some had bloated from decomposition. Yet they were moving nonetheless.

And their eyes shone with the same blood-colored light as the pillar of flame rising from the trees.

"Qazarl!" roared Kharlacht. The orc snatched his fallen greatsword and pointed it at the trees. "Qazarl! What treachery is this? You agreed that if I was defeated our army would withdraw from the field! Have you betrayed your word?"

Mzalacht laughed. "Fool! Do you think Qazarl would keep his word when given to human vermin? The wrath of the blood gods has come, and you will perish alongside the humans!" His eyes gleamed with battle fury. "Kill him! Kill them all!"

Mzalacht charged, roaring, and his guards did the same. Ridmark sprang to meet them, staff in both hands, and killed Mzalacht with a single powerful blow that snapped the orc's head back. One of the warriors lunged at him, only to meet Caius's descending mace. Bone crunched, and the orc fell lifeless to the field.

The last warrior drew back his sword to strike, but Kharlacht moved first. Blue steel blurred, and the warrior's head jumped off his shoulders with a spray of green blood. The corpse toppled, and the head rolled away.

Ridmark glanced at Kharlacht in surprise.

"Qazarl has betrayed his given word," spat Kharlacht, "and he has betrayed me as well. He swore that if you prevailed in the trial, he would withdraw from the field. He is a liar...and he has made a liar of me. I must aid you until this crime is expunged."

Ridmark nodded. "Glad for your help."

"Stand fast!" shouted Caius. "The dead are coming!"

Two of the undead orcs staggered towards them, broken arrows jutting from their chests. One drew back its fist to punch at Ridmark, and he raised his staff in a block. The sheer power of the undead orc's fist hammered into the staff like a missile from a catapult, and Ridmark stumbled back. He caught his balance and went on the attack, swinging his staff. The dead orc was supernaturally strong, but it was slow and Ridmark was not. In quick succession he shattered its knees and its elbows, and the orc collapsed as its legs would no longer support its weight.

Yet still the vile thing crawled towards him. The dead would not feel pain. Would Ridmark have to cut the corpse to pieces to stop it?

That would be a challenge with his staff.

Kharlacht bellowed as the second undead orc charged him, dodged its blow, and brought his sword around. His strike took the orc's head from its shoulders, a spurt of congealed, greenish-black blood bursting from the stump. The corpse collapsed, and Ridmark waited for it to get back up.

But it remained motionless.

"Their heads," said Kharlacht. "Removing their heads seems to cancel whatever black sorcery Qazarl used to animate these fools."

"Indeed." Ridmark hurried to the corpses of Mzalacht and his guards and plucked an axe from a dead warrior's back. It was a crude weapon, the haft rough, the crescent steel blade showing spots of rust. Yet it was heavy enough, and with it Ridmark could take off a head or two.

"We need to get back to the town," said Caius.

"Aye," said Ridmark. Hundreds of dead orcs had risen, and now all of them attacked Dun Licinia's northern wall. Arrows and crossbows did not slow them, and the undead orcs pulled themselves up the wall by sheer strength. "Qazarl will launch an attack while the undead distract the defenders." He looked at Kharlacht. "Will you come with us, or will you leave? Qazarl might have betrayed us, but he is still your blood kin, and..."

"No," said Kharlacht. "I will follow you into battle, Gray Knight. Qazarl is my blood kin, but he used me to work deception. The same blood ties that bound me to him now bind me to oppose him."

"Good," said Ridmark. He looked at the melee raging along the ramparts. "They dare not open the gates for us. Let us make for the western rampart and scale the wall." He secured the axe to a loop on his belt, turning the weapon so it would not slice his leg open. "Then we can aid Sir

Joram against…"

Blood-colored light danced over the slain herald and his guards, and the dead orcs rose in eerie silence. Ridmark turned to face them and felt a chill, his eyes straying to the slender pillar of bloody fire rising from the trees. Qazarl's spell was still active. That meant that any orcs slain in the fighting would rise as undead.

Even as the thought crossed his mind, the drums boomed, the orcs shouted, and the Mhalekite host surged forward.

They were charging right towards Ridmark.

"Qazarl," said Ridmark. "We've got to get to Qazarl. If we can kill him, it will cancel the spell and break the sorcery upon the undead."

"Aye," said Caius, "but how are we to reach him?"

The orcish warriors charged towards them, howling. They did not bother with shieldbearers to protect the ladders now, not with the defenders of Dun Licinia struggling to hold the undead at bay.

Ridmark opened his mouth to answer, and the blast of a trumpet rang out.

But it came from the southeast, not from the walls of the town.

From the road leading to Castra Marcaine.

Ridmark whirled and saw horsemen galloping past the town, knights and men-at-arms in steel plate and chain, gleaming lances and swords in their hands. At their head flew a green banner with a white hart, the sigil of the Dux of the Northerland.

And beneath the banner he glimpsed the white light of a Soulblade drawn in battle, burning in the hand of a Swordbearer.

Help had come from Castra Marcaine at last.

Ridmark only hoped that it hadn't arrived too late.

CHAPTER 22
CALLING THE FIRE

"They said the dead have risen and fight alongside the Mhalekites," said Elaine, her voice full of fear.

"Yes," said Calliande, closing her eyes. "I know."

She felt the pulse of the blood magic to the north, of the dark and filthy power Qazarl had conjured. She knew Qazarl was strong, but she had thought such a feat of sorcery beyond his reach. Yet she felt something…augmenting his magic, something old and strong and dark as the Black Mountain itself. Some relic of ancient sorcery, she suspected, something he had found.

No. Something that Shadowbearer had told him to find.

She was sure of it.

"Perhaps…perhaps we should move out of the church, my lady, before it's too late," said Elaine.

Calliande opened her eyes. "Why should we do that? If the town falls, there is nowhere to run."

"Before the dead below the church rise," said Elaine, her voice trembling.

"Oh," said Calliande. "No, we needn't worry about that. Qazarl's spell will only raise slain orcs. I think he used his own blood to empower it. Trying to use orc blood in a spell to raise a human corpse would be like…oh, trying to drink water to get drunk. You'd just make a mess."

Elaine stared at her. "How do you know that?"

"I don't really know," said Calliande, "but I do." She took a deep breath. "Get ready for more wounded. The undead are terrible foes, and…"

She blinked.

She felt the wrath of Qazarl's spell writhing to the north, a dark fire

201

that entered the orcish dead and commanded them to fight. But she felt another power, a closer power.

Something within the town.

And she recognized it.

Shadowbearer.

He was here. Somehow he had gotten inside the town.

"My lady?" said Elaine. Some of Calliande's fear must have shown on her face.

"I have," said Calliande, swallowing, "I have to go."

Shadowbearer was here, and he would come for her. And he would kill anyone who tried to stop him. He would butcher everyone in the church, all the wounded and all the women and all the halfling servants, just to get at her. She would bring more death upon these people, just as her presence had brought Qazarl and his Mhalekites and his undead to Dun Licinia.

Calliande had to flee, at once. She would take the soulstone and escape through the southern gate. With luck, that would draw Shadowbearer and his black magic away from the town, away from these innocents...

But something within her, something hard and cold, recoiled at the prospect.

No. She was through running. Shadowbearer and his servants had pursued her from the Tower of Vigilance, through the Deeps, and into Dun Licinia. And if she had indeed slept in that vault since the defeat of the Frostborn, that meant he had pursued her across the centuries.

And she was done running, done letting other people die for her.

"Elaine," said Calliande, "you are in charge here. There is something I must do."

"But my lady..." said Elaine.

But Calliande was already running for the doors, her skirts gathered in her hands.

Ridmark struck again and again, his staff vibrating in his hands.

Mzalacht's corpse came at him, his grating voice forever stilled, and reached for Ridmark's throat. Ridmark dodged, his staff spinning, and shattered first the herald's right knee and then his left. Mzalacht fell, and Ridmark dropped his staff, snatched the axe from his belt, and took off the orc's head in two chops.

Mzalacht's corpse slumped motionless to the ground. Ridmark spun, saw Caius shatter the knee of another undead, staggering the creature, and allowing Kharlacht to behead it with a single mighty blow of his dark elven steel.

"Gray Knight!" boomed Kharlacht, turning to the north. "They come!"

The tide of orcish warriors rushed at them, brandishing weapons.

Ridmark shoved the axe back into its loop, snatched up his staff, and met the enemy.

Kharlacht and Caius fought back to back, the huge orc towering over the dwarven friar. Caius's heavy mace stunned and disabled the orcish warriors, leaving them open for Kharlacht's sword. The two turned around each other, carving a bloody swathe through the tide of charging orcs. Ridmark fought at the edge of the chaos, his staff stabbing and thrusting and swinging. His blows cracked skulls and crushed throats, and sent the Mhalekites tumbling to the earth. Or his strikes stunned the orcs long enough for Kharlacht to take their heads off with a sweep of his dark elven steel.

It was more efficient that way. A beheaded orc could not rise again as an undead. For the dead orcs did rise again, and attacked anew. Whenever they did, Caius, Kharlacht, and Ridmark had to turn their attention to the undead, forcing Ridmark to abandon his staff for the far heavier and slower axe.

Even worse, the living orcs were surrounding them. The orcish host had fallen into disarray, with some charging for the walls of the town, and others attempting to form up to face the horsemen galloping from the southeast. But more and more were surrounding Ridmark and the others, forcing Ridmark back towards Kharlacht and Caius step by step.

Soon he would not have enough room to swing his staff or raise his axe, and then they would die. Ridmark slammed the butt of his staff into another orc's throat, dodged a thrust, and raised the staff in an overhead swing, stunning a second orc. Both crumpled to the ground, but four more rushed to take their place, and three undead staggered towards him.

He could not take them all at once.

Then a wall of horsemen slammed into the orcs.

Two of the orcs went down at once, trampled beneath steel-shod hooves. Another turned with a snarl, raising his axe, only for a lance to pierce his chest. One of the undead orcs turned towards a knight, but the knight swung a crescent-bladed war axe, all the strength of his arm and the momentum of his horse driving the blow. The blade sheared through the undead orc's neck and sent its body toppling to the bloody grass.

The knight turned towards Kharlacht and raised his axe.

"No!" shouted Ridmark, moving between the knight and Kharlacht. "He is on our side. Hold!"

The knight squinted at him, and the horsemen thundered around them, driving back the orcs.

"My lord Swordbearer!" shouted the knight, turning in his saddle. "You were right! It is him!"

Another horseman rode closer, a white light shining in his hand. As he drew closer, Ridmark saw that the light came from a longsword of gleaming steel, a rough white crystal shining at the base of the blade. Waves of magical power seemed to roll off the weapon.

A Soulblade, the enchanted blade of a knight of the Order of the Swordbearers.

A wave of longing and pain shot through Ridmark as he gazed at the weapon. He had once carried the Soulblade known as Heartwarden into battle, had used it to slay an urdmordar and numerous other creatures of dark magic. But then Mhalek had come and Aelia had perished, and Ridmark had been stripped of the blade, the brand burned upon his cheek.

The Swordbearer reined up and removed his helmet. He had a lean, olive-skinned face, with curly black hair and bright green eyes. He was young, no more than twenty-five, and Ridmark recognized him with a shock.

Sir Constantine Licinius, the Dux Gareth Licinius's eldest son.

And Aelia's sister.

Calliande ran into the square, following the pulse of icy magic against her senses, and headed for the castle.

The keep was deserted. Every last man able to hold a spear or carry a shield had been called to the wall, and Calliande heard the sounds of frantic battle ringing over the town.

The cellar. Shadowbearer's presence was coming from the cellar of the keep. Alamur was down there. Had Shadowbearer come to rescue his wayward minion?

Or to discipline him?

Calliande took a deep breath to steady herself and touched her belt. The dagger Ridmark had given her still rested there. It would be of little use against a wizard of Shadowbearer's might.

But it made her feel better nonetheless.

She passed through the courtyard and headed the keep's doors.

"Sir Ridmark Arban," said Constantine. "My God, it really is you. Father and I thought you died years ago. We heard the tales of the Gray Knight, of course, and we thought of that cloak Ardrhythain gave you after Urd Morlemoch. But I never dreamed you were still alive."

"I am," said Ridmark, his fingers tight around his staff. He had feared he might meet Constantine or his father here, and he had expected anger, fury, even an outright attack.

Not amazement.

"Why didn't you come back to Castra Marcaine?" said Constantine, bewildered.

"You know why," said Ridmark.

Constantine smote his saddle's pommel. "Damn it, Ridmark, it was not your fault. It was not!" Brightherald, his Soulblade, blazed brighter in his fist in response to his anger. "I do not care what lies Tarrabus Carhaine poured into the ears of the High King, lies that you seemed to believe. And what Imaria said...well, she was half-mad with grief. It was not your fault. You should have come back to Castra Marcaine. Father would gladly have made you a knight of his household, even one of his Comites. We..."

The dead orcs at the hooves of his horse started to move.

"Constantine!" said Ridmark. "Beware!"

The dead orcs surged to their feet and lunged at Constantine's horse.

But the Knight of the Soulblade was ready for them.

Brightherald came down in a blaze of white light, and took off the first undead orc's head in a flash. Two others came at the Swordbearer, and Constantine loosed powerful strokes. The magic of his Soulblade enhanced his strength and speed when he called upon it, and the power of the Soulblade was proof against dark magic.

In a matter of heartbeats all five undead orcs had been dispatched.

"God and his saints," said Constantine. "Undead? Are these orcs followers of an urdmordar? Or perhaps a dark elven necromancer?"

"Neither," said Ridmark. "They follow Qazarl, one of Mhalek's disciples."

Constantine's eyes hardened. "I remember Qazarl. Father thought he might have escaped your victory. He has returned to work mischief?"

"Aye," said Ridmark. "It is a long story. Qazarl worked a spell to raise his slain warriors as undead. If we do not find him and kill him, I fear the town will fall."

"Then let us find Qazarl," said Constantine, "and put an end to him at last." He glanced at Kharlacht and frowned. "Your orcish companion bears curious armor."

Kharlacht bowed, and Ridmark said, "This is Kharlacht of Vhaluusk, a baptized son of the Church and a most valiant warrior."

"Is he? Your word is good enough for me," said Constantine.

It should not have been. Ridmark wanted to tell him that, but then Constantine spotted Caius.

"Brother Caius!" said Constantine. "It is good to see you are well. Castra Marcaine's halls are darker without your preaching. I take it your mission to bring the holy word to the orcs of the Wilderland did not go well?"

Caius shrugged. "I fear not, my lord knight. Though it is with a small note of relief that I point out this attack is not in response to my preaching."

Constantine laughed. "The gravest fear of every preacher, I am sure. Come! Let us strike down Qazarl and deliver the town from its peril!"

He sounded so confident. Ridmark had known confidence like that once. He had known victory after victory, and had even led the host of the High Kingdom to victory over Mhalek himself...

Aelia's screams echoed in his ears.

He shoved aside the memories the sight of Constantine had stirred up. He could not afford to rebuke himself, not until Qazarl had been slain and the people of Dun Licinia saved.

"He is in the trees," said Ridmark. "This way."

And to his unease, Constantine and his escort obeyed without question.

Calliande slipped into the cellar below the keep.

Into the dungeon.

Though the dungeon was really more of a storeroom. Narrow windows close to the ceiling admitted grainy light, revealing sacks of grain stacked against one wall. A third of the cellar had been divided off with a row of iron bars, a door set in their middle.

Alamur, the Magistrius, sat in the center of the impromptu cell, bound wrist and ankle to a wooden chair, a blindfold over his eyes and a gag over his mouth to keep him from working magic.

Yet Calliande felt Shadowbearer's power in the cellar. Was the renegade high elf lurking the shadows, preparing to strike her down? She suddenly felt foolish for bringing the empty soulstone with her. Yet if she had left it behind, Shadowbearer could find it just as easily once she was dead.

A shadow moved, and Calliande stepped back.

Alamur's shadow was moving, rotating around him.

She saw the disgraced Magistrius shiver, saw sweat trickling down his brow and into his stained white robes.

Then the shadow reached over him, covering him like a shroud...and the gag in his mouth turned to dust. Alamur spent a few moments coughing and spitting, but then began to speak in a rapid, terrified voice.

"Master, I...I have done as you commanded," said Alamur. "I..."

"Be silent."

Calliande flinched, recognizing Shadowbearer's strange, reverberating voice. She looked around, expecting to see the wizard.

But the voice was coming from the shadow enveloping Alamur.

"I did as you bade me, Master," said Alamur, a terrified whine in his voice.

"Did you?" said Shadowbearer. "I told you to secure the woman and the soulstone once they came to Dun Licinia. Instead I find you bound and gagged like a pig trussed for the slaughter."

"But I kept your secrets, Master!" said Alamur, his terror intensifying. "I did not tell them the truth! I said...I said I served you for blood spells, for forbidden magic. I said nothing of your true intent."

"How admirable," said Shadowbearer. "How shall I repay such...daring initiative? I am sure I can think of a suitable reward. Perhaps I ought to make an example of you..."

"Please, Master!" said Alamur, shuddering. Calliande saw his eyes darting back and forth behind the blindfold. "Please! Give me another chance! One more chance, and I will prove to you that I am worthy." Tears streamed into his beard. "Please, just don't...don't..."

"Give you immortality...of a sort?" said Shadowbearer, the alien voice thick with amusement. "Oh, don't worry, Alamur. I wouldn't give you immortality. The thought of listening to you whine for the next thousand years is appalling. But you are fortunate. I have only thirteen months before the influence of the great conjunction passes, and I am in something of a hurry. So you are going to get one more chance. Exactly one."

The shadow slithered around the bound Magistrius, and the ropes on his wrists and ankles turned to dust.

"Find the woman Calliande and the empty soulstone," said Shadowbearer, "and bring them to the standing stones south of the Black Mountain. Bring her to me unharmed, Alamur. Unharmed! And the soulstone must be empty. If I find a single scratch upon her, or you attempt to work a spell using that soulstone...I shall be most displeased."

"I will not fail you, Master," said Alamur. "I swear it."

"Your devotion is ever so touching," said Shadowbearer. "Now go. Qazarl has launched his final assault upon the town. He may prevail, or he may not. It is of no concern. But the fighting occupies the woman's defenders. Now is your best chance to take her."

"Yes, Master," said Alamur.

"Go," said Shadowbearer, and the strange shadow vanished.

And as it did, the remaining ropes and the blindfold crumbled into dust.

Calliande took a step back. She had to find Ridmark, or Sir Joram, and warn him that Alamur had broken free.

Then the Magistrius's dark eyes fell upon her.

Sir Constantine and his escorts carved their way through Qazarl's host.

Ridmark jogged alongside their horses, striking at any target that presented itself, but few did. The massive charge of Constantine's horsemen had broken the orcish host, and most of the survivors fled for the foothills of the Black Mountain. Those that remained offered little resistance against a charge of heavy horsemen. Ridmark remembered the power of such a charge, his horse thundering beneath him, Heartwarden shining in his fist…

He pushed aside the thought.

But every orc they slew would only rise again as an undead puppet, dancing on the strings of Qazarl's sorcery, and Constantine's Soulblade could not be everywhere upon the field. Sooner or later the undead orcs would wear down the horsemen and seize the town.

Unless they found Qazarl first.

The horsemen reached the edge of the trees and slowed. Ahead Qazarl's strange pillar of flame rose into the sky, painting the nearby trees with a bloody light. Ridmark hurried forward as the horsemen picked their way over the roots and the needles, Kharlacht and Caius following him. The ancient orcish burial mounds lay off the road, in a clearing ringed by pine trees.

He stepped past the last tree and into the clearing, the space dominated by a grass-covered mound about twenty feet tall. Someone had dug into the mound's southern slope, and the air shivered and buzzed with the presence of potent dark magic.

Qazarl stood atop the mound, a strange staff in his right hand.

Its length had been fashioned from orcish leg bones bound with corroded bronze wire, and the tusked skulls of three orcs adorned its top. The empty eyes of the orc skulls blazed with crimson fire, and the staff shivered and pulsed in Qazarl's hand in time to the fire rising overhead.

A flame, Ridmark realized, that appeared directly above the bone staff itself.

"Gray Knight!" shouted Qazarl, his voice gleeful, his white beard rippling in the icy wind. "I had hoped you would come here. You defeated Mhalek here…and here you shall die. Poetic, no?"

Ridmark said nothing, Kharlacht and Caius joining him.

"And you, traitorous cousin," said Qazarl, pointing the staff at Kharlacht. "I am glad you have declared your allegiances at last. If you love the god of the humans so much, then you can perish with the humans."

"Qazarl," said Kharlacht as the horsemen entered the clearing. "This is madness. Do you think this plan of yours will bring you victory? You cannot conquer the Northerland, let alone the realm of Andomhaim."

Qazarl laughed. "Do you think this is about conquest? Fool boy! The world is changing. Did you not see the blue fire fill the sky, just as Shadowbearer predicted? The old era of the world is passing. A new age has come…and the humans shall be slaves. If they even survive at all."

Constantine swung down from the saddle and pointed Brightherald at the orcish shaman. "Qazarl of the Wilderland! I am Constantine, Knight of the Soulblade and son of the Dux of the Northerland. By his authority, I command you to cease your black magic, gather your host, and depart the realm, never to return. Otherwise you shall face my justice."

"Shall I, boy?" said Qazarl. "Your wretched little sword is useless here."

"This Soulblade was forged to defeat dark magic," said Constantine, "as you shall soon find out."

"Yes," said Qazarl, his voice heavy with mockery, "you shall break my spells with your sword, and then the Gray Knight shall beat me to death with his stick. Or you shall all die here. Shall we find out who is right?"

He struck the butt of the staff against the earth, the jaws of the tusked skulls clattering.

The ground shuddered…and hunched shapes erupted from the earth. Orcish skeletons, wearing corroded bronze armor, ancient swords in their bony hands. Long ago they had been buried here, to attend their chieftain in the next world.

And now they rose to kill at Qazarl's bidding.

A dozen of the undead warriors charged at Ridmark and Constantine.

"Ah," said Alamur. "Isn't this fortuitous?"

Calliande turned to run, but Alamur was faster.

The Magistrius gestured with his good hand, summoning power. Invisible force slammed into the cell door and ripped it free from its hinges with a shriek of tortured iron. Calliande flung herself to the side, and the edge of the door clipped her leg. The impact knocked her from her feet. Alamur strode out of his cage, and Calliande tried to stand, but the Magistrius gestured again.

She felt the surge of magic as invisible force seized her, threw her across the cellar, and slammed her against the stone wall. The same force kept her pinned against the wall, her boots dangling a few inches above the floor. Calliande strained against the force, trying to move, but it was too strong.

Alamur walked towards her, hand extended, white light glimmering around his fingers.

Again Calliande reached into her mind, trying to find some memory of magic. If she could find a way to counter Alamur's spell, she could break free of him.

But again, nothing happened.

"The Master was right," murmured Alamur, stopping a few paces away. "He did give me one more chance." He laughed. "And here you are, walking right into my grasp. Why?"

"I sensed him," spat Calliande. "Shadowbearer."

Alamur raised an eyebrow. "And you thought to...confront him? To defeat him?" His dark eyes widened. "Which means...you have the means to defeat him..."

He took several alarmed steps back. He was terrified of her, Calliande realized. But why?

Did he believe she had the power to destroy him?

"Yes," she said, hoping to delay. "I came to destroy him, but I suppose I shall have to settle for you."

Terror flashed over Alamur's face, and she thought he would run from the cellar.

"No," he said at last. "No. If you had the power to kill me, you would have done so already. You wouldn't let me hold you like this." The fear faded from his expression, the confidence returning. "Which means...it will be easy enough to subdue you and deliver you to the Master."

"Are you so sure of yourself?" said Calliande.

"Yes." He smirked. "You don't even know who and what you are, do you? The Master knows. But you don't. And when I deliver you to the Master...you will die in your ignorance."

He strode towards her, hand raised.

###

The skeletal orcs charged at Ridmark and Constantine, their bronze swords flashing in the bloody light.

"Take the shaman!" shouted Constantine, raising Brightherald over his head.

"Kill them!" screamed Qazarl, gesturing with the staff. "Kill them all!"

Ridmark met the first of the skeletal orcs. The undead thing stabbed at him, and Ridmark sidestepped, sweeping aside the thrust with a jerk of his staff. He began raining blows down upon the skeletal orc, sending cracks through the yellowed bones. His fifth blow ripped the tusked skull from the skeleton and sent it tumbling across the grass.

The skeleton wavered and collapsed.

Constantine proved even more effective. Brightherald blazed in his fist, and he struck down three of the undead in rapid succession. The magic binding their bones burned away at the touch of the soulblade, and the

Swordbearer cut through them with ease. Ridmark smashed another of the skeletons, his eyes turning to Qazarl at the top of the mound. The shaman's defenses were crumbling, and if Ridmark could get close enough to strike a killing blow…

Qazarl shouted, struck the staff against the mound, and flung out his hand. A torrent of blood-colored fire erupted from his fingers, the grass withering to ash beneath its passage, and slammed into Constantine. The Swordbearer stumbled, raising his sword in guard. A Soulblade had the power to ward its bearer from hostile magic, and the blade shone with white light, Qazarl's bloody fire snarling and snapping.

The trees rustled, and more undead orcs emerged from the forest, summoned from the battlefield.

"Their heads!" shouted Ridmark, smashing the skull of another skeletal orc. "Take their heads!" He saw the undead driving back Constantine's knights. Kharlacht and Caius fought back to back, the dwarf's mace smashing the bones of the undead, Kharlacht's whirling greatsword taking their heads.

But there were too many of the creatures, and Qazarl loosed blast after blast of magic, keeping Constantine pinned in place. The Swordbearer could deflect the shaman's blasts, but he could not advance, not while Qazarl continued his attack.

And with that strange bone staff, it seemed unlikely that Qazarl's strength would wane.

"Perish!" roared Qazarl, and the undead closed around them.

"I'm afraid," said Alamur, stopping just out of reach, "that this will inflict a considerable amount of agony on you."

Calliande struggled, trying to tear free of his spell, but his will was too strong.

"A simple spell, that is all," said Alamur, "to dampen your will and make you a bit more…tractable." Purple light glimmered around his hand. "A spell I learned from the Master, as it happens. You yourself held the scroll. Now you shall get to experience it firsthand. A privilege, no?"

"You are a traitor and a coward," spat Calliande.

Alamur smiled. "On the contrary. I am a man with the vision to see that the order of the world shall soon change, and the courage to seize the opportunities for power. Like this."

He gestured, a pulse of purple light washing over Calliande, and she felt his will hammer into her mind, his magic sinking into her thoughts.

###

The undead orc toppled before him, its dead black eyes staring up at him. Ridmark snatched the axe from his belt, raised it high, and brought it down onto the orc's neck.

Two blows later, the undead orc's head rolled from its shoulders, and the corpse collapsed to the ground.

Ridmark grabbed his staff, the melee swirling around him. A limping orcish corpse staggered towards one of Constantine's knights, and Ridmark attacked from behind, his quick blow breaking one of the orc's legs. The undead thing fell to one knee, and the knight beheaded it with a powerful swing.

And for a moment, just a moment, Ridmark was free to move.

He shot a quick look around the clearing. Qazarl flung another gout of fire at Constantine, and the young Swordbearer swayed beneath the fury of the attack. Brightherald's light was starting to dim. The sword had great magic, but the weapon's strength matched the power of its wielder, and no man could bear up under such an assault for long. Sooner or later, Constantine would fall.

And then Qazarl could turn his magic against the rest of them.

Ridmark had to get to the shaman.

But he could not do it alone.

He raced forward, knocking down an undead in his path, and made his way to Kharlacht and Caius. The friar and the warrior battled together, keeping any of the undead from making their way to Constantine. A skeletal orc stabbed at Caius, and the dwarf blocked the blow on his mace. Ridmark came up from behind and swung once, twice, three times. His staff shattered the bones of the orc's right leg, and the undead thing tottered.

Caius's mace came down upon the top of its skull, shattering the yellowed bone to a dozen fragments.

"Qazarl," said Ridmark, breathing hard, and both Kharlacht and Caius looked at him. His arms and shoulders ached, sweat dripping down his face...but the battle was not over yet. "This isn't over until we get Qazarl."

"Then I suggest," said Caius, "that we get him."

Kharlacht nodded, and the three of them cut their way through the undead, making for the burial mound.

"You will obey me," said Alamur, his voice echoing in Calliande's ears and thundering inside her head. "You will obey me. By the power of this spell and the strength of my will, I compel you to obey me. Obey!"

Calliande shuddered, his magic sinking deeper into her thoughts. She felt it reshaping her thoughts, forcing her to obey.

But as before, when she had faced Talvinius, fury rose up inside her, rage that Alamur should abuse his magic, rage that he had betrayed the people in his care to their deaths at Qazarl's hands.

And with that rage the white fire welled up inside her again.

The fire burned away Alamur's spell, though his will still held her fast.

"That is not possible!" hissed Alamur. "You don't know who you are. You can't do that!"

Calliande gritted her teeth. "Try that again and I'll show you what I can do."

"No," said Alamur. He surged forward, his uninjured hand locking around her throat, and Calliande felt his thumb digging into her windpipe. "When you pass out, I'll carry you out of here like a sack of meat. The Master wants you alive. I suppose he will forgive a few bruises."

Calliande gagged, pawing at his hand, but the Magistrius was stronger than she was. Her arms twitched, her hands falling to her sides.

Her right hand brushed the handle of the dagger Ridmark had given her.

With a last desperate burst of strength, she yanked the dagger free of its sheath and stabbed.

The blade sank into Alamur's side.

The Magistrius fell back with a scream, and Calliande fell in a heap, coughing, as both his magical and physical grasp released. Alamur grabbed his side, his eyes wide as blood stained his white robes.

"You...you stabbed me," he whispered. He sounded more surprised than anything else.

Calliande staggered to her feet. "Then you should not have tried to take me to Shadowbearer."

Rage blossomed over his face. "Then die!" He lifted his left hand, purple light snarling and hissing around his fist. Calliande recognized the spell. It was an attack of dark magic, a spell that would shatter her mind and stop her heart.

He was going to kill her.

Alamur thrust out his fist, shouting in rage as a ball of purple flame leapt from his hand, and Calliande reacted on instinct.

Her hands came up, calling the fire within her, and a hazy shield of white light appeared before her. Alamur's spell struck the shield with a sound like a sword hitting a cuirass, and she felt the strain of his will pressing against hers.

But her will was stronger.

He flinched in sudden horror.

Much stronger.

Calliande's will drove back his...and the ball of purple fire rebounded from her shield and slammed into him.

Alamur screamed and fell, his eyes bulging, the purple fire dancing up and down his limbs. He struck the ground and lay motionless, his face forever frozen in a mask of utter horror.

Calliande walked towards him, numb, and yanked her dagger free, cleaning the bloody blade upon his robes before returning it to its sheath. She had learned to do that, somewhere.

She stared at the corpse…and a fact impressed itself upon her mind.

The white fire still shimmered below her thoughts.

She raised her left hand and stared at it, calling the fire. Patterns flashed through her mind, spells and symbols and formulae, and a pale glow surrounded her fingers.

Magic. The white fire was magic, called from the ancient Well at Tarlion's heart, and it was hers to summon and command.

She was a Magistria. Or, at least, she had once been a Magistria.

But now she was again.

Her head turned towards the stairs, Alamur's corpse forgotten. Even in the cellar, the distant sounds of fighting came to her ears. The town of Dun Licinia was about to fall without aid.

The people of the town needed her.

Ridmark needed her.

Calliande grabbed her skirts and ran for the stairs.

Ridmark charged for the burial mound, Kharlacht on his right and Caius on his left. Qazarl's fire surged past them, hammering into Constantine. Qazarl's magic could keep Constantine pinned in place, preventing the Swordbearer from bringing his soulblade to bear against the undead. Once the undead had disposed of Constantine's companions, the undead could tear the Swordbearer to pieces.

Unless Ridmark killed Qazarl first.

An undead orc lunged at him, and Ridmark dodged, his staff driving into the orc's knee. The undead stumbled, and Kharlacht moved into the gap. His heavy blade sheared through the undead orc's neck, and corpse and head both tumbled down the side of the burial mound. A skeletal orc attacked Caius, and he swung his heavy mace with both hands. The joint of the skeleton's left knee exploded into powder, and the undead fell.

The path was clear to Qazarl himself.

The shaman stood atop the burial mound, left hand gripping the staff of bones, right thrust towards Constantine. A constant stream of blood-colored fire erupted from his fingers, the air shivering with the power of it. A nimbus of crimson light swirled around him. Qazarl looked like a demon risen from the pits, a horror come to wage war upon the living.

He looked, Ridmark thought, a little like Mhalek.

He charged at the shaman, and Kharlacht and Caius raised their weapons.

But Qazarl reacted first, leveling the bone staff, the tusked skulls clattering. A pulse of red light, and a wall of unseen force slammed into Ridmark. The blast knocked him over, but he tucked his shoulder and rolled, regaining his feet. He saw Kharlacht lying motionless, saw Caius rolling to the base of the hill. Had the spell knocked them unconscious?

Or had Qazarl simply killed them?

"A pity," said Qazarl, looking at Kharlacht. "He was such a capable…"

Ridmark attacked, all his strength behind his blow.

His staff plunged towards Qazarl's head, only to rebound from the nimbus of red light.

"Did you not think I would ward myself against your weapons?" said Qazarl. He shook the staff, the skulls grinning at Ridmark. "All that power…and I would spare none to protect myself? In the end, I am stronger in than Mhalek ever was." He leveled the staff. "Farewell, Gray Knight."

The red light glowed brighter, filling Ridmark's vision.

Calliande ran up the stairs and reached the ramparts of the northern wall.

The battlements were slick with blood, and all around her men-at-arms and militiamen struggled against the undead orcs. The dead things climbed up the walls by sheer strength, throwing themselves upon the living men. The defenders were holding their own, but barely. Beyond the ramparts she saw the chaos of the battlefield, saw horsemen flying the banners of Castra Marcaine and Dux Gareth Licinius.

And she saw the pillar of crimson flame rising from the burial mounds in the woods, felt the harsh wrath of Qazarl's magic.

"My lady!"

She saw Sir Joram standing behind the struggling militiamen, his armor and surcoat spattered with blood both red and green.

"Go back to the castle!" he said. "I do not know if we can hold here. Go…"

But Calliande sensed the black magic animating the dead orcs, the blood spell that made them dance and jerk upon the strings of Qazarl's will.

And she knew the spell to break those strings.

Calliande closed her eyes, crossed her arms over her chest, and reached for the white fire within her. It came at her call, and her mind directed the power through the structure of a spell.

"My lady!" shouted Joram. "Go!"

She opened her eyes, saw three of the undead break through the line and reach for her with cold, dead hands.

Calliande smiled and released the spell.

A ring of white light erupted from her, passing through the living men and the dead orcs alike, spreading over the northern rampart. The light touched the living men without harm. But wherever it touched the dead orcs, they fell like puppets with cut strings, smoke pouring from their mouths and nostrils.

In a matter of heartbeats Calliande's magic destroyed every last undead orc attacking the walls of Dun Licinia.

She swayed as a wave of dizziness washed through her. Expending that much power had taken a great deal. Magic, she realized, was limited by stamina. What she had just done was like carrying a dozen forty-pound sacks of flour up a flight of stairs.

All at once.

"My lady!" Sir Joram grabbed her arm. She was grateful for the support. She had not survived Shadowbearer and Qazarl and Alamur only to lose her balance and fall to her death from the walls. "Are you...are you well?"

"I think so," said Calliande, blinking as the spinning stopped.

"That spell...it was well-timed," said Joram. "Those fiends would only stop fighting once we chopped off their heads. You...you are a Magistria?"

"It would appear so," said Calliande. "Ridmark, where is Ridmark?"

"I do not know, my lady," said Joram. "He fought the duel with the orcish champion, and then the horsemen from Castra Marcaine arrived, and he followed Sir Constantine into the woods."

Calliande slipped from his grasp and moved to the battlements. In the distance she saw the pillar of Qazarl's magic rising from the trees, felt the power rolling off it in burning waves. Qazarl himself was likely there.

Which meant Ridmark was almost certainly there, if Qazarl had not killed him already.

She knew what she had to do.

"Get ready to catch me," she told Joram. "I'm going to cast a spell, and then I'm likely going to pass out."

Joram started to speak, but she ignored him and summoned power, as much as she could handle, the white fire blazing around her. Calliande gestured, her mind forcing the magic into the shape she desired, and flung out her hands.

A ball of dazzling white flame erupted from her palms and shot over the battlefield, plunging into the woods.

She saw the white flash of its impact, and then everything went black.

The crimson nimbus around Qazarl shone brighter, and then the world exploded around Ridmark.

White fire filled his vision.

But the flame passed through him without harm. The burial mound shook beneath his boots, and he drove his staff into the earth, leaning on it to keep his balance. The white flame faded away, and he saw Qazarl staggering back and forth, his eyes glassy.

And his crimson nimbus had vanished.

The white fire, whatever it was, had broken the shaman's protective spells.

It was Ridmark's last chance.

He ran forward, his staff coming up, and struck. Qazarl shook out of his stupor and raised a hand to cast a spell, but it was too late. Ridmark hit him across the face with the staff, and the shaman staggered back. His next blow ripped the staff of bones from Qazarl's grasp. Qazarl roared and lifted his hands, bloody fire brightening around them.

Ridmark brought his staff down with enough force to break Qazarl's right wrist. The shaman howled in pain, and Ridmark drove his staff into Qazarl's gut, reversed it, and swung it against Qazarl's knee.

The shaman collapsed upon his back, clutching his wounded wrist, and Ridmark raised his staff to land the killing blow.

"It won't matter!" spat Qazarl.

Ridmark hesitated.

"You've beaten me," said Qazarl. "Killing me changes nothing. The new order is coming, Gray Knight. Shadowbearer has foreseen it. The world shall change...and the Frostborn will return." He grinned, his mouth full of blood from the staff's impact. "Kill me...and the Frostborn will still return."

"Perhaps," said Ridmark, "but you will not see it."

He hammered the staff down.

CHAPTER 23
THE HERO OF DUN LICINIA

Calliande drifted in a strange white mist, cool and clammy.

The mist filled her mind.

She saw the sad-eyed old man in the white robe, the old man whose image had greeted her as she awakened beneath the Tower of Vigilance. She realized his white robe was the robe of a Magistrius, the same kind of robe Alamur had worn. He had been one of the Magistri...as had she.

"I knew you, didn't I?" said Calliande.

The old man offered a sad nod, his tangled gray beard brushing his collar.

"Who are you?" said Calliande. "Tell me. Who am I? Please, tell me."

"I cannot," said the old man. "You have denied yourself your memories, for good and proper reasons. I admit I thought your plan folly. I still do. But it was wise to conceal your memory. Otherwise Shadowbearer would have plucked your secrets from your mind...and now all would be lost. The gate would be open, and ice would devour the world."

"Please, say plainly what you mean," said Calliande. "Speak not to me in riddles."

"I cannot," said the old man, "for you have forbidden it."

"Then what can you tell me?" said Calliande.

The old man thought for a moment. "Only that you may call me the Watcher, and that you must not tell anyone of me. Your plan...your plan has gone badly awry. The Order of the Vigilant was to greet you upon awakening, to take you to the appointed place, but they fell victim to their own corruption and perished. So you must carry on in the Order's stead. Beware Shadowbearer. He knows that you are a threat to him and his servants...and he will be hunting you."

"I will," said Calliande. "But can you tell me nothing more?"

"Only this. To find your answers, you must find your staff."

"My staff?" said Calliande. Shadowbearer had asked her about a staff. That, and a sword. He had seemed very eager to find both. "Where is my staff?"

"At Dragonfall," said the old man.

"I don't know where that is," said Calliande.

"Few do. You did. Shadowbearer does. And he will seek you," said the Watcher. He closed his eyes. "Be careful, my lady. A great burden lies upon you...and you alone can carry it."

"I shall," said Calliande. She felt a great affection for the old man, and desperately wished she could remember more about him. "Thank you."

"My prayers go with you," said the Watcher.

He began to fade into the mists.

"Will I see you again?" said Calliande.

"I will await you," said the Watcher, "at Dragonfall."

He vanished, and Calliande felt herself drifting again. The mist flickered with visions. Again she saw herself speaking to the council of old men in robes, arguing her case. She saw armies marching to war, herself riding at their head. Sheets of glowing blue ice spreading to cover the land, tall figures in armor the color of pitted ice walking before the glaciers, swords that burned blue in their hands.

A knight wielding a sword of red gold that burned with flame.

A twisted staff of oak, shining with a pale white light.

And a laughing shadow in a long red coat, a shadow that hunted her across the centuries...

The mist swallowed Calliande, and she knew no more.

Calliande's eyes fluttered open.

She sat up, confused. She lay in a narrow bed, clad in a loose nightshirt. The bed occupied a small castle room, the walls and ceiling of stone, a shaft of sunlight falling through the narrow window. Brother Caius sat in a chair below the window, eyes closed and a book open upon his lap.

She heard a rasping noise, and realized that Caius was snorting.

"Caius?" she said.

"Eh?" said Caius, his strange blue eyes opening in his gray-skinned face. "I was not sleeping. I was merely resting my eyes."

"What happened?" said Calliande. "Where am I?"

Caius closed his book. "You, Magistria, are in your chamber at the keep. Sir Joram brought you here."

"What happened with the battle?" said Calliande. "Qazarl and the orcs? And Ridmark...did he fall..."

"No, Ridmark was fine, when last I saw him," said Caius. "When you attacked Qazarl, it broke his protective spells. Ridmark was able to strike him down, and once the shaman was dead, his spell over the undead broke. Sir Constantine's men were able to sweep the Mhalekites from the field." He sighed. "I fear it was a great slaughter. Some of the orcs escaped, but not many. If Qazarl gathered all that remained of Mhalek's followers, then the Mhalekites have been reduced to only a few ragged bands."

"How long have I been asleep?" said Calliande.

"Two days," said Caius.

She rubbed her face. "I fear I might have overexerted myself."

"Your overexertion decided the battle and restored your memory," said Caius. "The effort appears to have been worthwhile."

"No," said Calliande. "My memory did not return. Just...just my powers. It appears I was indeed a Magistria during the war against the Frostborn two centuries ago. But none of my memories have returned. Just my skills with magic. Or some of them."

Caius snorted. "Give that your skills with magic saved my life, I am grateful for them. Qazarl would have slain us all, had you not struck."

"Was Ridmark hurt?" said Calliande.

"No," said Caius. "He came through the battle unscathed." He hesitated. "He...spoke with me, to make sure you were well, once the battle was over. And then he departed Dun Licinia."

"He departed?" said Calliande. "Why? He saved the town! He slew Qazarl, you said so yourself."

Caius stood. "Perhaps you should speak to Sir Joram and Sir Constantine. They asked to talk with you, once you awakened." He bowed. "I shall send one of the servants to help you dress."

A short time later Calliande entered the great hall of the keep, wearing a clean gown, the dagger Ridmark had given her sheathed at her belt. Caius walked at her side, his heavy boots clicking against the flagstones.

Sir Joram Agramore waited at the table, clad again in mantle and tunic. At his side sat a handsome man of about twenty-five, with curly black hair, olive-colored skin, and bright green eyes. A sheathed longsword hung at his belt, and Calliande felt the power of the magic gathered in the weapon...and in the soulstone worked into the blade.

The sword was a Soulblade, which meant that black-haired knight was a Swordbearer.

Both men rose as she approached.

"My lady Calliande," said Joram with a bow, "you do us honor. Or shall I address you as the Magistria Calliande now?"

"For all your kindnesses to me," said Calliande, "you may address me however you wish."

"And since your magic defeated the traitor Alamur and helped us defeat Qazarl," said Joram, "I wish to address you with the highest honor." He gestured to the younger man. "This is Sir Constantine Licinius, son of the Dux Gareth Licinius of Castra Marcaine, and a Knight of the Order of the Soulblade."

Constantine bowed, and Calliande gripped her skirts and did a curtsy.

"My lady Magistria," said Constantine, "I thank you for your aid. With Alamur turned traitor, we were at a sore disadvantage against Qazarl. If you had not unleashed your magic when you did, I fear we would all have been slain, and Dun Licinia would now be ashes."

"Thank you, my lord Swordbearer," said Calliande, "but the credit properly goes to the man known as the Gray Knight, Ridmark Arban. He saved my life, not once but many times, and his skill at arms helped Sir Joram defend the town."

Joram snorted. "Now you do me a kindness. Ridmark defended the town. I was merely along for the ride, as it were."

"Ridmark refused all reward," said Constantine, "and departed for the north as soon as he was sure you were safe."

"Why?" said Calliande. He had promised to help her find the truth of her past. "Why did he leave?"

Constantine sighed. "I fear it was my fault. I...reminded him too much of the past."

"What past?" said Calliande. "My lords, forgive me for being blunt...but what happened to Ridmark? He utterly refused to speak of it."

"Aye," said Caius. "I have rarely seen a warrior of such boldness and skill, whether among my own kindred or yours. For a man like him to bear the brand of a craven and a traitor...I cannot fathom it."

Constantine and Joram shared a look.

"He was the best of us," said Joram. "We were all squires together, in Dux Gareth's court, and he was the boldest and the most skilled. He achieved everything he set his mind to accomplish."

"I hated him at first, I admit," said Constantine. "But I was just a boy, and I was jealous that his father, the Dux of Taliand, had greater prestige than my own father. But Ridmark had no pride in him. He befriended us all...and helped teach me and my brothers the use of the sword."

"He became a Swordbearer at eighteen," said Joram, "one of the new-made knights that old Master Galearus selected. And he did deeds of tremendous renown. At eighteen, he slew the urdmordar Gothalinzur. A lone, new-made Swordbearer, and he slew an urdmordar matriarch. Such a feat...I would not have believed it, had any other man than Ridmark done it."

"He told me a little of it," said Calliande, remembering their discussion in the Deeps as the others slept.

"When the high elven archmage Ardrhythain himself came to my father's court to ask for a Swordbearer to undertake a perilous quest," said Constantine, "my father chose Ridmark. He ventured into the ruins of Urd Morlemoch and confronted the Warden, the dark elven sorcerer that rules over that evil place. And he was victorious!" He looked at the ceiling and sighed. "And my sister Aelia loved him. Ridmark asked my father for her hand in marriage, and he consented gladly."

"And then Mhalek came," said Joram. "He declared himself a living god, and led a huge host into the Northerland. He invited the leaders of the High King's host to a parley and slaughtered them. It would have been a disaster…but Ridmark took command of the host and crushed the Mhalekites utterly."

"But Mhalek escaped," said Constantine.

Suddenly the haunted looked in Ridmark's blue eyes made sense.

"And when he escaped, he went to Castra Marcaine, didn't he?" said Calliande.

Joram nodded. "You are wise, Magistria."

"Ridmark left the army and pursued," said Constantine. "Mhalek had taken Aelia captive."

"What did Ridmark do?" said Calliande, horrified.

Constantine looked away.

"He killed Mhalek," said Joram, "before the Dux's seat in the great hall of Castra Marcaine. But he did not know that Mhalek had worked a spell joining his blood to Aelia's. One final cruelty. Any wound Mhalek received would be dealt to Aelia as well."

"God's mercy," said Caius. "So when Ridmark struck down Mhalek…"

Constantine nodded. "I fear my sister perished as well."

She remembered Ridmark's grim face, the echo of pain in his blue eyes.

"But why did the Order expel him?" said Calliande. "He did nothing wrong. His wife's death was on Mhalek, not him! He couldn't have known about the spell."

"I thought the same," said Constantine, "as did my father, and most of the other chief nobles. But Tarrabus and his lot thought otherwise."

"Tarrabus?" said Calliande. She did not recognize the name.

"Tarrabus Carhaine," said Joram, "the Dux of Caerdracon. We were squires together, at Castra Marcaine…and he always hated Ridmark. He blamed Ridmark for Aelia's death, accused him of cowardice for leaving his army in the field. The new Master of the Order was undecided, but

Tarrabus can be persuasive. And Ridmark…I think Ridmark agreed with them. The heart went out of him after Aelia died. He did not even try to defend himself. Tarrabus forced the Order to expel him, strip him of his Soulblade, and brand him as a coward. His father and brothers turned their back on him."

"How is he still alive?" said Calliande. "From what I understand…if a Swordbearer is severed from his Soulblade, he quickly loses the will to live."

"It does not often come to pass that a Swordbearer is expelled from our Order," said Constantine, "but when it does, the former Knight usually wastes away. But Ridmark…Ridmark is not the sort of man to lie down and die."

"The Frostborn," said Caius. "He believes the Frostborn are returning."

"The Frostborn are extinct," said Joram. "Some of the things Gothalinzur and the Warden told him made him believe the Frostborn would return. But they are extinct, a relic of the past." He sighed. "Or so I thought. After your arrival, my lady, and Qazarl's attack…I am not so sure."

"He believes the Frostborn shall return," said Constantine, "and has spent the past five years searching. And along the way, he has helped people, saved them from pagan orcs and creatures of the wild and worse things. Hence the legend of the Gray Knight." Constantine spread his hands. "And that, my lady, is the tale of Ridmark Arban. I fear he is condemned by a harsher judge than any other in the realm."

"His own conscience," said Joram.

Calliande stood in silence for a moment. Many of the things Ridmark had said and done made a great deal of sense now. Little wonder he regarded his own life so lightly.

He did not care if he lived. Perhaps he even believed he deserved death.

"If you will forgive the question, my lady Magistria," said Constantine, "what shall you do now?"

Calliande blinked. "Oh?"

"We thought you might go to Tarlion," said Joram, "to speak with the Masters of the Order of the Magistri. They might have the spells to repair at least some of your lost memories."

Calliande thought of Talvinius and Alamur. How many more Magistri were like them?

"Perhaps," she said.

"If not," said Constantine, "you would be welcome at my father's court. The Northerland is a perilous land, and Qazarl and his Mhalekites are hardly the only dangers we face. A valiant Magistria would have a place of honor among us."

"Or you could stay here, if you forgive my presumption," said Joram. "Since Alamur was a traitor, we now have no Magistrius among us, and the Masters of the Order will investigate his death before they deign to send a replacement. It could be months before we have a new Magistrius, and Dun Licinia sorely needs one. We are at the very edge of the realm, and your magic would be a welcome aid."

Calliande thought it over. She could see herself settling here, helping the people of the Northerland to build their homes and keep the dangers of the Wilderland at bay.

But she still didn't know who she was. She was a Magistria, that was plain, but that told her very little.

And Shadowbearer would hunt for her and the empty soulstone in the pouch at her belt.

And the Watcher had told her to find him and her staff at Dragonfall.

"I think," said Calliande, "that I know what I must do now."

CHAPTER 24
THE FOUR

Ridmark strode alone through the trees, the dark mass of the Black Mountain rising to the east.

The vast wilderness of the Wilderland stretched before him, forest and swamps and mountains and plains.

Of course, the wilderness wasn't empty. Tribes of pagan orcs lived beneath the trees, warring against each other and their neighbors. Urdmordar built petty kingdoms from the shadows, feasting upon their victims. Packs of beastmen migrated across the land, hunting prey and their foes. Kobolds raided from the tunnels of the Deeps, as did dark elven princes. Wyverns flew overhead, and beasts of ancient dark elven sorcery hunted in the darkness.

Ridmark knew it well. He had spent five years wandering the Wilderland, traveling to lands no man of Andomhaim had ever seen, seeking for evidence of the return of the Frostborn.

And now he had seen blue fire fill the sky, just as the Warden had predicted...and Ridmark knew where he had to go.

Urd Morlemoch awaited him.

It lay far to the northwest, on the shore of the cold northern sea, near the border between the Wilderland and the Three Kingdoms of the dwarves. It had once been a mighty fortress of the dark elves, tens of thousands of years old, and from there the dark elves had waged their endless war against the high elves.

And then the dark elves had summoned the urdmordar, intending to use them as slave soldiers against the high elves...only to find themselves enslaved by the urdmordar. The High King, the Magistri, and the Swordbearers had smashed the urdmordar, wielding magic taught to them by Ardrhythain, but Urd Morlemoch remained, ruled by its undead Warden.

The undead dark elven wizard who had taunted Ridmark with his warning of the blue fire, the omen that would herald the return of the Frostborn.

Now that omen had come, and Ridmark would wring the truth of it from the Warden.

He kept walking, the ground smoothing as he left the foothills of the Black Mountain behind.

Caius might have come with him, had he asked, and possibly Calliande. Joram would have sent an escort of men-at-arms, and Constantine would have convinced his father to summon his knights and Comites, and march to Urd Morlemoch in force.

But if they went with Ridmark, many of them would die, and he did not want any more deaths on his conscience.

Again he heard Aelia screaming, her eyes staring up at him, full of shocked betrayal, the blood pooling around her...

Ridmark shook his head and kept walking.

It was better to go alone.

He had promised Calliande that he would help her find her memory, and he regretted leaving her behind. But it was just as well. She had come into her full powers as a Magistria, and the Masters of the Order of the Magistri could help her recover her memories.

And she was somehow connected to the Frostborn. For some reason the Order of the Vigilant had put her into a magical sleep for centuries below their castle. Ridmark suspected if he solved the riddle of the Frostborn, he would also answer the question of Calliande.

He kept walking.

But right now, he had more immediate problems.

Such as the fact that someone had been following him for the last mile.

Ridmark entered a clearing and looked around. He would have enough room here to wield his staff effectively. Of course, if his pursuers had archers among their number, they could shoot him. But he did not think they had any bows.

In fact, he thought there was only one man after him.

Ridmark waited, and after a moment a tall figure in gleaming blue armor stepped into the clearing.

"Kharlacht," said Ridmark.

"Gray Knight," said Kharlacht. The hilt of Kharlacht's greatsword rose over his right shoulder, and various cuts and bruises marked his face. He walked with a slight limp, but seemed otherwise unharmed.

"I sought you after the battle," said Ridmark, "but you were gone."

"Aye," said Kharlacht. "It seemed wisest to go. With Qazarl slain and his host broken, the knights from Castra Marcaine would kill any orc they could catch. Better to be gone, rather than try to explain myself."

"Sensible," said Ridmark.

Kharlacht nodded, his topknot bobbing, and said nothing.

"You're here to kill me, then?" said Ridmark, fingers loose around his staff. "I slew the last of your blood kin, and now you're here to kill me in turn?"

"No," said Kharlacht. "Qazarl…was the last of my blood kin, aye. But now he is slain. And he brought his death upon his own head. Even if I had never met you, Gray Knight, Qazarl still would have met his doom. Sooner or later he would have been overwhelmed and slain."

"If you are not here to kill me," said Ridmark, "then why are you here?"

"I wish to follow you into battle," said Kharlacht, "and aid you in your quest."

Ridmark blinked. "Why?"

"Because I owe you a debt," said Kharlacht. "You spared my life outside the walls of Dun Licinia. You could have slain me fairly and honorably…but you did not. I owe you my life, and I would see that debt repaid." He paused. "And your quest seems a good one."

"My quest?" said Ridmark.

"You did not speak of it to me, but I am neither blind nor deaf," said Kharlacht. "You seek to stop the return of the Frostborn."

"The Frostborn are extinct," said Ridmark. "The High King wiped them out two and a half centuries ago."

"So your nobles claim," said Kharlacht, "yet you have heard rumor of their return. And I listened to Qazarl and Shadowbearer speak in the dark hours of the night. They, too, were certain the Frostborn would return. Loyalty to my kin bound my tongue before, but Qazarl claimed the Frostborn would return the on day of the blue fire. That was why he wished to assault Dun Licinia. He desired to seize the town and offer it as a gift to the Frostborn, that he might earn the favor of the new masters of the world."

Ridmark nodded. That explained much.

"A terrible danger is coming," said Kharlacht, "and it seems that only you see it and seek to stop it. I would aid you, if I can."

"I am going to Urd Morlemoch," said Ridmark.

Kharlacht's expression did not change, but the skin around his eyes tightened. "A name of dread and fear among my kindred."

"A name of dread and fear among all kindreds," said Ridmark. "Nine years ago, the Warden that rules over the ruins told me of the omen of blue fire. Now it has happened. I will return to Urd Morlemoch and force the Warden to tell me more…and I will learn how the Frostborn will return.

And if it is in my power, I will find a way to stop it."

"I shall aid you," said Kharlacht.

"We might die," said Ridmark. "If there is anything else you wish to do, anywhere else you wish to go…you should do it now."

"I have nowhere else to go," said Kharlacht. "All my kin are dead. I was once betrothed to a woman of my kindred…but she, too, is dead, and I hope she resides with the Dominus Christus in paradise."

"I can understand that," said Ridmark.

"There is nothing else for me to do," said Kharlacht. "So I will follow you. If you will have me."

"Come," said Ridmark. "If we start now, we can likely make another ten miles before nightfall."

They walked into the woods.

"Are you sure about this?" said Caius as they walked through the woods.

"Absolutely," said Calliande.

She had traded her gown for a leather jerkin, trousers, heavy boots, and a thick cloak to ward off the chill. Behind them walked a train of four pack mules, laden with supplies. She had asked Sir Joram for modest supplies, and he had given her ten times what she needed.

"Do you know where he is now?" said Caius.

"Not far," said Calliande, touching the dagger at her belt. "Perhaps two days to the northeast. Urd Morlemoch is north of the Three Kingdoms, and he's heading there now."

Ridmark had given her the dagger as a gift, and it had saved Calliande's life. That gave the dagger a sort of…resonance, an echo, of his presence. And with the proper spell, that meant Calliande could use the dagger to follow him.

"Then let us continue," said Caius, tugging at the reins. "Were gambling not a sin, I would wager that we could make another ten miles before nightfall, even with these truculent beasts."

Calliande nodded. She would find Ridmark and lend him her aid. Together they would find the secret of the Frostborn.

And by doing so, perhaps she could find the truth of herself.

EPILOGUE

He had once been an archmage of the high elven kindred, an honored servant of his people, respected and renowned.

That had been a very long time ago.

So long that the humans had not yet come through the gate from Old Earth, that their ancestors had still been living in caves and hunting with sticks.

A very long time.

He was much more now…and yet, less than he should be.

The rage of it burned inside him, so hot that if it burst forth, it would devour the world.

But soon enough, he would make it right.

The creature that had once been an archmage of the high elves, the creature that some called Shadowbearer, walked alone in the Deeps. The clumps of ghost mushrooms clinging to the floor provided only a little light, but that did not trouble him. He needed very little light to see. In truth, he saw by things other than light, with senses other than mere eyes of flesh.

And with those senses he saw things that troubled him.

Qazarl dead, slain outside the walls of Dun Licinia.

Alamur dead, devoured by his own magic.

Calliande's powers returned. Only a portion of them, true, but even a portion was dangerous to him.

Even a portion could destroy him.

"Ridmark Arban," hissed Shadowbearer.

He had not considered the disgraced Swordbearer before. True, Ridmark had stopped Mhalek, but Mhalek had only been a…diversion, a distraction, a ploy to wear down the strength of the High King until the moons reached their proper conjunction and the real work began. And

Mhalek had died, but he had broken Ridmark in his death. Shadowbearer had not spared the man a thought since.

That had been a mistake.

But humans were like that. Such short lives, and they bred and died as quickly as rabbits. But the best of them, the bravest and the boldest, could reshape the world in the few short decades of their lives.

As Calliande had, centuries ago.

As Ridmark might yet do.

Idly, Shadowbearer wondered if the former Swordbearer knew just how many lives he had saved in the last ten days. If Ridmark had not been there, if that idiot Vlazar had managed to kill Calliande upon the altar and activate the soulstone…well, the defenders of Dun Licinia would have faced foes more potent than a ragged band of Mhalekites.

Far more potent.

But it was not too late. A year and a month after the omen, that was how long the threshold would remain, how long the thirteen moons would remain aligned, their magical fields interlocking just so. Shadowbearer's first plan had been undone, but he had been preparing for a very long time…and there was always another plan.

For corruption riddled Andomhaim like a rotten fruit, and his servants were everywhere.

Shadowbearer strode into a large cavern, the village of the Blue Hand kobolds waiting at the other end. The gate was closed, of course, but a simple effort of his vessel's power, and it crumbled into ruin. He strode into the village, and a score of kobolds surrounded him, leveling their obsidian spears, their crests flaring as they hissed at him. The fattest kobold of the lot, no doubt their Warchief, stepped forward.

"Who are you, high elf?" snarled the kobold.

"A traveler," said Shadowbearer in the kobold tongue. Such an uncouth language. Of course, all aspects of material world were uncouth. "I wish to speak with the shaman of the Blue Hand."

"He is dead!" snarled the Warchief. "Murdered by outsiders. I think you have come to attack the kobolds of the Blue Hand. But we are not weak. We will kill you, for daring to threaten the Blue Hand."

"Indeed?" said Shadowbearer, smiling.

The kobolds charged, and Shadowbearer raised his hands.

Fire came at his call.

A few moments later, he had killed every last kobold man, woman, and hatchling in the village. He spotted the Warchief trying to crawl away using his remaining arm, smoke rising from the hideous burns covering his sides and tail.

Shadowbearer walked after him.

"You," rasped the Warchief, "you are a dark elf, you…"

"No," said Shadowbearer, watching the flames consume the roofs of the stone houses, "I am not." He smiled. "Do you know the difference between the dark elves and me?"

The Warchief gaped at him, yellow eyes twitching, tongue flickering over his teeth.

"The dark elves," murmured Shadowbearer, "worshipped the shadow." He leaned closer. "I am the shadow."

The Warchief screamed, fire consuming him.

Shadowbearer left the smoking corpse behind and climbed to the cavern the wretched shaman of the Blue Hand, once the Magistrius Talvinius, had occupied. The kobolds of the Blue Hand had turned the cavern into a crypt for their dead god, placing his charred bones upon a bier in the center of the chamber.

Talvinius had grossly underestimated Calliande.

Shadowbearer had made that mistake once, centuries ago. He would not do so again.

He drew a chalk circle around the bier, ringing it in intricate symbols. Once the sigil was complete, he cast a long and elaborate spell. Cold air blew through the cavern, and the bones upon the bier stirred.

A voice whispered in his ears.

"Who disturbs my torment?" Even death had not removed the petulance from Talvinius's voice. "Who dares to summon me? I will pull you into the abyss with me," the spirit's voice dripped menace, "and we shall burn together."

"Talvinius," said Shadowbearer, smiling. "Have you forgotten me already? It has only been a century."

The spirit's menace dissolved into shock. "You! No...no! It is not possible!"

"You said that often as a living man," said Shadowbearer. "A pity you failed to learn otherwise. But no matter."

"You have come to free me, master?" said Talvinius, his voice full of cringing, desperate hope. "Give me a body, and I will eagerly serve you. I will do whatever you command."

"Actually," said Shadowbearer, "I don't need you at all. But when you died the final death, you were inside Calliande's mind. I need your memories. I had thought her broken. But since she destroyed both you and Alamur, it seems she recovered more of her strength than I thought."

"Master! No!" screamed Talvinius. "I will..."

"Stop talking," said Shadowbearer, and he sent his will digging into the spirit's memories.

He sorted through them, ignoring Talvinius's agonized screams. Images of the dead Eternalist's final moments flashed before his eyes. He saw Calliande's terror, saw her wrath as the power rose up in response to her anger…

"I see," said Shadowbearer. He released the spell, let Talvinius's maimed spirit fall gibbering back into the abyss, and left the cavern.

He stood in the midst of the slain kobolds, thinking.

Calliande had recovered some of her power, but none of her memories. That made her dangerous…but not nearly as dangerous as she could have been. Still, Shadowbearer would not confront her himself. He was so close, and he would not risk a confrontation with her, not now.

Even without her full powers, she could still destroy him.

But he needed her dead. And he needed the soulstone she carried.

And if she was not at her full strength, that would make it all the easier for his many servants to deal with her.

Or, perhaps, some new servants.

He cast a spell, shadow and blue fire dancing around his fingers, and a shadow-wreathed wind blew through the cavern, the flames in the ruined houses flickering.

And the dead kobolds, hundreds of them, rose as undead at his command.

"Go forth," said Shadowbearer. His will burned an image of Calliande into their minds. "Find this woman, overpower her, and bring her and the stone she carries to me." He sent an image of Ridmark into their minds. "And if you encounter this man, kill him."

The undead kobolds raced from the cavern to do his bidding.

Shadowbearer followed them from the ruined village.

He had a great deal of work to do.

THE END

Thank you for reading FROSTBORN: THE GRAY KNIGHT. If you liked the story, please consider leaving a review at your ebook site of choice.

Ridmark Arban will return in early 2014 in FROSTBORN: THE EIGHTFOLD KNIFE. To receive immediate notification of new releases, sign up for my newsletter at http://www.jonathanmoeller.com, or watch for news on my Facebook page.

ABOUT THE AUTHOR

Standing over six feet tall, Jonathan Moeller has the piercing blue eyes of a Conan of Cimmeria, the bronze-colored hair a Visigothic warrior-king, and the stern visage of a captain of men, none of which are useful in his career as a computer repairman, alas. He has written the DEMONSOULED series of sword-and-sorcery novels, the TOWER OF ENDLESS WORLDS urban fantasy series, THE GHOSTS series about assassin and spy Caina Amalas, the COMPUTER BEGINNER'S GUIDE sequence of computer books, and numerous other works. Visit his website at:
http://www.jonathanmoeller.com

Made in the USA
San Bernardino, CA
22 May 2018